Oriental Odyssey - I

In the Shadow of the Padishah
Through the Desert

Unabridged Translation of the
Original Karl May Manuscript Published under the Title

Giölgeda padischahnün
[In the Shadow of the Padishah]

A Travel Narrative
by
Karl May

Translated by
Michael M. Michalak

Original German text by Karl May [1842 – 1912]
First published 1881-1888
in 'Deutscher Hausschatz' in serial format

English translation by Michael M. Michalak

ISBN: 0-9718164-0-9

This book is printed on acid free paper.

Nemsi Books - rev. 06/20/02

Acknowledgements

We would like to thank the following people for their encouragement and advice during the arduous and sometimes frustrating task of translating the original Karl May work from German into English.

Walther Ilmar – For his encouragement and suggestions as well as his investigation of the legality in using the original work published on the Karl May Gesellschaft web site.

Karlheinz Everts - For giving us the permission to use the texts published at the Karl May Gesellschaft web site.

James Patrick Adair - For reading the manuscript in the early, unpolished stage. And for providing us with some foresight as to how our intended audience might receive the final manuscript.

To all these people, thank you for your input. It was much appreciated.

Michael M. Michalak – Translator
Elaine Adair Michalak – Editor

I also wish to give special thanks to my wife, Elaine, for the difficult work she undertook in editing the initial translated text. Despite her struggles with cancer during the closing chapters of this book, she persevered to complete the editing of the entire manuscript. Thank you, Elaine, for your labor of love.

Michael

Foreword

This book represents the first part of what we called an 'Orient Odyssey'. The old collected series was originally composed of six books, which embodied the collection of Karl May's 'Travel Adventures in the Orient'. The original manuscripts, however, were not written as separate books, rather they appeared in serialized form in the 'Deutscher Hausschatz' [German Home Treasure] from 1881 to 1888.

The tale '*Giölgeda padischahnün*' consists of thirty-six serialized parts and these, along with the travel narrative *'Durchs Wilde Kurdistan'* - 'Through Wild Kurdistan' - have subsequently been published as the first two books of May's 'Travel Adventures in the Orient' entitled 'Through the Desert' and 'Through Wild Kurdistan'.

We have chosen not to follow this division as the first book in the original collection entitled 'Through the Desert' terminates in the middle of the 25th chapter. This chapter continues in the second book, entitled 'Through Wild Kurdistan' and the action started in the first book is interrupted. Since the entire narrative of '*Giölgeda padischahnün*' runs for eleven more chapters in the second book before actually commencing the narrative from where this second book takes its title, we felt that the reader would be left unsatisfied at the end of the original first book if we were to adopt the same manuscript division.

Since our second book will not be immediately available to the reader, we believe that our audience might likewise be dissatisfied with the original layout. Therefore we have opted to divide the thirty-six chapter tale, originally entitled *'Giölgeda padischahnün'*, into two parts. The first, covering the desert travels and culminating in a desert battle, the second, opens with a new scene in Mosul and describes the adventures with the 'Devil Worshippers', which paves the way for further exploits in wild Kurdistan.

The 'Oriental Odyssey' concerns the adventures of a German traveler (told in the first person by the original author), Kara Ben Nemsi, and his friend and servant Hajji Halef Omar in the Orient. The journey is eventful insofar as it crosses strange and wonderful territories, which are carefully described for the readers' enjoyment. The first book tells a tale of murder, deceit, betrayal, kidnapping and a long chase over the sands of the world's largest desert.

When I first read this book in the original German in the early 1960's, it struck a chord within me and I avidly read about the other adventures of this German traveler in both the Orient and the Wild West territories of the United States of America. Later, after my family emigrated to Australia I lost touch with Karl May's works as no English language versions appeared to exist, at least in Australia. When I came to the United States, I was initially elated to discover that some English versions did exist, however, I was disappointed in reading these renditions, as what I had read in the original German version had not survived translation. I have heard that it is difficult to translate Karl May's works because his unique style is difficult to render into English – yet his books have been translated into some 30 languages other than English. I believed that the task could be done and have undertaken to translate and publish the 'Oriental Odyssey' in an unabridged manner. I hope that I will do justice to the man who gave life to those many beloved characters with his pen.

I started the first volume of the 'Orient Odyssey' in January 1999. The initial translation of the first book was completed by the end of that year, but many reviews were conducted to polish the translation for style and accuracy. Our task was not just translating the original work from one language into another, but rather it was a matter of extensive research. This translation is based on the original texts published more than one hundred years ago and the German language has undergone changes in spelling and use of idioms since then. Terms such as '*Barbier*' [barber] and other professions are no longer in common usage and could not be found in even the most comprehensive translation dictionaries. The spelling of certain words such as '*Muth*' [courage], and '*Thier*' [animal], still use the old 'th', which was discontinued some time ago and replaced with the singular 't'.

We also grappled with the terseness of dialog that was employed in the original German version. We strove to best represent this without ambiguity, and still keep the translated version true to the original author's style. Our solution was to retain the abruptness where possible; we simply added that a character 'said', 'muttered' or 'grumbled' his or her dialog whenever it became unclear as to who was speaking. We also broke apart long and convoluted sentences and added the name or title of the specific character when the referential terms to the same became unclear.

In those instances where the German idioms could not be rationally translated, we have translated the idiom practically verbatim and added an annotation explaining the meaning of the idiom to our best ability. (See: Author's Notes, at the end of this book).

We have also retained the many glaring errors that exist in Karl May's original work, preferring to render an authentic translation with supplementary notes, rather than editing these errors in the text itself. Yet we strove to make our final version fluent and readable, as well as enjoyable, for today's readers.

We hope that you, the reader, will enjoy this first tale in the series of gripping adventure narratives of the 'Oriental Odyssey'. And yes, there will be more. Our next project is the completion of 'In the Shadow of the Padishah: The Devil Worshippers', and the following tale that takes the reader 'Through Wild Kurdistan'.

Michael M. Michalak – Translator
Elaine Adair Michalak – Editor

DISCLAIMER

The translator and editor wish to advise that they do not endorse or confirm any of the views, interpretations, representations, or conjectures of the original author. Where we have recognized an inaccuracy of fact we have added a footnote to that effect; but it was not our intention to correct or edit the original text, nor censor or enhance the work of Karl May.

On the whole we have made no attempt to anglicize the foreign words (i.e. Turkish, Arabic etc.) that appear in the text. They appear in the original Germanic form, with a few exceptions – e.g. 'sh' being substituted for '*sch*', and 'j' replacing the Germanic form of '*dsch*'. We do not attest to the accuracy or authenticity of these foreign words, or to their spelling or definition, except where specified.

Two forms of parentheses have been utilized in this translation.

Brackets ( )	Contain commentary by the original author.
Square brackets [ ]	Contain notes or references by the translator or editor.

For Elaine

(24th September 1963 – 31st May 2001)

Abu el Nassr

[Father of Victory]

Chapter 1

"Is it really true, *Sihdi* - Master, that you wish to remain a *giaur* - an infidel, who is reckoned to be lower than a dog and more repulsive than a garbage-eating rat?"

"It is so." I replied.

"*Effendi*, I hate the infidels and relish the thought that after their deaths they go to *Jehenna*, where Lucifer dwells; but I wish to save you from this eternal damnation, which will be your fate if you do not become an *Ikrar bil Lisan* - a 'Holy Witness'. You are not like other *Sihdis* whom I have served and I recognize the good in you. Therefore I am going to convert you, whether you wish it or not."

Thus spoke Halef, my servant and guide. We had traveled through the gorges and crevasses of Jebel [Mount, Mountain] Aures together and then descended to the Dra el Haua, so that we could travel to Seddada, Kris and Dgashe via Jebel Tarfaui. A path leads from that place to Fetnassa and Kbilli by way of the notorious Chott [See Translation Notes Ch. 1.1] Jerid.

Halef was a curious little man. He was short enough to walk under my outstretched arm with ease, he was also remarkably lean and slight; one could almost contend that he had spent an entire decade pressed between two blotters in an herbarium. His face disappeared under his huge turban, which was easily three feet in diameter. His once white burnoose now shimmered with an array of hues on account of its secondary service as a napkin and washcloth. The cloak was intended for a much larger man, so that Halef, upon alighting from his horse, needed to gather it about him as a woman would gather her skirts and petticoats. But despite his unimpressive outward appearance, one had to admit a certain respect for the little fellow. He possessed an unusually acute brain, a great deal of courage, ability and perseverance, which enabled him to endure and conquer any adversity he might encounter. And since he also spoke all the dialects between his home, Uëlad Bu Seba, and the Nile delta, it is easy to understand that I was more than satisfied with his services, so much so that I regarded him more as my friend than my servant.

Unfortunately Halef had one characteristic which made me uneasy at times. He was a devout, almost fanatical Moslem and out of his concern for my eternal soul he had a relentless desire to convert me to Islam. Upon reflection, I suppressed a smile as I recalled the comical antics that had accompanied his most recent, fruitless, attempt.

I rode a small, half-wild Berber stallion, and my feet almost dragged along the ground. Halef, on the other hand, to bolster his image, rode an old, and in contrast to mine, sky-high *Hassi-ferdshahn* mare and sat so tall in the saddle that he had to bend down when he addressed me. Our conversation was very lively and was supplemented by both his hands and feet, which he whirled about in all directions to punctuate his sentences; as well as by the amazing grimaces that danced across his face to accentuate the importance of his words. This performance appeared so humorous to me that I had, at times, difficulty remaining earnest.

As I failed to respond to his previous words, he continued:

"Do you know what happens to a *giaur* after death, *Sihdi*?"

"Well, tell me?"

"After death, all people, may they be Moslem, Christian, Jew or whatever, pass into *Barzakh*."

"And that is the state between death and resurrection?"

"Yes, *Sihdi*. The sound of trumpets awakens the sleepers in *Barzakh*. *El Jaum el akbar* - the Beginning, and *el Akhiret* - the End, have passed and afterwards all is in ruin except *el Kuhrs* - the Throne of God, *el Ruhh* - the Holy Ghost, *el Lauhel mafus* and *el Kalam* - the Book and the Pen of Fate."

"Apart from that nothing else exists?"

"No."

"But what about Paradise and Hell?"

"*Sihdi*, You are wise and clever; you notice at once that which I forget to mention, this is why it is so sad that you wish to remain an accursed *giaur*. But I swear by my beard, I will convert you one way or another."

With these words his forehead wrinkled into a frown, he pulled at the seven strands on his chin and tugged at the nine wispy hairs on either side of his nose, known as a *summa summarum* beard. He twitched his legs and thrust his free hand very roughly into his mare's mane, as though she were Lucifer himself, from whom I needed to be saved.

His animal, so cruelly treated, began to rear up on her hind legs in protest but, as though realizing that such actions were beneath her breeding, she quickly settled down.

Halef continued his speech undeterred:

"Yes, *Jennet* - Paradise, and *Jehenna* - Hell, will also remain, otherwise where would the worthy and unworthy go? But before anyone can reach their destination, they must all walk across the Ssirath Bridge, which spans Lake Handh and is as narrow and as sharp as the well-honed cutting edge of a sword."

"You forgot one thing."

"What?"

"The coming of the *Deddshel*."

"Absolutely! *Sihdi*, You know the Koran and all holy books and yet you will not make the effort to be converted! But fear not; I will make a 'True Believer' of you yet! Anyway, before the final judgment the *Deddshel* will appear, he who is known to the *giaurs* as the Antichrist - is that not so, *effendi*?"

"Yes, that is so Halef."

"After that comes the *Hisab* where the deeds of every person are read from the *Kitab* [book], in which good and bad deeds are tallied. The consideration of the deeds will take about fifty thousand years, a time that, for the good will pass in an instance - but for the wicked will appear to be an eternity. That is the *Hukm* - the weighing of all human deeds."

"And afterwards?"

"Afterwards comes the final judgment. Those who have performed more good deeds than bad are permitted to enter Paradise, the infidel and the sinner go to Hell, but the Moslems whose bad deeds outweigh the good are only punished for a short time in Hell. You see, *Sihdi*, what awaits you as a 'True Believer'? But you will be saved; you shall go with me into *Jennet* - Paradise. I shall convert you, whether you be willing or not!"

And again his legs and arms danced about energetically as though he was performing a visual declaration of his enthusiasm for the task at hand. The ancient *Hassi-ferdshahn* mare, now becoming accustomed to this behavior, only twitched her ears and offered a curious glance in his direction.

"And what am I to suffer in your Hell?" I asked him.

"In *Jehenna* eternal flames will roast you. Streams of stinking water flow all around you and although you are plagued by an eternal thirst, the stench prevents you from quenching that thirst. There are also fearsome trees all around you and among them is the terrible *Zakum* tree, the branches of which bear devils' heads like fruit."

"Ugh!"

"Yes, *Sihdi*, it is terrible! The ruler of *Jehenna* is the dark angel Thabek, and there are seven sections, to which seven gates are opened wide. *Jehennem*, the first section, is where the Moslem sinners do penance for their misdeeds. *Ladha*, the second section, is for the Christians. *Hothama*, the third section, is for the Jews. *Sair*, the fourth section, is for the Sabier. *Sakar*, the fifth section, is for the Magi and fire-worshippers, and *Gehim*, the sixth, is for all those who prayed to idols and love fetishes. *Zaoviat*, the seventh and final region, which is also known as *Derk Asfal*, is the deepest and most fearful region. Here all hypocrites are assembled. The damned are carried through burning rivers to each of these sections by evil spirits and are forced to eat the terrible fruits of the *Zakum* tree whereupon their insides are shredded eternally. Oh, *effendi*, acknowledge the Prophet, so that you will spend but a short time in *Jehenna*!"

I shook my head and said: "If I am destined for Hell, I will go to the Christian Hell, which is as terrible as yours."

"Don't believe that, *Sihdi*! I promise you by the Prophet and all of the caliphs that you shall go to *Jennet*. Shall I describe it to you?"

"If you wish!"

"*Jennet* is located above the seventh heaven and has eight gates. First you come to the great Hawus Kewser Well, from which one hundred thousand souls can drink at one time. The water is whiter than milk; the fragrance is more delightful than *moshus* – musk and myrrh, and on the rim of the well stand a million golden goblets, which are encrusted with diamonds and other precious stones. From here you go to the place where the souls rest on golden cushions and are served delightful sweetmeats and nectar by immortal youths and *houris* – beautiful maidens. You will hear the most heavenly music, which accompanies the songs sung by the angel Israfil. A soft breeze, at Allah's command, passes through the trees and stirs the bells hanging in the branches in a most delightful harmony. Each soul is sixty els [distance from elbow to tip of middle finger] long and eternally thirty years old. In the midst of the trees the *Tubah* towers above all. This is the tree of good fortune; its trunk grows out of the center of the palace of the Prophet and its branches reach into the homes of the blessed; it is laden with all the fruits that are desirable. The roots of the *Tubah* tree are the fountainhead of all the rivers of Paradise, in which milk, wine, coffee and honey flow unceasingly."

Despite the sensual description of this concept of Paradise, I had to note that Mohammed could well have taken a Christian depiction and remodeled it for consumption by the Bedouin nomads. Halef looked at me expectantly and it was clear that he was convinced that his portrayal of Paradise had overwhelmed me.

"Now, what do you think?" he asked, as my silence began to vex him.

"I must tell you that I am not at all happy with the idea of swelling to the length of sixty els and I want nothing to do with *houris* as I am not at all comfortable with the female gender."

"But why?" he asked in amazement.

"Because the Prophet says: 'The woman's voice is like the song the *bulbul* - nightingale, but her tongue is full of poison like that of the viper.' have you not read this?"

"I have read it."

He lowered his head; I had beaten him with the words of his own Prophet. After a while he asked, with a little less confidence.

"But our belief is nevertheless beautiful? It is not required that you even look at a *houri*!"

"I will remain a Christian!"

"But it is not difficult to say: *La Illa illa Allah, we Mohammed Resul Allah*!"

"Is it more difficult to pray: *Ja abana 'Iledsi, fi 's - semavati, jata - haddeso 'smoka*?"

He cast an angry glance in my direction.

"I know well that Isa Ben Marryam, he whom you call Jesus, has taught you this prayer; you call it the Lord's Prayer. You wish to convert me to your belief, but do not hold out any hope that you will succeed in diverting me from *Tauhid*, the Belief of Allah!"

I was well aware that my comparison of our belief systems had always been a futile exercise, but it was, I discovered, the only approach to this discourse that would silence him. I used it again with predictable success.

"So leave me to my belief and I will leave you to yours!"

He grumbled something unintelligible at my words and then growled:

"Yet I will convert you, be you willing or not. And I shall succeed because you too have a *tesbih* - a rosary [See Trans. Notes Ch 1.2]. What I desire I will have as sure as I am Hajji Halef Omar Ben Hajji Abul Abbas Ibn Hajji Dawud al Gossarah!"

"So you are the son of Abul Abbas who is the son of Dawud al Gossarah?"

"Indeed."

"And both were pilgrims?"

"Yes."

"And you too are a hajji?"

"Yes."

"So all three of you were in Mecca and have seen the holy *Kaaba*?"

"Not Dawud al Gossarah."

"Ah! But why do you call him a hajji?"

"Because he was one. He lived on the Jebel Shur-Shum and as a young man he began his pilgrimage. He made it successfully across the *el Juf*, which is known as the body of the desert; but he became ill and had to remain at the Well of Trasah. There he took a wife, saw the birth of his son Abul Abbas and died. Should he not be a hajji, a pilgrim?"

"Hmm! But Abul Abbas made it to Mecca?"

"No."

"But he too is a hajji?"

"Yes. He began his pilgrimage and made it to the Admar Plain, where he had to remain."

"Why?"

"He beheld Amareh, the 'Pearl of Juneth', and fell in love. Amareh became his wife bore him Halef Omar, the very person you see next to you. Then he died. Was he not a hajji?"

"Hmm! But you have been to Mecca?"

"No."

"But you too call yourself a pilgrim!"

"Yes. When my mother died, I began my pilgrimage. I wandered towards the sunrise and towards the sunset, after midday and after midnight; I learned of all the oases in the desert and of all places in Egypt. I have not yet made it to Mecca, but I will eventually get there. Am I not a hajji?"

"Hmm! I thought that only one who had completed the hajj - pilgrimage and was actually in Mecca was permitted to call himself a hajji?"

"Actually, yes. But I am on the journey to Mecca!"

“That is admirable! But you too will eventually find a beautiful woman and remain with her; your son will also have the same kismet. Then after a hundred or so years your great grandson will say: ‘I am Hajji Mustafa Ben Hajji Ali Assabeth Ibn Hajji Saïd al Hamza Ben Hajji Schehab Tofaïl Ibn Hajji Halef Omar Ben Hajji Abul Abbas Ibn Hajji Dawud al Gossarah’ - and not one of these seven pilgrims from seven generations will have seen Mecca and become a true hajji. What do you think?”

As earnest as he was, he had to laugh at the possibility. There exist among the Mohammedan many who call themselves hajji, especially in the presence of foreigners, despite the certainty that they have never viewed the Kaaba with their own eyes nor managed to complete the journey from Ssafa to Merweh. They were never in Arafah nor had their hair and beard cut in Minah. My dear Halef was exposed, but he took it in good spirit.

“*Sihdi*,” he asked humbly, “will you tell anyone that I have not yet been to Mecca?”

“I will only mention it if you try to convert me to Islam; otherwise I will be silent. Look, are there not tracks in the sand?”

We had turned into the Wadi [a seasonal stream, or the dry channel of this, an oasis] Tarfaui some time ago and were now at a place where the wind-borne sand spilled over the escarpment. In this sand were distinct imprints.

“Some people rode through here.” Halef dismissed the hoof prints.

“So we will dismount and examine the tracks in detail.”

He looked at me bewildered.

“*Sihdi*, that is unnecessary. It is enough to know that people rode through here. Why should we examine hoof marks in the sand?”

“It is always good to know who is ahead of you.”

“If you stop to examine all the tracks that cross your path, it will take you some two moons before you reach Seddada. What concern is it to you who is ahead of us?”

“It has been my experience from my travels in far-off lands that a man’s very existence can depend on his awareness of what is happening about him. It is most advisable to examine all spoors and tracks to determine, if possible, whether they were made by friend or foe.”

“You will not encounter enemies here, *effendi*.”

“We can't know that for sure.”

I dismounted. There were the distinct tracks of three animals, one camel and two horses. The first was clearly a riding camel, as was evident by the dainty impressions. On closer examination of the remaining prints I was drawn to the curious placement of the impressions made by one of the horses. It was evident that it suffered some minor deformity of the legs. In a land where horses are wealth, to ride such a horse did not make sense unless the owner was an extremely poor Arab or a foreigner.

Halef, amused at my diligence in inspecting the tracks asked me, as soon as I had finished:

"What did you see, *Sihdi*?"

"The hoof prints of two horses and one camel."

"Two horses and one *jemmel*! Allah preserve your eyes; I see exactly the same thing without having to climb down off my animal. You, a *taleb* - an educated man, do things that a *hamahr* - a donkey driver would laugh at. What use is this treasure of knowledge you have uncovered here?"

"I know firstly that three riders passed this place about four hours ago."

"And what is this knowledge worth? You men from the *Belad el Rumi* - from Europe, you are strange people!"

His expression implied incredible pity for me. I preferred to ignore this and we continued on our way in silence.

Chapter 2

We followed the tracks for about an hour, until we reached a bend in the wadi where our horses stopped unexpectedly. Three vultures sat on the crest of a dune not far from us, upon uttering a dry squawk they lifted themselves into the air on broad wings.

"*El büdj* - the vulture," said Halef. "Where you find him there you will surely also find carrion."

"Yes, there must be a dead animal around here." I replied as I followed him up the dune.

Halef spurred his horse on and I was left in his wake. He had barely reached the top of the dune when he abruptly halted his horse and uttered a cry of surprise.

"*Mash Allah* - Miracle of God! What is this? Is that not a man lying there, *Sihdi*?"

I had to agree; it was indeed a man whose corpse was providing a meal for the vultures. I leaped quickly from my horse and knelt beside the body. The vultures' talons had torn the clothing but I discovered when I touched the body that not too much time had passed since the poor fellow had expired.

"*Allah kerihm* - God is merciful! *Sihdi*, did this man die from natural causes?" asked Halef.

"No. Do you not see the wound at his neck and the hole in his skull? He was murdered."

"Allah punish the man that did this! Or did this man die as the result of an honorable fight?"

"What do you call an honorable fight? Perhaps he was the victim of a blood feud. We will examine his clothing."

Halef assisted in this task. We found nothing of consequence until my attention focused upon the left hand of the deceased. I noticed a simple golden band of the customary style of a wedding ring. I removed the ring from the finger and discovered on the inner surface, in small but clear characters, the inscription – 'E· P· 15· Juillet 1830.'

"What did you find?" asked Halef.

"This fellow is no Ben Arab."

"What else would he be?"

"A Frenchman."

"A Frank, a Christian? On what do you base this?"

"If a Christian takes a wife, the bond is usually symbolized by the exchange of rings, in which their names and the date of the union are inscribed."

"And that is such a ring?"

"Yes."

"But how do you know that this man was a Frank? He could just as well have been an *Inglis* or a *Nemsi* like yourself."

"There are French references in the inscription."

"Still, that alone does not make him a Frank for certain *effendi*. It is just as possible that he found or even stole that ring?"

"That is true. But look at his shirt, the one that he wore under his clothes, it is definitely of European origin."

"Who killed him?"

"His two companions. Don't you see how the sand all around here is churned up, clearly evidence of a struggle? And do you notice that ..."

I stopped in mid-sentence. As I had been talking I had also risen to examine the surrounding area, I noticed the beginning of a wide bloody spill that began not far from the corpse and led sideways among the rocks nearby. I followed this trail with a cocked weapon in my hands as the murderers could still be in the vicinity. I did not have to go far when I heard the flapping of wings as more vultures made a hurried retreat from this second feast, a camel, that had died from the huge wound in its chest. Halef clapped his hands together and in a mournful voice cried:

"A gray *hedjihn*, a gray *tuareg-hedjihn*, and these murdering dogs, these spawn of *Shaïtan* - Lucifer, have killed it!"

It was clear that he was more concerned by the death of a beautiful riding camel than by the death of the Frenchman. As a true son of the desert, for whom the smallest material item might present an object of great value, he knelt by the camel and rummaged through the saddlebags - they were empty.

"The murderers have already taken it all, *Sihdi*. May they burn in *Jehenna* for all eternity! Nothing, not a thing have they left behind, just the camel - and those papers in the sand over there."

His words drew my attention to the place, some distance from us, where some crumpled pieces of paper had obviously been thought worthless and discarded. Since these papers might contain information that could assist in explaining what had happened here, I walked over to pick them up. There were several pages from newspapers and I straightened them and pieced them together. Now I had two pages from the '*Vigie algérienne*' and also two from the '*L'Indépendant*' and the '*Mahouna*'. The first is an Algerian newspaper, the second from Constantine and the third from Guelma. Despite their different origins, I discovered, upon quickly reviewing the content, that each paper reported an identical story about the murder of a French merchant in Blidah. The most likely murder suspect was an Armenian merchant, who had immediately fled and was then rigorously pursued. The description of the person by all three reports was identical in all aspects.

For what reason did the dead Frenchman, who was obviously also the owner of the dead camel, carry these papers? Did the incident described therein concern him personally? Was he a relative of the merchant from Blidah, was he the murderer, or was he a policeman who was on the trail of the murderer?

I took the papers and placed them in my pocket and put the ring on my finger for safe keeping as I returned to Halef, who had remained near the carcass. Above us the vultures circled, as soon as we had departed a short distance they descended onto the camel's carcass once more.

"What should we do now, *Sihdi*?" asked my servant.

"There is nothing we can do at present other than to bury the poor fellow."

"You want to dig a hole and put him into it and then cover him with dirt?"

"No, to do that we would need tools that we do not have. We will cover him with stones so that no animal can disturb his rest."

"And you think that he really is a *giaur*?"

"He is a Christian."

"It's still possible that you are wrong, *Sihdi*; he might have been a Moslem. Therefore permit me one request!"

"That being?"

"Let us lie him in such a position so that he faces Mecca!"

"I have no objection to that since he will at the same time be facing Jerusalem where our Christian Savior suffered and died. So lend a hand!"

It was a sad task that we performed in deep silence. As the stone mound that we had piled upon the corpse grew to a size that would protect it from the desert animals, I placed enough additional stones to style it into the shape of a cross. I then folded my hands in prayer and said a few words. This completed, Halef turned his eyes towards the east and began to recite the one hundred and twelfth *sura* of the Koran:

"In the Name of the ever-loving God! Speak: Allah is the one and eternal God. He is invisible and no being is His equal. Man loves his brief life and is not concerned with eternity. Your end has come and now you shall join your maker in a new life. May the number of your sins be small and the number of your good deeds be as great as the grains of sand in the desert in which you sleep!"

After these words he knelt in the sand and used it to clean his hands, which had been defiled by the handling of the corpse.

"So, *Sihdi*, now I am once more *tahir*, what the children of Israel call kosher, and may again touch what is clean and holy. What do we do now?"

"We try to catch up with the murderers."

"You will kill them?"

"I am neither judge nor jury. I wish to speak with them to discover why they committed this crime - then I will know what I should do next."

"They can't be very clever, otherwise they would not have killed a *hedjihn,* which is worth far more than their horses."

"The *hedjihn* would have exposed them. Look, do you see their tracks.

Come on! They are perhaps five hours ahead of us; possibly we will catch up with them in the morning before they reach Seddada."

Despite the oppressive heat and the wearisome stony ground we raced as though in pursuit of gazelles, it was therefore difficult to make conversation. This enforced silence was extremely difficult for Halef.

"*Sihdi*," he called from behind me, "*Sihdi*, do you wish to lose me?"

I turned to face him.

"Lose you?"

"Yes. My mare has older bones than your Berber stallion."

The ancient *Hassi-ferdshahn* mare was indeed slick with sweat and foam flew from her mouth.

"But today we cannot rest as usual during the hottest part of the day, instead we have to ride until sunset or we will not catch up with our quarry."

"The quick do not necessarily reach the finish before the slow, *effendi*, so - *Allah akbar*, look over there!"

We stood before a large drop in the wadi and saw in the distance, perhaps a quarter of an hour's ride from where we were, two riders, or more precisely two men who sat at the edge of a small *sobha* – pool, which held brackish water. Their horses nibbled at the dry and spiky mimosa that grew in the vicinity.

"Ah, there they are!"

"Yes, *Sihdi*, that is them. It got too hot for them and they decided to await the passing of the great heat."

"Or they decided to divide the loot. Back, Halef, back, so they do not see us! We leave the wadi and ride westward for a short time so it appears as though we came from Chott Rharsa."

"Why, *effendi*?"

"So that they will not suspect that we have discovered the body of their victim."

Our beasts climbed over the rim of the wadi and we rode straight into the desert in a westerly direction. After a while we turned and headed back to the position where the two men rested. As they were down in the deepest part of the wadi they did not see us approaching, but they could not fail to hear us as we drew near.

As we had anticipated, they heard our approach and had already arisen as we crested the rim. Equally foreseen, they had armed themselves and now regarded us with suspicion. I naturally did likewise, as would anyone who is suddenly confronted by strangers in this lonely wilderness. I did not, however, consider it necessary to arm myself.

"*Salaam aaleïkum*!" I hailed, as I reined in my horse.

"*Aaleïkum*," replied the elder of the two. "Who are you?"

"We are peaceable riders."

"Where do you come from?"

“From the west.”

“And where are you heading?”

“To Seddada.”

“To which tribe do you belong?”

I pointed to Halef and replied:

“He is from the Admar Plain, and I belong to the Beni-Sachsa. And you?”

“We are from the famous Uëlad Hamalek tribe.”

“The Uëlad Hamalek are good riders and courageous warriors. Where do you come from?”

“From Gafsa.”

“That means that you have had quite a long journey. Where are you bound?”

“To the Bir Sauidi, where we have friends.”

That they came from Gafsa and were on their way to the Sauidi Well were certainly lies, but I continued as though I believed every word and asked:

“Would you allow us to join you for our rest?”

“We intend to remain here until the early morning,” was the reply, which suggested neither a refusal nor an invitation.

“We too are thinking of remaining here until sunrise. You have enough water for us all as well as our horses. Permit us to rest with you?”

“The desert belongs to everyone. *Marhaba* - You are welcome in our midst!”

Despite their offer it was not difficult to detect that they would have preferred we continue our journey immediately. We guided our horses down the side of the wadi and dismounted at the water’s edge, where we immediately settled ourselves.

As I was now able to study the two in greater detail, my earlier misgivings regarding their characters gained in strength. The elder, with whom I had been speaking, was tall and gaunt. The burnoose hung from his body as it would from a scarecrow. Two small, piercing eyes glowered from beneath the dirty blue turban. Above the thin, bloodless lips a dry straggly mustache held a meager existence. The pointed chin tended to thrust upward, and the nose, yes, this nose; it was unlike the beak of an eagle or a hawk. It reminded me more of the vultures that only a short time ago I had chased from the murder victim’s corpse.

The younger fellow was noticeably handsome; but his passions had weakened his eye and his nerves and marred his forehead and cheeks prematurely. He did not present a trustworthy demeanor. The elder spoke Arabic with an accent that indicated he came from the Euphrates, and the younger I suspected was not at all of Oriental origin but rather a European. Their horses, which stood nearby, were not the best of their breed and had obviously been ridden hard recently. Their garments appeared to have suffered much, but their weapons were in extremely good condition. Where they had previously rested lay several items that one seldom sees in this area. Obviously they did not have time to conceal these upon our arrival: one silken handkerchief, one golden watch including chain, one compass, one truly magnificent revolver and one morocco-[a soft fine leather or goatskin tanned with sumac] bound journal.

I acted as though I had not noticed these items and took from my saddlebag a handful of dates, which I nonchalantly began to eat.

"What will you do in Seddada?" asked the elder of the two.

"Nothing. We will pass through." I replied.

"To where?"

"Over the Chott Jerid to Fetnassa and Kbilli."

The unguarded glance he gave his companion indicated to me that it was the same route that they had intended to take. He now asked:

"Do you have business in Fetnassa or Kbilli?"

"Yes."

"You wish to sell your herds there?"

"No."

"Or your slaves?"

"No."

"Or perhaps wares that you are shipping from the Sudan?"

"No."

"What then?"

"Nothing. A son of my tribe does not trade in Fetnassa."

"Or do you intend to fetch yourself a wife there?"

I threw him an angry look.

"Do you not know that it is an insult to speak to a man about his wife! Perhaps you are a *giaur*, and lack that knowledge?"

It appeared as though I had hit upon the truth because the fellow appeared quite concerned. He did not have the physical characteristics of a Bedouin; a face such as his was more likely Armenian - ah, was it not an Armenian merchant, who was suspected of murdering the French merchant at Blidah, and whose description I had in my pocket? I had not taken the time to read the description carefully and as this thought raced through my mind, my eye was caught by the silver plate on the revolver handle, upon which a name was engraved.

"Allow me!" I said as I simultaneously picked up the weapon and read: 'Paul Galingré, Marseille'.

That was certainly the name of the owner rather than the name of the factory. I did not betray my interest however, but asked instead:

"What kind of weapon is this?"

"A . . . a . . . a rotary gun."

"Would you tell me how one shoots with it?"

He described it to me. I listened with attentive fascination and concluded:

"You are no Uëlad Hamalek, but a *giaur*."

"Why do you say that?" He demanded.

"See, I am correct! If you were a son of the Prophet, you would have shot me on the spot for calling you a *giaur*. Only infidels have revolvers. How would such a weapon come into the hands of a Uëlad Hamalek! As a present?"

"No."

"So you purchased it?"

"No."

"Then it was loot from some raid?"

"Yes."

"From whom was it taken?"

"From a Frank."

"Whom you fought fairly?"

"Yes."

"Where?"

"On the battlefield."

"Which one?"

"At El Guerara."

"You lie!"

With that last retort his patience was at an end. He rose and reached for the revolver.

"What say you? That I lie? Shall I shoot you down like ..."

I finished the sentence for him:

"Like that Frank up there in the Wadi Tarfaui!"

The hand that held the revolver dropped to his side and he turned several shades paler. But he quickly gathered his wits and demanded with threatening undertones:

"What do you mean by these words?"

I reached into my pocked for the papers and quickly scanned them to find the name of the alleged murderer.

"I shall tell you what I mean; you are no Uëlad Hamalek. Your real name is well known to me; it is Hamd il Amasat."

Now he backed away from me and put out both hands in a warding off motion.

"How do you know me?"

"I know you, that is enough."

"No, you do not know me, I am not who you say, I am a Uëlad Hamalek, and I will shoot anyone who says otherwise!"

"To whom do these things belong?"

"They belong to me."

I picked up the handkerchief. It was monogrammed with the letters 'P · G'. I opened the watch and found the same letters engraved on the inside of the case.

"Where did you get them?"

"What does it matter to you? Put them down!"

Instead of obeying him, I opened the journal. On the first page I read the name 'Paul Galingré'; but the content was unfortunately in shorthand, which I am unable to read.

"Put the book down, I tell you!"

With these words he knocked the book from my hand and it flew into the watering hole. I tried to recover it but was suddenly confronted with another adversary. The younger man had placed himself between the water and me. Halef, who had expressed no interest in the dispute, had however followed the conversation and I noticed that he now had his finger on the trigger of his flintlock. It would only take a signal from me and he would shoot. I bent down and picked up the compass.

"Stop; that is mine! Give it back!" The elder of the two cried.

He grabbed my arm to lend authority to his words; but I said in a calm voice:

"Sit down, we have much to talk about."

"I have nothing to discuss with you!"

"But I have with you. Sit down, otherwise I will shoot you down!"

This threat apparently had the desired impression. He lowered himself to the ground and I did likewise. I then took hold of my revolver and began:

"See, I too have a revolver! Put yours away or else this one goes off!"

He put the weapon down carefully to his side but made sure that it was within easy reach.

"You are not a Uëlad Hamalek?"

"I am one."

"You do not come from Gafsa?"

"I come from there."

"How long have you ridden through Wadi Tarfaui?"

"What is that to you!"

"It means quite a lot to me. Up there is the body of a man whom you murdered."

A nasty expression moved over his face.

"And if I had done this thing, what have you to say about it?"

"Not a lot; just a few questions to ask."

"Which are?"

"Who was the fellow?"

"I did not know him."

"Why did you kill him and his camel?"

"Because I wanted to."

"Was he a Moslem?"

"No. He was a *giaur*."

"You took all his possessions?"

"Should I have left them?"

"No, you should have kept them for me."

"For you ...?"

"Yes."

"I don't understand you."

"You should make an effort to understand me, that man was a *giaur*; I am also a *giaur* and I am going to demand retribution."

"You intend to avenge his death?"

"No, if it were revenge that I had in mind you would already have taken your last breath. We are in the desert, where the only law is that of the strongest. I will not try to prove which of us is the stronger, rather I will leave you to the vengeance of your God, who knows all, sees all and leaves no evil deed go unpunished. One thing I do demand from you, and you would do well to heed my words: you will hand over everything that you have taken from your victim."

He looked at me with a calculating smirk.

"Do you think that I will actually do this?"

"I know it."

"So take what you will!"

He made a rapid movement towards the revolver on the ground beside him, but quickly decided against it as he faced the dark maw of my own revolver barrel.

"Stop, or I will shoot you!"

It was certainly a strange situation in which I found myself. Luckily my opponent was easily intimidated and possessed little courage. He withdrew his hand quickly and appeared undecided as to what to do next

"What are you going to do with the Frank's belongings?"

"I am going to make sure that they are returned to his relatives."

He now regarded me with an expression that was almost sympathetic!

"You are lying. You want to keep them for yourself!"

"I do not lie."

"And what do you intend to do with me?"

"At present, nothing; but beware if you should ever cross my path again!"

"You are truly going to Seddada from here?"

"Yes."

"And if I give you all the things I took from the Frank will you let me and my companion go to Bir Sauidi unhindered?"

"Yes."

"You promise this to me?"

"Yes."

"You will swear it!"

"A *giaur* never swears, his word is like an oath of truth."

"Here, take the revolver, the watch, the compass and the cloth." He thrust these items at me.

"What else did he have on his person?"

"Nothing."

"He had money."

"That I will keep."

"I do not begrudge you this but give me the pouch or whatever it was held in."

"You shall have it."

He pulled a pearl encrusted wallet from his belt and handed it to me, once he had emptied it of its contents.

"And he had nothing else?"

"No. Do you want to search me?"

"No."

"So we can go?"

"Yes."

His disposition changed as relief swept over him. His companion was certainly a timid person who plainly beamed with delight to have escaped justice in this manner. They quickly took their remaining possessions and mounted their horses.

"*Salaam aaleïkum* - Peace be with you!"

I did not reply and they took this impoliteness in their stride. Within the blink of an eye they had reached the rim of the wadi and disappeared over it.

Halef had not uttered a word during the entire episode; now he broke his silence.

"*Sihdi*!"

"What?"

"May I say something?"

"Certainly."

"Have you heard of the ostrich?"

"Yes."

"Do you know what they are like?"

"Well, tell me?"

"Foolish, quite foolish."

"Go on!"

"Forgive me, *effendi*, but you appear to be much worse than the ostrich."

"And why is that?"

"Because you let those crooks go."

"I can't hold them prisoner and neither can I just kill them."

"Why not? If they had murdered a 'True Believer', you can be certain that I would have dispatched them to *Shaïtan*. But since he was a *giaur* I am not too concerned whether or not they are made to face justice. You, however, are a Christian and you let the murderers of a Christian go!"

"Who says that they will escape justice?"

"They are already gone! They will reach Bir Sauidi and then go to Debila and El Uëd, so that they can disappear in the *areg* (region of the dunes)."

"That they will not do."

"What else would they do? They said that they will go to Bir Sauidi."

"They lied. They will go to Seddada."

"What tells you this?"

"My eyes."

"Allah bless your eyes, with which you behold the marks in the sand. Only an infidel would handle this matter as you are doing now. But I will eventually open your eyes to the ways of the Prophet, of that you can be certain - may you like it or not!"

"Then I will call myself a hajji without ever having been in Mecca."

"*Sihdi* . . . ! You promised me not to speak of this!"

"Yes, as long as you do not try to convert me."

"You are my master, and I must endure it. But what do we do now?"

"First we make sure that we are safe. Here we are easy targets for a bullet. We must make sure that these villains are really gone."

I climbed to the rim of the wadi and saw that the two riders had already covered a great distance on a southwesterly trek. Halef had followed me to the crest.

"There they ride." he said. "That is the direction to Bir Sauidi."

"Once they are out of sight they will turn towards the east."

"*Sihdi*, I believe your brain is turning soft. If they did that they would once again walk into our hands!"

"They think that we are going to leave here in the morning and that makes them confident that they will be a great distance ahead of us."

"You guess and have no way of knowing if you are right."

"You think so? Did I not notice up there that one of their horses had a peculiar gait?"

"Yes, I saw that too as they rode away."

"So I will also be proven right that they go to Seddada."

"Why don't we follow them right now?"

"We would get ahead of them if we did that because we will travel the direct route. That means that they would encounter our tracks and avoid meeting us again. Let us therefore return to the water and rest until it is time for us to follow them."

Chapter 3

We made our way down from the crest of the wadi. I lay down on my blanket and used the loose end of my turban to cover my face like a *lisham* – veil. I then closed my eyes, not to sleep but to aid in my contemplation of recent events. But who has the ability to concentrate on anything for long in the terrible heat of the Sahara? I did actually nod off for about two hours and when I awoke it was time for us to be on our way.

The Wadi Tarfaui opened onto the Chott Rharsa; we therefore had to leave the wadi if we wanted to go eastwards towards Seddada. After about an hour we encountered a trail, made by two horses, which came from the west and went into the east.

"Now, Halef, do you recognize this *ethar* - this spoor?"

"*Mash Allah*, you were right, *Sihdi*! They are going to Seddada."

I dismounted and took a closer look at the impressions.

"These tracks were made about half an hour ago. Let us slow our progress, otherwise they will see us coming up behind them."

The foothills of the Jebel Tarfaui slowly fused into the lower plain, the sun had set and after a short time, as the moon rose, we saw Seddada below us.

"Do we ride down?"

"No. We sleep among those olive trees by the outcrop of that hill."

We diverged from our original trail and found a comfortable place in the olive grove for our bivouac. We were both accustomed to the howling of the jackal, the yelping of the fennec fox and the deeper tones of the furtive hyena, therefore the sounds of the night did not disturb us and we soon fell asleep. Upon awakening I made it my first task to inspect our quarry's tracks from the previous day. I was certain that this close to a town it would reveal nothing of further use, but I was pleasantly surprised when it did not lead into Seddada but instead turned towards the south.

"Why did they not go into the town?" asked Halef.

"To avoid being seen. A hunted murderer must take care." I replied.

"But where are they going now?"

"Obviously to Kris, so that they might ride across the Jerid. Then they will have left Algiers behind them and attained temporary refuge."

"We are already in Tunisia. The border is the line between Bir el Khalla and Bir el Tam, over the Chott Rharsa."

"That will not be enough for people such as these. I would wager that they will go via Fezzan to Kufarah, only then can they be certain of safety."

"They are already quite safe here, if they have a *Bu-Djeruldu* - travel pass from the Sultan."

"That would not help them if they encountered a consul or an agent of the police."

"You think so? I would not advise anyone to sin against the mighty '*Giölgeda padischahnün*'! (Literal: In the Shadow of the Padishah)"

"You say that and profess to be a free Arab?"

"Yes, in Egypt I have witnessed what the Sultan is capable of, but here in the desert I do not fear him. Will we go to Seddada?" Halef asked.

"Yes, to buy dates and to drink some good water. After that we go on."

"To Kris?"

"To Kris."

Within a quarter of an hour we had restocked our provisions and were on the road that led from Seddada to Kris. Below us on our left the surface of Chott Jerid shimmered brilliantly, reflecting up into our faces, a sight that I fully intended to appreciate.

The Sahara is a great and still unsolved riddle. Way back in the year 1845, Virlet d'Aoust proposed that a part of the desert should be flooded by the sea, thereby turning the surrounding area into arable and fruitful land that would also facilitate in bringing the benefits of civilization to the inhabitants. Whether this project is feasible and whether it would have the desired effect upon the region is still being debated.

At the foot of the southern slopes of the Jebel Aures and along the easterly continuation of this mountain range, which is composed of the Dra el Haua, Jebel Tarfaui, Jebel Situna and Jebel Hadifa, an immense undulating plain reaches out beyond the horizon. At its depths this unique plain is covered with salt crusts and salt extrusions that are the remnants of a huge dried-out lake. In the Algerian sector it is given the name *chott* and in the Tunisian sector it is called *sobha* or *sebcha.* The boundary of this curious and remarkable area is marked in the west by the foothills of the Beni-Mzab-Plateau, in the east by the Gulf of Gabes and in the south by the dune region of Ssuf and Nifzaua, which adjoins Jebel Tebaga. Perhaps this depression explains the existence of the Gulf of Triton, which is written of by Herodotus, the 'Father of History'.

Apart from the great number of small swamps, which dry out in the summer, this area consists mainly of three large *sebcha*, namely, from west to east, the Chotts Melrir, Rharsa and Jerid, the last of which is also referred to as El Kebir. These three basins form a domain, the western half of which is deeper than the Mediterranean at Gabes during low tide.

The depression of the chott area is nowadays, to a large part, filled with drift sand and only in the middle of each basin does there exist a considerable amount of water. Due to its appearance the chott has been likened to, by Arabian writers and travelers, a camphor carpet, or crystal coverlet, even a silver plate or the surface of molten metal. This aspect of the chott, to which these comparisons refer, may be attributed to the salt crust that covers it, the thickness of which varies between ten and twenty centimeters. Only in certain places is it possible to stand on this crust without danger to life or limb. Woe to him who deviates from the safe path by even the width of a hand! The crust gives way and the victim is swallowed up in the blink of an eye. Immediately afterwards, the crust closes again as though nothing had happened. The small paths that lead across the chott are especially dangerous during the rainy season when the rain lays bare the sand-covered crust and washes it away.

The water of the chott is green and denser than fresh water and saltier than the sea. An attempt to measure the depth has not been successful but it may be assumed that these salt swamps are not deeper than fifty meters. The real danger of breaking through the crust lies in the mass of fluidic, moving sand, which flows fifty to eighty centimeters beneath a layer of light green water. This is the product of the *samums* [hot desert winds], which for a thousand years drove the sand from the desert into the water.

The oldest Arabic geographers, including Ebn Jobeir, Ebn Batuta, Obeidah el Bekri, El Istakhri and Omar Ebn el Wardi, all agree that there are very real dangers for any traveler on the chott. The Jerid has already swallowed thousands of people and camels without a trace. In 1826 a caravan that was comprised of more than one thousand camels attempted to cross the chott. An unfortunate incident caused the camel at the head of the long train to step off the designated path. It disappeared into the chott and was followed by all the other animals. As soon as the caravan was swallowed up, the crust reappeared as it had before, not a single trace of the event remained. It would seem impossible for a catastrophe of such magnitude to occur. To believe it one has to first realize that a camel is accustomed to following the leader and that it is usually tied to the camel in front. Secondly, the path over the chott is often so narrow that it would be impossible for an animal, much less a caravan, to turn about.

The deceptive appearance of the plains, beneath which death lurks, is in places suggestive of a shimmering blue-tinted mirror not unlike molten lead. The crust is at times hard and translucent like a bottle, and when it is struck it sounds like the floor of the Solfatara in Naples. For the most part though it consists of a soft, gruel-like mass, which appears perfectly firm but is at best able to support only a light layer of sand. Anything heavier than this would be engulfed without a trace.

The guides who cross these regions use small stones as markers at regular intervals along the path. In earlier times on the Chott El Kebir, palm branches were pushed into the ground. The branch of the date palm is called '*jerid*', and that is probably how the chott received its other name, 'El Jerid'. The stone heaps are called '*gmaïr*', and are generally absent at such points where the ground is covered with water for several meters, sometimes as deep as a horse's chest is high.

The crust of the chott is not at all even, but consists of waves that may at times reach a height of some thirty meters. The troughs of these waves appear as furrows and are used by caravans; it is in these lower regions that death and destruction lurk. Even a gentle wind can cause the salt crust to oscillate and water is forced upward under considerable pressure, spouting from available fissures like fountains.

This glittering but deadly plain was on our left as we followed the route to Kris, from there a path to Fetnassa leads across the chott along the Nifzaua Peninsula.

Halef indicated the chott below; "do you see the chott, *Sihdi*?"

"Yes."

"Have you ever ridden across a chott?"

"No."

"Then thank Allah; if you had, you might have already joined your ancestors! We are really going to cross it?"

"Certainly."

"*Bismillah* - In God's Name! May my friend Sadek still live."

"Who is he?"

"My brother Sadek is a famous guide of the Chott Jerid; he has never taken a wrong step. He belongs to the Merasig tribe, was born to his mother in Muï Hamed but lives with his son, a brave warrior, in Kris. He knows the chott like no other and he is the only one that I would trust, *Sihdi*. Do we ride directly to Kris?"

"How far is it?"

"A little over an hour."

"So we head a little westward. We must see if we can pick up the trail of the murderers."

"You really think that they have gone to Kris?"

"They too have certainly spent the night in the open and are already ahead of us with the intention of crossing the chott."

We left our path and headed west. Not far from our original route we came across many tracks; the further we went the less numerous the spoor became until finally none remained. At last, on the path that leads to El Hamma, I spied the hoof prints of two horses in the sand, and after diligently inspecting these tracks, I was certain that our quarry had made them. We followed their trail to the vicinity of Kris, where we lost it among others on the broad path. I was therefore assured that the murderers could be found here. Halef had become pensive.

"*Sihdi*, shall I tell you something?" he said.

"What is it!"

"It is certainly good if one can read the language of the sand."

"I am glad that you have realized this. But there is Kris. Where is the home of your friend Sadek?"

"Follow me *Sihdi*!"

We rode through an area where a number of tents and huts squatted beneath several palm trees, beyond this we entered a grove of almond trees. In the shelter of these stood a broad, low hut; upon our approach an Arab emerged from this dwelling and excitedly ran towards my little friend Halef.

"Sadek, my brother, you beloved of the caliph!"

"Halef, my friend, you blessed of the Prophet!"

They embraced each other like lovers. The Arab then turned to me and said:

"Forgive me that I have not attended you! Enter into my house; it is yours!"

We did as he bade us. Sadek was alone in the dwelling and he presented us with all kinds of refreshments, which we happily accepted. Halef now thought it proper to introduce me to his friend.

"This is Kara Ben Nemsi, a great *taleb* from the west who can speak with the birds and read the secrets of the sand. We have accomplished many great deeds together and I am his friend and servant and will eventually convert him to the way of the Prophet."

This steadfast fellow had once asked my name and had truly remembered the word Karl, but being unable to pronounce it, he had quickly converted it to Kara and added Ben *Nemsi*, 'offspring of the Germans'. Where or when I was supposed to have talked with the birds totally escaped me, in any case this claim raised me to the same level as Solomon who was said to have had the gift of being able to converse with animals. As to the alleged great deeds, I could likewise not recall, unless Halef was referring to the incident where I had become caught up in some scrub and was smoothly plucked from my Berber horse, who then took the opportunity to play a game of 'catch' with me. But the high point of Halef's diplomacy was his claim that I desired to be converted to Islam. This deserved a swift rebuttal; I therefore asked Sadek:

"Do you know the entire name of your friend Halef?"

"Certainly."

"And it is?"

"He is Hajji Halef Omar."

"That is incomplete. He is Hajji Halef Omar Ben Hajji Abul Abbas Ibn Hajji Dawud al Gossarah. You should know therefore that he is from a dutiful and devout family whose members were all hajjis, although ..."

"*Sihdi*," interrupted Halef with an astonishing pantomime of shock and terror, "do not speak of the virtues of your servant! You know that I will always be obedient to you."

"I hope so Halef. You should not speak of you and I; rather ask your dear friend Sadek the whereabouts of his son, whom you have spoken of to me "

"Has Halef actually told you of my son, *effendi*?" asked the Arab. "Allah bless you, Halef, that you were so thoughtful of the ones that love you! Omar Ibn Sadek, my son, went over the chott to Seftimi and will return today."

"We too desire to cross the chott, and we would have you guide us," said Halef.

"You? When?" Sadek asked us.

"Today." I replied.

"Where do you wish to go to, *Sihdi*?"

"To Fetnassa. What is the path like?"

"Dangerous, very dangerous. There are only two safe paths to the other shore, that is El Toserija between Toser and Fetnassa and Es Suida between Nefta and Sarsin. The path from here to Fetnassa is the worst and there are only two who know it with certainty, that is I and Arfan Rakedihm from Kris."

"Does your son not also know the way?"

"Yes, but he has never traveled it alone. Truly, he knows the road to Seftimi better."

"This, after a time, joins with the one to Fetnassa." I ventured.

"After about two thirds of the way, *Sihdi*."

"If we start after noon, when will reach Fetnassa?"

"Before sunrise, if your animals are strong."

"You travel the chott even by night?"

"If the moon shines, yes. But if it is dark then one has to rest on the chott, specifically where the salt is so thick that there will be no problem with the load of the camp."

"Will you guide us?"

"Yes, *effendi*."

"So let me first study the chott!"

"You have not yet crossed a chott?"

"No."

"Then come! You shall see the swamp of death, the place of despair, the sea of silence, over which I shall guide you with confident steps."

We left the hut and turned to the east. After we crossed a wide, marshy boundary we arrived at the actual shore of the chott; due to the salt crust the water was not visible. I started to dig with my knife and discovered that the crust was of a depth of fourteen centimeters and yet it was solid enough to bear the weight of an average man. It was covered with a thin layer of drifting sand, which had been blown away in some areas. These patches shimmered a bluish-white color. While I was still engrossed in my observations a voice called from behind us:

"*Salaam aaleïkum* - Peace be with you!"

I turned around. Before us stood a slim, bow-legged Bedouin who appeared to have lost his nose either to some infection or perhaps even a bullet.

"*Aaleïkum*!" replied Sadek. "What is my brother Arfan Rakedihm doing here on the chott? He wears traveling clothes. Will he guide foreign travelers over the *sobha*?"

"That is so," replied Arfan Rakedihm. "Two men, who will arrive shortly."
"Where are they going?"
"To Fetnassa."

Chapter 4

Arfan Rakedihm gestured toward Halef and myself and asked Sadek:

"Do these two foreigners also wish to cross the lake?"

"Yes." Sadek replied.

"To go where?"

"Also to Fetnassa."

"And you are to guide them?"

"You have guessed it."

"They can just as well go with me; that will save you the trouble."

"They are friends, who are no trouble to me."

"I knew it: you are miserly and allow me nothing. Have you not consistently snatched the richest travelers from me?"

"I have snatched no-one from you; I guide those people who come to me of their own free will."

"Why did Omar, your son, become a guide to Seftimi? You take my livelihood from me by force, so that I starve; Allah shall punish you and lead your steps so that the chott will swallow you up."

It may well have been that competition had created adversaries here, but even if this were not so, this man was not to be trusted, one could see it in his eyes and one thing was certain, I would not have chosen him as my guide. Arfan Rakedihm turned and walked along the shore, where some distance away two riders appeared; those he would lead over the chott.

"*Sihdi*," called Halef. "Do you recognize them?"

"I do."

"Should we let them go unhindered?"

He had already raised his gun and was ready to shoot. I forestalled him.

"Leave them! They will not escape us."

"Who are those men?" asked our guide.

"Murderers." replied Halef.

"Have they killed a member of your family or your tribe?"

"No."

"Have you a blood debt to settle with them?"

"No."

"So let them go! It is not worth getting mixed up in the affairs of strangers."

This fellow spoke like a true Bedouin. He did not even feel it necessary to look at the men described to him as murderers. They too had noticed and recognized us. I watched them hasten out onto the salt surface. As soon as they had done so they turned their backs on us with contemptuous laughter.

We walked back to the hut, rested until noon, replenished our provisions and then commenced our perilous journey.

I have trudged many winter miles in snowshoes upon unfamiliar foreign rivers, where one needed to be ever vigilant against breaking through the ice, but I have never experienced the feeling that crept over me now as I stepped out onto the unpredictable chott. It was neither terror nor fear, but rather the feeling a tightrope walker might experience if he were not entirely sure whether the rope that carries his weight has been correctly anchored. Instead of ice, a salt crust - this was quite new to me. The strange sound, the color, the crystallization of the crust – this was all so alien, it did little to bolster my sense of well-being. I tested each step and sought assurance of the firmness of the surface. In places it was so hard and smooth that one could have used skates upon it, in other places it had the dirty, loose appearance of trampled snow and would not bear the least amount of weight.

Only after I had become reasonably comfortable with this new sensation did I mount my horse, and then trusted first in our guide and secondly in my animal's instincts. The little stallion behaved as though this were not his first such trek. He walked, where it was safe, with great confidence but when that confidence faltered he identified the safe areas in a tentative, almost tender fashion, on a path that was often less than a foot wide. He laid his ears either forwards or backwards, sniffed the ground, snorted with indecision or consideration and was so careful in places that he first tested the ground by stamping it with his foreleg.

Our guide paced ahead, I followed him and behind me rode Halef. The trek placed such a heavy toll on our attention that we spoke little. Therefore, some three hours had passed before Sadek turned to me:

"Take care, *Sihdi*!" He cautioned, "Now comes the worst part of the whole journey."

"Why the worst?"

"The path often crosses deep water and is very narrow for long stretches - barely the width of two hands."

"The surface will remain sound enough?"

"I am not certain; the firmness frequently varies."

"So I will dismount to halve the load." I suggested.

"*Sihdi*, don't do it. Your horse walks with more certainty than you."

Since the guide was in charge, I consented and remained in the saddle. But even today I shudder when I think about what happened in the following ten minutes. Just ten minutes, but under such circumstances this short span can seem like an eternity.

We had reached terrain where hill became valley and valley became hill. The wave-like rises were composed of hard, compacted salt, the valleys, however, were a thick, gruel-like mass, where scant patches existed that could hold both man and beast, and great concentration as well as a healthy respect for the accompanying peril was required. Despite the fact that I was upon my horse, the green water often reached up to my thigh. This meant that the safe areas needed to be detected below the surface of the water. The worst of it was that the guide and then the animals had to first find and then test these areas before each could be trusted with the full weight of rider and mount. Even then the ground was so precarious, so treacherous, that one dared not remain a moment longer than necessary if one did not wish to sink - it was nerve-racking.

Now we came to a section of the path that was not altogether dependable and barely deviated from a ten-inch width for some twenty meters.

"*Sihdi*, watch out! We are standing in the midst of death." Called our guide.

He turned his face towards the east whilst he probed the surface and prayed in a loud voice the holy *fatcha*:

"In the name of the all-forgiving God. Hail and praise God, the Master of the world, the Forgiver, who rules on the Day of Judgment. You Whom we wish to serve and to You we do direct our plea that You guide us on the righteous path, the path that enjoys Your mercy and not the path, on which . . . "

Halef, who was behind me, had joined in the prayer; suddenly both halted at the same moment: - from between the next two crests a shot rang out. Our guide threw both his arms upwards, uttered a wordless cry, lost his footing and disappeared in an instance below the salt crust, which immediately closed over him.

It is in instances such as this when human reason is bestowed with an acuity that enables it, almost instantaneously, to arrive at a range of conclusions that would otherwise have taken minutes or even hours to process; thrusting them, with blinding clarity, upon the conscious mind. The echo of the shot had not yet receded and our guide was not yet fully submerged, nevertheless I comprehended everything. The two murderers wished to dispose of their accusers; they had persuaded their guide, all the more compliant because he was envious of Sadek. They did not need to harm us, for when they killed our guide we too were surely lost. They had ambushed us here, at the most dangerous section of the path, and shot Sadek. Now they needed only to watch and wait for us to make a wrong move and then we too would vanish beneath the surface of the chott.

I noticed, despite the suddenness with which it all happened, that Sadek had taken the bullet in the head. Had the bullet penetrated Sadek and continued on to strike my horse, or had the beast simply been startled by the sudden sound? Either way the small Berber stallion shied violently lost his rear footing and broke through the crust.

"*Sihdi*!" Came Halef's anguished howl from behind me.

I was doomed, but for one thing that saved me: while my horse was sinking and desperately trying to find solid ground, I placed both my hands on the saddle-horn, threw my legs back and into the air and vaulted over the animal's head. Due to the excess pressure I exerted on the poor beast he plunged instantly through the salt crust. In that moment, as I flew through the air, I prayed to God the most devout prayer of my life. Long words and numerous minutes are not necessary for prayer; when one flies between life and death, there are neither words nor measurements of time.

I hit solid ground, which immediately began to subside beneath me. I sought and found my footing, sinking, searching and finding a foothold once more. I struggled, stumbled, and found ground in spite of this; I was pulled down and yet managed to move forward and still I did not sink. I heard nothing, I felt nothing, I saw nothing except for the three men over on the salt-crest, two of them waited for me with guns at the ready.

There, at last I had solid ground beneath my feet; solid, abundant ground, just salt, but it carried me to safety. Two gunshots cracked near by - God decided that I should live; I tripped and fell; the bullets whistled by me. I still carried my guns on my back; it was a wonder that I had not lost them; but I did not consider the weapons at that moment, instead I threw myself with clenched fists upon the two villains. They were not expecting this. The guide fled; the elder of the two knew that without the guide he was finished, so he immediately hastened after him; I seized the younger man. He tore free and raced off; I was hard on his heels. He was blinded by fear just as I was blinded by rage; we did not care where our chase led - he let loose a terrible, ragged shriek and I threw myself quickly backwards. The salty brew swallowed him up and I stood just thirty inches from his treacherous grave.

Behind me a fearful cry sounded.

"*Sihdi*, Help, Help!"

I turned about. There at the place where I had found solid footing, Halef fought for his life. He had broken through the surface, fortunately he was able to support himself by clutching the strong salt-crust. I sprang across to where Halef lay, pulled my carbine from my back and thrust it towards him while I laid myself flat on the ground.

"Grab the strap!" I urged him.

"I have it, *Sihdi*! *O, Allah illa Allah*!"

"Throw your legs up; I can't get any closer. Hold tight!"

He used the last of his strength to heave himself upwards; at the same time I pulled with all my might; it worked - he lay safely on the surface of the swamp. As soon as Halef got his breath back, he knelt and prayed the four hundred and sixtieth *sura*:

"All that is in heaven and on earth, praise God; it is His kingdom, and we should hail Him, as He is all powerful!"

He, a Moslem, prayed; but I, a Christian, could not. I must admit I could not find the words. Behind me lay the terrible saltpan, so dazzling, so tranquil and enduring, and yet it had swallowed our guide and both our animals. Ahead of us I saw the murderer escaping, he who was responsible for everything! Every fiber quivered within me, and it took an extended period of time before I could calm myself.

"*Sihdi*, are you wounded?"

"No. But my friend, in what manner did you manage to save yourself?"

"I jumped from my horse, just as you did, *effendi*. And beyond that I remember nothing. I could begin to think again only when I was hanging on the salt lip. But we are still done for."

"Why?"

"We have no guide. Oh, Sadek, friend of my soul, may your spirit forgive me, that I was responsible for your death. But I will avenge you, that I swear by the beard of the Prophet; I will avenge you, if I do not die here first."

"You will not die, Halef."

"We will die, we will die from hunger and from thirst."

"We will get a guide."

"Who?"

"Omar, Sadek's son."

"How will he find us here?"

"Did you not hear, he went to Seftimi and is to return today?"

"He will still not find us."

"He will find us. Did Sadek not say that the path to Seftimi and to Fetnassa is the same for two thirds of the way?"

"*Effendi*, You give me new hope and new life. Yes, we will wait until Omar passes by."

"For him it will be a blessing when he finds us. He too would otherwise be swallowed up, behind us the original path is gone yet he would not be aware of this."

We settled next to each other on the salt crust; the sun's glare was so intense that our clothes were dry in a matter of minutes and we ourselves were covered with a salty film wherever we had been wet.

The afternoon passed; it was just two hours before nightfall when we saw a figure slowly approaching our position from the east. The figure drew nearer and nearer until he also noticed us.

"It is he, "decided Halef and placed his hands either side of his mouth like a megaphone "Omar Ben Sadek, hurry to us!"

The man doubled his pace and soon stood before us. He recognized his father's friend.

"Be welcome, Halef Omar!" he greeted.

"Hajji Halef Omar!" corrected Halef.

"Pardon me! The joy of seeing you is to blame for my error. You came to Kris to see my father?"

"Yes." replied Halef.

"Where is he? If you are on the chott, he must be nearby."

"He is nearby." Halef replied formally.

"Where?"

"Omar Ibn Sadek, it is proper that the faithful remain strong when they encounter kismet."

"Speak, Sadek, speak!" [He cried, then turning toward us he asked.] "Was there an accident?"

"Yes."

"What happened?"

"Allah has called your father to his ancestors."

The youngster stood before us, speechless. He stared at Halef with despair in his eyes, and his face had become terribly pale. At last he gained control over his voice, but what he said was quite unexpected.

"Who is this *Sihdi*?" he asked.

"He is Kara Ben Nemsi, whom I led to your father. We followed two murderers, who traveled over the chott. "

"My father was your guide?"

"Yes, he led us. The murderers bribed Arfan Rakedihm and ambushed us. They shot your father down; he and the horses sank in the swamp; Allah protected the *Sihdi* and I."

"Where are the murderers?"

"One died in the salt, the other went with the c*habir* – guide, to Fetnassa."

"So the path here is spoilt?"

"Yes. You cannot tread here."

"Where did my father sink?"

"There, thirty steps from here." Halef indicated the spot where our guide had disappeared into the chott.

Omar walked as far forward as the crust permitted, gazed ahead for a time and then turned to face the east:

"Allah, Almighty God of justice, hear me! Mohammed, God's prophet, hear me! All you caliphs and martyrs of Islam, hear me! I, Omar Ben Sadek, will not laugh, nor cut my beard, nor enter a mosque, until the murderers of my father burn in *Jehennah*! I swear it!"

I was deeply shaken by this oath, but could say nothing against it. Now he sat down next to us and with almost unnatural calm said: "Tell me about it!"

Halef did as requested. When he was finished, the youth arose.

"Come!" Was the only word he uttered, then he walked ahead, in the direction from whence he came.

We had already covered the most difficult stretch of the path; there was no longer the same sense of danger, despite the fact that we marched through the evening and the whole of the night. In the morning we reached the shore of the Peninsula Nifzaua and saw Fetnassa before us.

"What now?" asked Halef.

"Just follow me!"

These were the first words that Omar had uttered since yesterday. He strode to the nearest hut on the shore. An old man sat before it.

"Salaam aaleïkum!"

"Aaleïkum."

"You are Abdullah el Hamis, the salt weigher?"

"Yes."

"Have you seen the *chabir* Arfan Rakedihm, from Kris?"

"He stepped onto the shore at daybreak with a stranger."

"What did they do?"

"The *chabir* rested here and then went to Bir Rekeb, from there he intends to return to Kris. The stranger bought a horse from my son and asked about the way to Kbilli."

"I thank you, *Abu el Malah*! - Father of the Salt!"

Omar walked on in silence and led us to a hut, where we ate some dates and drank a bowl of *lagmi* (date palm juice). Then we headed towards Kris, by way of Beshni, Negua and Mansurah, where our inquiries consistently confirmed that we were still hot on the heels of our quarry. From Mansurah it is not at all far to the great Oasis Kbilli. There was at that time still a Turkish *Wekil* – Governor, who, under the direction of the Regent of Tunis, administered the Nifzaua. For this purpose he was provided with ten soldiers.

We went first of all to a coffeehouse, where Omar did not remain long. He left to gather intelligence, and returned to us after an hour had passed.

"I have seen him." Omar reported.

"Where?"

"With the *Wekil*."

"With the Governor?"

"Yes. He is the Governor's guest and wears elegant robes. If you wish to talk with him, then you must hurry, it is the time of the audience."

My interest was highly stimulated. A hunted murderer was the guest of the local administrator!

Omar led us across the open ground to a low, stone house, the walls of which bore no sign of a window. In front of the door stood nine *nefers* - soldiers, who exercised before an *onbashi* - commander of ten men, while the s*aka* – drummer, leaned against the door and watched them. We were permitted to enter and were asked by a Moor about our business. He led us into the *selamlük* - a bare-walled room, adorned with just a worn carpet, which barely covered one corner of the room. On that carpet sat a man with graven facial features, he smoked tobacco from an ancient Persian *hookah* – water pipe.

"What do you want here?" he asked.

The tone in which this question was spoken was not at all to my liking, I therefore answered with a question:

"Who are you?"

He looked at me with stark astonishment.

"I am the *Wekil*!"

"We want to talk with your guest, who arrived here yesterday or today."

"Who are you?"

"Here is my passport."

I placed the document into his hand. He threw a quick glance over it, folded it and placed it into the pocket of his wide harem-trousers.

"Who is this man?" he continued, indicating Halef.

"My servant."

"What is he called?"

"He calls himself Hajji Halef Omar."

"Who is the other?"

"He is our guide Omar Ben Sadek."

"And who are you?"

"You have just read who I am!"

"I have not read who you are."

"It is written in my passport."

"That was written with the symbols of the infidel. Where did you get it?"

"From the French government in Algiers."

"The French government in Algiers has no jurisdiction here, your passport has as much value as a blank piece of paper. Now, who are you?"

I decided to keep the name that Halef had bestowed on me.

"My name is Kara Ben Nemsi."

"You are a son of the *Nemsi*? I don't know them. Where do they live?"

"West of Turkey before one reaches the borders of the lands of France and England."

"Is this oasis large where they live, or do they have many small oases?"

"They live in one oasis, which is so large that fifty million people occupy it."

"*Allah akbar* - God is great! There are oases that abound with life. Does this oasis also have streams?"

"It has five thousand rivers and millions of streams. Many of the rivers are so big that they can bear ships that carry as many people as the number of inhabitants of the towns Basma or Rahmath."

"*Allah kerihm* - God is merciful! What kind of disaster it would be if all these ships were to be swallowed up by the rivers within the very same hour! In which God do the *Nemsi* believe?"

"They believe in your God, but they do not call Him Allah, they call Him Father."

"Then they are not Sunnites, but Shiites?" [See Trans. Notes Ch 4.1]

"They are Christians."

"*Allah iharkilik* - God burn you! Then you too are a Christian?"

"Yes."

"A *giaur*? And you dare to speak to the *Wekil* of Kbilli! I will give you the *bastinado* [See Trans. Notes Ch 4.2] if you do not at once remove yourself from my sight!"

"Have I done something wrong according to your laws, or done something that has insulted you?"

"Yes. A *giaur* may never take it upon him to appear before me. Now, what is the name of your guide?"

"Omar Ben Sadek."

"Good! Omar Ben Sadek, how long have you been in the service of this *Nemsi*?"

"Since yesterday."

"That is not a long time. I will therefore deal with you mercifully and sentence you to twenty strokes on the soles of your feet."

Turning to me, he said:

"And what is the name of your servant?"

"*Allah akbar* - God is great, but he has regrettably made your brain so small that you cannot remember two names! My servant is called, as I have already told you, Hajji Halef Omar."

"You wish to insult me, *giaur*? I will pronounce your sentence soon enough! Now, Halef Omar, you are a hajji and serve this infidel? You deserve double strokes. How long have you been with him?"

"Five weeks." Halef replied.

"That comes to sixty stokes on the soles of your feet and afterwards five days without food and water! And you, now what was your name again?"

"Kara Ben Nemsi."

"Good, Kara Ben Nemsi, you have committed three great crimes."

"Which are, *Sihdi*?"

"I am no *Sihdi*; you address me as *Jenabin-iz* or *Hazretin-iz*, that is, 'Your Grace' or 'Your Excellency'! Your crimes are as follows: You have firstly misled two of the faithful, for which you will receive fifteen strokes; you have secondly dared to disturb me during my *kef* (midday rest), that is another fifteen strokes; and thirdly you have questioned my memory, that is another twenty strokes; all together that is fifty strokes on the soles of your feet. And since it is my right to collect a *wergi* - a fee, all your possessions are confiscated and assigned to me."

"Oh, great *Jenabin-iz*, I hold you in awe; your justice is sublime, your wisdom most sublime, your grace yet more sublime and your intelligence and cleverness the most sublime of all! But I request, noble *Bei* of Kbilli, let us see your guest, before we receive the stokes."

"What do you want from him?"

"I believe that he is an acquaintance of mine, and I wish to behold the happiness on his face upon seeing me."

"He is no acquaintance of yours. He is a great warrior, a noble son of the Sultan and a firm believer in the Koran, and he was never an acquaintance of any infidel. But so that he sees how the *Wekil* of Kbilli punishes criminals, I will let him come. The happiness on his face will not be from seeing you, it will be there as a result of every stoke you receive. He knew that you would come."

"Ah! How did he know that?"

"You passed him earlier, without seeing him, and he reported you to me immediately. Had you not come, then I would have had you apprehended."

"He reported us? For what?"

"That you will hear shortly. You shall then receive a second sentence, which will be greater than the one I have just given you."

This was indeed a strange and surprising turn of events taking place during our audience with this official. A *Wekil* with ten soldiers in a remote, forgotten oasis - he was, once upon a time, either a *tshaush* – sergeant, or a *mülasim* – lieutenant, and one knows what to expect from a Turkish lieutenant. These subalterns are, or were, no different from the boot-polishers and pipe-stuffers of those higher up. This man had been posted to Kbilli to give him the opportunity to fend for himself, and was then promptly forgotten, as the *Bei* of Tunis had already chased all Turkish soldiers from this land. Furthermore, the Bedu tribes were only under the protection of the Sultan insofar as that he annually sent their leaders his worn out robes of office, they in turn showed their thanks by not thinking about him at all. The dependable *Wekil* was therefore forced to support himself through extortion, and since this was a tricky affair when employed against the locals, the opportune appearance of a foreigner was entirely to his advantage. He knew nothing about Germany, he knew nothing of the meaning of a consulate, he lived among thieving nomads, and he believed me to be without protection and assumed that he could do as he wished without consequence.

Certainly it was correct that I could count only upon myself, but the thought that I should fear 'His Eminence' never once crossed my mind, instead I found it amusing that he intended to introduce us to the *bastinado* in such a genial manner. At the same time I was also curious to find out whether his guest was truly the one we pursued. Omar could have been wrong, which I doubted when I considered that this guest had reported us. What crime he accused us of I could only guess. In any case, he was clearly known to the *Wekil* and had used this to render us harmless.

The Governor clapped his hands, and at once a black servant appeared, he threw himself before the *Wekil* as one would before a Sultan. The *Wekil* whispered a few words to the servant, who then departed. After a time the door opened, and ten soldiers with their *onbashi* entered. They were a sad sight to behold in all their patched attire, which no longer resembled a military uniform;

most of them were barefoot, and all carried guns with which one could do all sort of things, except shoot. They also threw themselves before the *Wekil*, who, in what was apparently supposed to be a military manner, inspected them before conveying his order:

"*Kalkyn*! – Stand up!"

They rose, and the *onbashi* drew his mighty *sarras* from its scabbard.

"*Kylyn syraji*! - Into line!" He barked in a tenor voice.

They arranged themselves next to each other and held their guns comfortably in their brown hands.

"*Has - dur*! - Shoulder arms! " He commanded.

The guns flew into the air, knocked against each other, against the walls and even against the heads of these imposing heroes, but did after some time land luckily on the shoulders of their owners.

"*Isalam - dur*! Present arms!"

Once again the weapons became such a confused tangle that it came as no surprise when, during the act of bringing it under control, one of the hero's guns lost its barrel. The soldier bent down leisurely, picked up the barrel, looked at it from all sides, held it against the light to see if the hole through which one shoots was still present, pulled a palm-fiber strand from his pocket and bound the barrel into the position from whence it had absconded, namely, the butt. Then finally, with a satisfied look, he brought the restored weapon into the position that the last order had dictated.

"*Sessiz, söjle-me-niz*! Stand still and no talking!"

At this command they all pressed their lips together with visible force and intensity and made it plain by their earnest eye twitching that they were committed to preventing a single sound from escaping them. They had noticed that they were being called upon to guard three criminals and therefore it was important that we should be impressed. I really had to work hard to appear serious during these exercises and I noticed that my failure to do so had the effect of imparting courage to my companions.

Once again the door opened. The man we were waiting for entered. He was the one we were pursuing.

Without honoring us with a glance, he moved to the carpet, sat down next to the *Wekil* and took the pipe from the hand of the black servant who had entered with him and had just finished stoking the pipe for him. Only then did he raise his eyes and offer us a look of scorn that was beyond belief. The Governor then spoke to me:

"This is the man that you wished to see. Is he your acquaintance?"

"Yes."

"You spoke correctly; he is your acquaintance, that is, you know him. But he is not your friend."

"I would not be very thankful for his friendship. What does he call himself?"

"He is called Abu el Nassr."

"That is not true! His name is Hamd il Amasat."

"G*iaur*, do not dare to call me a liar, otherwise you will receive twenty more stokes! Of course my friend is called Hamd il Amasat; but know this, you dog of an infidel, when I was still *miralai* at Stambul [The old quarter of what is now Istanbul, Turkey], I was ambushed one night by Greek bandits. Hamd il Amasat came and spoke with them and saved my life. Since that night he is known as *Abu el Nassr*, 'Father of Victory', whom no one can oppose, not even a Greek bandit."

I could control myself no longer and shook my head in laughter.

"You, a *miralai* in Stambul, in other words a colonel? With which troop?"

"With the Guard, you son of a *shakal* - jackal."

I stepped one pace closer to him and lifted my right hand.

"I dare you to insult me again, if you do I will give you such a *ssille* - clap around the ears, that in the morning you will think that your nose is a minareh! You are some fellow - a colonel, you claim to be! You may put that past these oasis heroes but not me, understand!"

He rose with unaccustomed speed. This had never happened to him before, it was totally beyond his scope of understanding; he stared at me as though I were some spirit, and then spluttered – in rage or embarrassment, I do not know which:

"Listen, I could even have made *lawi-pasha* - major-general, if this post here in Kbilli had not been preferable to me!"

"Yes, you are the true epitome of courage and valor. You have fought with bandits, whom your friend conquered with mere words; do you not hear how that sounds? He was certainly well acquainted with them or even a member of their clan. He committed plunder and murder in Algiers; he killed a man in Wadi Tarfui; he killed our guide, Omar's father, on Chott Jerid because he wanted to be rid of me. I followed him to Kbilli, and I find this man is a friend of a supposed colonel in the service of the Sultan. I charge him with murder and I demand that you take him prisoner!"

Now Abu el Nassr stood up and exclaimed:

"This man is a *giaur*. He has drunk wine and does not know what he is saying," he charged disparagingly. "He must sleep off his intoxication and then be answerable for his accusations."

This was finally enough for me. I quickly grabbed him, lifted him into the air and threw him to the ground. He jumped up and pulled out his knife.

"Dog, you dare to touch one of Allah's faithful! You will die!"

With these words he threw himself upon me with all his might, but I delivered such a well-aimed blow with my fist that he fell down and stayed there without further movement.

"Seize him!" the *Wekil* commanded his soldiers.

I expected that they would immediately leap upon me, but I was astonished at what happened next. The corporal took up position in front of his squad and ordered:

"*Komyn silahlari*! - Ground arms!"

They all bowed low and placed their guns on the floor and returned to their previous positions.

"*Döndärmek sagha*! - Right turn!"

They made a quarter turn to the right and were now standing in single file.

"*Gityn erkek tshewresinde, koshyn-iz*! - Surround that man. March!"

As though on a parade ground they started with the left foot; the lead man called the pace.

"Left - right, left - right, left - right!" They marched until they had encircled me and stopped at the command of the corporal.

"*Onu tutmyn*! - Seize him!"

Twenty hands with an even one hundred dirty, brown fingers reached out from all around me and took hold of my burnoose. The affair was so absurd that I could easily have made a move for my freedom.

"*Dshenabin-iz, bizim - was herifu* - Excellency, we have the fellow!" announced the high commander of this courageous troop.

"*Brakyn-jok onu tekrar azad* – Do not let him go!" commanded the Governor with a stern expression.

One hundred fingers clawed a firmer and still firmer hold upon my burnoose, the stiff, Oriental dignity with which this all had transpired and the ludicrous marionette maneuvers of the troop almost caused me to laugh aloud.

As this was going on, Abu el Nassr had risen. His eyes glinted with fury and a murderous hunger for vengeance, he said to the *Wekil*:

"You will have him shot!"

"Yes, he will be shot; before that though he shall have a hearing, I am a fair judge and do not like to condemn anyone without a hearing. Bring forward the accused!"

"This *giaur*," began the murderer, "crossed over the chott with a guide and his servant; he met us and hurled my companion into the depths, so that he drowned miserably."

"Why did he do this?"

"For revenge."

"For what reason did he seek vengeance?"

"He killed a man in Wadi Tarfaui; we were passing by and attempted to arrest him, but he eluded us."

"Can you vouch for your words?"

"By the beard of the Prophet!"

"That is enough! - Have you heard these words?" the *Wekil* asked me.

"Yes."

"What do you have to add?"

"That this man is a scoundrel. He was the murderer and he has reversed the positions of the persons involved."

"He has vowed by the Prophet, and you are a *giaur*. I do not believe you, but him."

"Ask my servant! He is my witness."

"He serves an infidel; his words have no value. I will summon the great Council of the Oasis to hear my words and decide this case."

"You choose not to believe me because I am a Christian, and yet you believe this *giaur*. This man is an Armenian and a Christian not a Moslem."

"He has sworn by the Prophet."

"That is infamy and a sin, for which God will punish him. If you do not want to hear me, then I will accuse him before the Council of the Oasis."

"A *giaur* can not accuse one of the faithful, and the Council of the Oasis could not do anything to my friend because he holds the *Bu-Djeruldu* and is therefore protected by '*Giölgeda padischahnün'*, he stands 'In the Shadow of the Padishah'."

"And I am under the protection of *Giölgeda senin kyralün*, I stand 'In the Shadow of my King'. I too have a *Bu-Djeruldu*; you have it in your pocket."

"It is written in the language the *giaurs*; I would defile myself if I read it. Your case will be investigated today; but first you will experience the *bastinado*: You will receive fifty strokes on the soles of your feet, your servant sixty and your guide twenty. Lead them into the courtyard; I will follow!"

"*Alykomün elleri*! - Release him!" Commanded the corporal at once.

The one hundred fingers immediately released me from their grip.

"*Alyn-iz tüfenkleri*! - Take up arms!" The corporal continued.

The heroes lunged to take up their weapons.

"*Wirmyn hep - ütsh*! - Surround all three!"

In no time they had Halef, Omar and myself encircled. We were led into the courtyard, in the midst of which was a seat-like block. The construction and design of this block suggested its purpose, namely the dispensation of the *bastinado*.

While I conducted myself in a composed manner, my two companions had likewise followed without resistance, but I saw in their eyes that they awaited my move to make an end of this farce.

When we had stood before the block for a while, the *Wekil* and Abu el Nassr appeared. The black servant carried the carpet ahead of them and spread it on the ground, once they had seated themselves he passed them fire for their pipes. Then the *Wekil* pointed towards me and ordered:

"*Wermyn ona elli* - Give him fifty!"

The time had come.

"Do you still have my *Bu-Djeruldu* in your pocket?" I asked him.

"Yes."

"Give it to me!" I demanded.

"You will never get it back!"

"Why not?"

"So you may never again defile any of the faithful with it."

"You really mean to beat me?"

"Yes."

"Then I will show you how a *Nemsi* acts when he is forced to procure his own justice!"

The small courtyard was bordered on three sides by a high wall and on the fourth by the building; there was no passage out except the way we had come in. There were no spectators, therefore we were three against thirteen. They had allowed us to keep our weapons, as was the courteous custom of the desert; the *Wekil* was harmless enough, as were his soldiers, only Abu el Nassr might present a problem. I had to disable him.

"Do you have a rope?" I asked Omar quietly.

"Yes; my burnoose sash."

"Loosen it!" I advised him, turning to Halef I said: "You run to the exit and let no one through!"

"Procure it then!" challenged the *Wekil.*

"At once!"

With these words I leaped without warning, through the rank of soldiers and upon Abu el Nassr, I wrenched his arms behind his back and drove my knee so hard against his neck that he was unable to move from his sitting position.

"Bind him!" I commanded Omar.

This order was really not necessary, Omar immediately knew what to do and was already securing the rope around the arms of the Armenian. Before anyone could make a move against us, he was tied fast. My sudden attack had confounded both the *Wekil* and his bodyguard; he looked at me in consternation. I now drew my knife with my right hand and grabbed the *Wekil* by the nape of his neck with my left. In terror he extended his arms and his legs as though he were already dead, but this did animate the soldiers.

"*Hatshyn, aramin imdadi*! - Escape, bring help!" howled the *onbashi*, who was the first to find his voice.

His saber had become an inconvenience and he threw it away as he ran for the exit. The rest of the soldiers followed his lead, but there stood the stouthearted Halef with his flintlock at the ready.

"*Geri; durar-siz bunda*! - Back! You stay here!" he barked at them.

They stopped, turned and ran in all four directions hoping to find protection in the corners.

Omar had also drawn his knife and with a grim look in his eyes, stood ready to plunge it into the heart of Abu el Nassr.

"Are you dead?" I asked the *Wekil.*

"No, but you will kill me?"

"That depends on you - you the embodiment of justice and courage. But I tell you that your life hangs by a very thin thread."

"What do you want from me, *Sihdi*?"

Even before I could reply, there came the fearful wail of a woman's voice. I looked up and caught sight of a short, plump female figure that had appeared at the entrance; she rolled toward us with the greatest effort.

"*Tut*! - Stop!" she screamed. "*Öldirme onu*; *you benim kodsha*! - Do not kill him; he is my husband!"

So this large, round madam who, beneath her extensive cloth cocoon, steered towards me with what resembled a swimmer's strokes, was the *Wekil's* wife. Clearly she had expected to view an interesting execution from the wood-shuttered women's quarters but soon came to the horrible realization that her husband was about to be executed instead. I asked her calmly:

"Who are you?"

"*In kary wekilün*, I am the wife of the *Wekil*," she replied.

"*Ewet, you benim awret, gül Kbillinün* - Yes, she is my wife, the 'Rose of Kbilli'," confirmed the *Wekil* with a groan.

"What is her name?"

"*Demar-im Mersinah* - I am Mersinah," she volunteered.

"*Hey, demar Mersinah* - Yes, she is called Mersinah," echoed the *Wekil.*

She was the 'Rose of Kbilli' and her name was Mersinah, that is myrtle. I needed to be courteous in the presence of such a tender creature.

"If you show me the blush of your face, oh flower of the oasis, then I will remove my hand from your man." I said.

At once the *yashmak* - the veil, flew from her face. She had lived a long time among the Arabs, whose women do not cover their faces, and was therefore less restrained than she would have been among Turkish women. Besides, this situation concerned the precious life of her husband. I looked upon a flat, drab and dreary female face, which was so fleshy that one could not distinguish the eyes from the small blunt nose. Madame *Wekil* was perhaps forty years old and had tried to paralyze the consequences of time with high, black painted eyebrows and red rouged lips. Two black dots of kohl, which were drawn in the middle of each cheek, gave her a picturesque appearance, and as she now exposed her forearms from beneath the ample gowns, I noticed, that she had not only dyed her nails but also her entire hands with henna.

"I thank you, you 'Sun of Jerid'!" I flattered her. "If you promise me that the *Wekil* will remain calm and seated, no harm will come to him."

"*Kaladshak-dir* – He will remain seated - I promise you!"

"He may give thanks to your devotion that I did not crush him like an *indshir*, like a fig, that is pressed before drying. *Senin seda benzemar sedaja düdükün* - Your voice is like the voice of the flute; *senin göz perdahlamar nasyl göz güneshün* - your eyes shine like the eye of the sun; *ile senin shekl shekla Sheheresahdenün benzemar* - and your figure is like the figure of Scheherezade. To you alone do I make the offering of permitting him to live!"

I released my grip on the *Wekil*; he straightened himself with a relieved groan, but remained obediently seated. She inspected me with close attention from head to foot and asked amiably:

"Who are you?"

"I am a *Nemsi*, a foreigner, whose home is far across the sea."

"And are your women beautiful?"

"They are beautiful, but they can not rival the women of the Chott El Kebir."

She nodded, smiling with satisfaction, and I realized from her manner that I had found grace in her eyes.

"The *Nemsi* are quite clever, a very brave and courteous people, I have heard this said frequently."

She then decided. "You are welcome among us! But why have you bound this man; why do our soldiers flee before you, and why do you wish to kill the mighty Governor?"

"I have bound this fellow because he is a murderer; your soldiers fled from me because they realized that I would defeat all eleven of them, and the *Wekil* I have seized because he intended to beat me and then perhaps sentence me to death, without granting me justice."

"You shall have justice!"

I was forced to conclude that the slipper in the Orient had the same magical quality that it had in the West [See Trans. Notes Ch 4.3]. The *Wekil* saw that his authority was being threatened and attempted to reclaim it:

"I am a fair judge and will . . . "

"*Sus-olmar-sen* - You will be silent!" She commanded him. "You know that I am acquainted with this man, who calls himself *Abu el Nassr* - 'Father of Victory'; he should call himself *Abu el Jalani* – 'Father of Liars'. He was responsible for your posting to Algiers, just before you could become *mülasim*; he was also responsible for your posting to Tunisia, where you are forgotten in this desolate place, and every time that he has appeared, you have had to do something that caused you harm. I hate him, I hate him and I have no objection to the fact that this foreigner wishes to kill him. He deserves it!"

"He must not be killed; he stands in '*Giölgeda padischahnün*'!"

"*Tut aghyzi* - Shut your mouth! He stands in '*Giölgeda padischahnün'*, that is, he stands 'In the Shadow of the Padishah'; this foreigner however stands in *Giölgeda wekilanün*, thus he stands 'In the Shadow of the *Wekil's* wife' - my shadow; do you hear me? And he, who stands in my shadow, shall not be burned by you. Stand up and follow me!"

He arose; she turned to go; and he made a move to follow. That was of course totally contrary to my intent.

"Stop!" I commanded, whilst again taking hold of the scruff of his neck. "You will remain here!"

She turned around.

"Did you not say that you would free him?" she asked.

"Yes, but only on the condition that he remains in his place."

"He cannot sit here for all eternity!"

"You are right, oh 'Pearl of Kbilli'; but he can remain here until I have concluded my affairs."

"This is already done."

"How so?"

"Have I not said to you that you are welcome among us?"

"That is correct."

"You and your companions are therefore our guests and shall remain with us for as long as you desire or until you decide to leave."

"And Abu el Nassr, whom you called Abu el Jalani?"

"He is yours, and you can do with him as you please."

"Is that true, *Wekil*?"

He hesitated to give an answer, but a stern look from his lady prompted him to speak:

"Yes."

"You swear it?"

"I swear it."

"By Allah and his Prophet!"

"Must I?" he asked Madame, the 'Rose of Kbilli'.

"You must!" she replied with conviction.

"Then I swear by Allah and his Prophet."

"Now may he come with me?"

"He may."

"You will follow and join us in a meal of mutton and couscous."

"Do you have a place where I can safely keep Abu el Nassr?"

"No. Bind him to the trunk of that palm tree by the wall. He will not escape you, because he will also be guarded by our troops."

"I will guard him myself." replied Omar before I myself could.

"He will not escape; he will pay for my father's life with his own death. My knife will be as sharp as my eye."

The murderer had, from the instant of his being bound, not uttered a word; but his eyes followed us with a malevolent glare as he was led to the palm tree to which he was to be bound. It was truly not my intention to take his life; but he had fallen foul in a 'blood feud', and I knew that no plea from me would save him from Omar. *Ed d'em b'ed d'em*, or as the Turks would say, *kan kanü ödemar* - blood pays for blood. As long as he was either my captive or my quarry I had to view him as an enemy and a murderer and deal with him accordingly. Yet it would have been preferable to me, despite all that had happened, if he were to slip away without my knowledge. It was certain that he would not show me similar concern should I be unlucky enough to fall into his hands.

I left him in Omar's care and went with Halef to the *selamlük*. On the way my little servant asked me:

"You said that this man is not a Moslem. Is that true?"

"Yes. He is an Armenian Christian and pretends to be a Moslem whenever it is convenient for him."

"And you believe he is a bad person?"

"A very bad person."

"Do you see, *effendi*, that the Christians are very bad people! You must become one of the 'True Believers' if you do not wish to burn for an eternity in *Jehenna*!"

"But you yourself will burn in *Jehenna*!"

"Why?"

"Have you not told me that all liars and hypocrites will burn in *Derk Asfal* - in the seventh and deepest Hell, and be forced to eat the devils' heads from the *Zakum* tree?"

"Yes, but what does that have to do with me?"

"You are a liar and a hypocrite!"

"I, *Sihdi*? My tongue speaks only the truth, and there is no falsehood in my heart. Whomsoever would accuse me as you have, him my bullet shall dispatch!"

"You do lie, you claim to have seen Mecca, and feign to be a hajji. Shall I relate this to the *Wekil*?"

"*Aman, aman* - Forgive me! You would not do that to Hajji Halef Omar, the most loyal servant that you will ever find!"

"No, I will not do it; but you know the condition of my silence."

"I know and will take greater care, but despite that you will still become a 'True Believer', regardless of whether you may want to or not, *Sihdi*!"

We entered and were welcomed by the *Wekil*. It was not the friendliest welcome with which I have been greeted.

"Please sit!"

I followed his invitation and sat very close to him, while Halef busied himself with the pipes, which were stood in readiness in the corner of the room.

"Why did you ask to see my wife's face?" he began the conversation.

"Because I am a *Nemsi*, who is accustomed to seeing the face of one to whom he speaks."

"You have wicked customs! Our women conceal themselves, yours display themselves. Our women wear clothes that are long on top and short below; yours wear clothes that are short on top and long below and even sometimes short at both ends. Have you ever seen our women with the *Nemsi*? No! Yet your girls come to us - why is this? *Oh jazik* - Oh woe!"

"*Wekil*, is this hospitality which you offer me? Since when is it your custom to greet a guest with insults? I need neither your mutton nor your couscous and will now return to the courtyard. Follow me!"

"*Effendi*, forgive me! I only wished to tell you what I thought, but I did not intend to insult you."

"He who does not intend to insult may not always speak his mind. A chattering man is like a broken pot, of use to no one, because he holds nothing."

"Sit yourself down and tell me how you met Abu el Nassr."

I gave him a comprehensive report of our adventure. He listened in silence and finally shook his head.

"You believe that he murdered the merchant from Blidah?"

"Yes."

"Were you there!"

"I deduced it."

"Allah alone may deduce; he knows everything, and the thoughts of men are like riders who sit on disobedient horses and are carried away to places they did not intend to go."

"Allah alone may deduce; He knows everything? Oh *Wekil*, your spirit is tired from the excess of mutton and couscous you have eaten! Because Allah is 'all-knowing', He has no need for deduction; only he who searches for a solution by reasoning, without knowing the answer, deduces."

"I hear that you are a *taleb* - a learned one, who attended many schools, you speak in words that no one can understand. You also believe that Abu el Nassr killed that man in Wadi Tarfaui?"

"Yes."

"Were you there?"

"No."

"So did the dead man tell you?"

"*Wekil*, even the mutton that you feast upon knows that a dead man cannot speak!"

"*Effendi*, now you are impolite! You were not there, and the dead man could not speak; how then can you know that Abu el Nassr is the murderer?"

"I deduced it."

"I have already told you that only Allah may deduce!"

"I saw the tracks and followed them, and when they led me to Abu el Nassr he admitted that he had committed the murder."

"That you have found his trail is not proof that he is a murderer, because no one has ever been slain by tracks in the sand. That he admitted to the murder does not concern me either; he is a *kush-shakanün* - a joker, whose intention was to have some fun."

"One does not joke with murder!"

"But one does joke with a man, and you were such a man. You also believe that he shot your guide, Sadek?"

"Yes."

"Were you there?"

"Certainly."

"And you saw it?"

"Quite clearly. Hajji Halef Omar is also a witness."

"Well now, so Abu el Nassr shot your guide; and because of that you really want to claim that he is a murderer?"

"Naturally!"

"*Sihdi*! May Allah restore your judgment, you will soon realize that a man should not deduce!"

"And why not?"

"Because you were a witness to the shooting of your guide, you deduced that Abu el Nassr is a murderer?"

"That is self-evident."

"Wrong! Not if it was the result of a 'blood feud'. Does blood feud exist in your land?"

"No."

"Then I say to you, that a blood avenger is never a murderer. No judge would ever condemn him; only those to whom the victim was related have the right to pursue him."

"But Sadek did not insult him!"

"Then the clan to which Sadek belonged insulted him."

"Even that is not the case. *Wekil*, I wish to tell you that I personally want to have no dealings with this Abu el Nassr, who is really Hamd il Amasat and before that bore some Armenian name, so long as he leaves me in peace. But he has slain our guide Sadek, whose son is Omar Ben Sadek and he, as you told me earlier, has a right to take the life of this murderer. Sort it out with him, only make sure that this 'Father of Victory' never crosses my path again, otherwise I will settle the score with him!"

"*Sihdi*, now your words become wise. I will speak with Omar, he will let him go; but you are my guest for as long as you desire."

He arose and made his way to the courtyard. I already knew that it would be impossible to sway Omar from his intentions. Truly, the *Wekil* returned after a while wearing a dark expression and remained silent as the spit of mutton, which was prepared by the lovely hennaed fingers of the 'Rose of Kbilli', was carried in. Halef and I dug in bravely. At this moment, just as the *Wekil* chose to announce that Omar should receive his meal in the courtyard, as he could not be convinced to leave his prisoner, there came from outside a loud cry. I looked up and the plea came again:

"*Breh, effendina* - Help me!"

This entreaty was surely meant for me. I leaped up and hurried into the courtyard. Omar lay on the ground struggling with the soldiers; the prisoner was nowhere to be seen. By the exit stood the black servant, looking at me with a gloating grin on his face he sneered:

"Gone, *Sihdi* - there he rides!"

Three steps brought me to the front of the house, and I then saw Abu el Nassr disappear among the palms trees. He rode a racing camel, which obviously proceeded at a fantastic pace. I guessed at what had transpired. The *Wekil* had failed in the courtyard, but he was determined to save Abu el Nassr; he had commanded the black servant to prepare a camel and had ordered the soldiers to hold Omar while they cut the prisoner loose. These eleven courageous heroes dared to tackle this one, and the plan had worked. Certainly the success had been bought at a high price. Omar had used his knife, and as I pulled apart the tangle that the fighters formed, I saw more than one man bleeding.

"He is gone, *Sihdi*!" the young guide gasped with rage and exertion.

"Yes, I saw him."

"Which way did he go?"

"That way." I indicated the direction with my hand.

"You punish these here, *effendi*, but I am going after the escapee."

"He had a riding camel."

"I will catch him despite that."

"You have no animal!"

"*Sihdi*, I have friends here who will grant me a noble animal, and dates and water-skins. Before he can disappear over the horizon, I will be on his trail. You too will find my trail if you decide to follow."

He hurried away.

Halef had seen it all and had also helped me to disentangle Omar from the soldiers. He burned with rage.

"Why did you free this man, you dogs, you offspring of mice and rats . . . "

He would surely have continued this chastising liturgy, had not the *Wekila* entered the courtyard. She was again heavily veiled.

"What happened?" she asked me.

"Your troops jumped my guide . . . "

"*Murdarlar, tshapkinler* - You villains, you knaves!" She shouted, stamping her foot and squeezing her red fists from beneath her garments.

"And have freed the prisoner . . . "

"*Tshodshukler, dolandyryshler* - You deceitful knaves, you frauds!" she continued, and it appeared as though she were about to attack them physically.

"By the order of the *Wekil*." I added.

"The *Wekil*? - *Bu kurd, bu jalangdshy, bu faidasitzlikler, bu imaddshilikler* - That worm, that disobedient, useless, pighead! My hand shall deal with him, *ile gertshekki hemen shimdi* - and certainly at once, in this very instant!"

She turned and steered, full of anger, towards the *selamlük*.

Oh the delightful reign of the slipper, its scepter is identical in the north as in the south, in the east as in the west! (See Trans. Notes Ch 4.3). Halef wore a satisfied expression as he said.

"She is the *Wekil* and he the *Wekila*, and we stand better in *Giölgeda wekilanün* - 'In the Shadow of the *Wekil's* wife', than if we had a *Bu-Djeruldu* and were protected by '*Giölgeda padischahnün'*. *Hamdulillah* - Allah be praised, that I am not so lucky to be the *Wekil* of this *Wekila*!"

The Tschikarma

[The Kidnapping]

Chapter 5

It was that time of day when the Egyptian sun blazed with searing intensity and anyone who was not compelled by necessity to be in the open took shelter beneath any available cover and strove to find coolness and consolation.

I too was resting on a divan in my rented apartment, slurping spiced mocha and reveling in the aroma of spiced *djebeli*, which wafted from my pipe. The solid, windowless exterior walls offered some defense against the sun's burning rays. Nile water evaporated through the porous sides of the clay pots that stood everywhere about the room, making the atmosphere bearable - so effectively in fact that I noticed very little of the usual noontime commotion.

The scolding voice of my servant Halef Agha came from outside.

Halef Agha? Yes, my worthy little Halef had become an *Agha* - a Lord, and who had bestowed this honor upon him?

Amusing question! Who other than he himself!

We had reached Egypt via Tripoli and Kufarah, there we visited Cairo - which the Arabs classically call *el Masr* - the Capital, or more preferably *el Kahira* - the Victorious. We then traveled up the Nile as far as my limited resources would permit, thereafter renting an apartment for a prolonged rest. I would have been more than happy here if the otherwise fine divan and carpets were not also home to a multitude of jumping, biting beings, of which good old Fischart [Johann Fischart ca. 1546-1590] wrote:

"*Mich bizt neizwaz, waz mag daz seyn*? [Something is biting me, what may it be?]"

And from whom one learned that apart from the large-eyed *Pulex casins* and the red *Pulex musculi*, there were also the most enjoyable *Pulex irritans* and the furious *Pulex penetrans*. Sadly I must say that Egypt is not the hunting ground of '*irritans*', but rather of '*penetrans*', and I need not add that my *kef* - my noon rest, did not pass without interruption.

In any event, the scolding voice of my servant Halef Agha arose from outside, rousing me from my reverie:

"What? How? Who?"

"The *effendi*." came the bashful reply.

"You want to disturb the *Effendi el Kebihr* - the great Lord and Master?"

"I must speak with him."

"What - you must? Now, during his *kef*? Has Lucifer - Allah protect me from him! - Filled your head with Nile sludge, that you cannot comprehend what it means to be an *effendi*, a *hekim*, a man that the Prophet has endowed with wisdom, so that he can do all things, even raise the dead, if they can tell him the cause of their death!"

Ah well, I will have to admit that Halef had changed a lot whilst in Egypt! He had become exceedingly proud, consistently abrupt and an unashamed braggart, and in the Orient that is saying a lot.

In the Orient, every German is considered to be a great gardener and every foreigner is regarded as being an excellent marksman or an eminent healer. Now it so happened that whilst in Cairo I rather unfortunately came into possession of an old, partially stocked, homeopathic apothecary from Willmar Schwabe [manufacturer of herbal medicine and other natural products]. I had experimented here and there, and had administered five kernels of one-thirtieth potency to strangers and acquaintances; and then during the Nile trip I had prescribed for my fellow passengers' imagined ills a knife-point of milk-sugar. Thus with incredible speed I became known as a doctor who, in league with *Shaïtan* and with the aid of three kernels of durum wheat, could bring the dead back to life.

This notoriety had created a kind of delusion of grandeur in Halef's mind, which luckily did not hinder him in the performance of his duties as my trusted and attentive servant. That he was the principal contributor to the promotion of this reputation was self-evident; he was wholly in the ignominious vice of the late Baron Münchhausen senior and he further tried to bolster his image with his coarseness, the latter threatening to become a standard of his behavior. So he had, amongst other things, purchased a Nile-whip with his meager earnings, without which he was now never seen. He knew Egypt from an earlier visit and declared that nothing could be accomplished without such a whip, proclaiming that it could achieve more than courtesy or money, the latter of which I was indeed short of.

"God preserve your speech, *Sihdi*," I heard that pleading voice again; "but I really must see and speak with your *effendi*, the great doctor from Frankistan."

"You may not disturb him now."

"It is very important, otherwise my master would not have sent me."

"Who is your master?"

"He is the rich and mighty Abrahim-Mamur, may Allah grant him a thousand years."

"Abrahim-Mamur? Who is this Abrahim-Mamur, and what was the name of his father? Who was the father of his father and the father of his father's father? To whom was he born and where do they, who gave him his name, live?"

"That I do not know, *Sihdi*, but he is a mighty Lord, as his name says."

"His name? What do you mean?"

"Abrahim-Mamur, *Mamur* means 'leader of a province', and I tell you he was truly a *Mamur*."

"Was? He is no longer?"

"No."

"That is what I thought. Nobody knows him, even I, Halef Agha, the courageous friend and protector of my master, have never heard of him and never seen the tip of his tarboosh. Go away, my master has not the time!"

"Please tell me, *Sihdi*, what must I do to gain an audience with him!"

"Do you not know the sound of the silver key, with which the places of wisdom are unlocked?"

"I have this key with me."

"So turn the key!"

I listened attentively and heard the soft clinking of what sounded like silver pieces.

"One *para*? Indeed, I say to you, that the cleft in the lock is bigger than your key; which does not fit because it is too small." Halef indignantly responded.

"Then I must enlarge it."

Again I heard the soft metallic sound of small silver pieces. I did not know whether to laugh or be vexed. This Halef Agha had become an extraordinarily sly porter!

"Three *para*? Good, now one might at least inquire what it is you wish to tell the *effendi*."

"He must come with me and bring his magical medicine."

"Fool, what is wrong with you! For three *para* I shall coax him to give away his medicine, which is brought to him on the first night of every new moon by a white fairy?"

"Is this true?"

"I, Hajji Halef Omar Agha, Ben Hajji Abul Abbas Ibn Hajji Dawud al Gossarah, say it is. I have seen it myself, and if you do not believe me, then you will meet my *kamtshilama* - my Nile-whip!"

"I believe it, *Sihdi*!"

"That is fortunate for you!"

"And I will give you another two *para*."

"Give them to me! Who is ill in the house of your master?"

"That is a secret, which only the *effendi* may know."

"Only the *effendi* may know? Villain, am I, who have also seen the fairy, not an *effendi* as well? Go home; Halef Agha will not be insulted!"

"Forgive me, *Sihdi*; I will tell you!"

"I care not. Get out of here!"

"But I implore you ..."

"Go!"

"Shall I give you another *para*?"

"I will not take one anymore!"

"*Sihdi*?"

"But two!"

"Oh, *Sihdi*, your brow radiates compassion. Here, accept these two *para*."

“Good! So who is ill?”

“The wife of my master.”

“The wife of your master?” asked Halef with curiosity. “Which wife?”

“He has only this one.”

“And he was supposed to have been a *Mamur*?”

“He is so rich that he could have a hundred wives, but he loves only this one.”

“What is wrong with her?”

“Nobody knows; but her body is ill, and her soul is even worse.”

“*Allah kerihm* - God is merciful, but I am not. I stand here with this Nile-whip in my hand and long to beat your back with it. By the beard of the Prophet, your mouth utters such wisdom, as though your sense fell overboard during your trip on the river. Don't you know that a woman has no soul and therefore cannot enter heaven? How can the soul of a woman be ill - even more so than her body?”

“I do not know, but I was told so, *Sihdi*. Let me in to see the *effendi*!”

“I shall not do it.”

“Why not?”

“My master knows the Koran and despises women. The most lovely pearl of womanhood is to him but a scorpion in the sand. His hand has never touched the garment of a woman. He may love no earthly woman, otherwise the fairy would never come again.”

I had to commend Halef Agha's talent; my admiration grew moment by moment, despite this though I felt like giving him a taste of his own Nile-whip.

The response came: “You must know, *Sihdi*, that he will not be permitted to touch her costume, nor see her body. He may only converse with her through a screen.”

“Truly I am amazed at your clever words and the wisdom of your speech. Does it not occur to you that it is precisely because of the screen that he cannot talk to her?”

“How so?”

“The healing power that the *effendi* shall radiate will not reach the woman because it will be blocked by the screen. Go away!”

“I cannot leave because I will receive one hundred strokes on the soles of my feet if I do not bring the wise *effendi*.”

“Thank your kind master, you slave of an Egyptian, that he illuminates your feet with his favor. I do not wish to cheat you of your fortune. *Salaam aaleïkum*, Allah be with you and receive the hundred well!”

“Yet let me say one more thing, courageous Agha. The master of our house has more moneybags in his treasury than you can possibly count. He has ordered me to fetch you also and you shall be given a *bakhshish* - a gift, so generous that even the Khedive of Egypt could not equal it.”

At last this man had recognized Halef's soft spot and chosen to use it to his advantage, as one should always do when dealing in the Orient. The little master of my domain altered his tone at once and in a very friendly voice answered:

"Allah bless your tongue my friend but a *piaster* in my hand is preferable to ten bags in someone else's hand. Your hand, however, is meager, like a jackal in a snare or like the desert facing Mokattam."

"Do not hesitate to follow the advice of your heart, my brother!"

"Your brother? Think again - you are a slave and I am a free man, companion and protector of my *effendi*! The advice of my heart remains undecided. How can a field bear fruit, when so few drops of dew fall from heaven!"

"Here are three more drops!"

"Three more? I will see if I am permitted to rouse the *effendi*, if your master will truly provide such *bakhshish*."

"He will indeed."

"So wait!"

Now finally he is convinced that he is 'permitted to rouse' me, that clever fox! Still, he was only bargaining according to local custom, however much of a bad habit that might be, so in one sense he could be excused, especially considering that what he demanded of me for his services was hardly worth speaking of.

What sparked my interest in the affair was the fact that I was required for a female patient rather than a male. However, since a Moslem, apart from the wandering nomadic tribes, does not permit the inhabitants of his harem to be seen, the patient must be an older woman rather than a younger one, who, perhaps because of quality of character or spirit, enjoyed the special love of Abrahim-Mamur. Halef Agha entered.

"Are you asleep, *Sihdi*?"

The rogue! Here he called me *Sihdi*, and outside he caused himself to be addressed likewise.

"No. What do you want?"

"Outside is a man who wishes to speak with you. He has a boat on the Nile and says that I should accompany you."

The clever scoundrel only added this last to ensure himself of the promised *bakhshish*. I did not wish to embarrass him and behaved as though I had heard nothing of his conversation.

"What does he want?"

"Someone is ill."

"Is it urgent? "

"Quite, *effendi*. The soul of the patient is ready to depart this earth. That is why you need to hurry if you wish to keep it here."

Hmm, he was not a bad diplomat!

"Let the fellow enter!"

Halef walked out and pushed the messenger through the door. He bowed deeply, pulled off his shoes and waited humbly, until I was ready to speak with him.

"Come closer!"

"*Salaam aaleïkum*! - Allah be with you! Oh master, let your ears be open to the humble plea of a lowly servant."

"Who are you?"

"I am a servant of the great Abrahim-Mamur, who lives upstream from here, by the river."

"What do you wish to ask of me?"

"A great agony has come over the house of my master, because Güzela, the crown of his heart, is in the shadow of death. No doctor, no fakir and no wizard have been able to slow the pace of her illness. Then my master, may Allah bring him joy, heard of you and your fame and that death flees from your voice. He sent me to you with this message; 'Come and take the dew of ruin from my flower, then shall my gratitude be sweet and bright like the gleam of gold'."

This description appeared a bit pretentious for an aged woman.

"I do not know the place where your master lives. Is it far from here?"

"He lives on the shore and has sent a boat for you. In one hour you shall be with him."

"And who will bring me home?"

"I."

"I will come. Wait outside!"

He picked up his shoes and withdrew. I got up, threw on another garment and took my small case containing aconite, sulfur, pulsatilla and all the other items that can be had in abundance from any apothecary. Within five minutes we were sitting in a boat that was propelled by four oarsmen. I was lost in thought, but Halef Agha was as proud as a 'Pasha of three horsetails'. In his belt he carried the silver-plated pistols that were given to me in Cairo and a sharp burnished dagger; in his hand he held the ever-present Nile-whip, the most effective instrument with which to secure his esteem, reverence and regard with the local populace.

Certainly the heat was not agreeable, but the upstream movement of our transport provided us with a cooling breeze.

We traveled past durum, tobacco, sesame and senna plantations, in the background palm trees reached skywards. Further upstream were open flats covered with low mimosa and sycamore scrub; finally in the midst of desolate barren rocks and thousand year old stone blocks that were strewn all about, arose a square wall, in which there must surely be an entrance.

As we pulled alongside, I noticed that a small canal led under the wall from the river, ensuring that the occupants had access to vital water without needing to leave their abode. Our guide strode ahead, led us around two corners to the side farthest from the water and gave a signal at the gate located there, which soon opened in response.

The face of a black man grinned at us, but we paid little heed to his deep, floor-sweeping bow and strode past him. I did not expect to find architectural beauty in this splendid Oriental building; I was, therefore, not surprised by the bare, unadorned windowless facade that confronted me. The climate of this land had ravaged the old walls; this was not a dwelling I would have recommended for a frail, sick woman.

Some time ago there had been ornamental foliage adorning the space between the outer wall and the building, this had provided the inhabitants with a pleasant diversion; these plants were now long wilted and parched. Wherever the eye could see there was a stark forbidding bleakness, and only the flocks of swallows, which nested in the numerous cracks and fissures of the building, brought some life and movement into the sad drear scene.

The messenger led us through a dark, low gate into a small courtyard, in the middle of which was a well. Here the canal that I had noticed earlier ended; the builder of this lonely house was clever enough to ensure the supply of those elements that are vital in the blistering climate of this land. At the same time I noticed that the building was designed to withstand the yearly flooding of the Nile without damage.

The inner walls of the courtyard had many wooden gratings, behind which the rooms that served as guests' quarters were certainly located. I did not have the time to admire this place, instead I gave my servant a wink, indicating that he should wait there with the apothecary case that he carried, and I followed the guide into the *selamlük* of the house.

We entered a spacious room, high-ceilinged and dusky, the subdued and pleasing light filtered through the grated window openings. The tapestries, arabesques and ornaments gave the room a lived-in appearance and the clay cooling pots in their niches created a pleasant atmosphere. A balustrade divided the room into two sections, the immediate area being for the servants and the hindmost for the master and visiting guests. The elevated rear area sported a wide divan, which reached from one corner to the other, and upon which Abrahim-Mamur, the 'bearer of many satchels', reclined.

He arose as we entered, but remained, as was the custom, before his seat. Since I was not wearing the traditional footwear of the region I was unable to remove it in the customary manner, I therefore stepped across the costly carpet unmindful of my leather boots and sat down by his side. The servant brought the requisite coffee and the even more important pipe, and life could now continue.

I naturally examined this man's pipe first, because as anyone acquainted with the Orient knows, one can learn a great deal about the owner from his pipe. The silver wire-bound tube was long, aromatic and heavily gold-plated, certainly it had cost a thousand *piasters*. Even more expensive was the amber mouthpiece, which consisted of two parts that were joined by a gemstone-encrusted ring. This man appeared to truly posses 'many satchels'; still this was not reason enough for me to be overly impressed, as many an owner of such a pipe as was worth ten thousand *piasters* had obtained their riches by squeezing their bonded subjects. Thus it was a more valuable exercise to scrutinize his face!

Where had I seen these elegant and noble, yet in their disharmony, diabolical, features before? His small unblinking, extraordinarily astute eyes bored incisively into mine and then expressed a look of cold satisfaction.

Violent, burning passions had etched grievous traces upon this face; love, hate, vengeance and ambition had all alternately aided in dragging a great character into the gutter and infused the countenance of this man with an indefinable aura, which to the good and pure is a certain warning sign.

Where had I encountered this man before? I knew I had seen him somewhere; I must only remember where; but I suspected that it had not been under cordial circumstances.

"*Salaam aaleïkum*!" The words resounded slowly from behind the splendidly full, dyed-black beard.

The voice was aloof, toneless, lacking life or spirit; to hear such a voice was like feeling a cold shiver running down one's spine.

"*Aaleïkum*!" I replied.

"May Allah cause balm to flow from your footsteps and honey to drip from your fingertips so that my heart no longer hears the voice of my sorrow!"

"God give you peace and let me find the poison that gnaws at the essence of your happiness." I answered his greeting, since not even a doctor may ask about the wife of a Moslem without violating courtesy or custom.

"I have heard that you are a wise *hekim*. Which *Medresse* (higher school of the Orient) have you attended"

"None."

"None?"

"I am not a Moslem."

"No? What then?"

"A *Nemsi*!"

"A *Nemsi*! Oh, I know the *Nemsi* are clever people; they know of the philosophers' stone and the abracadabra, which drives away death."

"Neither the philosophers' stone nor the abracadabra exist."

He looked coldly into my eyes.

"You do not have to hide anything from me. I know that the wizard may not speak of his art and I have no intention of enticing it from you, all I require is that you use it to help me. How do you drive the sickness from a being, through words or with a talisman?"

"Neither by word nor with talisman, but with medicine."

"You shall not hide from me. I believe in you, although you are no Moslem, your hand is endowed with victory as though the Prophet had blessed you. You will discover the sickness and defeat it."

"The Lord is almighty; He can save or corrupt, and only to Him belongs that honor. But if I am to help, speak!"

This direct invitation, to reveal a critical household secret was abhorrent to him, even though he must surely have been prepared for it; at once he tried to hide his weakness and followed my invitation:

"You are from the land of the infidels, where it is no shame to speak of the daughter of a mother?"

I felt myself inwardly amused by the circuitous way he referred to his wife, but I remained grave and answered rather coldly:

"You want me to help you but you insult me?"

"In what respect?"

"You call my homeland the land of the infidels."

"But you are infidels!"

"We believe in God, the same God whom you call Allah. In your opinion I am an unbeliever; from my vantage point I could rightly call you the same; but I do not because we *Nemsi* never violate the rule of courtesy."

"Let us not speak about belief! The Moslem may not speak of his wife; but you will permit that I speak of the women of *Frankistan*?"

"I permit it."

"If the wife of a Frank is ill . . . "

He looked at me, as though he expected a comment; I indicated that he should continue.

"So, if she is sick and takes no food ..."

"None?"

"None at all!"

"Go on!"

"Then loses the sparkle in her eyes and the fullness of her cheeks - if she is tired but no longer knows the delight of sleep ..."

"Go on!"

"When she can stand only with support and only walk slowly, almost crawling - shivers with cold and burns with heat . . . "

"I am listening. Continue!"

"Is frightened and flinches at every sound - when she wishes for nothing, desires nothing, hates nothing and trembles with every beat of her heart ..."

"Go on, go on!"

"If her breath is as shallow as that of a small bird - if she neither laughs nor cries, nor speaks - if she utters no word of joy and no word of pain and does not even notice her sighs - if she shuns the light of the sun and at night cowers in the corners ..."

Again he looked at me, and in his fervent eyes I recognized fear, which apparently fed and grew with the recounting of each symptom of the malady. He must love the patient with the last dim and desperate fire of his almost desolate heart; and here he had unwittingly exposed his whole relationship to me.

"You are not yet finished!" I said.

"If she at times expels a sudden cry, as though a dagger were plunged into her breast - when she unceasingly whispers a foreign word."

"What word?"

"A name."

"Go on!"

"If she coughs and afterwards blood flows over her pale lips ..."

He now stared at me with such apprehension that I realized my verdict was a judgment for him, one that offered liberation or annihilation. I did not hesitate to give him the latter:

"She will die."

He sat motionless for some moments, as though struck, then he jumped up and stood before me stretched to his full height. The red fez had slipped off his shorn head, his pipe had fallen from his hand; his face twisted with conflicting emotions. It was a strange and terrible face; it resembled that image of the devil rendered by the hand of Doré [Gustave Doré (1832-1883), was probably the greatest illustrator of the 19th century. One of his most impressive works was The Illustrated Bible]. Not with tail, cloven hooves and horns, but with the highest symmetry of bodily structure, every facial feature bestowed with beauty, and yet the features, in their entirety, so repulsive, so vile, so diabolical. His eyes rested upon me with a look of horror that changed to anger and was finally replaced by undeclared malice.

"*Giaur*!" he thundered.

"What did you call me?" I asked coldly.

"*Giaur*! I said. You dare to tell me this? You dog! The whip shall acquaint you with who I am and the fact that you must obey my commands. If she dies, you die; but make her well and you shall demand from me whatsoever your heart desires!"

Slowly and with great composure I arose, stood upright to my full height before him and asked:

"Do you know what the greatest shame of a Moslem is?"

"What?"

"Look down at your fez! Abrahim-Mamur, what does the Prophet and the Koran say with regard to exposing the shame of your head to a Christian?"

In the next instant he had covered his head and with dark rage suffusing his face he had ripped his dagger from his sash.

"You must die, *giaur*!"

"When might that be?"

"Now, at once!"

"I will die, when it pleases God, not you."

"You will die now. Say your prayers!"

"Abrahim-Mamur," I replied as calmly as before, "I have hunted bears and swam after hippopotami; the elephant has heard my shot, and the lion – the 'strangler of herds', has felt the sting of my bullet. Thank Allah, that you are still alive, and ask Him to subdue your heart. You yourself are not able to because you are too weak and you will die if it does not happen at once!"

This was a new insult, harsher than the first, and with a twitching jump he made as if to grab me but pulled back at once when he saw the flash of the weapon in my hand, which one must never place out of reach in these lands. We stood opposite each other, and since he had dismissed the servants as soon as the coffee and pipes had been served, so that they would not overhear our delicate discussions, we were alone. With my brave Halef close at hand I did not have the least cause to fear the inhabitants of this old house. If necessary the two of us could have dealt with the few men that lived here; but I had a fair idea of the fate of the afflicted woman, and had begun to develop an uncommon interest in this. I had to see her and if possible, exchange a few words.

"You would shoot me?" he asked furiously whilst indicating my revolver.

"If necessary."

"Here, in my house, on my divan?"

"Certainly, if I am forced to defend myself."

"Dog, it is true, what I first suspected when you entered!"

"What is true, Abrahim-Mamur?"

"That I have seen you before."

"Where?"

"I don't know."

"When?"

"That I don't know either; but one thing is certain, it was not a friendly encounter."

"Just as today, I would be surprised if this meeting ends agreeably. You called me 'dog', and I say to you that the very moment after you utter that word again, my bullet will rest in your brain. Remember it well, Abrahim-Mamur!"

"I will call my servants!"

"Call them, if you want to see their corpses lying dead around you."

"Oho, you are not God!"

"Not God but a *Nemsi*. Have you ever felt the hand of a *Nemsi*?"

He laughed contemptuously.

"Take heed that you do not feel it! It is not bathed in rose oil like yours. Nevertheless, I will leave you the peace of your home. Live well. You do not wish me to conquer death; may your wish be fulfilled; *rabbena chaliëk* - the Lord keep you!"

I holstered the revolver and stepped towards the door.

"Stay!" he called.

I strode on.

"Stay!" He called in a commanding tone.

I had nearly reached the door and did not turn around.

"So die, *giaur*!"

Now I turned instantly and had just enough time to lunge sideways. His dagger flew past me and buried itself deep into the paneled wall.

"Now you are mine, knave!"

With these words I leaped towards him, seizing him as he came within my grasp, I hoisted him up off his feet and hurled him at the wall.

He remained there for some seconds before he gathered himself and arose. His eyes were huge, the veins on his brow were swollen to bursting point and his lips were blue with rage; but I held my revolver on him, and he halted reluctantly before me.

"Now you have met with the hand of a *Nemsi*. Do not dare to provoke it again!"

"Allah!"

"Coward! What is it called when one asks a doctor for help, insults him with words and then tries to murder him when his back is turned? The belief of such a person has little worth!"

"Sorcerer!"

"What?"

"If you were not a sorcerer, my dagger would have hit you, and you would not have had the power to throw me about!"

"Now! If I were a sorcerer, I would have saved your wife Güzela."

I spoke that name with forethought. It had the desired effect.

"Who spoke this name to you?"

"Your messenger."

"An infidel may not the speak the name of a believer!"

"I only speak the name of a woman who may be dead tomorrow."

Again he looked at me with an icy stare, then he clapped his hands before his face.

"Is it true, *hekim*, that she may be dead tomorrow?"

"It is true."

"Can she not be saved?"

"Perhaps."

"Don't say 'perhaps', say 'certainly'. Are you willing to help me? If she recovers, then demand what you will of me."

"I am willing."

"Then give me your talisman or your medicine."

"I have no talisman, and medicine I cannot give you now."

"Why not?"

"A doctor can only heal the sick if he is permitted to examine them. Come let us go to her or let her come to us!"

He fell aback as though hit by a punch.

"*Mash Allah*, are you crazy? The spirit of the desert has burned your brain if you are unaware of what you demand. The woman that is seen by a strange man is condemned to die!"

"She will surely die if I am not permitted to go to her. I have to measure the pulse of her heart and obtain answers to many questions that concern her illness. Only God is all-knowing and need not inquire of anyone."

"You truly do not heal through a talisman?"

"No."

"And neither by word?"

"No."

"Or by prayer?"

"I pray for the suffering; but God has already given us the means with which to heal."

"What means are these?"

"They are flowers, metals and minerals, the juices and forces of which we extract."

"They are not poisons?"

"I do not poison the sick."

"Will you swear to it?"

"Before any judge."

"And you must talk with her?"

"Yes."

"What about?"

"I have to ask her about her illness and about everything that surrounds it."

"And not about other matters?"

"No."

"You will pose every question to me first, to see if it is acceptable?"

"I am satisfied with that."

"And you must also touch her hand?"

"Yes."

"I will permit it for one whole minute, no longer. Must you see her face?"

"No, she may remain veiled. But she must walk up and down in her room a number of times."

"Why?"

"From her gait and posture much can be learned that concerns her illness."

"I permit it and will now fetch her."

"That will not do."

"Why not?"

"I have to see where she lives; I need to examine her chambers."

"For what reason?"

"Because there are illnesses that can be attributed to unsuitable quarters and only the eyes of a doctor can detect these."

"You really wish to enter my harem? (The Arabian word harem means literally 'the holy, invulnerable' and it is used by Moslems to describe the women's quarters, which are separated from the rest of the rooms in the house.)"

"Yes."

"An infidel?"

"A Christian."

"I will not permit it!"

"Then she will die. *Salaam aaleïkum*, Peace be with you and yours!"

I turned to go. I had already noticed from the description of the symptoms that Güzela suffered from an acute illness of the mind, but I behaved as though I believed that her illness was merely physical. Though as I suspected that her affliction was caused by the domination of this man, I still needed to clarify everything in my mind. He let me reach the door, then he called:

"Stop, *hekim*, stay. You shall enter the chambers!"

I turned and walked back without betraying my satisfaction. I had triumphed and was more than pleased with his disclosure as it revealed a great deal to me, much more than I would have been able to discover from a European. The love that this Egyptian bore, its consequences and concerns was indeed quite exceptional if he was willing to expose himself in this manner. The grim resentment he felt towards me was clear in his every expression. I was the unavoidable intruder into the mysteries of his inner sanctum, and I nurtured the conviction that even if I should heal the sick woman I would be leaving behind an unwavering enemy, especially since he, like myself, was of the opinion that we had already met under hostile circumstances.

He left to arrange things himself as no servant must suspect that he permitted a stranger entrance to the sanctuary of his home.

He returned after some time. There was an expression of firm, defiant resolve in the way he pinched lips and a look of ill-concealed hatred in his eyes as he instructed me:

"You shall go to her . . . "

"You already agreed to that."

"And see her chambers ..."

"Naturally."

"And her person . . . "

"Veiled and cloaked."

" Must you also speak with her?"

"That is necessary."

"I permit you much too much, *effendi*. But by all the salvation of all the heavens and by all the agony of all the hells, the moment you utter one word that I do not consent to or do the slightest thing that is not acceptable, then I will kill her. You are strong and well armed, that is why my dagger will not be pointed at you but at her. I swear this by all the *surat* of the Koran and by all the caliphs, whose memory Allah may bless!"

He had come to know me and thought that this insurance was more effective than the boastful threats directed at me. Besides it never occurred to me to offend him within his rights; his behavior did, however, strengthen my opinion that his relationship with the patient had a sinister aspect.

"Is it time then?" I asked.

"Come!"

He proceeded to lead the way and I followed behind.

First we passed through several dilapidated rooms, within which a menagerie of fauna lived out its entire existence. Then, by way of a chamber that appeared to serve as a reception area, we entered a room that bore all the signs of being a woman's apartment. All the items that lay roundabout strongly suggested a feminine presence.

"These are the chambers that you wished to view. See if you can spy the demon of the sickness within!" Abrahim-Mamur said with a derisive grin.

"And the apartment next door ...?"

"The patient is within. You shall see it also, but I must first satisfy myself, that 'the Sun' has covered her face before the eyes of a stranger. Do not dare to follow me, instead await my return in peace!"

He exited the room and I was left alone.

So here at last was Güzela. The name meant 'the Beautiful'. This circumstance and the Egyptian's entire manner caused me to doubt my earlier presumption that this matter concerned an older person. I let my gaze sweep the room. It was entirely identical to the room of the master: the balustrade, the divan and the niches containing the clay cooling pots.

Chapter 6

After some time Abrahim reappeared.

"Have you examined the rooms?" he asked me.

"Yes."

"Well?"

"I shall withhold my opinion until I have seen the patient."

"Then come, *effendi*. But let me caution you again!"

"Not necessary! I know full well what I need to do."

We entered into the apartment. Wrapped in loose garments, a heavily veiled feminine figure stood against the back wall of the room. No part of her was visible other than her small feet, which were encased in velvet slippers.

I commenced my examination, the line of questioning being acceptable to the Egyptian. I asked that she be allowed to make small movements and finally requested that she give me her hand. I very nearly let loose a loud guffaw despite the gravity of the situation, her hand was swaddled in such a thick cloth, that it was impossible to distinguish either the lay or the form of even a single finger through it. Even her arm was swathed in a similar fashion.

I turned to Abrahim: "*Mamur*, these wrappings must be removed."

"Why?"

"Otherwise I cannot locate a pulse."

"Remove the cloth!" he commanded her.

She withdrew her arm into her cocoon and then extended a dainty hand, on the ring finger I noticed a very delicate band, set with a pearl. Abrahim watched my motions with tense vigilance. While I laid my three fingers on her wrist I also turned my head, as though to hear the pulse as well as feel it - I was not mistaken - her light breath carried these faint, almost indiscernible words through the veil: "*Kurtar Senitzaji* - Save Senitza!"

"Are you finished?" asked Abrahim instantly as he hastened closer.

"Yes, that is all."

"What is wrong with her?"

"She has a great, deep suffering, the greatest that exists, but . . . I . . . am . . . going . . . to . . . save . . . her."

These last six words I directed with casual emphasis towards the woman rather than Abrahim-Mamur.

"What is the name of this evil?" Abrahim asked.

"It has a foreign name, which only doctors understand." I replied.

"How long will it be before she is well?"

"That may happen sooner or later depending on how mindful you are of me."

"In what respect am I to obey you?"

"You must give her my medicine regularly."

"That I will do."

"She must remain isolated and spared from all annoyance."

"That shall be done."

"I must be permitted to talk with her daily."

"You? Why?"

"To customize the dosage of the medicine to the feelings of the patient."

"I will tell you myself how she feels."

"You are not able to do this because you cannot gauge the feelings of the patient."

"What have you to talk about with her?"

"Only that which you permit."

"And where shall these meetings take place?"

"Here in these rooms, just as today."

"Tell me exactly for how long you must come!"

"If you heed my instructions, then five days from today she will be . . . free of her affliction."

"Then give her the medicine!"

"I do not have it with me; it is with my servant in the courtyard below."

"Then come!"

I turned towards the woman to indicate a silent farewell. She raised her hands in a silent plea beneath her cocoon and dared to utter three syllables:

"*Eww' Allah* - With God!"

Abrahim snapped at once:

"Silence! You may only speak when you are spoken to!"

"Abrahim-Mamur!" I said very solemnly. "Have I not told you that she must be spared all annoyance and worry? One does not speak in this manner to a patient who is near death!"

"Then she must first ensure that she does nothing to provoke it. She knows that she should not speak. Come!"

We returned to the *selamlük* and I sent for Halef, who soon arrived with the apothecary's bag. I prescribed Ignatia, [aka St. Ignatius bean, named by the Spanish Jesuits who brought the bean to Europe from the Phillipines in the 17th century. Used as an amulet to protect against disease. Seeds contain strychnine] leaving the necessary instructions and dosage and then made ready to depart.

"When will you come tomorrow?"

"At the same hour."

"I will send a boat for you. How much do you demand for today?"

"Nothing. When the patient has regained her health then you may give me what you please."

He still reached into his pocket, pulled out a richly embroidered purse and withdrew some coins and handed them to Halef.

"Here, you take!"

The stouthearted Halef Agha reached out with an expression that acknowledged the grace of the Egyptian and pocketed the *bakhshish* unexamined; he then declared:

"Abrahim-Mamur, your hand is open and so is mine. I will not close it against you - as the Prophet says, the open hand is the first step to the abode of the holy. Allah be with you and with me!"

The Egyptian accompanied us up to the garden where a servant opened the gate in the wall. When we were alone, Halef pulled the coins from his pocket to see what he had received.

"Three gold coins, *effendi*! The Prophet bless Abrahim-Mamur and let his wife remain ill for as long as possible!"

"Hajji Halef Omar!" I cried indignantly.

"*Sihdi*! Do you begrudge me a few coins?"

"No; but more than this, we should not be reluctant to wish good health to the unwell."

"How often will we come here, before she is well?"

"Perhaps another five times."

"Five times three is fifteen gold coins; if she gets well perhaps another fifteen coins, that is thirty gold coins. I shall discover whether there are more sick women along the Nile."

We reached the boat and the oarsmen were already waiting for us. Our guide sat at the rudder as before and as soon as we were aboard we headed downstream, naturally at a greater rate than the trip upstream, so that within half an hour we had reached our destination.

We laid to in the vicinity of a *dahabiah* (Nile houseboat or barge, having sails), which had anchored before the shore during our absence. Her ropes were tied, her sails reefed and in accordance with devout Mohammedan custom the *reïs* - the captain, called his crew to prayer:

"*Haï al el salah* - come, prepare yourselves for prayer!"

I was already of a mind to depart but I halted and turned quickly when I heard these words. This voice sounded extraordinarily familiar. Did my ears deceive me? Was this truly old Hassan, he who was known as *Abu el Reïsahn* - Father of Captains? Halef and I had met him in Kufarah, where he had been visiting his son, we had then returned to Egypt together.

We had grown fond of each other, and I was certain that he would be happy to see me again. I therefore waited until the prayer was completed and then called to the deck above.

"Hassan el Reïsahn, Ahoy!"

At once his bearded, affable old face appeared over the side.

"Who is . . . oh, *Allah akbar* - God is great! Is that not my son, the *Nemsi* Kara *Effendi*?"

"It is he, Abu Hassan."

"Come up, my son; I must embrace you!"

I climbed up and was heartily welcomed by him.

"What are you doing here?" he asked.

"I am resting from my journey, and you?"

"I come with my ship from Dongola, where I loaded a cargo of senna leaves. My ship sprung a leak and I had to dock here."

"How long do you intend to stay?"

"Only until the morning. Where do you live?"

"There on the right in the house that is set apart."

"Do you have a good landlord?"

"The Sheik el Belet (magistrate) of the locality, a man with whom I am well pleased. You will come and keep me company this evening, Abu Hassan?"

"I will be there, if your pipes are not broken."

"I have only the one, you will have to bring your own, but you will smoke the most delicious *djebeli* that exists."

"I will certainly be there then. Do you plan to stay here long?"

"No. I wish to return to Cairo."

"So travel with me. I will dock at Bulakh (suburb of Cairo with harbor)."

At this offer an idea came to mind.

"Hassan, you called me your friend!"

"Indeed you are. Ask of me what you desire, I shall provide it if I own it or can get it!"

"I am going to ask you a big favor."

"Can I fulfill it?"

"Yes."

"Then it is already agreed. What is it?"

"That you shall discover this evening, when you drink coffee with me."

"I will come and . . . but, my son - I forgot, I already have an invitation tonight."

"Where?"

"Within the very same house in which you stay."

"With the Sheik el Belet?"

"No, with a man from Stambul who traveled with me for two days and disembarked here. He has rented a room for himself and his servant."

"What does he do?"

"I do not know; he did not tell me."

"But his servant may have spoken."

The captain laughed; for him this was an uncommon act.

"This person is a rogue, he has heard all languages but learned little. He smokes, whistles and sings all day and gives, if one asks, answers that are true today and false tomorrow. The day before yesterday he was a Turk, yesterday a

Montenegrin, today a Druze [Druze, Middle Eastern Moslem sect who live mainly in the mountain regions of Lebanon and S. Syria], and Allah knows what he will be tomorrow or the day after."

"Then you will not come to visit me?"

"I will be there, after I have smoked a pipe with him. Allah keep you; I still have work to do."

Halef had already gone ahead; I followed presently and upon entering my apartment stretched out on the divan to think over and evaluate the day's events. This however was not to be as my landlord presently entered the apartment and greeted me;

"*Salaam aaleïkum.*"

"*Aaleïkum.*"

"*Effendi*, I come to obtain your consent."

"For what?"

"A foreign *Sihdi* came to me and requested accommodation, which I gave to him."

"And where is this accommodation?"

"Upstairs."

"Then the man will not bother me, do as you like Sheik."

"But you have much to ponder over, and he has a servant, who apparently whistles and sings a lot."

"If it offends me, I will forbid him."

The concerned landlord thus departed and I was once again alone, though I was not to be permitted peace for reflection; I heard the footfalls of two people, one came from the courtyard and the other from outside my door.

"What do you want here? Who are you?" asked the one. I recognized the voice of Halef, my little servant.

"I should ask who you are first, and what you want in this house?" asked the other.

"I? I belong in this house!" announced Halef quite indignantly.

"I too!" came the reply.

"Who are you?"

"I am Hamsad al Jerbaja."

"And I am Hajji Halef Omar Agha."

"An *Agha*?"

"Yes; the companion and protector of my master."

"Who is your master?"

"The great doctor who lives in these chambers."

"A great doctor? What does he cure?"

"Everything."

"Everything? Do not try to deceive me! There is only one who can cure everything."

"Who is that?"

"I."

"Then you are a doctor also?"

"No. I am also a protector of my master."

"And who is your master?"

"One does not know. We only moved in a little while ago."

"You should have remained outside."

"Why?"

"Because you are impolite and don't answer questions when asked. Will you tell me who your master is?"

"Yes."

"Well?"

"He is, he is . . . my master - but not your master."

"Rogue!"

After these last words I heard Halef depart in a most undignified manner. The other remained by the entrance and whistled; then started to softly hum a tune; after a pause he began to sing in a sonorous voice.

I was happily surprised and almost leaped up when I heard the lyrics of the two verses that he sang in the Arabic dialect that is spoken in Algiers:

"*Fid-dagle ma tera jekun?*
Chammin hu Nabuliun
Ma balu-hu jedubb hena?
Kussu-hu, yes fitjanena!

Gema'a homr el-elbise
Wast el-chala muntasibe.
Ma bal hadolik wakifin?
Hallu-na nenzor musri' to!"

And these Arabic verses, which rhyme so well, sound something like this in German:

"*Was kraucht nur dort im Busch herum?*
Ich glaub', es ist Napolium.
Was hat er nur zu krauchen dort?
Frisch auf, Kam'raden, jagt ihn fort!

Wer hat nur dort im off'nen Feld
Die roten Hosen hingestellt?
Was haben sie zu stehen dort?
Frisch auf, Kam'raden, jagt sie fort!"

[The Literal translation would be:
Fid-dagle ma tera jekun? –
What crawls about in the bushes?
Chammin hu Nabuliun –
I believe its Napoleon.
Ma balu-hu jedubb hena? –
Why does he crawl about in there?
Kussu-hu, yes fitjanena! –
Flush him out, brave fellows

Gema'a homr el-elbise –
A lot of red pants
Wast el-chala muntasibe. –
Stopped in the midst of the field.
Ma bal hadolik wakifin? –
Why do they stand there?
Hallu-na nenzor musri' to! –
Let us quickly discover!]

The melody was also the same, note for note, tone for tone. I leaped for the door as soon as the second verse was completed, opened it and beheld the singer. He wore wide blue harem-pants, a jacket of the same color, leather half-boots and a fez upon his head; he was in all aspects quite ordinary. There was only one peculiarity - although he was aware of my scrutiny, he continued his song unperturbed:

"*Hum jəbroku we-jer'adu*
We-bi'l-medafe' jadribu
Ma bal hadik el-karka'a?
Ogsu-hum mitl ez-zoba'a!

Nabuliun, Nabuliun,
Ara gunud-ak judbirun!
Bi-aun Allahi naksod-ak,
Min es-serir nukebkib-ak

Yes ejuha 'l-Fransawiun,
Ruweda-kum teftahirun!
Barizu-kum lana tekun,
Gada geza-kum tahodun!"

When he finished, he placed his fists on his hips, stood as though he had little regard for me and asked:

"Did you like the song, *effendi*?"

"Quite! Where did you learn it?"

"I made it up."

"Tell that to someone else but not to me! What of the melody?"

"I especially made that up myself!"

"Liar!"

"*Effendi*, I am Hamsad al Jerbaja and will not be abused!"

"You are Hamsad al Jerbaja and you are still a big scoundrel! I know this melody."

"Then someone has sung or whistled what he overheard from me."

"And from whom did you hear it?"

"From no-one."

"You are incorrigible as is evident. This melody belongs to a German song."

"Oh, *effendi*, what do you know of Germany!"

"The song is called: *Was kraucht nur dort im Busch herum?*
Ich glaub', es ist ..."

"*Hurrjes, wat is mich denn dat*! - Hello, what is this!" he interrupted in a jubilant voice, speaking in a *Jüterbogk* dialect.

"Are you perhaps a German also?" he continued.

"Of course!"

"Really? A German *effendi*? From what region do you come, if I may ask, master *hekim-bashi*?"

"From Saxony."

"A Saxon! One could burst with happiness! And you have become a Turk?" [See Trans. Notes Ch 6.1]

"No, not at all. You are a Prussian?"

"That is self-evident! A Prussian from Jüterbogk."

"How did you get here?"

"By railway, by ship, by horse and camel and by my legs."

"What did you do originally?"

"I was a barber, also a surgeon, and a dentist – in short a quack. I was not happy at home, so I went out into the wide world, here and there and finally to this place."

"You must tell me everything. But whom do you serve now?"

"He is a son of a merchant from Constantinople by the name of Isla Ben Maflei, he has an incredible amount of money, that one."

"What business does he have here?"

"How should I know? He is searching for something."

"What is that?"

"Apparently a woman."

"A woman? That is odd!"

"But apparently close to the mark."

"And what kind of woman might this be?"

"A Montenegrin, a Senitsha or Senitza, or however that is pronounced."

"Wha-a-at? - She is called Senitza?"

"Yes."

"You are certain?"

"Of course! Firstly he has a picture of her; also he always . . . wait, he claps upstairs, Herr *effendi*; I must attend him!"

I did not sit down again, instead I was driven to pacing back and forth within my room. This barber from Jüterbogk, who referred to himself poetically as Hamsad al Jerbaja, was without doubt of enormous interest to me, even more intriguing was his master, he who searched along the Nile for a Montenegrin woman named Senitza. Unfortunately my thoughts were interrupted by the arrival of some fellows who were hoping to obtain relief from their suffering with the aid of my magical kernels. In Oriental fashion they tarried one whole hour with me before I could discover what ailed them and was able to minister to them, then they lingered in their places until it pleased them to break the audience.

So it was that evening drew near. The captain arrived and went upstairs, after a half an hour his shambling tread was heard again and he entered my chamber. Halef served the coffee and tobacco and then withdrew. After a short time I heard Halef wrangling with the Jüterbogker Turk.

"Have you had your leak repaired?" I asked Hassan.

"It has still not been mended. I could only plug the hole today and pump the water out. Allah will provide another day tomorrow."

"And when do you depart?"

"The day after tomorrow, early."

"Would you take me along?"

"My soul would be happy to have you with me."

"And if I brought yet another?"

"My *dahabiah* has a lot of room. Who is it?"

"Not a man but a woman."

"A woman? Have you bought yourself a slave, *effendi*?"

"No. She is the wife of another."

"And he will come with us also?"

"No."

"Then you have bought her from him?"

"No."

"He has given her to you?"

"No. I will take her."

"*Allah kerihm* - God is merciful! You want to take her without his knowledge?"

"Perhaps."

"Truly, do you know what it is you do?"

"Well?"

"A *tschikarma*, a kidnapping!"

"Certainly."

"A *tschikarma* is punishable by death. Has your spirit become so bleak and your soul so dark, that you seek death?"

"No. The whole affair is still quite doubtful. I know you are my friend and will keep silent on this. I will tell you everything."

"Open the door to your heart, my son. I listen!"

I recounted the events of the day and he listened intently. When I had finished he arose and beckoned: "Arise, my son, take your pipe and follow me!"

"To where?"

"You shall understand presently."

I suspected what he intended and followed him. He led me to the room of the merchant upstairs. The servant was not present and upon announcing our arrival with a polite cough, we entered.

The man that arose was still young, perhaps twenty-six years of age. The precious *tshibuk*, from which he smoked, told me that the Jüterbogker was correct in his statement of 'an incredible amount of money'. This man had an interesting, sympathetic appearance and I felt immediately that I could trust him with my life. Old Abu el Reïsahn began to speak:

"This is the merchant Isla Ben Maflei from Stambul, and here is the *effendi* Kara Ben Nemsi, my friend whom I hold dear."

"You are both welcome, please be seated!" answered the young man.

His face displayed his expectation, as he obviously realized that the captain must have good grounds to bring me to him without prior discussion.

"Will you grant me a favor, Isla Ben Maflei?" asked the captain.

"Willingly. Tell me what I should do."

"Tell this man the story you told me recently!"

The merchant's face expressed surprise and suspicion.

"Hassan el Reïsahn," he said, "you swore to me your silence and yet you have already betrayed my confidence!"

"Ask my friend if I revealed a single word!"

"Why do you bring him up here and ask that I should reveal all to him?"

"You said to me that wherever I lay to in the evenings, I should keep an eye open and make inquiries about that which you had lost. I have already opened my eyes and my ears and I bring you this man who may be able to provide information."

Isla cast aside his pipe and jumped up in a single motion.

"Is it true? You bear tidings?"

"My friend Hassan has not spoken a word to me, and I do not know on what subject I can offer you information. You must speak first!"

"*Effendi*, if you can tell me what I desire to hear, then I will reward you as only a Pasha can!"

"I do not desire a reward. Speak!"

"I am searching for a maiden, who is called Senitza."

"And I know a woman who bears that very name."

"Where, where, *effendi*? Speak quickly."

"Perhaps you should describe the maiden to me first?"

"Oh, she is beautiful like a rose and splendid like the dawn; she is fragrant like the bloom of the *reseda*, and her voice is like the song of the *houris*. Her hair is like the tail of the horse *Gilja*, and her foot is like the foot of Delilah, who betrayed Samson. Her mouth utters only words of kindness, and her eyes . . . "

I interrupted him with a wave of my arm.

"Isla Ben Maflei, that is not the description I need. Don't speak in the language of the betrothed, but with words that make sense! How long ago did she go missing?"

"Two moons ago."

"Did she have something by which she may be identified?"

"Oh, *effendi,* what would that be?"

"A piece of jewelry perhaps, a ring, a chain ..."

"A ring, a ring, yes! I gave her a ring, the gold of which is as thin as paper, but it held a beautiful pearl."

"I have seen it."

"Where, *effendi*? Oh, tell me quickly! And when?"

"Today, a few hours ago."

"Where?"

"In the vicinity of this place, not more than an hour away."

The young man knelt in front of me and laid both his hands on my shoulders.

"Is it true? You are not telling an untruth? You are not deceived?"

"It is true; I am not deceived."

"Then come, arise; we must go to her."

"That will not work."

"It will work, it has to work! I will give you a thousand *piaster*, two - three thousand *piaster* if you lead me to her!"

"And even if you gave me a hundred thousand *piaster* I cannot lead you to her today."

"When then? In the morning, very early in the morning?"

"Pick up your pipe, light it and sit down! He who acts in haste, repents at leisure. We need to discuss this."

"*Effendi*, I cannot. My soul is in turmoil."

"Light your pipe!"

"I do not have the time; I have to ..."

"Well! If you do not have time to order your thoughts, then I must leave."

"Stay! I will do everything that you demand."

He sat down and availed himself of a glowing coal from the brazier and lit his pipe.

"I am ready. Now speak!" he encouraged me.

"Today a rich Egyptian sent for me to attend his sick wife ..."

"His wife ...!"

"So he let it be known to me."

"You went?"

"I went."

"Who is this man?"

"He called himself Abrahim-Mamur and he lives upstream from here in a lonely, dilapidated house on the shore of the Nile."

"Does a wall encircle it?"

"Yes."

"Who would have suspected this! I have searched all cities, villages and camps along the Nile, but I never thought that this house was lived in. Is she truly his wife?"

"I do not know, but I do not believe she is."

"And she is ill?"

"Quite."

"*Wallahi* - by God, he shall pay if something vile has happened to her. What is the sickness from which she suffers?"

"Her illness is of the heart. She despises him; she is consumed with longing to escape him and she will die if it is not realized soon."

" She said this to you, not he?"

"No, I observed it."

"You have seen it?"

"Yes."

"You eavesdropped?"

"No. He led me to his harem so that I could talk with the patient."

"He himself? Impossible!"

"He loves her ..."

"Allah punish him!"

"And he feared that she would die if he sent me away."

"Then you spoke with her?"

"Yes, but only the words that he permitted. Nevertheless, she found a moment to whisper something to me: 'Save Senitza!' She used this name, although she is known as Güzela."

"What was your reply to her?"

"That I would rescue her."

"*Effendi*, you are dear to me; my life belongs to you! This man has stolen and kidnapped her. He has, through swindle, cleaved her to himself. Come, *effendi*, we will go. I must at least see the house in which she is held captive!"

"You will remain here! I am going there again tomorrow and ..."

"I go with you, *Sihdi*!"

"You stay here! Would she recognize the ring that you wear on your finger?"

"She knows it very well."

"Will you entrust it to me?"

"Gladly. But what for?"

"I will speak with her again tomorrow and will arrange for her to see the ring."

"*Sihdi*, that is wonderful! She will know at once that I am nearby. What then?"

"Tell me first all that I should know."

"You shall discover everything, *Sihdi*. Our business is one of the biggest in Istambul; I am my father's only son and while he manages the bazaar and supervises the servants, I undertake the necessary travels. I was often in Scutari and saw Senitza, as she and her female companion took a leisurely cruise on the lake. I saw her again after this. Her father does not live in Scutari, but in the Black Mountains; she came but occasionally to visit her friend. Some two months ago I visited the lake again; her companion had disappeared with a man, and Senitza as well!"

"Where did they go?"

"Nobody knew."

"Not even her parents?"

"No. Her father, the brave Osco, had left Czernagora to search the far reaches of the earth for his child; but I was obliged to go to Egypt to make purchases. On the Nile I encountered a steamer that was traveling upstream. As the *sandal*, on which I was a passenger, passed the steamer I heard my name being called. I looked across to the steamer and saw Senitza, who had removed the veil from her face so that I should recognize her. Next to her stood an elegant, foreboding man, who at once concealed her face with the *yashmak* - I saw nothing more. Since that hour I have been on their trail."

"You do not know for certain if she departed her homeland willingly or by force?"

"Not voluntarily."

"Did you know the man that stood next to her?"

"No."

"Good! Could you have been mistaken? Perhaps it was a different person that only resembled Senitza"

"Would she have called out my name and reached towards me, *effendi*?"

"That is true."

"*Sihdi*, you have promised to rescue her?"

"Yes."

"Will you keep your word?"

"I will keep it if it is truly her."

"You will not take me with you. How will you know if it is she?"

"Your ring will provide me that assurance."

"And how will you spirit her out of the house?"

"By telling you in what manner you may rescue her."

"I will rescue her you can depend on that."

"And then? Hassan el Reïsahn, would you be prepared to take her aboard your *dahabiah*?"

"I am prepared to do this, although I do not know the man whom she is with."

"He calls himself *Mamur*, as I have told you."

"If he was truly a *Mamur* - a ruler of a province, then he is powerful enough to destroy us if we are caught" said the Captain earnestly. "A *tschikarma* is punishable by death. My friend Kara Ben Nemsi, you will need to be very clever and move with great care tomorrow."

As far as I was concerned I was thinking less about the danger and more about the adventure. Of course it was clear that I would do nothing if Abrahim-Mamur truly had a right to the patient.

We continued to discuss this matter for a long time.

Since it had become late by the time we retired, it was no wonder that I awoke later than usual. I would have slept even longer, had the song of the barber not awoken me. This one leaned against the outside entrance and appeared to honor me with his entire repertoire of German songs. I permitted the singer entry so that I could talk with him for a time and found him to be an agreeable but frivolous lad whom I would not have traded for my Halef, despite our common German heritage. I never suspected under what evil circumstances we were to meet again in the future.

In the forenoon I visited Abu el Reïsahn on his ship, and no sooner had I finished my meal than the boat arrived to take me to see my patient. Halef had been keeping a busy lookout for it.

"*Effendi*, do I go with you?" he asked.

I shook my head and replied in jest:

"I will not need you today."

"What? You do not require me?"

"No."

"What if something happens to you!"

"What might happen to me?"

"You could fall into the water."

"Then I will swim."

"Or Abrahim-Mamur could kill you. I have seen it in him, he is not your friend."

"Then you could not help me either."

"No? *Sihdi*, Halef Agha is a man on whom you can always depend!"

"Then come!" I relented.

In truth, I think his enthusiasm had much to do with his *bakhshish*.

The journey was much as it had been before, today however, I paid more attention to things that could be useful to me. In the garden I noticed many long, sturdy poles. The outer as well as the inner doors were always locked with wide wooden bolts, the construction of which I committed to memory. There was no dog about, and from the helmsman I discovered that besides the master, the patient and an old female guard, eleven men belonged to the household and slept there. The master always slept on the divan in his *selamlük*.

As I entered, Abrahim approached me with a gladder countenance than he had worn at my departure yesterday.

"Be welcome, *effendi*! You are a great physician."

"How so!"

"She started to eat yesterday."

"Ah!"

"She spoke with her custodian."

"Pleasant?"

"Pleasant and more."

"That is good. Perhaps she will be completely cured in less than five days."

"And earlier today she even sang a little."

"That is even better. She has been your wife for a long time?"

At once a dark shadow moved over his face.

"The physicians of the infidels are quite inquisitive!"

"Thirsting for knowledge: but our thirst for knowledge has saved many lives and preserved the health of many of those that could not be helped by your physicians."

"Was your question really necessary?"

"Quite!"

"She is just a girl, although she belongs to me."

"Then help is assured."

"He led me to the room where I had been told to wait yesterday and in which I was to wait again today. I looked about with greater interest. Windows were nonexistent; the openings for light were covered with grilles. The wooden grating was mounted in such a manner that by pulling out a long, thin rod it could be opened. On the spur of the moment I pulled out one of these rods and put it behind the grille so that it would not be noticed. I had just finished when Abrahim reappeared. Behind him entered Senitza.

I walked towards her and posed my questions. All the while I played with the ring that Isla had loaned to me in a manner that suggested my eagerness for the task at hand. Suddenly I let it slip from my fingers. It rolled up to Senitza's feet; she bent down quickly and picked it up. Immediately Abrahim stepped forward and took it from her hand. As quickly as it happened, she still had enough time to glance at the ring - and to recognize it, as I noticed from her surprised movement and the unconscious placement of her hand over her heart. For the present I had nothing more to do here.

Abrahim asked about my conclusions.

"God is good and almighty," I replied; "He sends His aid, often before one thinks. If He desires it she will be well by tomorrow. She should take the medicine that I will send and await my return with confidence."

Today she let me go without daring a word. In the *Selamlük* Halef already stood in readiness with the apothecary's bag. I prescribed nothing more than powdered sugar, for which the little Agha received an even bigger *bakhshish* than yesterday. Then we were ferried back downstream.

The captain already awaited me at the merchant's abode.

"Have you seen her?" the merchant called to me.

"Yes."

"Did she recognize the ring?"

"She recognized it."

"Then she knows that I am nearby!"

"She suspects it. And if she understood my words correctly she knows that she will be rescued this night."

"But how?"

"Hassan el Reïsahn, have you repaired your leak?"

"It will be repaired this evening."

"Are you prepared to take us aboard and provide us with passage to Cairo?"

"Yes I am."

"Then listen to me! The house where Senitza is confined has two doors that are bolted from within; we cannot enter through these. But there is a second way, although it will be difficult. Isla Ben Maflei, can you swim?"

"Yes."

"Good. There is a canal that runs from the Nile under the walls into a well that is located in the middle of the courtyard. Shortly before midnight when all are asleep we will meet there and you will enter by way of the canal, up through the well and into the courtyard. The gate that you will find there is locked with a bolt that can easily be opened. When you have done this, you come to a garden, the gate there opens likewise. As soon as the gates are open - we enter. We grab some poles from the garden and lean them against the wall so that we can climb up to the grated opening, behind which the harem is located. I have already opened it from the inside."

"And afterwards?"

"What will happen afterwards will depend on the circumstances. We go by boat to the place where we shall carry out our first task, which is to sink Abrahim-Mamur's boat so that he cannot pursue us. In the meantime the *reïs* will make his *dahabiah* ready to sail."

I took a pencil to hand and drew a plan of the house on a piece of paper so that Isla Ben Maflei could orient himself when he climbed from the reservoir tonight. The day passed wholly under the many preparations; evening arrived and as the time came to begin I called Halef and gave him the necessary instructions for the adventure to come.

Chapter 7

Halef quickly packed our possessions. The rent was already paid in advance.

I made my way to Hassan and Halef soon followed with our belongings. The ship was ready to depart and needed only to be let go from the shore. After some time Isla and his servant also arrived and we then boarded the long narrow boat which belonged to the *dahabiah*. The two servants had to row and I was stationed at the tiller.

It was a night of such tranquility that one could easily believe that in the whole world not a single trace of peril existed.

The soft breezes, which had played with the shadows of twilight, were now calm. The stars of the south smiled benignly out of the darkening indigo heavens and the waters of this majestic river flowed gently and silently in its wide bed. This calm also dwelt within me, though the circumstances might make this difficult to believe.

It was not an easy task that we were to undertake but one only trembles before an event that is unplanned or unlaunched, once it is begun one may proceed without inner turmoil. A kidnapping by night would perhaps not have been necessary if we could have charged Abrahim-Mamur before a court. But we were uncertain of the situation and did not know what just or unjust means were available to him in support of his claim to Senitza. Only from her could we ascertain what we needed to know to make a case against him and that we could only discover if we succeeded in surreptitiously freeing her.

After about an hour the dark outline of the dwelling rose from the gray, stony surrounds. We laid to a short distance from the wall and I alighted alone to reconnoiter. I discovered that the entire perimeter of the building was deserted, and even within the wall it appeared to be so. In the canal lay Abrahim's boat with its oars. I boarded and brought it alongside our own.

"Here is the boat," I said to both servants. "Row it downstream a little, fill it with stones and let it sink. The oars, however, we can use. Leave them in our boat, which you will afterwards untie and hold fast so that it can be pushed off as soon as we return. Isla Ben Maflei, follow me!"

We left the boat and crept up to the canal. The water here did not look inviting. I threw a stone into its depths and discovered that the canal was not deep. Isla removed his clothes and slid into the water. It reached up to his chin.

"Is it all right?" I asked him.

"It is better to swim than to walk, I think. The bottom of the canal is coated with so much sediment that it almost reaches to my knees."

"Are you still determined?"

"Yes. Bring my clothes with you when you go to the gate. *Haidi!* - Here goes!"

He lifted his legs from the muck, stroked through the water with his arms and disappeared within the opening in the wall where the canal flowed.

I did not proceed to the gate at once, instead I waited where I was in case something unforeseen should occur, however unlikely that might be. My diligence paid off however, just as I decided to leave Isla's head re-appeared in the opening.

"You return already?" I asked.

"Yes. I could not go far."

"Why not?"

"*Effendi*, we cannot rescue Senitza!"

"Why not?"

"The wall is too high ..."

"It would not help if it were lower because the house is locked up."

"And the canal also!"

"Locked?"

"Yes."

"With what?"

"With a strong wooden weir-gate."

"Could you not remove it?"

"It withstood all my efforts."

"How far to this obstacle from here?"

"The gate has to be just by the foundation of the house."

"I have to see this. Get dressed, hold my clothes and wait here for me." I directed him.

I removed only my outer garment and slid into the water. Floating on my back I swam on. The canal was not open to the air in the garden, instead it was covered over with stone plates. When I reckoned that I had reached the house, I bumped into the gate. It was as high and as wide as the canal itself and was constructed from stout, well-bound wooden stakes and was mounted to the wall with iron brackets. The gate was obviously designed to keep animals such as rats and the like from the well. I shook the structure but it would not budge and I had to admit that it would be impossible to remove it in its entirety. I grabbed a single stake with both hands, braced my knees either side of the wall – with a hefty jerk the stake broke. Now there was a gap and within a period of two minutes I had removed four stakes so that an opening was created through which I could maneuver.

Should I go back, so that Isla could continue? No, that would be a waste of time. I was already wet and knew the place in greater detail than he. So I squeezed through the breach I had made and swam on in water that was thick with churned silt and sludge. When, according to my estimation, I should have been under the inner courtyard; the roof suddenly dipped and confirmed that I was nearing the well. The canal here resembled a pipe completely filled with water; so much so that it was difficult to take a deep breath as there seemed to be a complete absence of air. The remaining distance would have to be covered either by crawling or by diving through this pipe, an exercise that would be not only uncomfortable and arduous but also quite dangerous. What if I encountered a second obstacle further on, when it was too far to turn back for air? . . . Or if I was discovered when I breached the surface of the well? It was a real possibility that someone might be in the courtyard.

I could not permit such thoughts to weaken my resolve. I drew in a deep breath, plunged beneath the surface and propelled myself forward with a half-swimming, half-walking motion as fast as I was able.

I covered a considerable distance before I began to suffer from the lack of air, my hand touched a new obstacle. It was, by the feel of it, a perforated tin sheet that acted like a sieve or filter, it completely covered the entire cross-section of the pipe.

This discovery set tendrils of fear uncoiling within me.

I could not retreat, the distance back to where I could breathe was also the distance in which I would suffocate, yet the sieve appeared to be mounted in a most secure manner. There were truly only two alternatives: either I was successful in getting through the barrier or I drowned. There was not a moment to lose.

I braced myself against the sheet metal; I pushed and strained with all my strength, to no avail. What if I did break through and the well was not directly beyond this point - then I was done for. I only had strength and breath left for a few seconds; I felt as though a terrible force strove to burst my lungs and explode my body - one final, supreme effort; dear God in Heaven, help me to succeed! I felt the wet, icy hand of death close around my heart. It seized me in a ghastly, unrelenting grip and clamped down with fearsome might; my pulse faltered, my consciousness faded, my soul railed against the horror. A convulsive, deadly force radiated into stiffening sinews and muscles. I do not hear the rending of metal, nor any other sound, but the battle with death achieved what had been unattainable from life - the sieve gave way, pulling out of the wall brackets. I lunged upwards, drawing in a long, deep breath as I broke the surface, this revitalized me in an instant and I ducked back below the surface. Someone could still be in the courtyard and quite possibly see my head in the middle of the well. That is why I now arose warily near the rim and looked about.

There was no moon, but the stars of the south provided enough light to distinguish shapes. I climbed out of the well and prepared to creep over to the wall when I heard a soft creaking; I looked up at the grating behind which the harem was located. Right above me was the place where I had removed the rod and to the left of that I perceived a gap in the grating of the room I had not been permitted to enter. It was certainly Senitza's bedroom. Did she remain awake to await my coming? Did the sound come from the grating that she was opening in her room? If that was the case she could have seen me come out of the water but would have withdrawn again as it would have been impossible for her to recognize me.

I crept closer and placed my hands around my mouth.

"Senitza!" I whispered softly.

The gap grew larger and a dark little head appeared.

"Who are you?" she breathed down to me.

"The *hekim* who was with you earlier."

"You come to rescue me?"

"Yes. You heard and understood my words?"

"Yes. Are you alone?"

"Isla Ben Maflei is outside."

"Ah! He will be killed!"

"By whom?"

"By Abrahim. He does not sleep at night, he is on guard. And my aged guardian sleeps in the room next to me. Quiet - listen! . . . Oh, flee quickly!"

From behind the door, which led to the *selamlük*, a sound emanated. The gap above me closed and I hurried back to the well. Here was the only place where I could find cover. Carefully I lowered myself into the water so that no ripple would betray my presence.

I had barely done so when the door opened and the figure of Abrahim-Mamur cautiously appeared and began to wander about the courtyard. I stood in water that reached to my mouth and the rim of the well hid my head so that the Egyptian was not aware of my presence. He assured himself that the gate was locked and when he had completed his rounds, he retired to the *selamlük*.

I climbed from the water and stole over to the gate, unlocked the bolt and opened it. I was now in the garden. Swiftly I crossed the distance to the outer gate and opened that in the same manner. It was my intention to run around the corner to fetch Isla Ben Maflei, when he appeared.

"*Hamdulillah* - God be praised, *effendi*! You succeeded."

"Yes, but I had to contend with death. Give me my clothes!"

My pants and vest dripped water; I hastily threw my coat about my shoulders so that my movement would not be restricted.

"I have spoken already with Senitza."

"Is it true, *effendi*?"

"She understood me and awaits us."

"Oh come! Swiftly, swiftly!"

"Wait a moment!"

I walked back into the garden to fetch one of the poles that I had noticed upon my earlier visit. Then we entered the courtyard. A gap had again opened in the grille.

"Senitza (Senitza is Serbic and is in German 'Augapfel' - that is 'apple of the eye'), my star, my ..." Isla extolled in a muffled voice when I drew his attention to the gap. I interrupted him:

"For all the riches in the world, quiet! Now is not the time to be pouring out your heart. You will be quiet and only I shall speak!"

I then spoke to Senitza:

"Are you ready to go with us?"

"Oh, yes!"

"Can you go through the chambers?"

"No. But opposite, behind that wooden pillar, is a ladder."

"I will get it!"

We needed neither the pole nor the rope that we had brought along. I went to get the ladder. It was stable. As soon as I leaned it against the wall Isla climbed up. Meanwhile I crept to the door of the *selamlük* to listen.

It took some time before the figure of the girl appeared. She climbed down the ladder with Isla's support. The moment she reached the courtyard floor, the ladder was jolted, it swayed and fell to the ground with a crashing blow.

"Run! Quickly to the boat!" I hurried them along.

They rushed to the gate and in that same instance I heard steps from behind the *selamlük* door. Abrahim had heard the noise and was coming to investigate. I had to shield the escapees and therefore followed them at a slower pace. The Egyptian caught sight of me, saw the fallen ladder and the open grating.

He roared loudly enough to awaken every inhabitant of the house.

"*Chirsytz, hajdut* - Thief, bandit, stop! To me, to me, you men, you people, you slaves! Help!"

Whilst he bellowed these words Abrahim bounded after me. Now, the Oriental style of bed is quite different from its European counterpart, one sleeps mostly in one's clothes on a divan; so it was that the inhabitants of the house were also soon up and after me.

The Egyptian was hard behind me. At the outer gate I turned for a quick look. He was barely ten paces behind, a second figure had appeared at the inner gate, also in fast pursuit.

Once outside the walls I saw Isla Ben Maflei and Senitza to my right. Accordingly I turned to my left, Abrahim was fooled, he did not see the other two but chased after me. I ran around a corner in the direction of the river on the upstream side of the house, whilst our boat was on the downstream side. Then I ran around the second corner and along the shore.

"Stop, scoundrel! I will shoot!" Abrahim cursed from behind me.

So he was armed then. I hurried on. If a bullet hit me now I would be either dead or a prisoner, because close behind Abrahim were his servants, as was evident by their shouts. The shot cracked. He had fired on the run instead of stopping to aim; the bullet whistled past me. I pretended to be wounded and fell to the ground.

He ran past me because he had spied the boat, which Isla and Senitza had just boarded. The instant Abrahim had passed I leaped up, took several strides in his pursuit and seizing him by the neck threw him down to the ground.

The cry of the *fellatah* sounded close behind me. I had forfeited both time and distance in this little battle; but I reached the boat and jumped in. At once Halef pushed off from the shore and we were several boat lengths away before the pursuing band reached the point we had just vacated.

Abrahim had staggered to his feet. He now took in the situation.

"*Geri*," he bellowed: "*geri erkekler* - Aback, aback, you men! *Geri doghru kajika* - Back, to the boat!"

They all turned in the direction of the canal where their boat had been berthed. Abrahim was there first and let loose a cry of fury when he saw that the boat was gone.

We had in the meantime left behind the quieter waters close to shore and entered the faster moving current near the middle of the river. Halef and the barber from Jüterbogk rowed; Isla and I took one of the captured oars each and our boat soon shot downstream at quite a pace.

No word was spoken; the mood was not one in which words could be composed.

This whole adventure had taken some time and already the horizon flushed with the coming dawn and one could see far over the mistless waters of the Nile. We could still see Abrahim and his men standing on the shore; further upstream a sail appeared, luminescent with the dawn.

"A *sandal*!" said Halef.

Yes, it was a *sandal*, one of those ancient vessels that was well manned and able to sail so fast that it could race against a steamboat and win.

"He will call upon the *sandal* for help and then give chase to us," said Isla.

"Let us hope that the *sandal* is not a trader, and refuses to obey him!"

"If Abrahim offers the *reïs* a sufficient sum I doubt if it will be refused."

"Even if that eventuates, we will have gained a good lead. The *sandal* must pull to and Abrahim and the *reïs* will negotiate - time is passing. Also, Abrahim has to make sure that he has all that he requires for his trip before he boards, since he does not know how long this pursuit will continue."

The sail now disappeared from our view and we made such good and fast progress that in less than half an hour we saw the *dahabiah,* upon which we would continue our journey.

Abu el Reïsahn leaned over the gunwale at the stern. He saw that a female sat in our boat and therefore concluded that our endeavor had succeeded, at least thus far.

"Lay to," he called. "Lower the gangway!"

We climbed aboard, and our rowboat was fastened at the stern. Then the ropes were let go, the sails where hoisted and the vessel turned its bow from the shore; the wind filled the canvas and strove for the middle of the current which already carried us down river.

I approached the *reïs*.

"How did it go?" he asked me.

"Very well. I will describe it to you, but first tell me if a good *sandal* can catch your vessel."

"Are we being pursued?"

"I don't believe so, but it is possible."

"My *dahabiah* is quite worthy, but a good *sandal* can overtake any *dahabiah*."

"Then let us hope that we will not be pursued!"

I told him about our adventure and then entered the cabin to change out of my still-damp clothes. The cabin was divided into two sections, one small and one larger. The first was assigned to Senitza and the latter to the Captain, Isla Ben Maflei and I.

Perhaps two hours had passed since our departure when I noticed the tip of a sail upstream that grew larger with every passing moment. As the hull became visible, I recognized it as the *sandal* that we had seen earlier this morning.

"Do you see that ship?" I asked the *reïs*.

"*Allah akbar* - God is great, and your question is equally so," he replied. "I am a *reïs* and should not see this sail that steers behind me!"

"Is it a vessel of the *Khedive*?"

"No."

"How do you know that?"

"I know this *sandal* quite well."

"Ah!"

"It belongs to the *reïs* Chalid Ben Mustapha."

"Do you know this Chalid?"

"Indeed; but we are not friends."

"Why is that?"

"An honest man cannot be the friend of a dishonest one."

"Hmm, then something is becoming clear."

"What?"

"That Abrahim-Mamur can be found aboard."

"We will see!"

"What will you do when the *sandal* comes alongside the *dahabiah*?"

“I must permit it. The law says so.”

“And if I will not permit it?”

“How will you accomplish this? I am the *reïs* of this *dahabiah* and I must follow the rule of the law.”

“And I am the captain of my will.”

At this point Isla entered. I did not want to ask him any intrusive questions, but he proposed to clarify the situation himself:

“Kara Ben Nemsi, You are my friend, the greatest friend that I could have found. Shall I relate to you how Senitza fell into the hands of this Egyptian?”

“That I would dearly love to hear, but such a tale requires time and composure, which we do not have at present.”

“You are anxious? Why is this so?”

He had not noticed the vessel sailing behind us.

“Turn and behold the *sandal*.”

He turned about.

“Is Abrahim aboard?”

“I do not know, but it is quite possible because the captain is a scoundrel who would permit himself to be bought by Abrahim's bribe.”

“How do you know he is a scoundrel?”

“Abu el Reïsahn says so.”

“Yes,” the *reïs* confirmed; “I know this captain and his ship. Even if it was further from us, I would recognize its sail, which has been thrice mended and patched.”

“What will we do?” asked Isla.

“First we will wait to discover if Abrahim is aboard.”

“And if he is?”

“Then he will not pass us.”

Our captain measured the progress of the *sandal* and our own and then said:

“He is closing on us. I will set an additional *triketha* (small sail).”

This was done, but I noticed after some minutes that this action would at most delay, rather than avert, the final confrontation. The *sandal* continued to close the distance between us; finally there were only a few ship lengths separating us, the *sandal* had reefed one sail to reduce its speed. We could now see Abrahim-Mamur standing on the deck.

“There he is!” cried Isla.

“Where exactly?” asked the *reïs*.

“Right up front in the bow.”

“Him? Kara Ben Nemsi, what are we to do? They will hail us and we will have to reply.”

“Who, according to your law, has to answer?”

“I, the owner of this *dahabiah*.”

"Pay attention now to what I say, Abu el Reïsahn. Are you prepared to lease your ship to me until we reach Kahira?"

The captain looked at me in amazement, but comprehended the implication of my proposal at once.

"Yes," he replied.

"Then I am the owner?"

"Yes."

"And you as *reïs* must do as I command?"

"Yes."

"And you are not responsible for anything?"

"No."

"Good. Call your men together!"

At his call the crew assembled.

"Men, I tell you that this *effendi*, who is called Kara Ben Nemsi, has leased this *dahabiah* from here on, until we reach Kahira, " the captain explained. "Is it not so?"

"Yes, it is so." I confirmed.

"Can you confirm that I am no longer the master of this ship?" he asked his crew.

"We confirm it."

"Then return to your posts. But know this, I have been ordered by Kara Ben Nemsi to continue my duties as captain of this ship."

They departed, surely in a quandary about the strange tidings they had just received. In the meantime the *sandal* had drawn parallel with us. The captain, an older man – tall and very thin with a heron feather in his tarboosh, stood on the gunwale and called across to us:

"Oh *dahabiah*, who is your *reïs*?"

I leaned over and replied:

"*Reïs* Hassan."

"Hassan Abu el Reïsahn?"

"Yes."

"Ah, that is indeed wondrous, for I know this man." he observed smugly. "You have a woman aboard?"

"Yes."

"Hand her over!"

"Chalid Ben Mustapha, are you crazy!"

"That depends. We will come alongside."

"We will not permit that."

"How do you intend to stop us?"

"I will show you immediately. Pay attention to the feather in your tarboosh!"

I quickly raised my weapon, which I had surreptitiously held at the ready, I aimed and fired. The feather fluttered down. Even the worst disaster could not have upset the honorable Ben Mustapha as this warning shot had. He jumped so high, as though his long limbs were made of elastic rubber, held his head in both hands and fled behind the mast of his vessel.

"Now you know my marksmanship, Ben Mustapha," I called across. "If your *sandal* remains on our port side for another minute, then I will shoot - not the feather from your tarboosh, but the soul from you body; of that you can be certain!"

This threat had immediate effect. He hurried to the rudder, tore it from the hands of the person who had been steering the vessel up until that point and set course to move away from us. In two minutes the *sandal* had fled so far from us that it was out of range of my weapon.

"For the moment we are safe," I said.

"He will not come too close again," agreed Hassan; "but he will not lose sight of us, he will wait until we lay to at some shore where he can secure support from the law."

"I do not fear that."

"I do not fear it either, since the ship is yours. I fear something else."

"What would that be?"

"That!" He indicated the water ahead with his hand, and we grasped immediately what he had not expressed in words.

We had already begun to notice that for some time the waves were gaining in force and speed and were pulling us along at a faster clip, the shoreline was narrowing and had become craggy. We were close to the rapids and their hidden obstacles, which pose a very real hazard to vessels that navigate these stretches of the Nile. For now the hostility that existed between us had to take second place and the full concentration of every man must focus on the threatening elements before us. The voice of the *reïs* echoed over the deck:

"You men, keep your eyes open, there is the *shellahl* - the cataract! Come together and pray the holy *fatcha*!"

The crew obeyed the command and began:

"Protect us oh Lord from Lucifer, whom You turned to stone!"

"In the name of the ever-loving God!" intoned the *reïs*.

The crew joined in and prayed the *fatcha*, the first *sura* of the Koran.

I have to admit that this prayer touched me, not from fear of the impending danger but from the deep, heartfelt religious reverence that was displayed by these half-wild people who undertake no deed without the constant reminder that in this act of human weakness there is strength.

"Well then lads, you fearless rogues, to your posts," ordered the captain; "the current has us in its grasp."

The command of a ship on the Nile is not as routine as that of a European vessel. The hot blood of the south flows through the veins and drives men in moments of peril from their greatest expectation to their deepest despair. There are screams, calls, howls, prayers and curses in that instance of danger and in the next, when the danger has passed, loud jubilation, whistles, songs and cheer. Throughout all this each man works at his designated task with all his might and the captain jumps from one to another, spurring each man on, chastising the slow only as an Arab can and rewarding others with the sweetest, most affectionate praise, in which the word 'hero' is repeated most often. Hassan had been prepared for the passage through the cataract and had signed on a reserve crew. Every oar now had double the usual men, and the rudder was controlled by three strong coxswains, who knew every foot of this river and its hazardous places.

With terrible power the waves crashed upon the barely covered rocks and foamed over the deck. The thunder of the cataract drowned out everything, even the loudest command. The ship groaned and creaked in all its joints; the oars were useless, the rudder completely unheeding, the *dahabiah* raged through the boiling waters.

Now the black glassy rocks closed in and left but a small passage, almost too narrow for our ship. The waves were forced through this gap and exited in a mighty broad jet into the basin below that was sown with razor-edged and needle-sharp rocks.

In a screaming rush we entered the narrows. The oars were shipped. Now, now we were in the terrible canyon, the walls on either side were so close that I could have touched them with my hand. It was as though this canyon was trying to spit us up into the air, the torrent hurled us with immense power over the sharp rocks, out of the funnel and down into the chasm of a kettle. It boiled and raged, thundered and screamed about us: then we were grasped again with irresistible might and thrust into a plunging sheet of water, the surface of which was so calm and still, whilst directly below lurked a most monstrous horror. We did not float, no . . . we were falling, plunging with unimpeded fury down this course and ...

"*Allah kerihm* - God is merciful!" Hassan's shrill cry could be heard at last. "*Allah il Allah*, to the oars, to the oars, you lads, you heroic champions, you tigers, panthers and lions! Death is before you, do you not see it? *Amahl, amahl, ïa Allah amahl* - come on, come on, by God come on you dogs, cowards, villains and pussycats, work, work, you staunch, brave heroes, you peerless and proven hand-picked men!"

We shot towards pincer-like rocks that opened before us and which could in the very next moment destroy us. The rocks were so sharp, and the current so strong that a ship could be reduced instantly to wreckage no larger than a hand.

"*Allah ïa Sahtir* - Oh you Savior, help! Port, to port, you dogs, you vultures, you rat eaters, you devourers of carrion, to port, to port with the rudder, great and splendid fathers of heroes! *Allah, Allah, Mash Allah* - God performs miracles, may He be thanked!"

The ship had responded to the near superhuman efforts and flew past the rocks. For a few moments we were in calm waters and all fell to their knees to thank the Almighty.

"*Esh'hetu inu la il laha il Allah*!" the cries sounded jubilantly across the deck - "Witness that there is only one God! *Sellem aaleïna baraktak* - Bestow upon us Your blessing!"

The *sandal* appeared behind us as though shot from a bow, they had passed through the same dangers as we had. The *sandal* was swifter than our *dahabiah* and it was bound to pass us. But the passage here was so narrow that we could yield only with great difficulty and it raced past with little leeway between the two vessels. Abrahim-Mamur leaned against the mast, his right hand concealed behind his back. When we drew level he revealed a long Arabian gun which he brought level with his cheek - I threw myself down - the bullet passed over me and in the next moment the *sandal* was ahead of us.

Everyone had seen the attempt on my life but no one had time to wonder or to vent their anger because the current once again had us and was pulling us into a labyrinth of cliffs.

From ahead there came a loud scream. The *sandal* was thrown by the might of the *shellahl* into the rocks; the crew used the oars against the current and the slightly damaged vessel shot away, once again in the grip of the river. The collision had caused a man to fall overboard; he hung in the water and grappled desperately at the cliff face. I grabbed a handy date-fiber rope, hurried to the starboard and thew it to the endangered man. He reached for it - clutched it - and was pulled to safety; it was Abrahim-Mamur.

As soon as he was safely aboard, he shook the water from his clothes and leaped towards me with balled fists.

"Dog, you are a thief and a swindler!"

I awaited him with a confident stance, and my pose had the desired effect. He stopped before me, his fists unused.

"Abrahim-Mamur, be courteous, you are not in your home now. If you utter another word that displeases me, I will have you tied to the mast and whipped!"

The greatest insult for an Arab is to be whipped, the second greatest is the threat of being whipped. Abrahim made a move, but composed himself at once.

"You have my wife aboard!" he shouted.

"No."

"You are not telling me the truth!"

"I tell you that the woman I have aboard is not your wife but the betrothed of this young man standing next to me."

He rushed to the cabin, but Halef met him there.

"Abrahim-Mamur, I am Hajji Halef Omar Ben Hajji Abul Abbas; these here are my two pistols, and I will shoot you down the moment you go where my master forbids!"

My little Halef made such a face that the Egyptian could not doubt that this threat was made in earnest. He turned and snorted:

"Then I will have you charged as soon as we lay to, when you land the extra crew."

"Do so. Until then you are not my enemy but my guest, for as long as you behave in a dignified manner."

The cataract and its perils had been navigated successfully and we now had the necessary leisure to turn to our affairs.

"Will you now tell us in what manner Senitza fell into the hands of this man?" I asked Isla.

"I will fetch her," he replied; "she should tell you herself."

"No; she should stay in the cabin because her presence would only aggravate the Egyptian and push him to the limit. Tell us before anything else whether she is Moslem or Christian."

"She is Christian."

"From which denomination?"

"From the one you call Greek."

"She never became the Egyptian's wife?"

"He bought her."

"Ah! Is it possible?"

"Yes. The Montenegrins do not go about with veils. He saw Senitza in Scutari and told her that he loved her and that she should become his wife; but she laughed at him. So he went to Czernagora to Senitza's father and offered a great sum to purchase her from him; her father threw him out. Then the Egyptian bribed the father of Senitza's female companion, whom Senitza visited often, and that one agreed to the deal."

"How?"

"This man pretended that she was a slave, sold her to Abrahim-Mamur and handed him a paper to attest that she was a Circassian slave."

"Ah, that is why her female companion disappeared with her father so suddenly!"

"Only because of this. The Egyptian boarded a ship to Cyprus with her, and then traveled to Egypt. You know the rest."

"What was the name of the man that sold her?" I asked involuntarily.

"Barud el Amasat."

"El Amasat - el Amasat - this name is familiar. Where have I heard it? Was this man a Turk?"

"No, an Armenian."

An Armenian - - ah, now I had it! Hamd el Amasat, the Armenian who had tried to kill us on Chott Jerid and escaped in Kbilli – was this the same man? - No, he could not be - the timing was wrong.

"Do you know," I asked Isla, "if this Barud el Amasat has a brother?"

"No; Senitza does not know either; I have questioned her about that family extensively."

The servant Hamsad el Jerbaja approached and turned to me:

"Herr *effendim*, I have to tell you something."

"Speak!"

"What is the name of this Egyptian no-good?"

"Abrahim-Mamur."

"So! He claims to have been a *Mamur*?"

"Indeed."

"He cannot put one over me as I know this man better than he knows me!"

"Ah! Who is he?"

"I saw him when he was receiving the *bastinado,* and since it was his first I made some inquiries about him."

"Now, who and what is he?"

"He was an attaché to the Persian embassy or something like that and had betrayed some secret or the like. He would have been executed, but because he had a patron he was punished with the *bastinado* only. His name is Dawuhd Arafim."

That the barber from Jüterbogk knew this man was an amazing coincidence and now my eyes were opened. I had encountered this Dawuhd Arafim in Ispahan on the Almeidan-Shah, where he was bound on a camel in transit to Constantinople as a prisoner. My path was for a short distance the same as that of the caravan and so it happened that he had seen me as well and remembered.

"I thank you, Hamsad, for this information, but keep it to yourself for now."

Now there was not the least reason for concern over the possibility that Abrahim would accuse me. I am not certain why it was but I could not shake the suspicion that he and Barud el Amasat, who had sold Senitza, did not just meet on that occasion. Abrahim was a degraded official, a prisoner and had even received the *bastinado* - now he pretended to be a Mamur and had a fortune - these were circumstances which made me think.

I preferred to keep this information to myself so that Abrahim would not know that he had been exposed.

At the next landing the crew that had been taken aboard the *dahabiah* upstream of the cataract had to be discharged. Our vessel steered towards the shore.

"Will we anchor or not?" I asked the *reïs*.

"No, I will turn about as soon as the men have disembarked."

"Why?"

"To avoid the police."

"And Abrahim?"

"He will be put ashore with the crew."

"I do not fear the police." I said.

"You are a foreigner in this land and are under the protection of your consul. Nothing can be done against you. Ahhh!"

This last utterance concerned the approach of a boat which was filled with armed, and none too happy men. They were *khawassen* - police.

"I don't think that you will turn about." I said to Hassan.

"I will if you order it, I have to obey you."

"Then I command that you do not; I would like to get to know the police here."

The boat pulled alongside and all the occupants climbed aboard our vessel before we reached the shore. The crew of the *sandal* had disembarked here before us and had already informed the local *khawassen* about the *tschikarma* and that Abrahim had been drowned in the *shellahl*. Then, as we later discovered, the old *reïs* Chalid Ben Mustapha had hot-footed it to the nearest judge and spun such a terrifying tale about the unbeliever, the murderer, the kidnapper, the thief and felon that I should have been lucky only to have been sentenced to hang or drown.

Since the judiciary in these lands had not yet noted, nor made use of, the invention of the legal document, the law was applied in a quick and summary manner.

"Who is the *reïs* of this ship?" asked the leader of the *khawassen*.

"I." replied our captain.

"What is your name?"

"Hassan Abu el Reïsahn."

"Do you have aboard an *effendi*, a *hekim*, who is an infidel?"

"That is he, Kara Ben Nemsi."

"And is a woman named Güzela also aboard?"

"She is in the cabin."

"Well then, you are all my prisoners and you will accompany me to the judge, this vessel in the meantime will be guarded by my people!"

The *dahabiah* laid to, and her entire crew as well as all passengers were transported to the shore. Senitza, heavily veiled, was led to a sedan that had been provided and was forced to follow our procession, which grew with every step as young and old, great and small joined us. Hamsad al Jerbaja, the ex-barber, walked behind me and whistled, in time with the cadence of his feet, this tune; '*Muß i denn, muß i denn zum Städtele hinaus*!' [This German song is known as 'Wooden Heart' in English]

The *Sahbeth-Bei* or director of police sat with his secretary awaiting our arrival.

He wore the insignia of a *bimbashi*, a major or commander of a thousand men, but had neither a warlike nor overly intelligent appearance. As had the crew of the *sandal*, so he too had thought Abrahim-Mamur drowned and welcomed the resurrected with great respect, the complete opposite of the one given to us. We were separated into two groups - the first included the crew of the *sandal* along with Abrahim and the servants that had accompanied him, the second group was comprised of the crew of the *dahabiah*, Senitza, Isla and myself, as well as Halef and the barber.

"Do you command a pipe, master?" the *Sahbeth-Bei* asked the supposed *Mamur*.

"Let it be brought!"

He received the pipe and a carpet on which to sit. Then the procedure began:

"Excellency, tell me your name, blessed by Allah!"

"It is Abrahim-Mamur."

"Then you are a *Mamur*. Of what province?"

"Of En-Nasar."

"You bring the charge. Speak; I will hear and will judge."

"I accuse this *giaur*, who is a *hekim*, of *tschikarma*; I charge that man next to him of *tschikarma*, and I charge that the captain of the *dahabiah* assisted in the *tschikarma*. How deeply the other two men and the crew of the *dahabiah* are involved, I leave for you to decide, oh *bimbashi*."

"Tell me where and how the theft was accomplished."

Abrahim did so. When he had finished, his witnesses were examined, which resulted in the *reïs* of the *sandal*, Master Chalid Ben Mustapha adding attempted murder to the list of charges.

One could see lightning in the eyes of the *Sahbeth-Bei* as he turned to me.

"*Giaur*, what is your name?"

"Kara Ben Nemsi."

"What is the name of your homeland?"

"*Germanistan*."

"Where is this handful of earth?"

"Handful? Hmm, *bimbashi*, you prove how ignorant you are!"

"Dog!" he countered. "What are you saying?"

"*Germanistan* is a great country and has ten times as many inhabitants as has Egypt. But you do not know this. You are a bad geographer in any case, that is why Abrahim-Mamur can lie to you."

"You dare to say such words again and I will have your ears nailed to the wall."

"I dare it! This Abrahim says he is *Mamur* of the Province of En-Nasar. *Mamurs* exist exclusively in Egypt ."

"Is En-Nasar not in Egypt, *giaur*? I have been there myself and know this *Mamur* as well as my brother, yes, even as well as myself."

"You lie!"

"Nail him!" The judge commanded.

I drew my revolver, and as Halef saw this he also drew his pistols.

"*Bimbashi*, I tell you that I will gun down the first person that touches me, and then you! I say again - you lie. En-Nasar is one very small, tiny oasis between Homrh and Tighert in the land of Tripoli; there exists no *Mamur*, but a poor Sheik; he is called Mamra Ibn Alef Abuzin, and I know him quite well. I could permit you to amuse me further and allow you to ask more questions; but I will cut this short. How is it that you let the accusers stand while the accused, the criminal, remains seated, and is even provided with a pipe?"

The good fellow looked at me bewildered.

"What do you mean, *giaur*?"

"I warn you, do not abuse me with this word! I have a passport and a *Izingitish* (visa) from the Viceroy of Egypt; and this man, my companion, is from Istambul; he has a *Bu-Djeruldu* from the Sultan and is in '*Giölgeda padischahnün'*."

"Show me!"

I handed him my documents and Isla also laid his before him. He read them and returned them to us with an embarrassed expression.

"Go on."

This encouragement proved to me that he did not know what to do. I therefore continued:

"You are a *Sahbeth-Bei* and a *bimbashi* and yet you do not know what your duty is. When you are given a hand-written document from the Sultan to read then you must press it to your brow, your eyes and your mouth and everyone in attendance must bow as though his Eminence were present in person. I will tell the Khedive and the Grand Vizier in what esteem you hold them!"

He did not expect that. He was so alarmed, that his eyes popped and his mouth gaped wordlessly. I continued:

"You wished to know the meaning of my previous words. I am the accuser and I must stand, and he is the accused and may sit!" I pointed at Abrahim

"Who accuses him?"

"I do, and he and he, all of us." I indicated myself, Isla and Hassan.

Abrahim was astonished, but said nothing.

"What do you accuse him of?" asked the *Sahbeth-Bei*.

"The *tschikarma*, the same crime that he accused us of."

Now I saw that Abrahim was becoming anxious. The judge commanded me:

"Speak!"

"It grieves me, *bimbashi*, that you must experience such sadness."

"What sadness?"

"That you must condemn this man, he that you know like a brother, yes, even as you know yourself. You were even with him in En-Nasar and confirmed that he was a *Mamur*. But I say to you that I too know him. He is called Dawuhd Arafim, he was an official of the Shah of Persia, he was deposed and sentenced to the *bastinado*."

Now Abrahim arose and spluttered, "dog! - *Sahbeth-Bei*, this man has lost his reason!"

"*Sahbeth-Bei*, hear me further, then it will be shown whose head sits more firmly, mine or his!"

"Speak!"

"This woman is a Christian, a free Christian from Karadagh (Montenegro - both are the same just as the Slavic Czernagora – 'Black Mountains'); he kidnapped her and brought her by force into Egypt. My friend here is her rightful fiancé, and he therefore followed her to Egypt to rescue her. You know us, because you have seen our passports, but him you do not know. He is a kidnapper and a swindler. Let him show you his passport or I will go to the Khedive and tell him how you dispense justice in the position that he has bestowed upon you. I have been accused of attempted murder by the captain of the *sandal*. Ask these men! They all heard me say that I would shoot the feather from his tarboosh and I did. He that calls himself *Mamur* had every intention of killing me when he fired upon my person. I accuse him. Now decide!"

The good man was now in an embarrassing situation. He could not disprove my words or deeds but felt that I was right and so decided to do what only an Egyptian could do.

"The people shall leave and return to their homes!" he commanded. "I will deliberate upon this affair and pass judgment this afternoon. In the meantime you are all my prisoners!"

The *khawassen* drove the spectators out with blows from their sticks; then Abrahim-Mamur and the crew of the *sandal* were led away, and finally we were led out into the courtyard of the building, where we could move about freely, while the *khawassen* guarded the exits. After some fifteen minutes these men disappeared.

I suspected what the *Sahbeth-Bei* had in mind and stepped up to Isla Ben Maflei, who sat next to Senitza by the fountain.

"Do you think we will win this process?"

"I don't think so; I leave everything in your hands," he replied.

"And when we win, what will happen to Abrahim?"

"Nothing. I know these people. Abrahim will give the *bimbashi* money or one of the expensive rings that he wears on his fingers, and the *bashi* will let him go."

"Do you wish him dead?"

"No. I have found Senitza, that is enough for me."

"And how does your beloved feel?"

Senitza replied:

"*Effendi*, I was very unhappy, but now I am free. I will not think about him again."

I was satisfied. Now all that remained was to consult Abu el Reïsahn. He explained in a roundabout manner that he would be happy to escape unscathed; so I decided to unobtrusively reconnoiter our surroundings. I walked through the exit into the street. The hottest part of the day had arrived and the street was deserted. It was clear what the *Sahbeth-Bei* desired - that we analyze our situation and not wait for his decision; I returned to the courtyard and informed my companions of my intention and suggested that they follow me. They did so and not a soul hindered our action.

As we reached the *dahabiah* we discovered that it had been deserted by the *khawassen*. A friend or admirer of the cargo of senna leaves could have annexed it without bother.

The *sandal* was no longer at the shore; it was gone. It was clear that the honorable Chalid Ben Mustapha had recognized the judge's intentions far earlier than we had and disappeared with his ship and crew.

But where was Abrahim-Mamur?

We were not disinterested in such a discovery; it was possible, even probable, that he would keep us under surveillance. I at least had a feeling that sooner or later we would meet again.

The *dahabiah* weighed anchor and we continued our interrupted journey with the happy knowledge that we had escaped unharmed from a difficult situation.

Abu-Seïf

[Father of the Saber]

Chapter 8

"And the angel of God, which went before the camp of Israel, removed and went behind them; and the pillar of the cloud went from before their face, and stood behind them.

And it came between the camp of the Egyptians and the camp of Israel; and it was a cloud and darkness to them, but it gave light by night to these: so that the one came not near the other all the night.

And Moses stretched out his hand over the sea; and the Lord caused the sea to go back by a strong east wind all that night, and made the sea dry land, and the waters were divided.

And the children of Israel went into the midst of the sea upon the dry ground: and the waters were a wall unto them on their right hand, and on their left.

And the Egyptians pursued, and went in after them to the midst of the sea, even all Pharaoh's horses, his chariots, and his horsemen.

And it came to pass, that in the morning watch the Lord looked unto the host of the Egyptians through the pillar of fire and of the cloud, and troubled the host of the Egyptians,

And took off their chariot wheels, that they drive them heavily: so that the Egyptians said, Let us flee from the face of Israel; for the Lord fighteth for them against the Egyptians!

And the Lord said unto Moses, Stretch out thine hand over the sea, that the waters may come again upon the Egyptians, upon their chariots, and upon their horsemen.

And Moses stretched forth his hand over the sea, and the sea returned to his strength when the morning appeared; and the Egyptians fled against it; and the Lord overthrew the Egyptians in the midst of the sea.

And the waters returned, and covered the chariots, and the horsemen, and all the host of Pharaoh that came into the sea after them; there remained not so much as one of them.

But the children of Israel walked upon dry land in the midst of the sea; and the waters were a wall unto them on their right hand, and on their left.

Thus the Lord saved Israel that day out of the hand of the Egyptians; and Israel saw the Egyptians dead upon the sea shore.

And Israel saw that great work which the Lord did upon the Egyptians: and the people feared the Lord, and believed the Lord, and his servant Moses. ..."

I was prompted to think of these verses from the second book of Moses, (Exodus Chapter 14, Verses: 19 to 31) when I halted my camel in the Hiroth Valley, across from Baal Zephon, and cast my eyes over the sparkling waters of the Red Sea. I too felt something of the fear that must have gripped the hearts of the children of Israel. I did not feel a baseless dread for these elements however, rather a reverent awe swept over me; that which is felt by every faithful man when he stands in a place where biblical history tells us that here the foot of eternity rested and here the hand of the everlasting held sway. It was as though I heard the voice that once called to the son of Amram and Jochebeth:

"Moses, Moses, . . . draw not nigh hither: put off thy shoes from off thy feet, for the place whereon thou standest is holy ground!"

Behind me lay the land of Isis and Osiris, the land of the pyramids and the sphinx, the land where God's people had slaved under the Egyptian yoke and moved stone blocks from Mokattam to build such wonders that even today arouse astonishment in anyone travelling along the Nile. In the reeds of this ancient and venerable river a princess found an infant who was destined to free a people from slavery and to give to them the ten commandments of God's law, which, even after many millennia, still form the basis of all laws.

Before my feet, beneath the burning rays of the sun, glittered the waters of the Arabian Gulf. These waters had once obeyed the voice of *Jehovah Sabaoth* [See Trans. Notes Ch 8.1] and formed two walls, between which the slaves of the land of Goshen found their way to freedom and their pursuers - a gruesome demise. These were the same waters in which the '*Sultan Kebihr*', Napoleon Bonaparte, almost perished.

And across from the *Birket Faraun* - the 'Sea of the Pharaoh', as the Arabs call that place where the waters closed over the Egyptians, rises the rocky base of the Sinai, immense and abiding it is the most famous mountain on earth, where, amidst thunder and lightning, these words resounded:

"I am the Lord, thy God; you shall have no other gods before me!"

The history of this place, even more than the setting, created an impression that was difficult to ignore, even if I had been so inclined. How many times had I sat in the lap of my old and devout grandmother and listened with baited breath as she told me of the creation of earth, the first sin, the first murder, the flood; of Sodom and Gomorrah, and the gift of the ten commandments on Mount Sinai. She had folded my little hands so that I could repeat with the necessary reverence, the ten-fold 'Thou Shalt'. Now, the earthly shell of the good woman was long interred and I stood opposite the place that she had painted with such lively colors even though she had only ever seen it with her mind's eye. The truth of the poet's words force themselves upon me:

"Quite different are the Holy Words,
That only the Book of Books report,
Written by the Holy Ghost they stand.
Only to these may you credence give,
And deep within their wonder live,
For the breath of God is felt at hand."

Faith provides a firmer conviction than the proudest construct that human logic can render. It was this belief that I had been experiencing for the past hour, so real, so full of life; I would have continued in this manner, paused here on my camel, looking out across the sea, if the voice of Halef had not roused me:

"*Hamdulillah* - Praise to God that the desert has ended! *Sihdi*, here is water. Dismount from your camel and refresh yourself with a bath, as I will do."

One of the two Bedouin who had guided us stepped towards me and raised a hand in warning.

"Do not do it, *effendi*!"

"And why not?"

"Because here lives *Melek el newth*, the Angel of Death. He who enters the water here will either drown or receive the seed of death. Each drop of this water is one tear from the hundreds of thousands of souls that perished because they tried to slay *Sidna Musa* - Moses and his followers. Every boat and every ship hurries past here without stopping; for Allah, who is called *Jehuwa* by the Hebrews, has cursed this place." [See Trans. Notes Ch 8.2]

"Is it true that no ship will stop here?"

"Yes."

"I had planned to wait for a vessel and obtain passage."

"To take you to Suez? We will guide you, and you will get there faster on our camels than you would by ship."

"I do not wish to go to Suez, but to Tor."

"Then you must of course take a ship; but no ship will stop here. Permit us to guide you a way to the south, to a place where there are no spirits and where every ship would happily lay to and give you passage."

"How long a time will we have to ride?"

"Not quite three times the period that is know by the Franks as an hour."

"Then let us go!"

I had not chosen the usual route between Cairo and Suez to reach the Red Sea. The so-called desert between these two cities no longer deserves that term. In earlier times it was feared, probably due to its complete lack of water and the local Bedouins who supplemented their existence by robbery. These days it was very different and for that reason I had chosen a path further south. A ride through the desolation was more attractive to me than a trip along much-traveled paths. That is why I also wanted to avoid Suez, which could offer only what I had already seen and experienced.

During our ride the bare heights of Jekehm and Da-ad rose before us and as the summit of Jebel Gharib came into view on our right, we left behind the pharaoh's tomb. To our left a vessel lay at anchor in a bay formed by the Red Sea.

The vessel was one of those barks that are called '*sambuk'* on the Red Sea. It was approximately sixty feet long and fifteen feet wide and had a small quarterdeck beneath which a compartment was usually constructed to accommodate the captain or distinguished passengers. Apart from the row-locks – a *sambuk* can be rowed - it has two triangular sails, one of which is so far forward that when filled by the wind it extends over the bow of the ship and forms a kind of hemispherical balloon; much as one might see on antique coins and on old frescoes. One can confidently assume that the vessels on these waters, in respect of construction, management and tackling, are identical to those seen here in the dim past, and that the sailors of today still visit the same bays and anchorages that were already populated at the time when Dionysus undertook his famous trek to India. These coastal ships of the Red Sea are usually built from the Indian wood that the Arabs call *sadsh*, which with time and water hardens to the point where it becomes impossible to drive in a nail. For this wood to rot is unheard of, and thus one may find *sambuks* that have been navigating these waters for some two hundred years.

Seafaring in the Arabian bays is quite perilous; that is why no vessel will sail at night, seeking instead a safe anchorage each evening.

The *sambuk* lying before us had done just this. It was fastened with an anchor and rope and lay, without crew, by the coast. The sailors had left the ship and now sat or reclined beside a small body of water that flowed into the sea. One man sat apart on a rug, his bearing was grave and he was surely the captain or the owner of this vessel. I noticed immediately that he was not an Arab but a Turk. The *sambuk* flew the colors of the Sultan and the crew wore Turkish uniforms.

Not one of the men moved as we approached. I rode hard up to their leader, raised my right hand to my breast and greeted him, intentionally, in Arabic rather than Turkish.

"God protect you! Are you the captain of this ship?"

He raised his eyes with pride and inspected me for some time before he answered:

"I am."

"Where is your *sambuk* bound?"

"Everywhere."

"What is your cargo?"

"Various things."

"Do you take passengers?"

"I do not know."

That was more than reserved, it was rude. That is why I shook my head and said in a sorrowful tone:

"You are a *kelleh* - an unlucky one, whom the Koran advises the faithful to show compassion to. I feel sorry for you!"

He looked at me in angry astonishment.

"You feel sorry for me? You call me an unlucky one, why?"

"Allah has lent your mouth the gift of speech but your soul remains mute. Turn to *kiblah* (direction of Mecca, towards which Moslems face during prayer) and request that Allah return that ability to your soul also, otherwise it will not be able to enter paradise with you!"

He smiled contemptuously and placed his hand on his belt where two huge pistols rested.

"Silence is better than gibbering. You are a gibberer; *wergi-bashi* Muhrad Ibrahim prefers silence."

"*Wergi-bashi*? - High tax collector? You are a great and certainly famous man but despite that you will answer when I ask a question."

"Are you threatening me? I see that I thought correctly: you are an Arab Jeheïne."

The Arabs from the tribe Jeheïne, by the Red Sea, are known as smugglers and thieves. The tax collector took me to be one of them; that was the reason for his insulting manner.

"Do you fear the Beni Jeheïne?" I asked him.

"Fear them? Muhrad Ibrahim does not know fear!"

Despite the pride that these words kindled in his eyes, there was something in his face that made me doubt his courage.

"And if I were a Jeheïne?"

"I would not fear you."

"Naturally. You have twelve *gemi-taïfasyler* (sailors) at your side and eight servants, whilst I have but three men. But I am no Jeheïne; I am not a Beni Arab, I come from the west."

"From the west? You wear the clothing of a Bedouin and you speak the language of an Arab!"

"Is that prohibited?"

"No. Are you a *Fransez* or an *Ingli*?"

"I belong to the *Nemsi*."

"A *Nemtshe*," he said with a derogatory expression. "Then you are a *bostandshi* – gardener, or a *bazirgian* - merchant?"

"Neither. I am a *jazmakdshi*."

"A writer? *Oh jazik* - Oh woe, and I thought you a courageous Bedouin! What is a writer? A writer is not a man; a writer is a being who consumes feathers and ink; a writer has no blood, no heart, no courage, no ..."

"Stop!" my servant interrupted him. "Muhrad Ibrahim, do you see what I hold in my hand?"

He had dismounted and stood before the Turk with his Nile whip. The Turk frowned and answered:

"A whip."

"Brilliant. I am Hajji Halef Omar Ben Hajji Abul Abbas Ibn Hajji Dawud al Gossarah. This *Sihdi* is Kara Ben Nemsi, who is not afraid of any man. We have wandered through the Sahara and all of Egypt and have accomplished heroic deeds. We will be the talk in coffee houses and market places the world over, and if you dare to utter one more word that displeases my *effendi*, then you will taste this whip, even if you are a *wergi-bashi* and have many men at your side!"

This threat was extraordinarily effective. As a result of Halef's daring act, the two Bedouin, who had been our guides up to this point, moved back several paces; the sailors and remaining companions of the Turk quickly rose and gathered their weapons and the *bashi* did likewise. He reached for his pistols, but Halef already pointed the business end of his own weapon at the *bashi's* bosom.

"Get him!" the *bashi* commanded as he lowered his own weapons.

The good people maintained their threatening postures but no one dared to lay a hand on Halef.

"Do you know what it means to threaten a *wergi-bashi* with the whip?" asked the Turk.

"I know it," replied Halef. "To threaten a *wergi-bashi* with the whip means that he will be given a taste of it directly, should he dare to speak further in this manner. You are a Turk, a slave of the Sultan; but I am a free Arab!"

I directed my camel to kneel, dismounted and pulled out my passport.

"Muhrad Ibrahim, you see that we fear you even less than you fear us; you have made a big mistake in insulting an *effendi* who is standing in '*Giölgeda padischahnün*'!"

"In the protection of the Sultan, may Allah bless him? Who do you mean?"

"I."

"You? You are a *Nemtshe*, a *giaur* ..."

"You are insulting me!" I interrupted him.

"You are an infidel, and of the *giaurs* it is written in the Koran: 'Oh, you faithful, do not make friends with those that do not belong to your religion. They will not cease to mislead you and wish only your demise!' How can the Sultan, who is the protector of the faithful, protect an infidel?"

"I know these words which you speak; they are written in the third *sura* of the Koran, in the *surat Amran*; but open your eyes, and bow in supplication before the *Bjuruldu* of the Padishah. Here it is."

He took the parchment, pressed it to his forehead, eyes and breast, bowed almost to the ground and then read it. He then returned it to me.

"Why did you not say that you are an *arkadar* (one who is protected) of the Sultan? I would not have called you a *giaur*, although you are an infidel. Be welcome, *effendi*!"

"You welcome me and dishonor my faith in the same breath. We Christians know the rules of courtesy and hospitality better than you; we do not call you *giaurs*, because it is our God Whom you call Allah."

"That is not true. We only have Allah; but you have three Gods, a Father, a Son and a Holy Ghost."

"We have just one God, because Father, Son and Holy Ghost are One. You say: 'Allah il Allah, God is God!' And our God says: 'I am a strong, united God.' The Koran says in the second *surat*: 'He is the Living, Eternal; He is not subject to sleep nor slumber; to Him belongs all that is in heaven and on earth.' Our Holy Bible says: 'God is from eternity to eternity; everything is open and exposed before His eyes; He created the earth, and the heavens are His handiwork.' Is that not the same?"

"Yes, your *Kitab* ([Book], Bible [in this case]) is good, but your belief is false."

"You are wrong. The Koran says: 'Righteousness does not just consist of turning one's face east or west in prayer, but instead just is he who believes in God, in the first day, in the angels, in the Word and the Prophets; and with love distributes his earthly fortune among his kin, the orphans, the poor and the pilgrims, yes, among all who ask; who frees the imprisoned, who says his prayers, honors his contracts and accepts misfortune with patience. He is righteous, he is truly pious.' Our Holy Book tells us: 'You shall love God above all things and your neighbor like yourself.' Does our belief not demand the same as yours?"

"You have copied this from the Koran into your *Kitab*."

"How is that possible since our *Kitab* is two thousand years older than the Koran?"

"You are an *effendi* and an *effendi* must always find reasons and proofs, even if he is wrong. Where do you come from?"

"From the land of *Gipt* (Turkish for Egypt), there in the west."

"And where do you wish to go?"

"Across to Tor."

"And afterwards?"

"To the *manastyr* (monastery) on Jebel Sinahi."

"Then you must go by water."

"Yes. Where do you sail to?"

"Also to Tor."

"Will you take me along?"

"If you pay well and ensure that we are not defiled by you."

"Have no fear! How much do you ask?"

"For all four and the camels?"

"Only for my servant Hajji Halef and myself. These two men will return home with their camels."

"With what will you pay? With money or something else?"

"With money."

"Do you wish us to provide you with food?"

"No; you only need to provide water."

"Then you pay ten *misri* for yourself, eight for this Hajji Halef."

I laughed in this brave fellow's face. This was truly Turkish to demand eighteen *misri* (about thirty-four *Taler*) for a short trip and a few sips of water.

"You sail for one day to reach the vicinity of the Bay of Nayazat, where you will anchor overnight?" I asked.

"Yes."

"Then we are in Tor by midday?"

"Yes. Why do you ask?"

"Because I will not pay you eighteen *misri* for such a short journey."

"Then you will remain here and take passage with another who will demand even more."

"I will neither stay behind nor seek passage with another. I will go with you."

"Then you pay me the sum that I have demanded."

"Hear what I tell you! These two men have loaned me their animals and guided me on foot from El Kahira for four Maria Theresa *Taler* [See Trans. Notes Ch 8.3]. During the hajj every pilgrim is ferried across the sea for one Maria Theresa *Taler*; I will give you three *Taler* for my servant and myself; that is enough."

"Then you stay here. My *sambuk* is not a cargo vessel; it belongs to the Sultan. I have to collect the *zehka* (A tax, the sum of which is designated specifically for alms) and am not permitted to take passengers aboard."

"But if they pay eighteen *misri*, then you are permitted! It is precisely because the *sambuk* belongs to the Sultan, that you will have to take me aboard. Take another look at the *Bjuruldu*! There are the words '*heb imdad wermek, sahihlik itshin meshghul, ejertshe akdshesiz* - extend all aid, ensure safety, even without pay'. Do you understand this? An independent person I would have to pay; an official I do not need to pay. I give you three *Taler* of my own free will; if you do not agree, then you will have to take me for nothing."

He realized that he was cornered and commenced to lower his demand. Finally, after a long debate, he held out his hand towards me:

"So it shall be. You are in '*Giölgeda padischahnün'*, and I will give you passage for three *Taler*. Hand them over!"

"I will pay you when I leave the ship at Tor."

"*Effendi*, are all the *Nessarah* (Christians – Nazarenes) as miserly as you?"

"I am not a miser, just careful. Permit me to go aboard, as I would prefer to sleep on deck rather than on land."

I paid my guides, who, as soon as they had received their due and a *bakhshish*, mounted their camels and started their return journey despite the lateness of the hour. Halef and I then climbed aboard. I did not possess a tent. During a ride through the desert one has to suffer not only the heat of the day but also the extreme cold of the night. He who is poor and does not possess a tent sleeps close to his horse or camel for warmth. Since I did not have any animals and the chill of the night was greater by the water than further inland, I preferred to make use of the cabin under the *sambuk's* quarterdeck.

"*Sihdi*, have I done right to show this *wergi-bashi* the whip?" Halef asked me

"I cannot fault you."

"But why do you tell everyone that you are an infidel?"

"Should one be afraid to speak the truth?"

"No; but you are already on the way to becoming one of the faithful. We are on the water that is called *Bar-el-Hamra* (the Red Sea) by the Franks: there is Medina and further to the right is Mecca, the cities of the Prophet. I will visit both of them, and you, what will you do?"

He had asked frankly the question that I had, for the past few days, been asking myself. For a Christian who dared to enter Mecca or Medina, it meant death; so it is written in the books. Was it truly so? If one did venture there, must they openly admit that they are Christian? Is it perhaps possible to choose a quiet day over one when caravans of pilgrims arrive and the boiling point of fanaticism is quickly reached? I had often read that an infidel may not enter a mosque, yet had subsequently entered several - could it be the same with these holy cities? I had found the Orient in many, many ways tamer than one might imagine and could not envision that a short visit, of perhaps an hour's duration, to Mecca would truly be so terribly dangerous. The Turk had thought me a Bedouin; it stood to reason that others would be of the same opinion. Despite this I could not come to a decision.

"I don't know yet." I replied to the little Halef.

"You will come with me into Mecca, *Sihdi*, but beforehand you must accept the true belief in Jiddah."

"No, that I will not do."

A call from the shore interrupted our conversation. The Turk had called his people to evening prayer.

"*Effendi*," said Halef, "the sun is setting; permit me to pray!"

He kneeled and prayed. His voice joined in unison with the praying Turks. The sound of the prayer had not yet dissipated when a different voice was heard. It sounded from among the rocky crags, which hid the northern view of the sea.

"In Allah we are fully satisfied, and wonderful is He, our protector. There is no might and power, apart from God, the High, the Great. Oh our Master, ïa Allah, oh forgive us willingly, oh benevolent, ïa Allah, Allah hu!"

These words were intoned in a deep bass voice, but the name of Allah was uttered by everyone praying in a tone that was a quinte higher. I knew these words and these tones; so it was that the howling dervish were accustomed to praying. The Turks had arisen and now gazed in the direction where the voice had emanated from. There, a small raft appeared, barely six feet long and four feet wide, on which a man knelt and operated a paddle tiller, using the strokes to keep time for his prayer. He wore a red tarboosh about which a white turban had been wound, and the rest of his clothing was equally white. This was a sign that he belonged to the sect of fakirs from Kaderijeh, whose benefactor was Abdelkader el Gilani, most of whom were fishermen or sailors. As he saw the *sambuk*, he was astonished for a moment and then called:

"La ilaha illa lah!"

"*Illa lah*!" answered the others in chorus.

He altered course to meet our vessel, came to with his raft and climbed aboard. We, that is Halef and I, were not alone because the *kürekdshi* (coxswain) had followed us and it was to him that the dervish turned:

"God protect you!"

"Me and you!" came the answer.

"How are you?"

"As well as you."

"To whom does this *sambuk* belong?"

"To his Eminence, the Sultan, who is Allah's cherished."

"And who is her captain?"

"Our *effendi*, the *wergi-bashi* Muhrad Ibrahim."

"And what is your cargo?"

"We do not have cargo; we go from place to place to collect taxes that were ordered by the great Sherif of Mecca."

"Have the faithful given in abundance?"

"Nobody held out, as those who give alms receive two-fold from Allah."

"Where do you sail from here?"

"To Tor."

"You will not reach it tomorrow."

"We will lay to at Ras Nayazat. What is your destination?"

"Jiddah."

"On that raft?"

"Yes. I have vowed to go to Mecca on my knees."

"But think about the banks, the cliffs, the shallows, the ill winds that exist here and the sharks that will swarm about your raft!"

"Allah is the Almighty; He will protect me. Who are these two men?"

"A *gi* . . . a *Nemtshe* with his servant."

"An infidel? Where does he wish to go?"

"To Tor."

"Permit me to eat some dates here; then I will go on."

"Do you not wish to remain with us for the night?"

"I have to go on."

"That is quite dangerous."

"The believer has nothing to fear; his life and his end is written in the book."

He sat and produced a handful of dates from among his clothes.

I had found the entrance to the cabin bolted and had leaned over the railing. As the two speakers were a considerable distance from me and I appeared to be looking at the water with deep contemplation the two might think that I did not understand their exchange. The dervish asked:

"That one is a *Nemtshe*? Is he rich?"

"No."

"How do you know that?"

"He only gave a sixth-part of what we asked for the passage. But he possesses a *Bjuruldu* from the Sultan."

"Then he is surely a noble man. Does he have much baggage with him?"

"None, but many weapons."

"I have never seen a *Nemtshe*, but I have heard that the *Nemtshe* are quite a peaceful people. He carries the weapons purely for display. But now I am finished with my meal and will continue my journey. Inform your master that a poor fakir thanks him for permission to board his ship!"

Some moments later he knelt again upon his raft. He gripped the tiller oar and moved it to the rhythm of '*ïa Allah, Allah hu*!'

This man had made a unique impression upon me. Why had he come aboard this ship and not the shore? Why had he asked if I were rich, while he scanned the deck during the conversation with a keen interest that he could not entirely hide? I had not the slightest reason for any unease and yet the thought came to me that this man was suspicious. I could have sworn that he was no dervish.

When he became indistinguishable to the naked eye I used my telescope. Although twilight passed quickly in these climes, it was still light enough to recognize him through it. He was no longer kneeling in accordance with his declared vow, instead he had seated himself comfortably and steered his raft in another direction - - he aimed for the opposite shore. There certainly was something 'rotten in the state of Denmark'.

Halef stood by my side and studied me. He appeared to be busy trying to guess my thoughts.

"Do you still see him, *Sihdi*?" he asked me.

"Yes."

"He thinks that we can no longer see him and steers for the opposite shore?"

"That is so. How did you guess?"

"Only Allah is all-knowing, but Halef has sharp eyes also."

"And what have your eyes seen?"

"That this fellow is neither a dervish nor a fakir."

"Ah?"

"Yes, *Sihdi.* Unless you have seen or heard of a dervish of the Order of Kaderijeh who speaks or sings the litany of the *hawlajüp*? (The 'howling' – dervish)"

"That is correct. But why should he pretend to be a fakir when he is not?"

"We must try to discover that *effendi*. He says that he will also travel by night. Why does he not do so?"

The coxswain interrupted our conversation. He came up to us and spoke:

"Where do you intend to sleep, *effendi*?"

"I will retire to the *tachta-perde* (cabin)."

"That cannot be."

"Why not?"

"Because the tax money is stored there."

"Then you will provide us with a carpet in which we can wrap ourselves, and we will sleep on deck."

"You shall have it, *Sihdi*. What will you do if enemies board the ship?"

"Which enemies do you mean?"

"Bandits."

"There are bandits here?"

"The Jeheïne live near here. They are known as the biggest *chirsizler* (thieves) far and wide, and neither man nor ship is safe from them."

"I thought your master, the *wergi-bashi* Muhrad Ibrahim, was a hero, a courageous fellow, who is not afraid of any man, not even bandits, nor Jeheïne?"

"That he is; but what can he do, what can any of us do against Abu-Seïf, the 'Father of Sabers', who is more dangerous and terrible than the lion in the mountains or the shark in the sea?"

"Abu-Seïf? I do not know him; I have never heard of him."

"That is because you are a foreigner. During the grazing time the Jeheïne bring their herds to the two islands of Libnah and Jebel Hassan and leave but a few men with them. The others go to rob and pillage. They attack the barks and either take everything that they find on them, or demand a heavy ransom."

"And what does the government do about it?"

"Which government?"

"Do you not stand in '*Giölgeda padischahnün*'?"

"It does not extend to the Jeheïne. They are free Arabs who are protected by the great Sherif of Mecca."

"So help yourselves! Capture the bandits!"

"*Effendi*, you speak like a Frank, who does not understand. Who can capture and kill Abu-Seïf?"

"He is only a man."

"But he is in league with *Shaïtan*. He can make himself invisible; he can fly through the air and over the sea; he cannot be wounded by saber, knife or bullet and his saber is *faldshymish* (bewitched). He penetrates doors and walls and smites with one stoke a hundred and more enemies through body and soul."

"That I have to see!"

"Oh woe, do not wish it *effendi*! The Devil will tell him that you wish to see him, and you can be certain that he will come. I go to get you a carpet - you should then retire and pray to your God, that he will protect you from all dangers that threaten you."

"I thank you for your advice, but I pray in my usual manner before going to sleep."

He brought us the rugs and we wrapped ourselves in these and were soon asleep as we were weary from our ride.

During the night sailors had guarded those sleeping on shore and the money on board. In the morning all assembled on the ship. The anchor was weighed, the sail unfurled and set and the *sambuk* steered southwards.

Chapter 9

We had sailed for almost three-quarters of an hour when we saw a boat being rowed in the same direction as ourselves. As we neared it we saw that there were two men and two fully veiled women aboard.

The boat halted shortly and the men hailed the *sambuk*. The helmsman let the sails fall and reduced the passage of the vessel. One of the two rowers arose and called:

"*Sambuk*, where to?"

"To Tor."

"We also. Would you take us?"

"Will you pay?"

"Willingly."

"Then come aboard."

The ship laid to and the four people climbed aboard whilst their boat was taken in tow. Then the *sambuk* continued on course.

The *wergi-bashi* went to the cabin, probably to prepare a place for the women, where they could be hidden from the view of the men. They had to pass by me. As a European I did not have to avert my eyes from them and therefore I noticed, to my surprise, that there was no evidence of perfume about them; it was customary for women of the Orient to perfume themselves so heavily that one could detect the odor from afar. An odor did indeed assail my senses; it trailed behind them like an invisible veil. An inherently Oriental odor - part camel and part unfermented *rasr* tobacco, which is customarily smoked by many Bedouin and has the identical effect on both the nose and the taste-buds as had the contents of the French sea-grass mattresses, which was used, in the absence of anything better, to stuff the pipes of many a German hero during the last war. [This travel narrative was set in the 1870's] It gave me the impression that two camel drivers had just walked past me; at least it was certain that the famous Persian poet Hafis Shems-ed-Din Mohammed did not have these two beauties in mind when he sang this verse:

"If your sweet perfumed locks
Blow o'er my grave,
Then thousands of flowers sprout
Up from this little hill of mine – "

I scrutinized them attentively until they disappeared behind the door, but I noticed no additional peculiarity. Perhaps they had a long camel ride behind them, so that the aroma of the 'ship of the desert' was difficult to shake from their clothes.

Their two companions spoke for a long time with the coxswain and the *bashi*; then one of them tried to engage me in conversation.

"I hear that you are a Frank, *effendi*?" he asked me.

"Yes."

"Then you are a stranger here?"

"Yes."

"You are a *Nemtshe*?"

"Yes."

"Do the *Nemtshe* also have a Padishah?"

"Yes."

"And Pashas?"

"Yes."

"You are not a Pasha though?"

"No."

"But a famous man?"

"*Pek, billahi* - By God, certainly!"

"Can you write?"

"*Peh ne güzel* - and very well!"

"And shoot too?"

"*Daha ei*- even better!"

"You will probably travel to Tor on this *sambuk*?"

"Yes."

"Do you go even further south?"

"Yes."

"Are the *Ingli* known to you?"

"Yes."

"Do you have friends among them?"

"Yes."

"That is very good. Are you strong?"

"*Korkulu* - terribly, *arslandsha* - like a lion! Shall I prove it to you?"

"No, *effendi*."

"But I will, as your curiosity is much greater than the patience of any man. Go now and don't bother me again!"

I grabbed him, turned him around and gave him a shove so that he shot across the deck then greeted the same with his belly. But he was on his feet again quickly.

"*Wai sana* - Woe to you, you have insulted one of the faithful; you must die!"

He ripped out his *handscar* and sprang towards me. His companion followed suit with a bared weapon. I quickly pulled the hard Nile whip from Halef's belt to salute the attackers with; but they did not get far, at that moment the door of the cabin opened and one of the women appeared. She raised her hand in silence and then pulled it away again. The two Arabs slowed their steps and moved aside without a sound; but their looks told me that I could not expect anything good from them.

The Turks had watched the incident with great indifference. If a man was killed aboard, then it was his kismet. As far as I was concerned, the pointless questions of this person had made me defensive. But were they really pointless? Did they perhaps have a hidden purpose? The Oriental is not a chatterbox, and least of all does he waste his words on a stranger, especially one that he knows to be a *giaur*.

I had said, with anger-fuelled sarcasm, that I was a famous man and a great marksman. Why did he want to know if I was a 'Pasha', a famous man, a writer, and a good marksman? What use was it to him to know whether I intended to travel further south and whether I had friends among the English? Why did he say: 'that is very good' in response to my last affirmation and what purpose did it serve him to discover if I was strong and powerful? Furthermore he had asked these questions in a condescending manner as though I were an inferior, as a detective would address a suspected criminal. Most conspicuous of all was the immediate obedience that he and his companion had shown to the direction of the woman. That was uncommon, even suspicious here, where a woman is placed so much lower than a man, and where, in public life, a woman does not have the right of self-determination.

"*Sihdi*," said Halef, who had not moved from my side, "Did you see?"

"Who or what?"

"That beard?"

"The beard! Which beard?"

"The beard that the woman had ..."

"The woman? Did the woman have a beard?"

"She did not wear the *yashmak* doubled like before, it was simply cast over her face, and thus I saw the beard."

"A moustache?"

"A full beard. That is not a woman but a man. Shall I tell the *bashi*?"

"Yes, but so that no-one hears."

He went on his way. He certainly could not have been mistaken; I knew that I could trust his sharp eyes and involuntarily I brought this new circumstance and the dervish together. I saw Halef speak with the *bashi*; who shook his head and laughed; he did not believe it. Halef turned away from the *bashi* with an angry look on his face and returned to my side.

"*Sihdi*, this *bashi* is so stupid that he considers even me a fool."

"How so?"

"And he considers you even more foolish than I."

"Ah!"

"He says that a woman would not have a beard and that a man would never wear the clothing of a woman. *Sihdi*, what do you think of these women that sport full beards? Perhaps they are Jeheïne?"

"I suspect so."

"Then we must keep our eyes open, *Sihdi*!"

"That is the one thing that we will do and that means that we keep our suspicions to ourselves. Stay a little distance from me, but close enough that we can come to each other's aid!"

He moved a considerable distance from me, and I sat down on my carpet. I then busied myself making entries into my journal but kept my eyes on the cabin and the two Arabs. It occurred to me that I was waiting for something unpleasant to happen at any moment; despite this the day passed without any further suspicious events.

The evening twilight had arrived when we anchored in a small bay that was formed by a horseshoe bend of Jebel Nayazet, which belongs to the granite chain of the Sinai.

The beach was very small as only a few paces from the shore the deeply fissured cliffs reached steeply skywards. The anchorage, therefore, provided complete shelter from the wind, but would it also provide safety from other interruptions today . . . ? I would have liked to explore some of the crevices and fissures in the cliff but unfortunately it was already evening by the time the Turks had landed and, as usual, lit a fire.

The two evening prayers, *El Mogreb* followed by *El Ashia* an hour later, echoed ceremoniously up the steep cliffs. If someone was concealed in those cliffs they must surely hear of our presence even if our fire had not been spotted. Like yesterday, I preferred to spend the night aboard the vessel with Halef and arranged with him that we would rotate our watch. Later a sailor came aboard to keep watch and then the two women ventured up from the cabin to enjoy the evening air. They were again heavily veiled; I noticed this because the stars of the south illuminated the entire deck with a gentle glow, making it easy to see all. The women soon retired to the cabin, the door of which I could keep under close watch despite my position in the bow of the ship.

Halef slept about five paces from me. As midnight approached I woke him quietly and whispered:

"Have you slept?"

"Yes, *Sihdi*. Now you sleep!"

"I can depend on you?"

"As you would yourself!"

"Wake me if you have the slightest hint of suspicion!"

"That I will do, *Sihdi*!"

I wrapped myself tightly in the carpet and closed my eyes. I wanted to sleep but sleep eluded me. I went through the multiplication table in my mind - which did not help. I therefore used a means that would surely bring on sleep. I turned my eyes so that the pupils pointed upwards and concentrated on clearing my mind. Slumber approached and . . . wait, what was that?

I lifted my head from beneath the carpet and looked over to Halef. He too must have been alerted, as he had raised himself in an attitude of attention. I heard nothing more, but when I placed my ear to the deck once more, it being a better medium for conducting sound than air, I again heard the strange noise that had awoken me; apart from that everything was quiet.

"Do you hear something, Halef?" I whispered.

"Yes, *Sihdi*. What is it?"

"I don't know."

"Me neither. Listen!"

A soft, almost imperceptible splashing came from the stern. On the land the campfire had been extinguished.

"Halef, I will go to the stern in a few minutes; guard my weapons and my clothes!"

Of the three Turks that had returned aboard, two were sleeping on deck, the third was crouched down and was obviously also asleep. It was possible that I was being watched from the cabin; that was why I needed to use the utmost care. I left my 'Bear-killer' and my Henry carbine, as well as my turban and the *haïk* (Bedouin cloak) I had worn behind, the latter would have betrayed me because it was white in color. I then lay myself against the deck, proceeded to the edge of the same and crept slowly towards the stern until I reached the place on the port side where a kind of hen-house ladder led to the deck above the cabin and the tiller. I crawled up as softly as a cat since everything depended on it.

I accomplished this undiscovered and crept to the corner of the tiller deck. Ah . . . the strange noise was thus explained. The boat that the two women had traveled in, which had been taken in tow by the *sambuk*, had been positioned directly under the stern. Through the porthole a small but heavy object was being lowered with the aid of a rope, the sound it made rubbing against the sill could only be heard if one placed an ear against the ship's timbers. In the boat below there were three men who took charge of the object and then waited while the rope was raised and a second package was lowered.

Everything became immediately clear to me. The money that had been collected by the *wergi-bashi* was stowed in the boat, and . . . I had no time for further conjecture.

"*Alargha, iz chijanish* - Look up, we are discovered!" cried a deep voice from a point high up on the shore where one could overlook the deck; at the same time a shot cracked, the bullet bored its way into the plank very close to me. A second shot flared from the shore, a third; luckily the bullets flew past me but I could not risk further exposure. I had time enough to notice that the rope below had been cut and the boat was being rowed briskly away; I jumped from my position to the deck below.

In the same instance the door to the cabin opened, and I noticed two things; in the rear of the cabin some boards had been removed and through that gap a number of men had come aboard without being noticed. I did not see the women, but nine men leaped towards me.

"Halef, to me!" I called loudly.

I had no time to draw a weapon. Three men held me around the midsection and ensured that I could not reach my belt. Another three rushed towards Halef and the last three tried their best to hold onto my fists, with which I was attempting to defend myself. From the shore came the sounds of gunfire, curses and appeals for help, intermingled with commands shouted in a deep bass voice; a voice that I recognized - it was the voice of the dervish.

"It is the *Nemtshe*. Do not kill him, take him captive!" ordered one of the men that held me.

I tried to free myself, to no avail. Six against one! A pistol shot cracked not far from me.

"Help *Sihdi*! I am wounded!" cried Halef.

I gave a mighty wrench and dragged my opponents some paces with me.

"Knock him out!" a voice gasped.

I was held fast and despite my desperate resistance, received a blow on the head that knocked me down. There was a rushing sound, like a wildfire, in my ears. In the midst of the thundering roar I heard the report of gunfire and the cry of voices; then it felt as though my hands and feet were bound together and I was dragged away – finally, I felt no more.

When I awoke, I felt a wild, pounding ache in the back of my head, and it took some considerable time before I was able to piece together what had happened. All about me was complete darkness, but a loud lapping sound led me to believe that I was in the keel-space of a ship that was making fast progress. My hands and legs were bound so securely that I could not stir a limb. The bonds did not bite into my flesh however, as the material that bound me was cloth not rope or leather; but they prevented me from defending myself against the ship's rats, which inquisitively examined my person.

A very long time passed without my situation changing. Finally I heard the sound of footsteps but could see nothing. My bonds were removed and a voice commanded me:

"Get up and come with us!"

I raised myself. They led me from my prison through the gloom between the decks, upwards. On the way I examined my clothing and found to my surprise and delight that besides my weapons nothing else had been taken.

As I stepped out upon the deck I noticed that I was on a small, narrow, keel-hugging bark, which had two triangular and one trapezoidal sails. The rigging on this vessel, in view of the storms, squalls, rips and shallows abundant in these waters, required a captain who was confident of his knowledge and possessed as much courage as ferocity. The vessel was manned by three times as many men as were required and had a cannon on the fore-deck, which was so well concealed by boxes, bales and barrels, that it would not be seen from another ship. The crew was a band of weather-beaten men, every belt bristled with weapons capable of shooting, hacking or stabbing. On the quarterdeck sat a man in red trousers, green turban and blue kaftan. His long vest was richly embroidered with gold, and in the *bassora*-scarf that served him as a belt there glinted valuable weapons. I immediately recognized him as the dervish. Next to him stood the Arab that I had thrown to the deck of the *sambuk*. I was led before these two men. The Arab glared at me vindictively, the dervish with contempt.

Chapter 10

"Do you know who I am?" the dervish asked me.

"No, but I have my suspicions."

"Well, who am I?"

"You are Abu Seïf."

"I am he. Kneel down before me, *giaur*!"

"What are you thinking! Is it not written in the Koran that one should pray only to Allah?"

"That does not apply to you, you are an infidel. I order you to kneel and show your respect."

"I do not know if you deserve my respect, and even if I did, I would express my esteem in a different manner."

"*Giaur*, kneel or I will behead you!"

He had risen and grasped his curved saber. I moved a step closer to him.

"My head? Are you really Abu Seïf, or an executioner?"

"I am Abu Seïf and I keep my word. Kneel down, or I shall place your head before your feet!"

"Beware of your own head!"

"*Giaur*!"

"*Korkakdshi*!"

"What!" he hissed. "You call me a *korkakdshi* - a coward!"

"Why did you attack the *sambuk* by night? Why do you wrap your *jasusler* (spies) in women's clothing? Why do you show courage only when you are surrounded by your own men who will protect you? If you alone were confronting me, then you would speak differently!"

"I am Abu Seïf, the Father of Sabers, and ten men of your sort could do nothing against my blade!"

"*Aferihn* - Bravo! That is the way to talk when one is afraid to act."

"Afraid to act? Are the ten men here? If that were the case then I would prove to you that I tell the truth in an instant!"

"Ten are not necessary; one will suffice."

"And perhaps you would be that one?"

"Pah, you would not permit it!"

"Why not?"

"Because you are afraid. You kill with words, not with the saber."

I had expected the anger that my words had ignited to produce a stronger response, but I was disappointed. He hid his fury behind a cold and deadly calm, took the saber from his neighbor's belt and handed it to me.

"Here take it and defend yourself! But I tell you, even if you have the skill of Afram and the strength of Kelad, you will be a corpse upon my third stroke."

I took the saber.

I found myself in a unique position. The 'Father of the Saber' had to be an extraordinary swordsman by Oriental standards, which is to say that Orientals are on the average mediocre swordsmen and equally poor marksmen. The 'skill of Afram and the strength of Kelad' was not saying much of anything then. I had never crossed blades with an Oriental in accordance with the rules of fencing, but even if the saber that was handed to me was thin for the parry, and in weight and flexibility unfamiliar, I still had a great desire to show the 'Father of the Saber' the superiority of the European skill at weapons handling.

The entire ship's crew had closed upon us, and every face reflected the conviction that I was a dead man upon Abu Seïf's third stroke.

He pressed upon me so quickly, savagely and without form, that I had no time to take up position. I parried his undisciplined attack and attempted a circular transition to provide an opening for myself; to my surprise he managed to come in under my blade. He traversed and attempted a feint - which did not succeed. I traversed as well and made a *coup de temps*; my stroke found its target, although it was not my intention to wound him greatly. Now, filled with rage, he lost control, stepped back and again attacked; I moved in half a step, lunged with incisive firmness into the line of his attack and . . . his weapon flew from his hand and fell overboard.

A cry sounded round about. I stepped back and lowered my weapon.

My opponent stood before me and stared.

"Abu Seïf, you are a very skilled fencer!"

These words shook him from his stupor; but I saw, contrary to my expectation, no sign of anger only surprise in his face.

"*Giaur*, you are an infidel and yet you have bested Abu Seïf!"

"You made it easy for me, because your fencing is neither noble nor superior. My second thrust drew your blood, my third took your weapon; yes, I did not even follow through with my third, while your third should have killed me. Here take the saber; I am in your hands."

This positively daring appeal to his nobility worked.

"Yes, you are in my power, you are my prisoner; but your fate is in your own hands."

"In what respect?"

"If you do what I demand of you then you will be free again soon."

"What must I do?"

"Will you fence with me?"

"Yes."

"And teach me in the manner of the *Nemtshe*?"

"Yes."

"As long as you are on my ship, you will not let yourself be seen by any strange eyes?"

"Agreed!"

"And you will leave the deck upon my order when any vessel comes into sight?"

"All right."

"You will not speak to your servant."

"Where is he?"

"Here on this ship."

"Tied up?"

"No, he is wounded."

"Halef Omar is injured?"

"His arm is wounded and he has a broken leg, he cannot move."

"Then I cannot give you my oath. My servant is also my friend and I must tend to him; you will permit me to do this!"

"I will not permit it; but I promise you that he will be well cared for."

"That is not enough. If he has a broken leg, then I must set it for him. There surely is no one here that knows how to do this."

"I know how. I am as good as a *jerrah* (surgeon); I have bound his wound and splinted his leg. He does not suffer and is satisfied with my work."

"I need to hear it from his lips."

"I swear to you before Allah and the Prophets! If you do not give me your word that you will not attempt to speak to him then I will arrange it so that you will not see him at all. But I have more demands of you."

"Go on!"

"You are a Christian, so you will ensure that you do not defile my men?"

"Very well."

"Do you have friends among the *Inglis*?"

"Yes."

"Are they important people?"

"There are Pashas among them."

"Then I will exchange you?"

This was something unexpected! It meant that he did not want to kill me but to profit from my freedom.

"How much do you demand?"

"You have little gold and silver on your person; you cannot buy freedom for yourself."

So he had searched my pockets. But he had not found that which I had sewn into the sleeve of my Turkish jacket. Of course that would not have been enough for my ransom anyway. I therefore replied:

"I have nothing; I am not wealthy."

"I believe you, although you have excellent weapons and you carry instruments that are unknown to me. But you are noble."

"Ah!"

"And famous."

"Ah!"

"You have said as much to this man on board the *sambuk*."

"It was in jest."

"No, you spoke in earnest. Someone that is strong and knows how to handle a saber as you have done cannot be other than a great *zabit* (officer), for whom his Padishah would willingly pay a great ransom."

"My king would not pay for my freedom with money; he will demand it for nothing."

"I do not know the king of the *Nemtshe*; how then will he speak with me and force me to free you?"

"He will do it through his *eltshi* (ambassador)."

"I do not know him either. There is no *eltshi* of the *Nemtshe* here at Ma-el-Hamrech."

"The ambassador is in Stambul with the Sultan. I have a *Bu-Djeruldu*, which you call *Bjuruldu*, and am therefore one who stands in the 'Shadow of the Sultan'."

He laughed.

"The Padishah means nothing here; here only the Sherif of Mecca rules, and I am mightier than both. I will neither deal with your king or with his ambassador on your behalf."

"With whom then?" I asked.

"With the *Inglis*." He replied.

"Why with them?"

"To exchange you."

"For whom?"

"For my brother who is in their hands. He attacked one of their ships with his bark and was taken prisoner. They have taken him to Eden (as the Arabs call Aden by the Strait of Bab-el Mandeb) and intend to execute him; but now they will have to free him."

"Perhaps you are mistaken. I am no *Inglis*. They will leave me in your hands and execute your brother."

"Then you too will die. You can write - you will compose a letter to them in your own words. If the letter is well received, then they will exchange you; if not then you have determined your own fate. Think about the content of your letter; you have many days yet."

"How many?"

"We have a treacherous sea before us, but I intend to travel by night whenever possible. If the wind remains favorable, we will reach Jiddah in four days. From there to the region of Sanah, where I will hide my ship, it is almost as far again. So you have a week to think about the content of the letter, as I will send a messenger from Sanah."

"I will write the letter."

"And you promise that you will not attempt to escape?"

"That I cannot promise you."

He studied my face for some time.

"*Allah akbar* - God is great, and I did not believe that there were honest people among the Christians. So - you wish to escape?"

"I will take advantage of every opportunity."

"Then I will not fence with you; you could defeat me and jump overboard to swim to freedom. You can swim?"

"Yes."

"Remember that there are many fish in the sea that would eat you!"

"I know it."

"I will have you heavily guarded. This man next to me will remain always at your side. You have insulted him; and he will not let you out of his sight until you are either free or dead."

"What would happen to my servant in either case?"

"Nothing. He has committed a great sin in becoming a servant to an infidel; but he is neither a Turk nor a *giaur*, he will be granted his freedom when you are given yours or when you are dead. You can remain on deck for now; but when your guard gives the order you will go below where you will be locked in your cabin."

He turned away and I was dismissed.

I walked to the bow and then ambled along the railing; when I got tired, I lay down on the deck. Always the Arab remained close by so that the distance between us was never greater than five or six paces.

This was extreme as well as unpleasant. Nobody else appeared to bother about me; no one spoke a word to me. I was handed water, couscous and some dates in silence. As soon as another vessel was sighted I had to go down to my cabin and a guard remained at my door until I was permitted to go topside again, in the evening my door was bolted and barred with all sorts of clutter.

In this manner three days passed. I felt greater anxiety for my wounded Halef than for myself; but all my attempts to get to him were in vain. Obviously he was below deck like myself, but any attempt to pass a sign to my servant while my guard was not looking could have done us both harm.

As we had a quick and favorable journey, we soon arrived in the vicinity of Jebel Eyub and Jebel Kelaya, where the coast up to Jiddah consistently declined and became flatter. It was twilight. In the northern sky there were small, gauzy clouds as seldom seen in this region. Abu Seïf watched them with some trepidation. Night fell and I had to go below. It was much sultrier than before and the humidity rose from quarter-hour to quarter-hour. I still could not sleep when midnight approached. I heard a distant muffled roar, thundering and rumbling, which swiftly approached until the storm gripped our ship. I felt the bow plunge deep into the water, rise again and shoot forward with doubled speed. The vessel moaned and groaned in all its joints. The foot of the mast creaked in its wedges and on deck the feet of the crew drummed amidst fearful cries, yammering and prayers.

The distinct, booming commands of the captain could be heard amidst all this. It was essential that he not lose his resolve. In accordance with my calculations we were nearing the heights of Rabbegh, known as Rabr by the Arabs, south of which are a number of cliffs and coral reefs that make the passage of ships, even by day, extremely dangerous. There too is the island of Ghauat, and between it and the Ras Hatiba two coral reefs reach skyward. The passage between them is hazardous even by day and in calm weather, that is why the crews prepare themselves with prayer before they reach this spot. It is called 'the place of two ropes'; a name that indicates the means by which, in earlier times, sailors sought to ensure safe passage.

We were driven with the frenzied swiftness of the tempest towards this channel. A landing beforehand was impossible.

I had risen from my sleeping place. If the ship ran aground on a reef I would still be doomed as my cabin door was locked.

I thought I heard, amidst the roaring of the elements, a sound outside my door. I moved closer and listened. I was not deceived. The clutter that barricaded the door was being removed and the door opened.

"*Sihdi*!"

"Who is there?"

"*Hamdulillah* - God be praised that he let me find the right place! Don't you know the voice of your faithful Halef?"

"Halef? Impossible! It cannot be he because he cannot walk."

"Why not?"

"Because he is wounded and has a broken leg."

"Yes, I am wounded, *Sihdi*, by a ball in the arm - but only a little. My leg is not broken."

"Then Abu Seïf lied to me."

"No, I deceived him. I had to pretend so that I could help my good *Sihdi*. I lay with splints on my leg for three days in my cabin below, and during the night I took them off and crawled about investigating."

"Brave Halef, I will not forget this!"

"I have also found out some things."

"What?"

"Abu Seïf will lay to some distance before Jiddah, to make a pilgrimage to Mecca. He will pray there for his brother's freedom. A number of his men will go with him."

"Perhaps it will then be possible to escape."

"I will see. This will happen tomorrow. Your weapons are in his cabin."

"Will you come again tomorrow, if we do not perish tonight?"

"I will come, *Sihdi.*"

"But the danger, Halef!"

"Today it is so dark that no one could see me, and they do not have the time to watch out for us, *Sihdi*. But tomorrow Allah will help us."

"Does your wound give you pain?"

"No."

"What happened to the *sambuk*? I was unconscious and do not know."

"These pirates took all the money, which is now in the captain's *oda* (cabin), and the crew is in captivity. Only we two have been taken to free Abu Seïf's brother."

"You know about this?"

"I have listened to their discussions."

"And the bark from that night?"

"She lay at anchor not far behind the cliffs and waited for us. *Chajir ola* - Good night, *Sihdi*!"

"Good night!"

He left, closed the bolt and replaced the barricade as he had found it.

I had forgotten the storm during his visit, it had died down as quickly and as unexpectedly as it had come; although the sea was still high, as I noticed from the ship's movement, I suspected that the sky had cleared and the danger of shipwreck diminished in accordance. I went to sleep peacefully.

When I awoke, the ship was still; my door was opened and outside stood my guard.

"Do you want to go up?" he asked me.

"Yes."

"You can only stay on deck until *deghri* (midday prayer)."

I climbed on deck and found that all traces of the storm had vanished. The ship lay at anchor in a narrow bay that cut deep into the shoreline. The sails had been taken down and the masts had been stepped so that the vessel could not be easily spotted from the sea or the land, which appeared barren and deserted.

I remained on deck until midday without noticing anything out of the ordinary. At this time Abu Seïf had me brought before him. He was not on deck but in his cabin, where I saw my weapons hanging from the wall. Even my bullet-pouch was there, and many large *ketshikise* (goatskin bag. The hairy side turned to the outside) were on the deck, these obviously held powder. A *sandyk* (a wardrobe-like box) stood open, Abu Seïf closed it immediately upon my entry; but there was time enough for me to see that it contained many *kettshuwal* (canvas sacks), in which the stolen money from the *sambuk* could possibly be found.

"*Nemtshe*, I will have a few words with you."

"Speak."

"Will you still not give me your word that you will not attempt to escape?"

"I am no liar and I tell you truly that I will escape as soon as the opportunity presents itself."

"You will not get the opportunity; but you force me to be more stringent with you than I would wish. I will not be on board for two days; you may not leave your cabin for that time and will remain there with bound hands."

"That is harsh."

"Yes; but it is your own fault."

"I will have to comply."

"Then you can go. But know this, I will give the order that you shall be executed the moment you attempt to remove your bonds. If you were a believer then I would ask you to be my friend. You are a *giaur*, yet I neither hate nor despise you. I would have believed your promise; but since you will not give it, you will have to bear the consequences. Now go below!"

I was led below and locked into my cabin. It was an agony to lie there bound in the heat below deck. But I accepted the situation, although my guard extracted his vengeance by omitting to provide food or water. I put all my faith in Halef with such an expectation that I have seldom experienced. My situation was not improved by the fact that I was lying in the dark. I had heard the three prayers, *El Asr*, *El Mogreb* and *El Ashia*; then a long, long time passed, it must have been close to midnight when I finally heard a soft sound outside my door.

I listened attentively, but no further sound could be heard. I did not dare speak. Perhaps it was only a rat.

Chapter 11

It was quiet for some time; then I heard footsteps approaching, accompanied by a soft rustling that was like the sound of a carpet or mat being spread on the deck. What was it? It was certain that my guard had decided to spend the night in front of my door. My hope was now at an end, because if Halef came now . . . but listen! What was that? It required all my concentration to determine that the wooden bolt on my door was being opened ever so slowly. Some seconds later I heard a hard clap - it sounded like someone trying to rise but failing to manage it . . . a short, suffocating moan, then a soft voice whispered:

"*Sihdi*, come; I have him!"

It was Halef.

"Who?" I asked.

"Your guard."

"I cannot help you, my hands are tied."

"Are you tied to the wall?"

"No. I can come to you."

"Then come, the door is open."

As I exited, I felt the Arab lying on the deck, twitching as though he were having a convulsion. Halef was kneeling on the Arab with his hands around his neck, choking off the Arab's breath.

"Search his belt for a knife, *Sihdi*!"

"There is one; wait!"

I withdrew the knife with my hands, put the hilt between my teeth and sawed at the bonds that were tied around my wrists.

"How goes it, *Sihdi*?"

"Yes, my hands are free. Thank God that he is not dead!"

"*Sihdi*, he would deserve it."

"Nevertheless he shall live! We will tie him up and gag him, then put him into my cabin."

"Then he will groan through his nose and give us away."

"I will unravel his turban and wrap it around his face. Let go a little so that he can breathe! - Now - here is the gag . . . here, his belt, to bind his hands and feet . . . let go of his neck and hold his legs . . . like so – finished! Now into the cabin with him!"

I took a deep breath as soon as the door was bolted shut behind the prisoner and I was on the stairs with Halef.

"What now, *Sihdi*?" he asked me.

"Tell me how it all worked out now?"

"Oh, quite simple. I crawled out of the hold and listened."

"If they had discovered you ...!"

"They did not guard me because they thought that I could not move. Then I heard that the "Father of the Saber" went with twelve men to Jiddah. He took much money with him to give to the Sherif of Mecca. Then I heard that the Arab who was guarding you was going to sleep by your door. He hates you, would have killed you long before if he did not fear Abu Seïf. If I wanted to get to you then I had to get to him first and so I crawled across the deck without being noticed. You have taught me this in the desert. And just as I arrived, he came to."

"Ah, then it was you! I heard this."

"As he lay down, I grabbed him around the neck. The rest you know, *Sihdi*."

"I thank you, Halef! How does it look up there?"

"Very good. As I crept across the deck, it was the crews' intention to light their *afijon* (opium). Their master is gone so they dare to do this."

"So take the weapons that belonged to my guard; they are better than those that you had. Now come. I will lead."

As we crept to the deck above, I could not suppress a smile thinking about the fact that Abu Seïf was bringing a gift to the Sherif of Mecca that was a part of the booty that he had stolen from him in the first place. As I put my head through the opening I detected the fragrance that one encounters around every opium den. The men lay motionless about the deck; I could not determine whether they slept or waited for the rush of the narcotic poison to take effect. Luckily the path to the cabin was clear. We headed for it in a deck-hugging crawl and successfully reached the door. Thanks to Oriental carelessness it had no lock; the hinges would not squeak as they were made of strips of leather nailed both at the top and the bottom of the door and to the frame.

I opened the door only as far as was necessary to crawl through and as soon as we were both inside I closed it. Now I felt as secure and relaxed as I would if I were at home in my own room. Here hung my weapons and five paces from there was the side of the ship, from which a leap would be sufficient to reach the shore. The watch, the compass and the money I already had with me.

"What shall I bring along?" asked Halef.

"Take one of those blankets that are lying in the corner. We will need them - I will also take one."

"Nothing else?"

"No."

"But I have heard that there is a lot of money here."

"It is there in the *sandyk*; we will leave it because it is not ours."

"What are you saying, *Sihdi*? You will take no money with you? You will leave to bandits that which we have so much need of?"

"Do you wish to become a thief? No!"

"I? Hajji Halef Omar Ben Hajji Abul Abbas Ibn Hajji Dawud al Gossarah - a thief? *Sihdi*, if someone else should say this to me . . . ! Did you not order me to take the weapons from your guard below? Did you not order me to take the blanket?"

"That is not theft. We have lost our blankets and your weapons at the hands of these bandits and have a right to restitution. But we still have our money."

"No, *Sihdi*; they have taken mine."

"Did you have much?"

"Did you not pay me three Maria Theresa *Taler* every two weeks? I had kept every one; now they are gone and I will take what belongs to me."

He stepped towards the trunk. Should I stop him? In a way he was right. We found ourselves in circumstances where we had to take the law into our own hands. Where could we charge Abu Seïf and demand the return of the stolen money? I had to be very frugal with my money and whilst I could have replaced my servant's loss from what I had, any further debate would have detained us and placed us in danger; I therefore satisfied myself with the statement: "The *sandyk* will be locked. "

He stepped closer to it, examined it and said, "Yes. There is a lock and the key is missing, but I will open it all the same."

"No, you will not! If you break the lock, the noise will betray us!"

"*Sihdi*, you are right. I will not be able to get my money. Come, we will go!"

From the tone in which he spoke these words, I almost felt sorry that he had to forego restitution. Another Arab would not have done so, of that I was certain, and this caused me to promise:

"Halef, I will replace the Theresa *Taler* that you have lost!"

"Truly, *Sihdi*?"

"Yes."

"Then let us go!"

We left the cabin and made it undetected to the side of the ship. One could see by the light of the stars that the distance to the shore was not insignificant.

"Can you make it, Halef?" I asked anxiously.

I knew that he could jump well; but here there was no room to take a run-up.

"Watch me, *Sihdi*!"

He rose, set his foot on the railing and stood, in the next moment, on the shore. I immediately followed him.

"*Hamdulillah* – God be thanked! Now we are free. But what next?"

"We go to Jiddah."

"Do you know the way?"

"No."

"Or perhaps you have a *harjta* (map) that can show us the way?"

"No to that also; but we just need to head south. Abu Seïf had to walk; that is a sure sign that the city is not far from here. Let us first examine our weapons."

We went behind some euphorbia scrub, which hid us sufficiently well as it was not the small Arabian variety but rather the taller East Indian kind. My guns were loaded; certainly the pirates had not known how to handle my revolver or my Henry carbine and had undoubtedly marveled at my heavy 'Bear-killer' [See Trans. Notes Ch. 1.1]. The Arab is accustomed to a light firearm, and there are whole tribes who are still armed with flintlocks of strange and ancient construction.

After we had assured ourselves that our flight had gone unnoticed, we started out on our uncertain route. As far as possible we had to follow the coastline, which meant we had to walk around the many various sized bays, thus our progress was slow. In addition, the ground was thickly covered with colocynths [bitter apple, wild gourd, Vine of Sodom – a large melon-like fruit, not considered edible] and aloes, despite the close proximity of the sea, this made our passage extremely difficult. Finally dawn approached and our trek became easier and faster. We could see some distance ahead and decide which path to choose to avoid the curvature of the coast. It was about eight o'clock in the morning when we saw the minareh (This word is written minaret in the French manner and many Germans also speak it this way, which is incorrect) of a city, which was encircled by a high wall that was reasonably well maintained.

"Shall we ask if this is Jiddah, *Sihdi*?" asked Halef.

We had already encountered many Arabs during the past hour without speaking to them.

"No; it is certainly Jiddah."

"And what do we do here?"

"Firstly, I will look around the place."

"And I too. Do you know that Eve, the mother of all mankind, is buried there?"

"Yes."

"When Adam buried her, he grieved for forty days and forty nights; then he went to Selan-Dib [See Trans. Notes Ch 11.2], where he died and lies buried. That is an island of which only the faithful have knowledge."

"You are mistaken, Halef. This island was named Sinhala Dvipa by its inhabitants, wherefrom your language made Selan-Dib. Sinhala Dvipa is called Lion Island; it belongs to Christians, the *Inglis*, and I have already been there twice."

He looked at me in amazement.

"But our *talebs* (learned ones) say that every infidel who sets foot on the island will die!"

"Am I dead?"

"No. But you are loved by Allah, although you do not believe."

"I will give you another example. Is it not said that every infidel who enters the holy cities of Mecca and Medina must die?"

"Yes."

"But there are Christians who have been there."

"Is that true?"

"Yes. They behaved as Moslems."

"Then they must have comprehended our language and our customs."

"They understood them."

He looked at me anxiously and searchingly.

"*Sihdi*, you know our customs and language. Do you intend to go to Mecca?"

"Would you take me along?"

"No, *Sihdi*; if I did I would fry in the deepest *Jehenna*."

"Would you betray me if you saw me there?"

"*Effendi*, don't make me sad! I would have to betray you and yet I could not possibly. I could not live any more!"

I saw in him that the latter was his firm belief; it would be terrible to keep him in agony any longer.

"Halef, you care for me?"

"Even more than myself, *Sihdi* - believe this of me!"

"I believe it. How long will you still travel with me?"

"As long as you wish. I will go with you to the ends of the earth, even if you are a Christian. But I know that you will become a 'True Believer', because I will convert you, willing or not."

"Only a Hajji can say this."

"Oh, *Sihdi*, I will really become one now. There is Jiddah, where I will visit the grave of Eve. Then I will go to Mecca and will visit Arafah; in Minah I will let myself be shaved and participate in all the holy customs. Will you wait for me in Jiddah?"

"How long will you be in Mecca?"

"Seven days."

"You will find me again in Jiddah. But is your hajj valid, as it does not coincide with the month of pilgrimage. [See Trans. Notes Ch 11.3]?"

"It is valid. See, here is the gate. What is it called?"

"It is probably the north gate, the *Bab el Medina*. Will you grant me a request?"

"Yes, because I know that you will not order me to do anything that I may not do."

"You shall not tell anyone that I am a Christian."

"I will obey."

"You shall behave as though I were a Moslem."

"Yes. But will you grant me a request?"

"Which would be?"

"I have to purchase the *aziz-kumahsh* (Literally: 'Holy Stuff') and offer many gifts and alms ..."

"Be reassured; you shall receive your Theresa *Taler* today."

"I can perhaps not use them, as they are minted in the land of the infidels."

"Then I will give you the same sum in *piasters*."

"You have *piasters*?"

"Not now – but I will get some from a *sarraf* (money changer)."

"I thank you, *Sihdi*! Will I have enough to reach Medina?"

"I believe so, if you are frugal. The trip there will cost you nothing."

"How so?"

"I will ride with you."

"To Medina, *Sihdi*?" he asked in a concerned tone.

"Yes. Is this prohibited?"

"The way there is open; but you may not enter Medina."

"And if I await you in Jambo?"

"That is marvelous, *Sihdi*; that will work!"

"Then we are in agreement!"

"And where do you go from there?"

"Firstly to Medaïhn Saliha."

"Master, do you seek death! Don't you know that it is the city of ghosts, who tolerate no mortals?"

"They will have to tolerate me. It is a very mysterious place; I have heard wonderful things about it and that is why I must see it."

"You will not see it because the ghosts will bar your way; but I will not leave you even if I have to die with you. By then I will be a true hajji, to whom heaven is always open. And where do you want to go afterwards?"

"Either to Sinai, Jerusalem or to Bassra and Baghdad."

"And will you take me along?"

"Yes."

We had reached the gate. Outside the wall there were scattered many huts built from straw or palm leaves where the poor *hadhesi* (workers) lived, or the even poorer wood and vegetable sellers. A ragged fellow called to me:

"*Taïbihn, effendi, seiak, keif chelak* – Are you well, *effendi*, how goes it with you, and how do you feel?"

I stopped. In the Orient one must always take the time to answer a greeting.

"I thank you! I am well; it goes well with me, and I feel excellent; but how are you, son of a valiant father, and how goes your business, you the inheritor of the holiest tribe of the Moslems?"

I used these words because I saw that he wore the *m'eshaleeh*. Although in recent times Christians have been permitted to visit Jiddah, it is considered one of the holy cities, the inhabitants having the right to wear this sign. Four days after the birth of a child, the infant's cheeks are cut thrice and their temples twice, the scars remain for their whole life. That is the *m'eshaleeh*.

"Your words are like *zahari* (flowers); their perfume is like that of the *Benaht el Jennet* (Daughters of Paradise, the *houris*)", replied this fellow. "It goes well with me also, and I am happy with my business. It will also be of use to you."

"What kind of business do you have?"

"I have three animals available. My sons are *hamahri* (donkey drivers), and I help them."

"You have them at your home?"

"Yes, *Sihdi*. Shall I fetch two for you?"

"What shall I pay you?"

"Where do you intend to ride?"

"I am a stranger here and will search for a place to stay."

He surveyed me with a peculiar gaze. A stranger, and one on foot, was no doubt remarkable.

"*Sihdi*," he asked, "do you wish to go where I have led your brothers?"

"Which brothers?"

"Yesterday at the time of *mogreb*, thirteen men arrived on foot, just like you; I led them to the great *khan*."

That was certainly Abu Seïf with his men.

"They were no brothers of mine. I do not want a room in a *khan* or a *funduk* (guest house), I would prefer a private residence."

"*Ama di bacht* – What luck! I know of such a house where you can find rooms that are almost too good for a prince."

"What would you charge if we were to ride there on your donkeys?"

"Two *piaster*."

That was about twenty German pennies each.

"Fetch the animals."

He departed with ponderous steps and retrieved, from behind a palisade, two donkeys that were so small they could almost have walked between my legs.

"Will they carry us?"

"*Sihdi*, one of them could carry all three of us!"

That was an exaggeration, yet my animal did nothing to indicate that I was too heavy for it; rather it immediately went on its merry way once I had mounted, this was of course halted immediately inside the city wall.

"*Tut*," demanded a rattling voice from one side; "*tut, wermya-iz aktshe* – Halt, pay money!"

Within a crumbling brick wall to my right there was a square opening, in which could be seen a head; and upon the face of this head there hung a huge pair of frightful spectacles; in these spectacles there rested just one lens. Beneath this lens I saw a gigantic nose and below this, canted to one side, was a vast chasm, from the depths of which these words had apparently emanated.

"Who is that?" I asked our guide.

"The *radshal el bab* (gatekeeper). He collects the tax for the Sultan."

I encouraged my donkey to move in front of the opening and, for the sake of some fun, took out my passport.

"What do you want?" I asked.

"Money!" He replied.

"Here!"

I waved the splendid *möhür* (seal) before the eye that was not protected by the lens.

"*Lutf, jenabin* – Forgive me, your grace!"

The orifice below his nose snapped shut, the face disappeared and immediately I saw a gaunt figure leap sideways over some bricks. It was clad in an old, worn *Janissaire* [soldier in an elite Turkish guard organized in the 14th century and abolished in 1826.] uniform, wide blue trousers, red socks, a green jacket and upon the head sat a white cap with a tassel hanging from it. It was the brave *radshal el bab*.

"Why is he running away?" I asked the guide.

"You have a *Bu-djeruldi* and need not pay. He has therefore insulted you and fears your vengeance."

We rode further and after some five minutes were in front of the gate of a house that had four great barred windows facing the street, a rarity in Mohammedan lands.

"Here it is!"

"Who owns this house?"

"The *jewahirdshi* (jeweler)] Tamaru. He has given me a commission."

"Is he at home?"

"Yes."

"Then you may return. Accept this *bakhshish*!"

With profuse words of thanks, the man mounted one of his donkeys and rode away. I entered the house with Halef and was led by a Negro into the garden where his master was. I explained my requirements to him and he led me immediately back into the house and showed me a selection of chambers that were empty. I rented two for a week at a cost of two *talaris*, which was a decent price. For this price I was also spared an interrogation. I provided only the name that Halef had given me.

During the afternoon I wandered around the city sightseeing.

Jiddah is a pleasant city and it appears to me that it has justly earned its name – Jiddah means 'the rich one'. It is surrounded on three sides by a high, wide, turreted wall, and is further protected by a deep moat. To the seaward side it is defended by a fort and many batteries. The wall has three gates: the

Bab el Medina, the *Bab el Yemen* and the *Bab el Mecca*, the latter being the most magnificent, with two towers whose parapets are adorned with elaborate fretwork.

The city is divided into two halves; the *nysf* (halves) of Syria and Yemen; there are broad and reasonably clean streets and many beautiful open places. Most notable are the many houses that have windows in the outside walls. They are generally several stories high and are well constructed, with decorative arched doors along with balconies and sills.

The bazaar runs the full length of the city parallel to the sea and many side streets lead off it. Here can be found Arab and Bedouin, Fellatah, merchants from Basra, Baghdad, Maskat and Makalla, Egyptians, Nubians, Abyssinians, Turks, Syrians, Greeks, Tunisians, Tripolitans, Jews, Indians, Malayans: - All in their national costume; one might even come across the occasional Christian.

Beyond the walls, as is usual in most places in Arabia, the desert begins and there are the huts of those people who cannot find room in the city. Not far from the barracks near the Bab el Medina, is the cemetery, where the grave of the 'Mother of Mankind' is on display. This is sixty meters or almost ninety Prussian ells [cubits] long and in the center a small mosque is mounted.

That Jiddah is swarming with beggars is no great wonder. The largest contribution to their ranks comes from India. While the pilgrims from other lands search for work to earn their passage back to their homeland, the Indians are too indolent. If one were to give to each of these then one would soon become a beggar himself.

I went from the churchyard to the harbor and walked slowly along the water's edge. I thought about the possibility of seeing Mecca and did not notice that it had become more and more deserted around me. Suddenly a voice sounded from the water:

"*Jetst geh' I zum Soala*
Und kaf ma an Strick,
Bind 's Diandl am Buckl
Trog's überall mit."

[Now I go to Soala
And buy myself a rope,
Bind it to my belt
Carry it around everywhere]

A '*G'sangl*' [German slang: song] from my homeland! Here in Jiddah! I looked about and saw a boat, in which sat two men. One was a native. His skin color and his clothing indicated that he was a *Hadharemieh* – certainly the boat belonged to him. The other stood upright and presented a striking figure. He wore a blue turban, red Turkish harem-pants and over that a European frock in an old fashioned cut; a yellow silken kerchief was tied about his neck, on either side of this pointed two *jebel-pambuk-bezi,* which are usually attached to a collar called '*Vatermörder*' [Literally 'Father murder', name given to style of winged collar] in my homeland. Around his ample waist, the man had slung a sarras; the scabbard of this was so stout that one might have suspected that it held three blades.

This was the bard. He had noticed that I had halted in surprise, and perhaps thought that he had a song-loving Bedouin before him; he cupped his left hand beside his mouth, turned further to the right and sang:

"*Und der Türk und der Ruß,*
Die zwoa gehn mi nix o',
Wann i no mit der Gret'l
Koan Kriegshandl ho'!"

[And the Turk and the Russian,
Those two don't concern me,
When Gretel and I still have
War parley to do!]

This was highly entertaining, much more so than the earlier incident, when Jüterbogker Hamsad al Jerbaja had surprised me with his song at the house by the Nile! I too placed my hand beside my mouth.

"*Türkü tshaghyr-durmak* – Sing some more" I called to him.

I did not know if he understood me, but he continued immediately:

"*Zwischen Deiner und meiner*
Is a weite Gass'n;
Bua, wennst mi nöt magst,
Kannst es bleiben lass'n!"

[Between you and me
Is a broad street;
Boy, if you don't like me,
Then you can leave it alone!]

Now I had to test this yodeler, so I responded with:

"*Zwischen Deiner und meiner*
Is a enge Gass'n;
Bua, wennst mi gern magst,

Kannst herrudern lass'n!"

[Between you and me
Is a narrow street;
Boy, if you like me,
Then let yourself be rowed across!]

He let out a cry of joy, pulled the turban from his head, the sarras from the scabbard, and whirled both turban and saber high in the air; then, replacing both objects in their original positions, took hold of the tiller and steered to the shore.

I walked towards him. He leaped to the shore, but stood as if stunned as he examined me more closely.

"A Turk, who can speak German?" he asked doubtfully.

"No, a German, who tries a little Turkish."

"Then truly! I did doubt my ears. But you really look like an Arab. May I ask who you are?"

"A writer. And you?"

"A . . . a . . . Hmm; violinist, comedian, ship's cook, private secretary, bookkeeper, husband, merchant, widower, pensioner and presently, tourist on his way home."

He said this with such overpowering grandiosity that I had to laugh.

"Then you have experienced much! And you are on your way home?"

"Yes, to Triest, if I don't change my mind on the way. And you?"

"I will see the homeland again, possibly some months from now. What are you doing here in Jiddah?"

"Nothing. And you?"

"Nothing. Shall we assist each other?"

"Naturally, if it is all right with you!"

"Of course! Do you have a place to stay?"

"Yes, for four days already."

"And I for almost as many hours."

"Then you are still not settled. May I invite you to my place?"

"Certainly! At what time?"

"Right now. Come! It is not far."

He put his hand in his pocket and paid the boatman; then we walked back to the harbor. Along the way we exchanged only general comments until we reached a single story house, which we entered. It was divided at the entrance into two halves. He opened the door to the right half and we entered into a small chamber, the furniture within consisted of a low wooden frame, over which a long mat was laid.

"This is my room. Welcome! Sit down!"

We again shook hands and I seated myself on the *serir*, while he stepped into the next room and opened a large chest that stood within.

"With a guest such as you I would not withhold my precious wares " he called to me. "Observe what I bring you!"

There were a great many precious wares that he placed before me:

"Here is a pot of apple slices, cooked yesterday evening in the coffee machine; it is the best that one can enjoy in this heat. Here are two pancakes, baked in the tobacco tin over there – one each. There is still the rest of the English wheat bread, a little stale, but edible. You have good teeth, as I see. To this add half of a Bombay sausage – perhaps a little smelly – but it does no harm. In this bottle is genuine, aged cognac; even if it's not wine, it's better than water; I no longer have a glass, but that does not matter. Later, in this box . . . do you take snuff?"

"Regrettably no."

"Pity! It is excellent. But you smoke?"

"Very much."

"Here! There are still eleven pieces; we divide them – ten for you and one for me."

"Or reversed!"

"No, that won't work."

"We will see. And in that tin, what have you there?"

"You guess!"

"Show me!"

He handed me the tin and I sniffed it.

"Cheese!"

"You guessed it! Unfortunately the butter is missing. Now dig in! You certainly have a knife; here is a fork."

We ate with gusto.

"I am a Saxon." I said and told him my name. "Were you born in Triest?"

"Yes. My name is Martin Albani. My father was a shoemaker by trade. I should have become something greater, such as a merchant, but was better with my violin than with figures and so on. I became a pauper – you know how it is. I loved my father, but became acquainted with a group of Pressnitzer harp players and joined them. We went to Venice, Milan and further west and south within Italy, and finally even to Constantinople. You are acquainted with these players?"

"Certainly. They often travel overseas."

"First I played the violin, then I advanced to comedian; unfortunately we had bad luck, and I was happy that I found a position with a traveling merchant from Bremen. With him I went to London; from there I sailed with an Englishman to India. In Bombay I became ill and was sent to the hospital. The hospital's manager was an efficient man, but no champion when it came to writing and arithmetic; he engaged me when I was fit again. Later I joined a merchant as bookkeeper; he died from the fever, and I married his widow. We lived childless and happy until her death. Now I am homesick and on my way there ...”

“To your father?”

“He too no longer lives, but did – thank God! – not suffer. Since my success we had written each other often. Now I have sold my business and travel slowly towards home.”

I liked this man. He acted as he was. He may not have been called rich; but he behaved like a man that has just as much as he needs and is content with it.

“Why do you not travel directly to Triest?”

“I have to bring order to some figures in Maskat and Aden.”

“Then you have become accustomed to figures in the end?”

“Certainly,” he laughed. “And now – my affairs are not pressing; I am my own master – what does it matter if I look around the Red Sea? You are doing this also!”

“Of course. How long will you remain here?”

“Until a suitable vessel berths here. You did not expect to find a Bavarian or a Tyrolian when you heard me singing?”

“True; but I do not feel disappointed – we are Germans nevertheless and are happy to have met each other.”

“How long will you stay here?”

“Hmm! My servant is on a pilgrimage to Mecca; I will probably wait for him here for about a week.”

“That makes me happy; then we can be together for a bit longer.”

“I agree; but for two days we have to get along without each other.”

“How so?”

“I have a desire to visit Mecca.”

“You? I think that it is prohibited for a Christian!”

“That is so. But who will detect me?”

“That’s true. You speak Arabic?”

“Yes, as much as I need for my kitchen.” [Enough to get by, to fulfill daily needs.]

“And you know how a pilgrim must conduct himself?”

“That too; and it is certain that my conduct will not exactly be that of a pilgrim. Were I to follow the custom and do the prescribed ceremonies and even pray to Allah and his prophets – it would certainly be a sin against our holy belief.”

“You would know differently within yourself!”

“That does not minimize the guilt.”

“Might one not make a sacrifice for knowledge?”

"Yes, but not one such as this. Besides, I am not a man of science. Should I ever get to Mecca then it is worth only the story that I can tell my acquaintances. I would like to claim that one can visit the city of the prophets by playing at being a pilgrim and still not betray one's Christian beliefs."

"Probably not."

"Do you believe that only pilgrims visit Mecca?"

"One would think that merchants would also go there. They would also visit the holy places and pray there."

"It would surely be impossible to govern them. I reckon that it would take sixteen hours to reach Mecca on foot; one can ride the distance in eight hours. If I had a *bsharihn hedjihn*, then I would need just four hours. I arrive, dismount by some *khan*, wander around the city at a dignified, solemn pace, visit the holy places; I would need only a few hours. Everyone would take me for a Moslem and I return satisfied."

"That does not sound dangerous, but daring it is, nonetheless. I have read that a Christian may only come within nine miles of the city."

"Then we should not be in Jiddah either, if English miles are meant. On the way from here to Mecca are eleven coffeehouses; I will confidently dare to enter the ninth and even dare to say that I am a Christian. Time has changed much, now it is enough to deny Christians entry into the city. I dare to try."

I had persuaded myself so effectively that it became my firm decision to go to Mecca. I took these thoughts back to my room with me; they followed me down into sleep and were still present upon my awakening. Halef brought me coffee. I had kept my word and had given him his money yesterday.

"*Sihdi*, when do you permit me to go to Mecca?" he asked me.

"Have you already seen everything in Jiddah?"

"Not everything; but I will be done soon."

"How will you travel? With a *delyl*?"

"No, that costs too much. I will wait until more pilgrims are gathered and then rent a camel for the trip."

"You may go as soon as you wish," I consented.

Delyls are those officials who guide foreign pilgrims and ensure that no precept is overlooked. Among the pilgrims there are many women and girls. Since it is not permitted for an unmarried woman to enter the holy places, the *delyls* make a business of meeting with these unmarried female pilgrims in Jiddah, marrying them, guiding them to Mecca and on completion they hand them their divorce papers.

Halef had barely left the room, when I heard a voice outside ask:

"Is your Master at home?"

"*Dehm Arably* – Speak Arabic!" replied Halef to the question, which had been asked in German.

"*Arably*? I can't manage that, my boy; at most I could speak a little Turkish with you. But wait, I will announce myself; certainly he is just behind that door."

It was Albani, whose voice now proclaimed loudly:

"*Juchheirassasa!*
Und wenn d'willst, will i a,
Und wenn d'willst, so mach auf,
Denn deßweg'n bin i da!"

[Hello there!
And when you will, I will too,
And when you will, then open up,
Because that's why I am here!]

He brilliantly fashioned the lyric of his song to the circumstance. Certainly Halef stood outside, stock still in amazement and this would continue if I did not answer, so for his sake I did not because I thought he should hear a little more. It was not long before the Triester continued:

"*Soldat bin i gern*
Und da kenn' i mi aus,
Doch steh i nit gern Schildwach
In fremder Leut Haus."

[I like being a soldier
And I know the task well,
But I don't like standing guard
In the house of strangers.]

And as even that sweet remembrance had no effect, he threatened:

"*Und a frischa Bua bin i,*
Drum laß dir 'mal sag'n:
Wenn d'nit glei itzt aufmachst,
Thua i's Thürerl zerschlag'n!"

[And a fresh boy am I,
That's why I tell you:
If you don't open up at once,
Then I will break down your door!]

I could not permit it to come to that so I got up and opened the door for him.

"Aha," he laughed, "then that did help! I almost thought that you had already left for Mecca."

"Hush! My servant must not know of this."

"Sorry! Guess what favor I came to ask!"

"With a claim for reciprocation for your hospitality yesterday? I am sorry! I can at most repay you with munitions, but not with rations, at least not with ones as rare as those on your menu."

"Pah! But it is truly a request or rather a question."

"Speak it!"

"We spoke yesterday very little of your experiences; but I suspect that you can ride."

"I can certainly ride a little."

"Only horses or also camels?"

"Both; even donkeys, which I was forced to ride yesterday."

"I have never sat on the back of a camel. Now, I heard earlier today that there is a *dewedshi* (renter of camels, after the fashion of a renter of horses) nearby, from whom one can cheaply buy the chance to play at being a Bedouin ..."

"Ah, you wish to risk a little trip on a camel?"

"That is it!"

"Then you will experience a kind of seasickness –"

"That's nothing."

"Against which not even a dose of creosote will protect you."

"I am prepared for that. I have traveled along the coast of the Red Sea and yet have never ridden a camel. May I invite you to accompany me?"

"I have the time. Where do you wish to go?"

"That does not matter to me. Perhaps a trip around Jiddah?"

"I am with you. Who will acquire the camels? You or I?"

"I of course. Do you want to take your servant along?"

"I leave that up to you. One never knows what to expect in this land, nor whom one might encounter, a servant in the Orient is never superfluous."

"Then he comes with us."

"When shall we leave?"

"Within the hour."

"Good. But allow me to tell you this. Carefully examine the saddle and the blanket before you mount the camel; such caution is always advised as one can easily make the acquaintance of the six footed *bashi-bozuks*, which in the Orient are given the cute sounding name of '*bit'*."

"*Bit*? I am no bright spark in Oriental languages."

"But you have toyed with a little Latin?"

"Certainly."

"Then I refer to the creature that has the German name, written in Latin characters, of '*lob'*."

"Ah! Is it so bad?"

"Absolutely, at times. I have heard this parasite described in Hungary with the word '*bergleute*' (miners), probably because they work from top to bottom. On a camel ride you have to deal with the 'miners' of the Arabs and the 'miners' of the camels. It is lucky that the first have a touching allegiance to their lords and masters and avoid infesting a *giaur*. Therefore put one of your own blankets beneath the saddle and after the ride you take it to a pastry cook, who will 'de-infest' it in his oven, for a few *borbi* (one *para* is eight *borbi*)."

"Not bad! Do we take our weapons?"

"Of course! I, for example, am forced to take precautions as I might run into an enemy at any moment."

"You?"

"Yes, I! I was the prisoner of a pirate, from whom I escaped early yesterday. He is on his way to Mecca and might easily still be in Jiddah."

"That is amazing! He was an Arab?"

"Yes. I can't even have him charged, though my life would not be worth a penny where I to encounter him again."

"You did not tell me of this yesterday!"

"Why should I speak of it? One hears and reads so often that life is becoming more and more predictable and that there are no more adventures. Only a few weeks ago I spoke to a traveling scholar who declared this as a fact – that one could travel the Old World from Hammerfest to Capetown and from England to Japan, without finding a trace of that which could be called adventure. I did not contradict him, but I am certain that it depends on the personality of the traveler as to what kind of journey it will be.

A journey of enterprise or one taken courtesy of an agency is going to be very tame, even if one were to go to Celebes [See Trans. Notes Ch 11.4] or the Tierra del Fuego. I prefer the horse or the camel over the coach or the train, the canoe over the steamer and the gun over a many-visaed passport. I desire to travel to Timbuktu or Tobolsk rather than to Nizza or Helgoland; I do not depend on an interpreter or guide. On a journey to Murzuk I have less money at my disposal than many might need for a trip from Prague to the Imperial City – Vienna, for a stay of one week – and I have never complained of the lack of adventure.

He who visits the Old World or the western states of North America with huge resources, comes to find those resources a burden; but he who travels light is welcomed by the Bedouins and is their guest and makes himself useful. Over there in the Wild West one hunts for his food and combats a hundred dangers; for him an adventure is never far off.

I will wager that we will experience an adventure upon our ride, even if it is a little one? The warriors of old went out to seek adventure; the current heroes travel as commissioned voyagers, tourists, sun-seekers, beachcombers or pilgrims; they have their adventures under the umbrella of a hotel table, waited on by mock milkmaids, at the gaming table or on the skating-rink. Shall we wager?"

"You make me very inquisitive!"

"Yes, understand me well! You may perhaps call it an adventure if you meet two tigers who are fighting to the death in the jungle. I call it an even greater adventure if I meet two ant colonies at the forest edge, whose battle, in terms of daring and exertion, is equal to a battle between Hun and Goth. It also offers us an example of unselfish sacrifice, obedience and strategic or tactical calculation and cunning, so much so that we can but marvel over it. Almighty God shows his splendor in these tiny creatures as well as in the tigers, which make a greater impression only because we fear them. But go now and order the camels, so that we may find a well during the time of the great heat."

"I will go; but will you also keep your word in reference to an adventure!"

"I will keep it."

He left then. I had made this speech with forethought; because a maiden voyage on the back of a camel should most certainly be undertaken in a romantic frame of mind.

Chapter 12

When I stepped into Albani's abode three quarters of an hour later, Albani bristled with weapons.

"Come; the *dewedshi* waits impatiently for us. Or do you wish to partake of something first?" he asked me.

"No thank you."

"Then we take provisions with us. I have this pocket full."

"You want an adventure and yet take provisions with you? Away with them! If we feel hungry, then we find ourselves a *duar* (tent village). There we will find dates, flour, water and maybe a little *tshekir* as well."

"*Tshekir*? What is that?"

"Cake, baked from ground locusts."

"Ugh!"

"Pah, the taste is outstanding! To he who eats oysters, escargot, birds' nests, frogs' legs and rotten milk with cheese maggots, locusts must be a delicacy. Do you know who ate locusts with wild honey long ago?"

"I believe that this fellow was mentioned in the Bible."

"Certainly, and quite an esteemed and holy fellow he was. Do you have a blanket?"

"Here."

"Good. How long do we have the camels at our disposal?"

"For the entire day."

"Accompanied by the *dewedshi* or one of his people?"

"No, unaccompanied."

"That is good. You would certainly have had to provide security for this, but we will be happier and undisturbed. Come!"

The camel-renter lived two houses down from Albani. I immediately noticed that this man was not an Arab but a Turk. In his courtyard stood three camels, over which one could have shed tears.

"Where is your stable?" I asked him.

"There!"

He pointed to a wall that divided the courtyard into two sections.

"Open the door!"

"What for?"

"Because I wish to see if there are any *jemahli* in there."

"There are such beasts in there."

"Show them to me!"

He did not entirely trust me; that is why he only opened the door enough to let me get a glimpse into the space beyond. There stood eight of the best riding camels. I stepped closer and looked them over.

"*Dewedshi*, how much does this *Hazretin* (Excellency) pay you for the three camels that you have saddled for us?"

"Five *mahbubzechinen* (at the rate of 5 mark to a *summa* = 25 mark) for all three."

"And for such a price we get these pack animals with wounded legs and feet! Look here, you can see through their sides; their lips hang like your torn sleeve, and their humps – ah, *dewedshi*, they have no humps! They have a long journey behind them; they are quite emaciated and have little energy, such that they can barely carry their saddles. And what do the saddles look like! Look here, man! What is marching around on this blanket? Make haste and supply us with better camels, better blankets and better saddles!"

He looked at me with suspicion and anger.

"Who are you, that you give me such commands?"

"Look here! Do you see this *Bu-Djeruldu* of the Sultan? Shall I tell him that you are a swindler and that you abuse your poor animals to death? Quick, saddle the three *hedjihn* over there, the two brown ones on the right and the gray one in the corner, otherwise my whip will make you sprout extra hands!"

A Bedouin would have immediately reached for a pistol or a knife; but this fellow was a Turk. He hurried to obey my commands, and soon three of the best camels lay on their knees before us, fitted with clean tack. I turned to Halef:

"Now show this *Sihdi* how he should mount!"

He did so, and I stepped onto Albani's camel's kneeling forelegs.

"Watch out! As soon as you touch the saddle the *hedjihn* will rise, first with the forelegs, so that you will be thrown backwards. Then it will raise its hindquarters and you will be thrown forwards. You will have to counter these movements with your body." [See Trans. Notes Ch 12.1]

"I will try to."

He took hold and swung himself into the saddle. At once the animal rose despite the fact that I was standing on its forelegs. The good entertainer flew backwards, but did not fall as he gripped the front of the saddle; but now the camel raised its hindquarters and since Albani still held fast to the front of the saddle, he flew forward and tumbled from it, over the head of the camel and into the sand.

"Damn it, this thing is not so easy!" he grumbled as he picked himself up and rubbed the shoulder upon which he had landed. "But mount I must. Bring the animal to its knees again!"

"Rrree!"

Upon this command the camel again squatted down. The second attempt was successful, despite the rider having endured two substantial jolts. I found it necessary to give the camel-renter another rebuke:

"*Dewedshi*, can you ride a *jemmel*?"

"Yes, *Sihdi*."

"And also guide it?"

"Yes."

"No, I think you cannot because it seems you are unaware that you would require a *metrek*! (a small stick, the end of which is bent – used like a riding crop)"

"Forgive me, *Sihdi*!"

He gave a command and the switches were brought forth. Now I also mounted. Of course, we presented quite a different picture than would have been the case if we had accepted the wretched beasts of burden. The saddles we now had were very pleasing, tasseled and decorated with colorful embroidery, and the blankets were so large that they almost covered the entire animal. We rode out into the street.

"Where to?" I asked Albani.

"I leave that to you."

"Good; then out through the *Bab el Medina*!"

My new acquaintance drew the attention of all we met; his dress was that conspicuous. I therefore steered through many side streets and brought us, via several detours, out through the gate. We then rode at walking pace through the settlement of the Nubier and the Habeshaner and entered the desert beyond, which was not separated by a dwindling belt of vegetation but began directly beyond the outskirts, as it was with all the cities of the Hedshas.

Up to this point Albani sat well in the saddle. But now, without encouragement, our camels fell into a trot, which is their normal gait. This places the novice rider in the peculiar position whereupon they learn what seasickness is, without there being a drop of seawater in sight. During the first few steps Albani laughed at himself. He did not posses the skill necessary to minimize the jarring rhythm, forwards and backwards and from side to side; his long Arabian flintlock was a hindrance and his huge sarras bounced and rattled against the camel's side. He took the sarras between his knees, snapped his fingers and sang:

"*Mei Sabel klippert, mei Sabel klappert,*
Mei Sabel macht mir halt Müh,
Und das Kameel wickelt, das Kameel wackelt,
Das Kameel ist ein sakrisch Vieh "

[My saber clinks, my saber clanks,
My saber makes a lot of work for me,
And the camel wibbles, the camel wobbles,
The camel is a wicked beast.]

I gave my camel a light tap on the nose; it rose on its hind legs and shot ahead so that the sand whirled up behind me to a height of several cubits. The other two camels followed of course and that put an end to the singing. Albani held the switch in his left hand and the flintlock in his right; he used both as balance poles by whirling his arms in the air in an effort to maintain his balance. He presented a most comical appearance.

"Hang your flintlock around your neck and shoulder and hold tightly on to your saddle!" I called to him.

"Hang the . . . whoops! Hang the . . . oh, whoa, ahh! Hang the flintlock! I have not the . . . whoops, ow! . . . not the time to do it! Stop you . . . whoops, oh, whoa! . . . you wretched beast!"

"I am one with my mount!" I told him.

"Yes, but mine . . . oh, whoa, oh! . . . but mine runs like he is pos . . . oof, whoops! . . . like he is possessed, following yours!"

"Then halt your beast!"

"With what?"

"With your foot and the reins!"

"With my foot, I can't even . . . whoa! . . . even lift it, and the reins, I don't . . . stop – oh, stop, oh! I don't have them any more!"

"Then you must wait until your animal stops of its own accord."

"But I have no . . . whoa, oh! . . . no more breath left!"

"Then open your mouth; there is air enough!"

I turned forwards again and did not listen to his interjections. He was in good hands, as Halef rode at his side.

Within a short time we had crested a small rise and now open level ground stretched out before us. Albani appeared to have adjusted to the saddle by degrees; he complained no more. Thus within about an hour we had covered some two German miles when the silhouette of a single rider appeared. He was about a half a mile from us and rode an apparently excellent camel. The distance between us diminished quickly and after barely ten minutes we halted, facing each other.

He wore the clothes of a prosperous Bedouin, and the hood of his burnoose was pulled far forward to cover his face. His camel was worth more then the three of ours combined.

"*Salaam aaleïkum* – Peace be with you!" he greeted us, while he exposed his hand to remove the hood.

"*Aaleïkum*!" I replied. "Which is your way here in the desert?"

His voice sounded soft, almost like the voice of a woman; his hand was certainly brown, but small and dainty, and as the hood was removed I saw an entirely beardless face, from which two large brown lively eyes inspected me – this was no man, but in fact a woman.

"My way is everywhere," she replied. "Whereto does yours lead?"

"From Jiddah, I desire to exercise my animal and return again to that city."

Her face took on a less happy expression and her gaze turned suspicious.

"Then you live in the city?"

"No; I am a stranger there."

"You are a pilgrim?"

How should I answer? I did intend to pass as a Mohammedan; but since I was asked directly, I decided not to answer with a lie.

"No; I am no hajji."

"You are a stranger to Jiddah and are not here to visit Mecca? Either you were in the Holy City earlier or you are not one of the faithful."

"I have not yet been in Mecca, my belief is not as yours."

"Are you a Jew?"

"No; I am a Christian."

"And these two?"

"This one is a Christian like myself, and this one a Moslem who intends to visit Mecca."

Her face brightened suddenly and she turned to Halef.

"Where is your homeland, stranger?"

"In the west, far from here over the great desert."

"Do you have a wife?"

He was surprised by the question just as I was, as it is not the Oriental custom to ask about such matters.

"No." He replied

"Are you a friend or a servant of this *effendi*?"

"I am his servant and his friend."

She turned to me again:

"*Sihdi*, come and follow me!"

"Where to?"

"Are you a chatterbox or do you fear a woman?"

"Pah! Lets go!"

She turned her camel and back-tracked along the trail her animal had already made in the sand. I rode at her side and my two companions rode behind us.

"Now," I asked Albani over my shoulder, "was I right about the adventure that I promised you?"

Albani responded with song;

"Dös Dirndel ist sauba
Vom Fuaß bis zum Kopf,
Nur am Hals hat's a Binkerl,
Dös hoaßt ma an Kropf."

[The girl is clean
From head to foot,

Only her neck is marred,
With what one calls a wattle.]

The woman was certainly no longer young and the rays of the desert sun, as well as the strain and privation of desert life had darkened her face and etched furrows upon it; but at one time she had certainly been fetching, that was evident even today. What was she doing by herself in the desert? Why had she chosen the way to Jiddah and where was she now returning to with us? Why was she visibly overjoyed when she heard that Halef intended to go to Mecca, and why would she not say where she was leading us? – She was an enigma. She carried a flintlock and in her belt was a *yatagan*. A lance was tied to her saddle belt and in the hands of a skilful Arab this was a dangerous weapon. She gave the impression of being a self-sufficient, fearless Amazon and this description was quite correct as such warlike women exist more frequently in the Orient than the West, where women are given more freedom.

"What language is that?" she asked, as she heard Albani's tune.

"The language of the Germans."

"Then you are a *Nemtshe*?"

"Yes."

"The *Nemtshe* must be courageous people."

"Why?"

"The most courageous man was the 'Sultan el Kebihr', but still he was vanquished by the *Nemtshe-shimakler* (Northern Germans, Prussia), the *Nemtshe-memleketler* (Austrians) and the *Moskowler* (Russians). Why do you look at me so intently?"

She had heard of Napoleon and the outcome of the 'Freedom War'; she surely had an extraordinary past behind her.

"Excuse me, if my eye offends you," I replied. "I am not accustomed to meeting women such as yourself in this land."

"A woman that carries weapons? Who kills men? Who even rules her tribe? Have you never heard of Ghaliё?"

"Ghaliё?" I asked in contemplation; "was she not of the Begum tribe?"

"I see that you know of her."

"Was she not actually the Sheik of her tribe and conqueror of the troops of Mehemed Ali, who were commanded by Tunsun-Bei at the battle Taraba?"

"So it was. Do you now see that a woman can be like a man?"

"What does the Koran say of it?"

"The Koran?" she asked with a gesture of disdain. "The Koran is a book; here I have my *yatagan*, my *tüfenk* (flintlock) and the *jerid* (lance). In which do you believe? The book or the weapons?"

"In the weapons. You see then that I am not a *giaur*, I think as you do."

"You also believe in your weapons?" She asked incredulously.

"Yes, very much; much more than in the *Kitab-aziz* (Holy Book) of the Christians." I replied.

"I know it not, but I see your weapons."

This was certainly a compliment being paid to me, as Arabs are accustomed to judging a man according to the weapons he carries. She continued:

"Who has killed more foes, you or your friend?"

If it came to weapons, Albani was clearly bolder than I; but I was convinced that the good Triester had never endangered anyone with his sarras. I answered indirectly:

"I have not discussed this with him."

"How many times have you been involved in an *intikam* (blood feud)?"

"Never. My beliefs do not permit me to kill an enemy with my own hand; he will be dealt with by the law."

"But if Abu-Seïf came upon you now and tried to kill you?"

"Then I would defend myself and if necessary kill him, because self-defense is permissible. But you speak of the 'Father of the Saber' – do you know him?"

"I know him. You too are familiar with his name; have you heard of him?"

"I have not only heard of Abu-Seïf, I have seen him."

She quickly turned to face me.

"Seen? When?"

"Not too many hours ago."

"Where was this?"

"I saw him last aboard his ship. I was his prisoner and escaped him yesterday."

"Where is his ship?"

I indicated the direction in which I believed it to be.

"Over there, hidden in a bay."

"And he is still aboard?"

"No. He is in Mecca, delivering a gift to the Sherif."

"The Sherif is not in Mecca but in Taïf. I have to thank you for this vital information. Come!"

She encouraged her camel to greater speed and after some time veered to the right where a series of dunes could be seen on the horizon. As we approached I noticed that the range of hills consisted of the same beautiful gray granite that I would later also observe in Mecca. In the mouth of a valley stood several tents. She indicated these with her hand and said:

"There they dwell."

"Who?"

"The *Beni-küfr* (Damned) of the tribe Ateïbeh."

"I thought the Ateïbeh lived in El Zallaleh, Taleh and the Wadi el Nobejat?"

"You are well informed; but come. All shall soon be revealed!"

Before the tents stood some thirty camels, a number of horses and several thin, shaggy desert hounds, the latter launched into a frenzy of howling and barking as we approached, this resulted in the emergence of the inhabitants from the tents. They had taken hold of their weapons and appeared hostile.

"Wait here!" commanded the mistress.

She coaxed her camel into a kneeling position, dismounted and approached the men. Neither Albani nor Halef had overheard my conversation with her.

"*Sihdi*," asked Halef, "to which tribe do these people belong?"

"To the tribe Ateïbeh." I replied.

"I have heard of them. They are among the bravest men of the desert, and no pilgrim caravan is safe from their bullets. They are the greatest enemies of the tribe Jeheïne, to which Abu Seïf belongs. What does the woman want from us?"

"I still don't know."

"Then we will find out. But have your weapons at the ready, *Sihdi*; I don't trust them because they are outcasts and damned."

"How can you determine this?"

"Do you not know that all *Bedawis* (Bedouins) who live in the region of Mecca collect the drops of candle wax and the ash from the incense wood, as well as the dust from the threshold of the Kaaba and rub it into their brow? These men have unmarked brows; they are not permitted entrance to Mecca and may not approach the Kaaba; they are damned."

"On what grounds have they been outcast?"

"That we will perhaps discover from them."

In the meantime the woman had exchanged words with the men and now one of them approached us. He was an ancient one and presented a venerable bearing.

"Allah bless your arrival! Dismount and enter our tents. You shall be our guests."

This last assurance convinced me that we need fear no danger. Once an Arab has spoken the word *misafir* (guest), one could truly trust him. We dismounted from our animals and were led to a tent where we seated ourselves on a *serir* (a low wooden frame covered with rugs) and were served a frugal meal.

While we ate, no words were spoken. We were then handed a *bery* each and whilst we smoked the sharp *tombak* tobacco, which may have come from Baghdad or Basra, the conversation began.

Since we only received a single *bery*, it was proof that these people possessed no riches. In the vicinity of the Holy Cities, three types of pipe are smoked. The first and most costly is the *khedra*. It usually rests on a tripod and consists of finely decorated, pure silver and is fitted with a long tube which is called *leiëh* and is, depending on the wealth of the owner, ornamented with precious stones or other jewels. From the *khedra* one smokes only the most expensive tobacco from Shiraz. The second kind of pipe is the *shisheh*. It is similar to the *khedra*, only smaller and less costly. The third and most common kind is the *bery*. It consists of a water-filled coconut shell to which the bowl and a reed - in place of the tube, are fastened.

There were more than twenty men in the tent. The elder who had greeted us spoke:

"I am Sheik el Urdi (Leader of the camp), I have need to speak with you, *Sihdi*. Custom does not permit me to harry a guest with questions; but I do have some questions nonetheless. Will you permit me to ask them?"

"I permit it."

"You belong to the *Nessarah*?"

"Yes, I am a Christian."

"What are you doing in the land of the faithful?"

"I desire to learn about this land and its inhabitants."

A doubtful expression crossed his face.

"And once you have learned about it all, what will you do then?"

"I shall return to my homeland."

"*Allah akbar* – God is great, and the thoughts of the *Nessarah* are inscrutable! You are my guest, and I shall believe what you have said. Is this man your servant?" He indicated Halef.

"He is my servant and my friend."

"My name is Malek. You have spoken with *Bint-Sheik-Malek* (daughter of Sheik Malek); she informed me that your servant intends to go to Mecca to become a hajji."

"She has told you the truth."

"Will you wait for him until he returns?"

"Yes."

"Where?"

"I have not yet decided."

"You are a foreigner, but you know the language of the faithful. Do you know what a *delyl* is?"

"A *delyl* is a guide who makes a business of leading pilgrims to Mecca and showing them the marvels of the city."

"You are correct. But a *delyl* also does another kind of business. It is forbidden for single women to enter the Holy City. If a virgin desires to go to Mecca, then she first goes to Jiddah and enters into a formal marriage with a *delyl*. He takes her to Mecca as his wife, where she performs the *faradh* and *wadshib* (essential and requisite actions); once her hajj is completed he releases her from the bonds of marriage and she remains a virgin – he is paid for his services."

"I know this as well."

The preamble that the old Sheik employed made me inquisitive. What intention led him to associate Halef's pilgrimage with the duties of a *delyl*? I was soon to discover the significance as he explained without further ado:

"Permit your servant to act as a *delyl* for the duration of his hajj!"

This came as a surprise.

"To do what?" I asked him.

"I will tell you as soon as you have given your permission."

"I am not certain if I can. The *delyls* are officials who receive their status from the authorities."

"Who would forbid him to marry a virgin and release her again after his pilgrimage?"

"Who indeed. As far as I am concerned, I give my permission willingly if you think that it is necessary. Halef is a free man and you must discuss it with him."

It was delightful to watch the expression on Halef's face. He was completely baffled.

"Will you do it?" the elder asked Halef.

"May I see the girl first?"

The Sheik laughed a little and replied:

"Why do you wish to see her first? It is immaterial if she is old or young, beautiful or ugly, as you will release her after the hajj."

"Are the *Benaht el Arab* (daughters of the Arab) like the daughters of the Turks, in that they are not permitted to show themselves?"

"The daughters of the Arabs need not conceal their faces. You shall see the girl."

Upon a commanding movement of the Sheik's hand one of the men present rose from the floor and left the tent. After a short while he returned with a girl whose similarity to the Amazon allowed me to guess the relationship of the two.

"This is the girl, observe her!" said the Sheik.

Halef made full use of that permission. This beautiful girl, who was a mature fifteen years old with dark eyes, appeared to please him.

"What is your name?" he asked her.

"Hanneh (Anna)," she replied.

"Your eyes gleam like the *nur el kamar* (light of the moon); your cheeks shine like *zahari* (flowers); your lips glow like *römmahm* (pomegranates), and your eyelashes are as shady as the leaves of *el szemt* (the acacia). My name is Halef Omar Ben Hajji Abul Abbas Ibn Hajji Dawud al Gossarah, and if I am able, I will fulfill your wish."

Halef's eyes gleamed too, not just like the *nur el kamar* but also like the *nur esh shemms* (light of the sun); his words blossomed into poetic phrases. Perhaps he stood on the verge of the same abyss that had dashed the hajji hopes of his father, Abul Abbas, and grandfather, Dawud al Gossarah: The abyss of love and marriage.

The girl retreated again, and the Sheik asked Halef:

"What is your decision?"

"Ask my master. If he does not advise against it, I will fulfill your wish."

"Your master has already said that he permits it."

"That is right!" I confirmed. "But tell us now why this girl should go to Mecca and why she does not go to Jiddah and seek a *delyl* there?"

"Do you know Achmed-Izzet-pasha?"

"The Governor of Mecca?"

"Yes, you must know him, because every foreigner that enters Jiddah must seek him out to obtain his protection."

"He lives in Jiddah then? I did not seek him out; I don't need the protection of a Turk."

"You may be a Christian, but you are still a man. The protection of the Pasha is only available for a high price. Yes, he does not live in Mecca where he really belongs but in Jiddah because that is where the harbor is. His income is over a million *piasters*, but he knows how to increase it fivefold. Everyone must pay him, even the smugglers and pirates, that is why he lives in Jiddah. I was told that you have seen Abu-Seïf?"

"I have seen him."

"Now, this bandit is a good acquaintance of the Pasha."

"Impossible!"

"Why not? What is more advantageous - to kill a thief or to let him live and receive payment from him? Abu-Seïf is a Jeheïne; I am an Ateïbeh. Our two tribes are deadly enemies yet he dared to steal into our *duar* (tent village) and abduct my daughter. He forced her to become his wife; but she eventually escaped him and returned with her own daughter. You have seen both of them; you arrived with my daughter and her daughter was just here in the tent.

Since that time I have searched for him to demand retribution. I found him once; that was in the *seraj* (palace) of the governor. The governor safeguarded the thief and aided his escape while I lay in wait for him outside the city gate. Some time later the Sheik of my tribe sent me with these men here to Mecca to make an offering at the Kaaba. We camped not far from the *el Ramah* gap, there I saw Abu-Seïf arriving with some of his men, they also planned to visit the sanctuary. My anger got the better of me – although all disputes are forbidden around the Kaaba. I did not wish to kill him, only to force him to follow me outside the city walls where we could settle our feud. He defended himself and his men joined in. A fight ensued, which ended with the eunuchs interceding and taking us captive whilst letting Abu-Seïf and his men go free. Our penalty was banishment from the holy places. Our entire clan was damned and outcast to lay the curse to rest. Now we are outlaws. But we will avenge ourselves and depart from this place. You were a prisoner of Abu-Seïf?"

"Yes."

"Tell us about it!"

I gave a short report of that adventure.

"Do you know precisely where his ship is?"

"I could find it again even at night."

"Will you lead us to it?"

"Will you kill the Jeheïne?"

"Yes."

"Then my beliefs do not permit me to guide you."

"You are not permitted to avenge yourself?"

"No, our religion teaches that we should love even our enemies. Only the law has the right to punish the transgressor and you are not judges."

"Your religion is charming; but we are not Christians and we must punish our enemies ourselves, because our enemies are under the protection of the judge. You have described the place where they are and I will find it without your help. Only promise me that you will not alert the Jeheïne."

"I will not warn them, I have no desire to become their prisoner again."

"Then we are decided. When will Halef go to Mecca?"

"Tomorrow, if you permit it, *Sihdi*," replied Halef in my stead.

"You may go tomorrow."

"Then Halef shall stay with us," invited the Sheik. "We will accompany them to the Holy City, as far as we are permitted, and then return him to you."

An idea occurred to me that I voiced at once:

"May I also accompany you and await their return?"

I noticed at once that this request was received well all around.

"*Effendi*, I see, that you do not despise outcasts," replied the Sheik. "You shall be welcome among us! You shall remain with us and assist us this evening to perform the *ewlenma* (marriage)."

"That will not work. I must return to Jiddah to attend to my affairs. My landlord must know where I am."

"Then I shall accompany you to the city gate even if I may not enter. When will you ride?"

"At once if you prefer. I only need a little time and then I will return with you. Shall I bring a *kadi* or *mullah* to conduct the marriage ceremony?"

"We need neither a *kadi* nor a *mullah*. I am the Sheik of my camp, and that which I preside over is true and valid. However, you may bring parchment or paper, upon which we might record the contract. The *mohür* and *gemedsh* (seal and wax) I already possess."

In short order the camels stood ready and we mounted. The small troop consisted of Albani, Halef and myself along with the Sheik, his daughter and five

Ateïbeh. I followed the patriarch without objection, although I noticed that he did not choose the direct route but held towards the seaward path. Albani did not have as much trouble remaining in the saddle as on the outward journey and the long legs of the animals literally threw the ground behind them.

The Sheik halted and indicated a point to the side.

"Do you know what lies over there, *effendi*?"

"What?"

"The bay where the ship of the pirate lays at anchor. Have I guessed correctly?"

"You may assume that, but you must not ask me to confirm it."

He had guessed correctly and was silent. We rode on. After some time, two small specks appeared on the horizon in precisely the same direction as the location of Jiddah. It appeared they were not approaching us but were veering on a path that would lead them to the bay. Looking through my telescope I discovered that they were on foot. This was a conspicuous way to travel here in the desert, and the realization that they were Abu-Seïf's people dawned on me. It was conceivable that my guards had reported our escape to their captain and if that were the case, then the two men were probably returning messengers. Malek had also noticed them and was watching them intently. He turned to his men and whispered a command. At once three of them turned and rode back in the direction from whence we came. I knew his intent. Malek guessed the same as I and was determined to capture the two men. To achieve this, he had to cut them off on the path to the bay, but he had to do this in such a way as not to forewarn them. That is why his three men did not ride directly on, but rather appeared to turn about and then, once they were out of sight, rode in an arc to meet the pirates. While we continued on our way, Malek asked:

"*Effendi*, will you wait a little for us, or do you ride to the city where we will meet you at the gate?"

"You will want to speak to these men, I will remain with you until you have done so."

"They are perhaps Jeheïne!"

"I believe so too. Your men will cut them off on their way to the ship; you ride diagonally and I will continue on our present bearing with Halef so that they do not get the idea to escape to Jiddah."

"Your advice is good and I will follow it."

The Sheik turned away and I indicated to Albani that he should join him. It would be easier on him to travel with the Sheik as Halef and I had to ride at a gallop. The two of us flew along like a storm and steered towards their rear as we came into line with the hunted. The Jeheïne noticed our intention just then and hesitated. Behind them were Halef and I, Malek appeared at their flank and only the way in front of them appeared open. They moved forward at double the pace but did not get far before the three Ateïbeh appeared ahead of them. Although it was impossible for the pirates to recognize any one of us at this distance, they had to realize that we were enemies and they therefore tried to flee from us with the greatest haste. There was one prospect of escape open to them. They were armed – if they separated we would be forced to do likewise; it would then be possible for a solitary, cold-blooded marksman on foot to take on two or three mounted adversaries. But that strategy never occurred to them or they lacked the courage to carry it out. They remained together and were easily encircled. I recognized them immediately; they were indeed two of Abu-Seïf's crew.

"From where do you come?" the Sheik asked them.

"From Jiddah," replied one.

"Where do you go?"

"Into the desert to search for truffles."

"To search for truffles? You have neither animals nor baskets with you!"

"We want to see if these fungi grow here first, then we will fetch our baskets."

"To which tribe do you belong?"

"We live in the city."

This was of course an impudent lie, as these men must know that I recognized them. Even Halef was angered by their brazenness. He loosened his whip and said:

"Do you think that this *effendi* and I have become blind? You are rogues and liars! You are Jeheïne and in league with Abu-Seïf. If you do not admit it, my whip will teach you to speak the truth!"

"What does it concern you who we are?"

I leaped from my camel without waiting for it to kneel and took the whip from Halef's hand.

"Don't laugh it off, you rogues. Listen to what I tell you! What these warriors of the Ateïbeh tribe want from you is not my concern; but you will answer my questions. If you do, then you have nothing to fear from me; if you refuse then I will mark you in such a way that you will not dare to show yourself to any free and courageous Ibn Arab!"

To threaten a Bedouin with a whip is the greatest insult. Both pirates reached for their knives.

"We would kill you before you could whip us," threatened one of them.

"You apparently have not yet discovered how mighty a whip made from the skin of a hippopotamus is when it is in the hands of a Frank. It cuts like a *yatagan*; it descends more heavily than a club and is faster than a bullet from your *tabandshab* (pistols). Do you not see that the weapons of all these men are trained upon you? Leave your knives in your belts and answer! You were sent to find Abu-Seïf?"

"Yes," came the hesitant reply, as they realized that there was no escape.

"To tell him that I had escaped?"

"Yes."

"Where did you meet him?"

"In Mecca."

"How did you manage to get to Mecca and back so quickly?"

"We rented camels."

"How long does Abu-Seïf intend to remain in the Holy City?"

"Only a short time. He intends to go to Taïf, where the Sherif Emir resides."

"Then I am finished with you." I concluded.

"*Sihdi*, do you intend to let these bandits escape?" called Halef. "I will shoot them dead so that they will not harm anyone else."

"I have given them my word and you will keep it with me. Follow me!"

I mounted again and rode away, with some reluctance Halef followed me. Albani remained, he had pulled out his long sarras, although I trusted that the energetic pantomime was of a harmless nature. Indeed, he rested quite calmly on his camel while the Ateïbeh jumped from theirs to overpower the Jeheïne. They succeeded after exchanging a few non-lethal knife thrusts. The prisoners were bound onto the camels and the riders of the same turned back to deliver them to their camp. The others followed us.

"You have pardoned them, *Sihdi*; but they will die all the same," said Halef.

"Their destiny is not our concern! Think about what you are to become today. A bridegroom should be harmonious!"

"S*ihdi*, would you become a *delyl* for Hanneh?"

"Yes, if I were a Moslem."

"*Sihdi*, you are a Christian, a Frank, with whom one can speak about such things. Do you know what love is?"

"Yes. Love is a colocynth [bitter apple]. He who eats it gets stomach aches."

"Oh, *Sihdi*, who would compare love to a colocynth! May Allah enlighten your perception and warm your heart! A good wife is like a pipe of jasmine and like a tobacco pouch that never empties. And to love a virgin, it is . . . it is . . . like . . . a turban on a bald head and like the sun in a desert sky."

"Yes. And he who is struck by its rays gets sunstroke. I believe you have it already Halef. May Allah help you!"

"*Sihdi*, I know that you intend never to be a bridegroom; but I am one and that is why my heart is open like a nose that drinks in the aroma of the flowers."

Our short discussion came to an end when the others caught up with us. No words were lost over the incident and as the city came into view the Sheik halted his animals. He had brought two camels along that would carry us on our return journey.

"We will wait here, *Sihdi*," he said. "How much time will pass before you return?"

"I will be back before the sun's passage is equal to the length of your spear." I replied.

"And you will not forget the *tirsheh* or *kiahat* (parchment or paper)?"

"No. I will also bring *mürek* and a *kalem* (ink and a quill)."

"Do it. Allah protect you until we see you again!"

The Ateïbeh squatted next to their camels, and we three rode into the city.

"Now, was that an adventure?" I asked Albani.

"Certainly. And what an adventure! It nearly included deadly blows and murder. I really held myself ready to do battle."

"Yes, you had the appearance of a 'raging Roland' with whom one cannot eat cherries in peace. Did the ride agree with you?"

"Hmm! To begin with you had to get me into the swing of it; but then it went well. I promised myself a good German canapé! You wish to go with these Arabs? – Then we will not see each other again."

"Probably not, as you will take the first opportunity to secure a passage home. But I have experienced many instances of unexpected reunions, therefore I do not believe it impossible that we may meet again."

These words were to come true later. After we returned the animals to the *dewedshi*, we said our hearty farewells, as was proper for compatriots who meet in distant lands. Then Halef and I went to our abode to pack our belongings and to say good-bye to Tamaru, the landlord. I had not thought that I would be giving up my rooms so soon. On two rented donkeys we rode out of the city. There we mounted the waiting camels.

The ride passed with few words being exchanged. The most silent was the Sheik's daughter. She uttered no word, but her eyes glowed with a terrible fire and whenever she glanced to the left, in the direction where she believed Abu-Seïf's ship to be, her right hand either gripped her *handshar* or the butt of her flintlock, which lay across her saddle.

Chapter 13

As we reached the vicinity of the camp, Halef guided his horse alongside mine.

"*Sihdi*," he asked, "what are the customs of your homeland? Does a groom give his bride presents?"

"I would believe that everyone does so, with us as well as with your people."

"Yes, in *Jesirat el Arab*, as in the entire *Sharki* (East), it is the custom. But Hanneh is to be my pretend wife for just a few days, I am not certain if a gift is prudent."

"A gift is a courteous gesture that generates good feelings. I, in your place, would be courteous."

"But what shall I give her? I am poor and by no means prepared for a wedding. What do you think, should I honor her with my *adeshlik* (matchbox)?"

He had purchased a small box made from paper-maché in Cairo, in which he stored his matches. The thing was of great value to him because he had paid the merchant twenty times more than the thirty pennies it was worth. Love brought him to the heroic decision to part with this precious possession.

"Give it to her." I replied solemnly.

"Good, she shall have it! But will she give it back to me when she is no longer my wife?"

"She will keep it."

"*Allah kerihm*, God is merciful; he will not let me lose what is mine! What shall I do *Sihdi*?"

"If the *adeshlik* is so dear to you, then give her something else!"

"What else? I have nothing else. I cannot give her my turban, nor my gun, nor my Nile whip!"

"Then give her nothing."

He shook his head in consternation.

"That cannot be *Sihdi*. She is my bride and she must receive something. What will the Ateïbeh think of you, if your servant takes a wife without giving a gift?"

Ah! The crafty fellow intended to appeal to my ego and therefore the content of my pack.

"Allah, who enlightens your senses, be praised, Halef! As with you, it is equally with me. I can give your bride neither my *haïk*, nor my jacket, nor my gun!"

"Allah is fair and merciful *effendi*; he pays a thousand times interest for each gift. Does your camel not carry a leather pack, in which you have secreted many things that would delight a bride?"

"And if I gave her of its content, would it be returned to me once she is no longer your wife?"

"You must demand it!"

"That is not the custom with the Franks. But since you indicate that a thousand times interest will be mine, I will open the pack later and see if I can find something for you."

He straightened himself in his saddle with joy.

"*Sihdi*, you are the wisest and greatest *effendi* that Allah has created. Your goodness is wider than the Sahara, and your charity longer than the Nile. Your father was the most celebrated, and the father of your father the most awe-inspiring man among all the people in the kingdom of Nemsistan. Your mother was the prettiest rose, and the mother of your mother, the most charming blossom of the west. Your sons shall be as numerous as the stars in the heavens and your daughters as plentiful as the sands of the desert and the children of your children as countless as the drops of water that make up the sea!"

It was lucky that we had reached the camp, otherwise his gratitude would have married me to all the daughters of the Samoans, Tungus, Eskimos and the Papuans. As far as the leather satchel that he had indicated was concerned, it held various items that would make suitable gifts for a Bedouin girl. The merchant's son, Isla Ben Maflei, on our parting in Cairo after the Nile passage, could not be dissuaded from providing me with a collection of items that would be appropriate as gifts for the natives during the course of my travels. They were items that did not take up much space, nor were they very expensive in themselves, but for the desert dwellers they had enormous value insofar as they were rarely seen amongst them.

During our absence one of the tents had been cleared and prepared for me. When I had taken possession of it I opened the leather satchel and took out a locket; under its glass cover was a little devil that danced. It was crafted in a similar fashion to those cufflinks that hold miniature moving tortoises, it hung on a strand of facetted glass links, which by day or firelight sparkled with all the colors of the rainbow. The trinket would have cost two francs in Paris. I showed it to Halef.

He looked at it and drew back in alarm.

"*Mashallah*, Miracle of God! That is *Shaïtan*, may God curse him! *Sihdi*, how did you manage to get Lucifer under your control? *La illa illa Allah, we Muhammed resul Allah*! Save us Almighty, from the 'thrice-stoned devil'; as we wish to serve only You, not him!"

"He cannot harm you because he is locked up tight."

"He cannot get out, truly?" Halef asked with some trepidation.

"No."

"Can you swear by your beard?"

"By my beard!"

"Then show it to me again, *Sihdi*! But if he escapes, then I am lost and my soul will haunt you and your ancestors!"

He grasped the string of beads with his fingertips, and with the utmost care placed the locket on the ground and knelt before it to examine it.

"*Wallahi – billahi – tallahi* – by Allah, it is *Shaïtan*! Do you see how he opens his jaw and pokes out his tongue? He rolls his eyes and shakes his horns; he twists his tail, threatens with his claws and stamps his feet! Oh *jazik* – woe, if he crushes the case!"

"That cannot happen. It is an artificial figure!"

"An artificial figure crafted by the hand of man? *Effendi*, you deceive me to give me courage. Who can craft Lucifer? No man, no believer, no Christian or Hebrew! You are the greatest *taleb* and one of the most courageous heroes to walk on this earth because you have forced *Shaïtan* into this narrow *zindan* (prison)! *Hamdulillah,* now the Earth is safe from him and his minions, all descendents of the prophets can shout with joy and be happy over the pains that he has to endure in there! Why do you show me this necklace, *Sihdi*?"

"You shall give it to your bride as a gift."

"I? This necklace, which is worth more than all the diamonds in the throne of the great Mogul? Whoever owns this necklace will become famous among all the sons and daughters of the faithful. You really wish to part with it?"

"Yes."

"Then please, *Sihdi*, permit me to keep it for myself! I would rather give the girl my matchbox."

"No, you will give her this necklace. I command you!"

"Then I must obey. But where did you keep this and all the other things before you placed them in the leather pack yesterday?"

"From Kahira to this place is dangerous territory, that is why I hid them in the legs of my *shalwars* (wide, Turkish pants)."

"*Sihdi*, your wisdom and caution are beyond the wiles of the devil that you have forced to abide within your *shalwars*. When shall I give this necklace to Hanneh?"

"As soon as she has become your wife."

"She will become the most famous among all *Benat el Arab* (Benat is the plural form of bint, daughter), as all tribes will praise her and report that she holds *Shaïtan* imprisoned. May I also see the other treasures?"

It did not come to that because the Sheik had sent a messenger who requested our presence. We found all the Ateïbeh gathered in his tent.

"*Sihdi*, did you bring the parchment?" asked Malek.

"I have brought paper, which is as good as parchment."

"Will you write the contract?"

"If you wish it, yes."

"Then can we begin?"

Halef, to whom this question was directed, nodded, and at once one of the men present arose to question him.

"What is your complete name?"

"I am named Halef Omar Ben Hajji Abul Abbas Ibn Hajji Dawud al Gossarah."

"From which land do you come?"

"I come from the *garbi* (west), where the sun sets beyond the great desert."

"To which tribe do you belong?"

"The father of my father, may they both be blessed by Allah, lived with the famous tribes of the Uëlad Selim and Uëlad Bu Seba in the great Jebel Shur-Shum."

The man posing the questions, who must have been related to the bride, now turned to the Sheik.

"We all know you, oh brave, oh staunch, oh wise and righteous one. You are Hajji Malek Iffandi Ibn Achmed Chadid el Eini Ben Abul Ali el Besami Abu Shehab Abdolatif el Hanifi, a Sheik of the bravest tribe of the Beni Ateïbeh. Behold this man is a hero from the tribes of the Uëlad Selim and Uëlad Bu Seba, who live in the mountains that reach to the heavens and are known as the Jebel Shur-Shum. He is called Halef Omar Ben Hajji Abul Abbas Ibn Hajji Dawud al Gossarah and is the friend of a great *effendi* from Frankistan who is a guest in our tent. You have a daughter. Her name is Hanneh; her hair is like silk, her skin is like oil, and her virtues are as clean and shining as the flakes of snow that are blown about on the mountains. Halef Omar desires to take her as his wife. Speak, oh Sheik, what are your thoughts!"

The Sheik feigned dignified contemplation then answered:

"You have spoken my son. Now sit and listen to my thoughts. This Halef Omar Ben Hajji Abul Abbas Ibn Hajji Dawud al Gossarah is a hero, whose fame did reach us years ago. His arms are invincible; his tread is like that of a gazelle; his eye is as sharp as that of an eagle; he can throw the *jerid* many hundreds of paces; his bullet finds its target with certainty and his *handshar* has seen the blood of many enemies. He has also learned the Koran and in council he is the wisest and most experienced. Added to that, this mighty *Bei* of the Franks has thought him worthy of friendship . . . why should I refuse him my daughter if he is willing to fulfill my conditions?"

"What conditions do you set before him?" asked the previous speaker.

"The girl is the daughter of a mighty Sheik, which is why he cannot have her for the usual price. I demand a mare, five riding camels, ten pack camels and fifty sheep."

At these words Halef pulled such a face, as though he had swallowed the fifty sheep, ten pack camels and five riding camels as well as the mare, all with skin and hair. From where should he produce these animals? Luckily, the Sheik continued:

"Therefore I give her the customary husband's morning present comprised of one mare, five riding camels, ten pack camels and fifty sheep. Your combined wisdom will realize that it is entirely unnecessary to exchange the price and the morning gift. But I demand that he begin his pilgrimage to Mecca with his wife tomorrow at the *fagr* (prayer at the rise of the sun). They shall complete the required holy rituals and then return immediately. He shall treat his wife like a virgin and release her upon his return. For this service he shall receive a camel and a sack-full of dates. If he does not treat his wife like a virgin, then he shall receive nothing and shall be killed. You are witnesses to my demands."

The master of ceremonies turned to Halef.

"You have heard. What is your answer?"

It was evident from Halef's face that a certain point was not to his liking, namely the demand that he return his wife. But he was clever enough to befit himself to the current circumstances, and replied:

"I accept the conditions."

"Then write the contract, *effendi*," urged the Sheik. "Write it twice, once for me and once for him!"

I followed the demand and then read what I had written. It received the approval of the Sheik and once he and Halef had signed the documents he dripped sealing wax on to each copy and then used the hilt of his dagger as a seal.

With this, the formalities were completed and the essential wedding festivities could begin. They were, since it was only a sham marriage, very frugal. A sheep was slaughtered and roasted whole on a spit over a fire. While it cooked a mock battle was held, in which not a shot was fired; the reason for this was not difficult to guess.

As night approached, the meal began. Only the men ate, and only when we were satiated did the women then receive the remains. At this time Hanneh was to appear. Halef took the opportunity and arose from his place. The scene that occurred next cannot easily be described. The devil encased in the locket was a spectacle that no one could comprehend. All my attempts at explaining the mechanics did not help. They did not believe me, and all because the *Shaïtan* appeared alive. I was praised as the greatest hero and magician; but in the end, Hanneh did not receive the gift. The imprisoned *Shaïtan* was a wonder of such immense proportions that only the Sheik himself was considered worthy to keep this immeasurable wealth; of course this was only after I assured him, with all due ceremony, that the devil would never be able to escape and wreak havoc.

It was nearing midnight when I retired to my tent to sleep. Halef accompanied me.

"*Sihdi*, do I have to do everything that you wrote down today?" he asked.

"Yes. You have promised it!"

Some time passed before I heard his humble words:

"Would you surrender your wife?"

"No."

"But yet you say that I must keep my promise!"

"Certainly. If I took a wife, then I would not promise to surrender her."

"Oh, *Sihdi*, why did you not tell me that I should do likewise!"

"Are you a little boy, that you require my guidance? And how can a Christian advise a Moslem about marriage? I believe that you wish to keep Hanneh as your bride!"

"You have guessed it."

"Then you will leave me?"

"You, *Sihdi* ...? Oh . . . !"

He cleared his throat, but no words came. There was an unintelligible mumbling and later I heard a sob. He threw himself on one side, then on the other; it was clear that his liking for the girl and his attachment to me had placed him in a quandary. I left him to himself and soon fell asleep.

My sleep was so deep that I awoke only at the sound of thudding camels' feet. I arose and stepped out of the tent. In the east the horizon had already brightened, and in the direction of the bay the horizon was stained bright crimson. There was a fire, and the suspicion that formed in my mind at this sight was confirmed by the activity that was apparent in the camp. The men had been away and were now returning, they and their camels richly laden with plunder. Even the daughter of the Sheik had joined them, and as she dismounted from her camel I noticed that her garment was splattered with blood. Malek offered me the morning greeting and said, pointing to the fire cloud:

"You see that we found the ship? They slept as we came upon them and are now gathered with the dogs that are their fathers."

"You have killed them and plundered the ship?"

"Plundered? What do you mean by this word? Do not the possessions of the vanquished belong to the victor? Who will deny us what we have won?"

"The *zehka*, which was stolen by Abu-Seïf, belonged to the Sherif Emir."

"The Sherif Emir, the one who banished us? Even if the money belonged to him he will not see it again. But do you really believe that it was the *zehka*? You were deceived. Only the Sherif has the right to collect this tax, and he would never permit a Turk to do it. The Turk, whom you believe to be a tax collector, was either a smuggler or a tax collector for the Pasha of Egypt, may Allah crush him!"

"You hate him?"

"Every free Arab does. Have you not heard of the horrible deeds that occurred at the time of the Wachabites? Whether the money belonged to the Pasha or to the Sherif, it is mine now. But the time of the *fagr* draws near. Ready yourself to follow us. We cannot remain here any longer."

"Where will you erect your camp?"

"I will make camp at a place where I can watch the road between Mecca and Jiddah. Abu-Seïf shall not escape me."

"Have you also considered the other dangers that threaten you?"

"Do you think that an Ateïbeh fears danger?"

"No, but even the most courageous man must also be careful. If Abu-Seïf falls into your hands and you kill him, then you must leave the area immediately. You may then lose the child of your daughter, who will be in Mecca with Halef at that time."

"I will tell Halef where he can find us in such a case. Hanneh must go to Mecca before we depart. She is the only one among us who has not been to the Holy City and perhaps later it will be impossible for her to go there. That is why I have tried for so long to find a *delyl*."

"Have you decided where you will go?"

"We move into the El Nahman desert, towards Maskat, and afterwards we may send a messenger to the Beni Shammar at *El Frat* (Euphrates) or to the Beni Obeïde, to gain acceptance into their clan."

A short dawn ushered in the day. The sun touched the horizon, and the Arabs, who still reeked of spilled blood, knelt down in prayer. Soon afterwards the tents were taken down and the procession began to move. Now that it was daylight I realized how much plunder the Ateïbeh had taken from the ship. They had become wealthy people as a result of their raid. For this reason there was an atmosphere of unusual merriment about them. I could not join in the jubilation. I was disturbed because I was the innocent cause of the annihilation of the Jeheïne. Whilst I could not reproach myself for their actions, it was still valid to question my conscience – perhaps if I had acted differently . . . ?

The proximity of Mecca also weighed heavily on my mind. There it was – the 'Holy', the 'Forbidden'! Should I avoid it or dare to enter? All my limbs twitched towards it, yet still I had to consider the wisdom that spoke against entering with earnest contemplation. What would I gain if my visit were successful? I could say that I had been in Mecca – beyond that, nothing. And if I was discovered, then my death would be inevitable, and what a death it would be! But at the moment thinking about the pros and cons would lead nowhere, and I decided that I would be directed by circumstance when the time came. I had done so often before and had always been fortunate.

To keep any chance encounters to a minimum the Sheik made a detour. He permitted no rest until the evening. We were in a narrow ravine that was enclosed by steep granite walls; we rode for some distance within until we reached a kind of cul-de-sac from which no second exit was apparent. Here we dismounted, the tents were erected and the women started the campfires. This night there was a rich and multi-coursed meal that, of course, came from the content of the ship's galley. This was followed by the distribution of the much lusted after booty.

Since I had nothing to do with this, I left the group and took a walk around the cul-de-sac. At one place I discovered that it might be possible to scale the cliff-face and so I attempted this. The stars were bright and I managed the climb without too much difficulty. After about a quarter of an hour I stood at the top of the cliff and had a clear view all around. Towards the south I saw a row of bare mountains, above those a pale luminescence glowed, such as is produced by the lights of a city at night. Over there lay Mecca . . . ! From below me I heard the loud voices of the Ateïbeh as they squabbled over the distribution of their plunder. It was some considerable time before I rejoined them. The Sheik greeted me with these words:

"*Effendi*, why did you not stay? You must receive your part of all that we gathered from the ship!"

"I? You are mistaken. I was not with you and therefore am not entitled."

"Would we have found the Jeheïne if we had not met you? You were our leader without desiring to be so and that is why you shall receive what is your due."

"I will not accept it!"

"*Sihdi*, I am not familiar with your faith and because of this I will not berate you since you are also my guest; but it is wrong if your faith does not permit you to receive part of the plunder. The enemies are dead and their vessel is destroyed. Should we have also destroyed the things that are important to us?"

"Let us not argue – but keep my share!"

"We will not keep it. Permit us to give it to Halef, your companion, although he has already received his share."

"Give it to him!" I agreed.

The little Halef Omar gushed with gratitude. He received some weapons and clothes and a bag of silver coins. He did not let up – I had to count them to attest to the fact that he had become a rich man this night. The amount came to some eight hundred *piasters* and was more than sufficient to make a poor Arab happy.

"With this money you can cover your costs in Mecca more than fifty times over," noted the Sheik.

"When shall I enter the Holy City?" Halef asked him.

"Tomorrow between dawn and midday."

"As I have never been there, how should I conduct myself?"

"I will tell you. It is the duty of every pilgrim to go to the *El Hamram* – The Great Mosque, immediately upon arrival. You ride therefore to the *Beith-Allah* – 'House of God'; also known as the Great Mosque, leave your camels before it and enter. There you will surely find a *metowef* (guide), who will escort and direct you, but you must ask him the cost before, not after, otherwise you will be swindled. As soon as you see the Kaaba, you perform two *rikat* (prostration) along with the prescribed prayers, in gratitude for having reached the Holy City safely. Then you go to the *mambar* (pulpit, Turkish: mimbar) and remove your shoes. They remain there and are guarded; it is not permitted in *Beith-Allah* to hold your shoes in your hand, as in other mosques. Afterwards you commence the *towaf*, the journey around the Kaaba, which must be repeated seven times."

"In which direction?"

"To the right, so that the Kaaba is constantly on your left side. The first three laps are to be completed at an expeditious pace."

"Why?"

"In remembrance of the Prophet. It was rumored that he was dangerously ill, and to dispel the rumor he did three fast laps of the Kaaba. The subsequent circuits are performed at a reverent pace. You know the prayers that must be recited. After every circuit you must kiss the holy stone. Lastly, when the *towaf* is completed you press your breast to the door of the Kaaba, spread your arms and ask Allah aloud for the forgiveness of all your sins."

"Then I am done?"

"No. You have to go to the *El Madshem* (A small, marble-covered depression, from which Abraham and Ishmael are reputed to have taken the lime when they built the Kaaba). Then to the *Mekam-Ibrahim* (The stone that is reputed to have been used by Abraham as a stepping stone during the construction of the building) where you must perform two *rikat*. Afterwards you go to the sanctified fountain Zem-Zem and, after a short prayer, drink as much water as you like. I will provide you with a flask that you can fill and return to me, as the holy water is a remedy for all illnesses of the body and the soul."

"That is the ceremony at the Kaaba. What follows then?"

"Now comes the *say*, the journey from Szafa to Merua. On the Hill of Szafa stand three open arches. There you will position yourself facing the Mosque, lift your hands towards heaven and ask Allah to accompany you on the sanctified path. Then you walk six hundred paces to the altar [See Trans. Notes Ch 13.1] at Merua. On the way you will see four stone pillars that you must pass quickly. At Merua you pray once again and then you complete the same path six more times."

"Then all is done?"

"No, then you must have your head shorn and visit Omrah, which is as far from the city as Mecca is from us at present. Only then will you have completed the holy customs and may return to us. In the month of the great pilgrimage the pilgrims have to perform more and require more time as many thousands of pilgrims are present; but you will only need two days and can return to us on the third."

The instructions were followed by various hand signs that were of no interest to me as they were mostly directed towards Hanneh. I laid myself to rest. When Halef finally appeared, he listened to see if I was asleep. He noted that I was not and asked:

"*Sihdi*, who will attend to you during my absence?"

"I, myself. Will you do me a favor Halef?"

"Yes. You know that I will do anything for you that I can and may."

"You are to bring back a flask of holy water from the holy fountain of Zem-Zem for the Sheik. Bring one for me also!"

"*Sihdi*, ask anything of me, but not this, because this I cannot possibly do. From this fountain only the 'True Believers' may drink. If I brought you this water, nothing would save me from eternal hell!"

This information was imparted with such conviction that I did not press further. After a pause he asked:

"Will you fetch the holy water yourself?"

"That I am not permitted to do!"

"You may, if you first convert to the true faith."

"That I will not do; but now let us sleep."

The next morning he rode forth as a dignified husband with his wife. He would follow the advice he had been given and maintain that he came from a distant land, and not divulge that his veiled companion was an Ateïbeh. The warriors of the tribe, who were to guard the road between Mecca and Jiddah, rode with them for some distance. Guards were also posted at the entrance to our ravine.

The first day passed without incident; the second morning I sought out the Sheik to gain his permission for a little reconnaissance. He provided me with a camel and advised me to be careful, so that our presence would not be discovered. I had hoped to ride alone but the daughter of the Sheik approached me as I mounted my camel and asked:

"*Effendi*, may I ride with you?"

"You may."

As we left the ravine I followed the path to Mecca without thought. I expected my companion to warn me against this but she remained by my side without a word. After we had ridden for a quarter of an hour she steered me off the path and said:

"Follow me, *effendi*!"

"Where to?"

"I want to see if our guard is at his post."

Barely five minutes later we spied him. He sat on a rise and stared towards the south without turning.

"He does not need to see us," she said. "Come, *Sihdi*, I will lead you; where do you wish to go!"

What did she mean by these words? She led me to the left and looked at me with a smile. Then we allowed our animals to run until finally we stopped in a narrow valley, where she dismounted and seated herself.

"Sit next to me and let us talk." She said.

More than ever, she was an enigma to me, but I did as she asked.

"Are you convinced that your faith is the only true faith, *effendi*?" she began our strange conversation.

"Certainly!" I replied.

"I too," she spoke quietly.

"You too?" I asked with amazement, as this was the first time that I had heard such an acknowledgement from the mouth of a Moslem.

"Yes, *effendi*, I know that your faith is the true one."

"And how do you know this?"

"From within myself. The first place where people existed was Paradise; there, all beings lived together in harmony. That is how Allah desired it, and therefore the true religion is the one that proposes we live by this concept. That is the religion of the Christians."

"Do you know any Christians?"

"No; but an old Turk told me about them. He said that you pray to God: '*Ile unut bizim günahler, böjle unutar-iz günahler!'* (And forgive us our trespasses, as we forgive them that trespass against us!) – Is that correct?"

"Yes."

"And that in your 'Koran' it is written: *'Allah muhabbet you, ile muhabedda kim durar, bu durar Allahda ile Allah durar onada.*' ('God is Love, and who remains in that Love, remains with God and God with him.') – Tell me if this is also correct!"

" This is correct also."

"Then yours is the correct faith. May a Christian rape a virgin?"

"No! If he did then he would suffer extreme punishment."

"You see that your religion is better than ours? With you Abu-Seïf would not have been permitted to rape me and force me to be his wife. Do you know the history of this land?"

"Yes."

"Then you know how the Turks and the Egyptians fought against us despite our sharing the same beliefs. They besmirched our mothers and impaled our fathers by the thousands, quartered them, burned them, cut off their arms, legs, noses and ears, put out their eyes and smashed their children's skulls or tore them apart. I hate this faith, yet I must keep it."

"Why must you keep it? You can at any time ..."

"Quiet!" she interrupted harshly. "I tell you my thoughts, but you shall not be my teacher! I know what I need to do: I will have my revenge – revenge against all who wronged me."

"And yet you believe that the religion of love is the true one?"

"Yes; but shall I alone love and forgive? Even for our banishment from the Holy City I will seek revenge. Guess how?"

"You tell me!"

"It is your secret desire to enter Mecca?"

"Who told you this?"

"I guessed." She answered me.

"I certainly desire to see the city."

"That is most dangerous; but I demand revenge and have therefore led you to this place. Would you complete the prescribed tasks if you were in Mecca?"

"I would rather avoid them if possible."

"You do not wish to compromise your belief and you are right to try and avoid that. Walk to Mecca; I will wait for you here!"

Was this not extraordinary? She wanted to avenge herself against Islam by allowing an infidel to defile the streets of its Holy City. As a missionary I could have done a proper job of this – although it would have taken some time and effort, but as a 'globetrotter' this was an impossible task.

"Where is Mecca?" I asked.

"When you cross this mountain, you will see it in the valley beyond."

"Why should I walk and not ride?"

"If you were to ride, someone might think you a pilgrim and watch you. If you enter the city on foot then you will be thought of as someone who has already been there and are just taking a stroll."

"And you really will wait for me?"

"Yes."

"How long a time?"

"For a period that you Franks would call four hours."

"That is quite brief."

"Consider that you might be easily spotted if you remain too long. You may only traverse the streets once and visit the Kaaba; that is enough."

She was right. It was good that I had decided to be guided by circumstance. I arose. She pointed at my weapons and shook her head.

"You look quite the native, but does an Arab carry such weapons? Leave your gun and take mine instead."

Something akin to mistrust fleetingly intruded upon my mind but I had not the least reason to hold on to it. That is why I exchanged my gun for hers and started to climb the mountain. As I reached the summit I saw Mecca before me, at a distance of about half an hour's walk, nestled in the valley below between bare and unpopulated heights. I identified the Citadel Shebel Shad and the minarehs of several mosques. *El Hamram*, the main mosque, was located in the southern part of the city.

I directed my steps towards that place. On the way I felt what an experienced soldier might feel when he suddenly hears the rolling thunder of a mighty battle.

I reached the city without incident. As I had noted the location of the mosque beforehand I did not need to ask for directions. The houses between which I strode were constructed of stone and the streets were strewn with desert sand. Shortly, I stood before the great square that formed the *Beith-Allah* and I slowly walked around the same. The four sides consisted of colonnades above which rose six minarehs. I counted two hundred and forty paces for the length and two hundred and five paces for the width. Since I wished to admire the exterior later, I entered through one of the gates. Inside sat a *Mekkaui* (inhabitant of Mecca), who traded copper flasks.

"*Salaam aaleïkum*!" I greeted him with dignity. "What does such a *kuleh* cost?"

"Two *piaster*."

"Allah bless your sons and the sons of your sons, your price is cheap. Here have the two *piaster* and I will take the *kuleh*."

I took the flask and strode through the columns. I found myself near the pulpit and removed my shoes. Now I could admire the inside of the Holy House. Near the middle stood the Kaaba. Since it was clad with the *kisua* (black silken cloth) it presented a strange sight. Seven paved paths led up to it, between these were as many grassed areas. Next to the Kaaba I noticed the sanctified fountain Zem-Zem, before which stood a few officials who distributed its waters to the pilgrims. The whole shrine did not confer a holy impression to me. Baggage- and litter-carriers ran here and there with their loads; public scribes sat under the colonnades; there were even fruit and pastry merchants. A casual glance through the rows of columns revealed an exceptional riding camel preparing to kneel so that its master could dismount. Its owner had his back to me and he motioned to a servant of the mosque to stay with his camel. I noticed this only in passing as I strode up to the fountain. I wanted to fill my flask first, but I had to wait a while for my turn. I paid a small tribute, closed the flask and slipped it into my pocket. Then I turned and – stood not ten paces from Abu-Seïf!

A mighty shock infused my limbs but luckily it did not paralyze me. In moments such as this, thought and decision work at a tenfold pace. Without wishing to draw attention to my escape, I strode with the longest possible strides towards the columns, outside of which rested Abu-Seïf's camel. This animal alone could save me. It was a pale *hedjihn*, as is found in the Jammar mountain range.

My shoes were forfeit; I did not have time to retrieve them as already I heard the outcry behind me:

"A *giaur*, a *giaur*! *Onu tutyn, bekdshiler Jamenün* – catch him, you protectors of the shrine!"

The effect that this charge had was fantastic. I had not the time to look behind me but I heard a roar like that of a waterfall, a howling similar to that of a hurricane and a pounding and stamping equal to that of a herd of at least a thousand buffalo. The time for a measured pace was over. I darted across the square, leaped between the columns, up the three steps and stood before the camel, its legs had not been bound. A well-placed punch knocked the servant aside and in the next moment I sat in the saddle with my revolver in my hand. But – would the animal obey?

"Ee – oh – ah! – Ee – oh – ah!"

Thank heaven! At the familiar call it arose in two rapid motions and off we went like the wind. Shots cracked behind me – faster, faster!

If the camel had been a cantankerous beast, as one quite often finds, then I would have been finished. But in less than three minutes I was outside of the city and only when I had climbed half the length of the hill did I dare to look behind me. Below me a teeming mass of riders pursued me. The Moslems had obviously hurried to the nearest *serais* and *khans* and mounted whatever animals they could find there.

Where could I run? To the Sheik's daughter, who would be betrayed by such a move? But I had to warn her! I coaxed my mount with constant encouragement: its swiftness was incomparable. At the summit I glanced back once more and realized that I was safe. Only a single rider had managed to close the distance between us. It was Abu-Seïf. By chance he had managed to seize a horse that was able to achieve an extraordinary pace.

I flew across the summit and down the other side. Malek's daughter sighted me. That I returned on a camel and rode at a burning pace left no doubt about the situation. She immediately mounted her camel and took my earlier mount by the reigns.

"Who has discovered you?" she called to me when we were within shouting distance.

"Abu-Seïf." I shouted back.

"*Allah akbar*! Does the rogue follow you?"

"He is fairly close."

"And many others?"

"They are further behind."

"Then stay your distance from me and flee straight over hill and dale," she instructed me.

"Why?"

"You shall see."

"First I must draw near you. Give me my weapons!"

On riding past each other we exchanged weapons; then the daughter of the desert hid behind a rocky outcrop instead of following me. Now I understood her intention: she intended to place Abu-Seïf between herself and me. He appeared momentarily on the summit. I intentionally permitted my mount to slow a little and observed that his efforts doubled at the sight. As I climbed the next slope, he galloped down the first and across the valley floor without heeding the tracks that suggested I was not alone. When I reached the summit I saw that more of the hunters had crested the first hill and I also noticed that my companion was on the move. Her plan had succeeded: Abu-Seïf was between us; and since she no longer held the reigns of the second camel but simply let it follow, he would believe that she was just one of the pursuers, should he look around.

As for myself, I had nothing to fear now and since the rest of the horde fell further behind I needed only to concern myself with the capture of Abu-Seïf. I therefore searched for a passage that would lead out of the hilly terrain and onto the plane, in a direction that was away from the camp of the Ateïbeh. At the same time I gradually reigned in my *jemmel.*

The ride lasted for some three-quarters of an hour before I finally reached open desert. I headed into the same and diligently kept Abu-Seïf out of shooting range. Now the Sheik's daughter cleared the chain of hills, but I saw also that one of the pursuers had crested the last summit, he surely rode an exceptional camel, as he consistently closed the distance between us. His animal was far superior to Abu-Seïf's horse.

Concern began to spread within me, not for myself but rather for my companion; then I saw, to my surprise, that this rider steered sideward, as though to overtake us in an arcing maneuver. I halted my camel and peered intently behind me. Was it possible? The fellow on the flying *hedjihn* looked just like Halef. How had he managed to get his hands on such an animal and how had he come to be following us? I halted my camel again to take another, closer look. Yes, it was Halef and no other. He sought to make himself known to me and waved his arms about as though he was trying to catch swallows.

I remained calm and took my gun to hand. My pursuer was within earshot.

"Rrrreee, You 'Father of the Saber'! Stay your distance, otherwise I will send you my bullet!"

"Stay my distance? You dog!" he bellowed. "I will catch you alive and return you to Mecca, you defiler of the shrine!"

I could do nothing else: I aimed and fired. To spare him I had aimed at the chest of his horse. The beast tumbled and rolled, trapping Abu-Seïf beneath, it thrashed about on top of him - once, twice -and then died. I waited for him to extricate himself but nothing happened. Either he was wounded or pretended to be so in order to lure me closer. I rode cautiously towards him and reached him simultaneously with Malek's daughter. He lay there motionless, his eyes closed.

"*Effendi*, your bullet reached him before mine!" she moaned.

"I shot his horse not him. But he could have broken his neck or something else. I will see."

I dismounted and examined him. If he was not hurt internally then he was in good shape and only unconscious. The daughter of the Ateïbeh drew her *handshar*.

"What do you intend to do?"

"To take his head."

"You will not, because I have a claim on him."

"My claim is older!"

"But mine is greater: I have vanquished him."

"That is according to the customs of this land. Will you kill him?"

"What would you do if I do not; if I choose to give him his freedom or just leave him here?"

"Then you surrender your claim and mine is valid."

"I do not surrender it."

"Then we take him with us and it will be decided what will happen to him."

Halef now joined us.

"*Mashallah*, Miracle of God! *Sihdi*, what have you done?"

"How do you come to be here?" I asked him.

"I hurried after you!"

"I certainly see this. Explain in detail!"

"*Sihdi*, you know that I have quite a lot of money. Why should I carry it in my pocket? I wanted to buy myself a *jemmel*, so I went to a merchant who lived in the southern part of the city. Hanneh was with me. Whilst I inspected the animals, among which this one was the best and the most expensive – only a Pasha or Emir could afford to buy it, a great noise erupted outside. I hurried out with the merchant and heard that a *giaur* had defiled the shrine and escaped. I thought of you at once, *Sihdi*, and I saw you an instant later racing for the heights. Everyone scrambled into the courtyard to find animals on which to pursue you. I did the same and grabbed this *hedjihn*. After I commanded Hanneh to hurry to the camp and inform the Sheik of what had happened, I gave the merchant, who did not wish to lend me this animal, a slap and rode to catch you. The other pursuers fell behind; now I have you and also this *jemmel*."

"It is not yours."

"We will discuss that later, *Sihdi*. The pursuers are still behind us – we cannot stay here. What shall we do with the 'Father of the Saber and Deceit'?"

"We bind him on the spare camel and take him with us. He will eventually come to."

"And where do we run to?"

"I know of a place," replied the daughter of the Ateïbeh. " You know it also Halef; my father the Sheik told you in case we did not meet at the camp."

"You mean the Atafrah cave?"

"Yes. Hanneh would have guided you there. Only the leaders of the Ateïbeh know of this cave and they are not currently there. Come, help me bind the prisoner."

With the aid of six hands it was not difficult to bind Abu-Seïf upon the camel that had carried me from the camp to the vicinity of the city. Malek's daughter took everything that Abu-Seïf carried on his person; then we mounted and hurried towards the southeast.

Thus I successfully escaped. I did not think then that I would once again see Mecca, therefore I save the description of the city and its sights until later.

On the way I had to suffer Halef's reproaches.

"*Sihdi*," he said, "have I not told you that no infidel may visit the Holy City? You almost lost your life!"

"Why did you deny me my request when I asked for water?"

"Because I could not fulfill it."

"Now I have obtained the water myself!"

"You were at the sanctified fountain?"

"Look here! This is genuine water from Zem-Zem!"

"*Allah kerihm*, God is merciful, *Sihdi*! He has made you a 'True Believer' and even a hajji. A *giaur* may not enter the city; but he who has water from Zem-Zem is a hajji and therefore a true Moslem. Have I not constantly said that you would be converted, whether you were willing or not?"

It was a bold, though humorous, statement of the facts; but it also had the effect of calming the Moslem conscience of my good Halef, therefore I did not intend to set his perception to rights.

The landscape around Mecca is extraordinarily dry and wherever there is a well there surely is the center of a village or at least a transient camp. Such places we had to avoid and so it was that, despite the heat of the day, we did not stop until we had reached a place that abounded with broken rock. We followed the Sheik's daughter over gravel and scree and among mighty stone boulders until we reached a cleft as wide as a camel.

"This is the cave," said our guide. "Even the animals can enter if we remove the saddles."

"We stay here?" I asked.

"Yes, until the Sheik comes."

"Will he come?"

"He will surely come, because Hanneh has notified him. If an Ateïbeh does not come to the camp then he can be found here at the cave. Dismount and follow me!"

Abu-Seïf had regained consciousness, but had not uttered a word during the entire trip and his eyes remained closed. He was brought into the cave first. When one penetrated the cleft it got ever wider and finally became a room large enough for forty or fifty men and animals. The greatest advantage was the water that had collected in the rear of the cave. After we had moved the prisoner and the animals to safety we searched for large bundles of *rattam* grass outside, which had the unique quality of burning equally well whether it was green or dry. This would be used only at night, for during the day the smoke would easily betray our sanctuary. In any case, we did not really need to fear discovery. Our way here had been mostly over rocky ground, which would not make tracking easy.

I made a peculiar discovery when I searched the saddlebag of my camel: it contained a substantial amount of money.

Chapter 14

We were tired, as were our animals; the bonds of our prisoner were secure and we could sleep peacefully. Nonetheless, I divided the watch between Halef and myself. In this manner the last hour of the day passed and the night descended. At dawn I had the watch. Roused by the sound of an approach, I peered out of the fissure and saw a man, he was creeping carefully towards our hiding place. I recognized him as an Ateïbeh and stepped out of the crevice.

"Allah be thanked that I see you, *effendi*!" he greeted me. "The Sheik has sent me ahead to discover if you were here. Now I need not return, as that is the sign that I have found you."

"Whom did you expect to find here besides myself?"

"Your servant Halef, the *Bint el Ateïbeh* and perhaps even the captive Abu-Seïf."

"Why would you expect to find all of them?"

"*Effendi*, it is not difficult to guess. Hanneh came to our camp with just two camels and told us that you had been in Mecca and had then fled. The *Bint el Malek* accompanied you and surely would not have left you, even though you did commit a great sin. Halef chased after you and beyond the hills your pursuers found the horse of the Jeheïne shot dead, but Abu-Seïf was not there. You must therefore have captured him. Of course only we could have guessed this and no other."

"When will the Sheik arrive?"

"Perhaps within the hour."

"Then come inside."

He did not even honor the prisoner with a glance but immediately lay down to sleep. Within the time indicated a small caravan arrived at the cave. Everything was unloaded and moved inside. I expected to be reproached by the Sheik. However, his first question was,

"Have you captured the Jeheïne?"

"Yes." I responded.

"He is here?"

"Unharmed and in good health."

"Then I will pass judgment on him!"

It was noon by the time everything was organized. Now the court could commence. But before this happened I had an interesting conversation with Halef.

"*Sihdi,* permit me a question." He began.

"Speak!" I urged him.

"Is it not true that you are aware of all the things that you have written about me and Hanneh?"

"All of them."

"When must I release Hanneh?"

"As soon as you have completed the pilgrimage."

"But I have not yet concluded it!"

"What remains outstanding?"

"In Mecca, nothing. Since all went quickly I have completed everything there. But I desire to keep my wife and it occurred to me that a true hajj requires a trip to Medina."

"That is correct. What does Hanneh say to this?"

"*Sihdi*, she loves me. Believe it – she told me herself!"

"And you love her?"

"Very much! Is it not written that Allah took a rib from Adam and created Eve from it? Beneath the rib there is the heart and does not the heart of a man yearn for his wife."

"But what will the Sheik say?"

"That is what concerns me, *Sihdi*!"

"And you have no other worries?"

"No."

"And what about me? What might I have to say?"

"You? Oh, you will give your consent, for I will not leave you, as long as you will have me."

"Your wife could not travel with us; think about that!"

"Neither should she. I will leave her with her tribe until I can return."

"Halef, that is a sacrifice that I would not demand of you. But since you love each other I must do all that I can to see that you may keep her as your wife. Perhaps the Sheik can be persuaded so that you will not need to release her."

"*Sihdi*, I will not release her, even if we have to elope. Oh she knows that I am Hajji Halef Omar Ben Hajji Abul Abbas Ibn Hajji Dawud al Gossarah, and she would follow me to the ends of the earth!"

With this self-confident assurance he proudly departed. Meanwhile a circle had formed, into which Abu-Seïf had been carried. I was requested to take part in the trial and seated myself next to Sheik Malek.

"*Effendi*," he began, "I have heard that you have a claim against this man and I know that this is the truth. Will you surrender him to us or do you wish to participate in the deciding of his fate?"

"I will participate in the decision, I and Halef, as he too has a claim against Abu-Seïf."

"Then remove the prisoner's bonds!"

He was released but remained motionless, as though already dead.

"Abu-Seïf, arise before these men and prepare to defend yourself!"

He remained on the ground without opening his eyes.

"He has lost the power of speech, you all see it; why should we bother to speak with him? He knows what he has done as do we all; what use are words and questions? I say that he must die and serve as food for the jackals, hyenas and vultures. He who agrees with this verdict, let him declare it."

Everyone murmured approval. I alone wanted to veto the judgment but was hindered by an unforeseen event. Upon the Sheik's last words, the prisoner suddenly sprang up and darted between the Ateïbeh towards the fissure. A loud cry of despair echoed from all around and then everyone leaped up to pursue the escapee. I was the only one who remained behind. Abu-Seïf had burdened himself with huge transgressions and according to the laws of the desert deserved death; despite this it would have been impossible for me to agree with that verdict. Perhaps he would manage to escape. If this was the case, then we could not linger at the cave a moment longer.

I remained alone for some time. The first to return was the old Sheik. He had lagged behind the younger men.

"Why did you not pursue him, *effendi*?" he asked me.

"Surely your brave men will capture him without my aid. They will catch him, will they not?"

"I do not know. Abu-Seïf is a famous runner, and as we exited the cave he had already disappeared. If we do not catch him we will have to depart, as he now knows the location of the cave."

Moment by moment more men returned. They had not seen Abu-Seïf and neither had they spied his tracks. After some time Halef returned and lastly the Sheik's daughter, whose nostrils flared with rage. A short exchange of opinions yielded that no one had seen him. The frustrating circumstance that permitted only one person at a time to follow him through the narrow entrance had given him a lead, and the terrain outside had aided his escape.

"Listen, you men," said the Sheik, "he will betray our hiding place. Should we depart immediately or should we try to find and catch him with the aid of our animals? If we ride in circles around the area it is perhaps possible that we might spy him."

"We will not flee, we would rather seek him out," said the Sheik's daughter.

The others agreed.

"Well then, take your camels and follow me. Whoever returns the prisoner – dead or alive – will receive a great reward."

Halef now stepped forward and spoke: "I have already earned the reward. 'The Father of the Saber' lies outside – dead!"

"Where did you capture him?" asked the Sheik in surprise.

"Lord, you must know that my *Sihdi* is a master in battle and in the art of reading the *makam* (spoor); he has taught me to read tracks in the sand, in the grass, on the earth and upon the rock. He has taught me how to think when following quarry. I was the first who left the cave after Abu-Seïf; but I did not see him. I ran, first left then right, and since I did not find him I thought that he was clever enough to hide immediately upon leaving the cave. I looked behind the rocks and found him. There was a short struggle during which my dagger invaded his wicked heart. I will show you his body."

I again remained in the cave, as the others followed Halef to view the late Abu-Seïf.

Soon they returned, rejoicing.

"What do you demand as your reward?" asked the Sheik of brave little Halef.

"Lord, I come from a distant land, to which I will not return again. Do you consider me worthy to join your tribe."

"You want to become an Ateïbeh? What does your master say to that?"

"He is in agreement. Is that not true, *Sihdi*?"

"Yes," I answered. "I add my wish to his."

"As far as I am concerned, I would agree on the spot," declared the Sheik. "However I must question my people, as the adoption of a stranger is an important decision that may consume a great deal of time. Do you have relatives close by?"

"No."

"Are you burdened by a blood feud?"

"No."

"Are you a Sunnite or a Shiite?"

"A follower of the Sunna."

"You truly have never had a wife or children?"

"No."

"In that case, we can immediately bring it before the council."

"Then decide also upon another matter!"

"What other matter?"

"*Sihdi*, will you speak in my place?"

I arose from the ground and assumed a dignified posture. Then I started my speech:

"Listen to my words, oh Sheik, and may Allah open your heart so that my words find favor with your will. I am Kara Ben Nemsi, an Emir under the *talebs* and a hero of Frankistan. I came to Africa and to this land to meet the inhabitants and to perform great deeds. To achieve this I needed a servant who was conversant in all the dialects of the east and the west, one who was clever and wise and not afraid of any lion, panther or man. I found Hajji Halef Omar Ben Hajji Abul Abbas Ibn Hajji Dawud al Gossarah and am satisfied with him in all measures to this day.

He is as strong as a boar, loyal as a hound, clever like a fennec fox and fast as an antelope. We have battled on the chott; we breached the salt-crust there and yet saved each other. We have subdued the animals of the field and the desert.

We have defied the evil *smum* (samum – hot desert wind). Yes, we have even gone to the border of Nubia to rescue a captive, a flower of flowers, from the power of her tormentor. We traveled to the *Belad el Arab* and what we endured is already known to you, as you were witness to it.

Hajji Halef then took your granddaughter, Hanneh, to Mecca. She became his assumed wife and he signed a contract to return her. Now, however, Allah has guided their hearts with love and they do not desire to part. You are Hajji Malek Iffandi Ibn Achmed Chadid el Eini Ben Abul Ali el Besami Abu Shehab Abdolatif el Hanifi, the wise and brave Sheik of the sons of the Ateïbeh. Your insight will tell you that I would not easily part with a companion such as Halef; but I wish him only happiness and that is why I plead with you to adopt him into the tribe of the Ateïbeh and to tear up the contract in which he has promised to return his wife to you. I know that you will grant this wish, and I will spread your fame and the fame of your tribe through the entire west, once I return to my homeland. *Salaam*!"

All had listened intently. Malek responded:

"*Effendi*, I know that you are a famous Emir of the *Nemsi*, although your name is as short as the blade of a woman's knife. You ventured forth like a Sultan, who commits great deeds without being recognized, and yet the children of our children will relate your heroic deeds. Hajji Halef Omar is to you like a Vizier, whose life belongs to his Sultan, and you came into our tents in order to grant us a great honor. We love you and him – and we will unite our voices in order to make him a son of our tribe. Also I will speak with his wife, and if she wishes to remain with him, I will tear up the contract as you have requested, for he is a brave warrior, who killed Abu-Seïf, the thief and robber. Now, however, permit us to prepare a meal to celebrate the death of our enemy and to then undertake the discussion in a worthy manner. You are our friend and brother, although you have different beliefs than us. *Salaam*, *effendi*!"

A Desert Battle

Chapter 15

"The Lord will be terrible unto them: for he will famish all the gods of the earth; and men shall worship him, everyone from his place, even all the isles of the heathen. And he will stretch out his hand against the north, and destroy Assyria; and will make Nineveh a desolation, and dry like a wilderness. And flocks shall lie down in the midst of her, all the beasts of the nations: both the cormorant and the bittern shall lodge in the upper lintels of it; their voice shall sing in the windows; desolation shall be in the thresholds: for he shall uncover the cedar work. This is the rejoicing city that dwelt carelessly, that said in her heart, I am, and there is none beside me: how is she become a desolation, a place for beasts to lie down in? Every one that passeth by her shall hiss, and wag his hand." – (Zephaniah 2:11, 2:13-2:15) –

I thought of these words by the prophet Zephaniah as we pulled our boat over to the right-hand shore of the Tigris by the last glimmer of day. The whole area to the right and the left of the river is an immensely solemn, vastly desolate graveyard. The rays of the sun anoint the ruins of Rome and Athens, and the great monuments of ancient Egypt reach towards heaven. They speak clearly enough of the might, riches and art of the people who erected them. But here by the two rivers, the Euphrates and the Tigris, lie piles of devastated ruins over which the Bedouin carelessly ride, often without an inkling that below the hooves of their horses the joy and pain of thousands of years lies buried. Where is the tower that the people of the 'Land of Sinear' [Sinear or Shinar: an ancient country on the lower courses of the Tigris and Euphrates rivers – refers to the Tower of Babel] built when they spoke in one language: "Come, let us build a city and a tower, the tip of which touches heaven, so that we might make a name for ourselves!"?

They constructed the city and the tower, but those places are now desolate. They desired to make a name for themselves, but the names of the tribes that lived successively in this city and practiced their idolatry in the tower, as well as the names of the dynasties and governors who were steeped in gold and in the blood of millions, they have faded, and even the greatest efforts and the best research cannot guess at their identities.

But how did I come to be on the Tigris, and upon this steamer that carried us towards the rapids at Chelab?

I traveled with the Ateïbeh into the *El Nahman* desert, as I did not dare to show myself in the western part of that land. When we neared Maskat I was enticed to visit that city. I did so on my own and unaccompanied. I admired its famous walls, its well laid streets, its mosques and Portuguese churches; was awed by the *Belujitanian* [possibly gypsy mercenaries] bodyguard of the *Imam* and finally seated myself in one of the open coffee houses to enjoy a cup of *keshreh.* This beverage is brewed from the shell of the coffee bean and is spiced with cinnamon and cloves. My enjoyment was marred by a shadow that had darkened the doorway. I looked up and saw a figure that demanded lengthy scrutiny:

A tall, gray stovepipe hat sat atop a long, narrow head, which was, with regard to hair growth, an utter desert. An endlessly wide, thin-lipped mouth laid itself in the path of the nose, which was sharp and already quite long enough, yet it betrayed its intention to extend itself to the chin. The bare, desiccated neck jutted out of a very wide, wrap-around shirt collar that had been faultlessly ironed; this was followed by a gray-checkered tie, a gray-checkered vest, a gray-checkered frock-coat and gray-checkered trousers, likewise-patterned gaiters and dust-gray boots. In his right hand, the gray-checkered man carried an instrument that was similar to a hoe and in the left he held a double-barreled pistol. From his breast-pocket a folded newspaper peeped forth curiously.

"*Wermyn kahwe*!" he demanded in a jarring voice that sounded not unlike a sparrow-rattle. [a noisemaker].

He sat down on a *senïeh*, which would have ordinarily served as a table, but was employed by him as an armchair. He received the coffee, dipped his nose towards the brew and snuffled the aroma, then he poured the contents out onto the street and placed the cup on the ground.

"*Wermyn tütün* - give me tobacco!" he now ordered.

He was given an already lit pipe, drew upon it once, blew the smoke out through his nose, spat and threw the pipe down next to the cup.

"*Wermyn ...*" - he thought hard, but the Turkish word would not come, and perhaps he did not know Arabic either. Therefore he rattled abruptly: "*Wermyn* roast beef!".

The *kawehdshi* did not understand him.

"Roast beef!" he repeated, whilst enacting a pantomime with his mouth and ten fingers that indicated eating.

"*Kebab*!" I interpreted for the host, who immediately departed through the door to prepare the meal. This dish consists of small cubed pieces of meat that are placed on a skewer then roasted over a fire. The Englishman now turned his attention towards me.

"Arab?" he asked.

"No."

"Turk?"

"No."

Now he drew his thin eyebrows upward in expectation.

"Englishman?"

"No. I am a German."

"A German? What are you doing here?"

"Drinking coffee!"

"Very well! Who are you?"

"I am a writer!"

"Ah! What are you doing in Maskat?"

"Looking around."

"And then what?"

"I don't know yet."

"Do you have money?"

"Yes."

"And your name?"

I told him my name. His mouth opened in such a manner that his thin lips formed an even-sided rectangle, which permitted a clear view of his wide, long teeth. His eyebrows climbed higher than before and the tip of his nose wiggled as if it desired to scout out what the cavity beneath it intended to say. He then grabbed at his frock-coat and extracted a notebook, thumbed through the pages, shot up in the air, grabbed his hat and honored me with a bow.

"Welcome, sir; you are known to me!"

"Ah . . . me?"

"Yes, very!"

"May I ask, from where?"

"I am a friend of Sir John Raffley, a member of the Traveler-club, London, Near-Street 47." (See: >Deutscher Hausschatz<, VI. Jahrgang, Seite 47) [This is a referral by the author, Karl May, to an article or reference concerning the above mentioned club, appearing in the German magazine 'Deutscher Hausschatz' or 'German Home Treasure', the sixth (VI) annual publication, page number 47.]

"Really? You know Sir Raffley? Where is he now?"

"On a trip – here or there – who knows. You were with him in Ceylon?"

"Yes, of course."

"Elephant hunting?"

"Yes."

"Then at sea aboard the Girl-Robber?" [See Trans. Notes Ch 15.1]

"That is right."

"Do you have time to spare?"

"Hmm! Why do you ask?"

"I have read of Babylon – Niniveh – excavations – 'Devil Worshippers'. I want to go there – excavate – fetch a 'fowling-bull' – give it to the British museum. Cannot speak Arabic – would gladly procure a guide. Are you interested – pay very well!"

"May I ask your name?"

"Lindsay, David Lindsay – no title, won't need to call me Sir Lindsay."

"You really intend to go to the Euphrates and Tigris?"

"Yes. Have a steamboat – journey up there – disembark – steamboat waits, or goes back to Baghdad – buy a horse and a camel – travel, hunt, excavate, make gift to British museum, tell of adventures at the Traveler-club. Will you join me?"

"I prefer to be independent."

"Of course! You can leave me whenever – will pay well, very well – only come with me."

"Who else will be with us?"

"As many as you like – however I would prefer you, me and two servants."

"When do you intend to depart?"

"The day after tomorrow – tomorrow – today – immediately!"

This was an offer that could not suit me better. I did not think about it for long before I agreed. Of course I insisted on the condition that I was free to leave anytime. He led me to the harbor where the charming little steamboat was berthed and I concluded within a half an hour that I could not wish for a better companion. He wanted to hunt lions and all sort of beasts, wanted to see the 'Devil Worshippers' and most of all excavate a 'fowling-bull' as he called it – a winged bull, and donate it to the British museum. These plans were adventurous, and for this reason were to my liking. I had encountered many strange people during my travels and Lindsay was certainly one of them.

Unfortunately he did not permit me to return to the Ateïbeh. A messenger was sent to get my things and notify Halef of where I would be traveling. When the messenger returned, he told me that Halef, with one of the Ateïbeh, would travel to the land of the Abu Salman and Shammar-Arabs in order to negotiate the incorporation of the Ateïbeh into their tribe. He would take my *hedjihn* with him and eventually catch up with me.

I was glad to receive this message. That Halef had been chosen to act as ambassador proved to me once again that he had become the favorite of his father-in-law. We traveled up the Persian Gulf, saw Basra and Baghdad and afterwards steamed up the Tigris to the place where we docked today . . . .

Upstream of our landing place Zab-asfal joined the Tigris, and on the opposite shore was a thick bamboo jungle. As I have mentioned previously; night approached - yet Lindsay insisted that we erect the tents on shore. I really did not feel like doing this but could not leave them to it and so joined in. The crew of the steamboat consisted of four people; it would return to Baghdad at dawn, and therefore the Englishman decided, against my counsel, that everything, including the four horses that he had bought in Baghdad, should be unloaded.

"It would be better if we did not, sir," I warned him.

"Why?"

"Because we can do it tomorrow by the light of day."

"It can also be done this evening – I pay well!"

"The horses, as well as ourselves, would be safer aboard the vessel than on land."

"Are there thieves – robbers – murderers, here?"

"The Arabs should never be trusted. We are not yet prepared!"

"We will not trust them, but we will be prepared – we have guns; every scoundrel will be shot down!"

He could not be dissuaded from his design. Two hours later we were finished with the work; two tents were erected, and between these and the shore the horses were secured. After dinner, we bedded down. I had the first watch, the two servants the second and third and Lindsay took the fourth watch. The night was beautiful, before us the water rushed past in a broad bed and behind us rose the heights of the Jebel Jehennem. The brightness of the firmament illuminated everything sufficiently, but the land on which I stood was still an enigma. Its past was like the waters of the Tigris that disappeared below in the shadow of the jungle. Here were memories of a combination of great nations and great states bound together with the titles of Assyria, Babylonia and Chaldea, but these memories were like the reflection of a dream, the details of which have been forgotten.

When my watch was over, I awoke one of Lindsay's servants and instructed him with care. His name was Bill, he was an Irishman who gave the impression that the power of his muscles was thirty times greater than the power of his mind. He grinned very mischievously at my instructions and then commenced patrolling up and down. I retired to my tent and drifted off to sleep.

I did not wake voluntarily but was shaken by the arm. Lindsay stood before me in his gray-checkered suit, which he had decided to continue wearing even in the desert.

"Sir, wake up!" He implored.

I jumped to my feet and asked: "Did something happened?"

"Hmm – yes!"

"What?"

"Unpleasant!"

"What?"

"Horses are gone!"

"The horses? Have they torn themselves loose?"

"I don't know."

"Were they still there when you took over the watch?"

"Yes!" He confirmed.

"But you had the watch?"

"Yes!" He agreed.

"Where were you?"

"There." He pointed to an isolated hill, which was somewhat removed from our tents.

"There; why there?"

"Because it is probably a ruins hill – went there because of fowling-bull."

"And when you returned, the horses were gone?"

"Yes!"

I stepped outside and examined the stakes. The ends of the lines were still there; the animals had been cut loose.

"They did not tear themselves loose; they were stolen!" I announced.

He formed the familiar parallelogram with his lips and chuckled in amusement.

"Yes! By whom?"

"By thieves!"

He appeared to find this even more amusing.

"Very well, by thieves – where are they – what are their names?"

"I don't know!" I answered, exasperated.

"No – I don't know either – nice, very nice! – an adventure!"

"Not an hour has passed since the theft. If we wait another five minutes it will be light enough to read the spoor."

"Nice – wonderful! You were a scout – find tracks – chase – shoot dead – capital fun – pay well, very well!"

He stepped into his tent to prepare what he thought necessary. Shortly, by the light of dawn, I concluded that there had been six men and informed him of my discovery.

"Six? – How many are we?"

"Just two. Two must remain with the tents, and the boat must also remain here until we return."

"Yes! I will order it and then we go!"

"Are you a good runner or shall I take Bill?"

"Bill? Pah! Why did I come to the Tigris! Adventure! Run well – run like a deer!"

After the necessary instruction had been given, he threw the strange hoe, as well as his gun, over his shoulder and followed me. It was important to catch the thieves before they joined a larger group and that is why we hurried as fast as we could. The long checkered legs of my companion held out, it was enjoyable to have him run with me.

As it was springtime, the ground resembled not so much a desert as a meadow; the flowers erupted from the earth in clusters. We had not run far before our trouser legs were colored with pollen. Due to the height of the vegetation, the trail was easy to see. It finally led us to a tributary that flowed from the Jebel Jehennem in a lively fashion. On this shore the track led to a place that was trampled with the hoof marks of many horses, and closer examination revealed that from here on instead of the tracks of four horses there were ten. Two of the six thieves had walked back to this place from our camp, instead of riding. When they reached here they all mounted and continued on, leading our horses.

Lindsay grimaced, displeased. "Miserable – deadly annoyed!" he grumbled.

"About what?" I asked.

"They will escape!" He complained.

"Why?"

"They all have horses now – we are on foot."

"Pah! We will overtake them nevertheless, if you can keep pace; but this is not even necessary. One should not only look but also see and deduce."

"Then deduce!"

"Did these people come upon our camp by chance?"

"Hmm!"

"Perhaps, but perhaps not. It would appear to me that they followed our steamer by land, which laid to each evening. If that is the case, then their trail leads west, but only because they need to cross this river and they did not dare to do so with strange horses."

"Therefore the detour?"

"Yes. They will seek a ford or some place where they can cross easily before they will resume their original direction."

"Wonderful, good – very good!"

He threw off his clothes and stepped up to the riverbank.

"Well, sir, are you a good swimmer?" I asked him.

"Yes!"

"It is not without hazard here, if one wishes to keep his clothes as well as his weapons dry. Wrap your clothes like a turban around your hat!" I suggested.

"Good – very well – will do it!"

I too disrobed and fashioned a turban, which I placed on my head; then we entered the water. The Englishman was truly a good swimmer as well as an excellent runner. We reached the other shore without incident and clothed ourselves once more.

Lindsay let me lead without comment. We ran about another two English miles to the south and then turned west where the high ground would provide us with a good all round view. We climbed the hill and looked about. As far as the eye could see, not a living being was visible.

"Nothing! - Nothing - not a soul . . . miserable!"

"Hmm, I do not see anything either!"

"If you erred – Oho, what then?"

"Then we still have time to track them from the river on. No one has yet managed to steal a horse from me without punishment; even now I will not return until I have all four animals again."

"I too."

"No. You must remain with your property."

"Property? Pah!" He scoffed, "if it is gone, then I buy it again – I am happy to pay for adventure – very well."

"Wait! Does something move out there?" I cautioned.

"Where?"

"There!" I indicated the direction with my hand.

He opened his eyes and mouth wide and stood with legs spread wide. His nose quivered as he drew in air – it appeared as though this olfactory organ had the ability to see or at least possessed some crude optical or premonitory sense.

"Correct – I see it too!"

"It is coming towards us."

"Yes! If it is them, shoot them dead!" He declared.

"Sir, they are people!" I objected.

"Thieves! They must die – die unconditionally!" He stated flatly.

"Then I am sorry, but I must leave you," I said regretfully.

"Leave? Why?"

"I will defend my skin if I am attacked, but I murder no human being without reason. I believe you to be an Englishman!"

"Well! Englishman – nobleman – gentleman – will not kill them – only take the horses!" He acquiesced.

"It appears that it is truly them!"

"Yes! Ten creatures – agreed!"

"Four are rider-less and six mounted."

"Hmm! You are a good scout – you are right – Sir John Raffley spoke volumes – stay with me – pay well, very well!"

"Are you a good shot?"

"Hmm, rather!"

"Then come, we have to retreat so that we are not discovered. Our field of operation is between the hill and the river. Let us head south for another ten minutes, there the heights are so close to the water that it will be impossible for them to escape."

We ran at full tilt down the hill and soon reached the place that I had indicated. Reeds and bamboo bordered the river and at the foot of the hill there grew mimosa and wormwood scrub. We had enough room to hide ourselves.

"What now?" asked the Englishman.

"Conceal yourself here in the reeds and let the company pass. I will hide in the mimosa at the other end of this pass, and when the thieves are between us, we both come out of hiding. I alone will shoot, since I perhaps understand how to read the circumstances better, and you will use your gun only at my request or if your life is threatened."

"Well – good, very well – excellent adventure!"

He disappeared in the reeds and I chose my hiding place. After a short while we heard the sound of hooves. They approached and then passed by where Lindsay was hidden, without any sense of foreboding or need for vigilance. I saw the Englishman rise from the reeds and I likewise stepped from my hiding place.

The thieves immediately reigned in their horses. I had one gun slung over my shoulder and the other, the Henry carbine, I held in my hands.

"*Salaam aaleïkum*!" I said.

The friendly greeting astounded them.

"*Aaleïk* –" answered one of them. "What are you doing here?"

"I wait for my brothers who shall help me."

"What kind of help do you need?"

"You see that I am without a horse. How should I cross the desert? You have four animals to spare; will you sell me one?"

"We do not sell these horses!"

"I hear that you are Allah's favorites. You do not want to sell the horse because your heart desires to make a gift of it to me."

"Allah heal your senses! I will not give away a horse either."

"Oh, you example of mercy, you will taste the joy of paradise fourfold because you will not only give me one horse but all four, as I have need of all of them!"

"*Allah kerihm* – God is gracious! This man is delirious, certainly crazy."

"My brother, think about it, crazy people take what is not freely given! Look behind you! Perhaps you will give him what you deny me."

Only now, when they saw the Englishman did they comprehend their situation completely. They quickly took hold of their lances and readied themselves for a fight.

"What do you want?"

"Our horses, which you stole at the break of day."

"You are a crazy man! If we had taken your horses you could not have caught up with us on foot!"

"You think not? You know that these four horses belong to the Franks, who came by ship. What makes you think that the Franks will permit themselves to be robbed without retribution, and that they are not smarter than you! I observed that you made a detour at the river, so we swam across to get ahead of you. You however, permitted yourselves to be deceived. I do not wish to spill your blood; therefore I ask you to return the horses of your own free will. Then you can go where you will!"

He laughed. "You are but two men, and we are six."

"Very well! Then everyone does what he desires!"

"Get out of the way!"

He lowered his lance, which was decorated with ostrich feathers, and spurred his horse towards me. I raised the Henry carbine: my shot cracked and horse and rider crashed to the ground. In less than a minute I aimed and shot another five times. All of the horses dropped to the ground and only ours, which had been tied together, remained standing. The one who had held them, held them no more. We used the moment of confusion to mount and ride away.

Behind us arose the angry cries of the Arabs. We were unconcerned, we sorted out the reigns of our horses and rode away laughing.

"Magnificent – grand – wonderful adventure – worth a hundred pounds! Two of us, six of them – they took our four horses, we took their six – priceless – lovely!"

"Lucky everything went so remarkably well, sir. If the animals had spooked then we would not have got away so quickly and could easily have caught a few bullets."

"Do we also make a detour or do we go straight on?"

"Straight on. We know our horses; our crossing will be easy."

We reached our tents in good time and soon after our arrival the boat departed, leaving us alone in the desert. Lindsay had wanted to take much luggage as well as provisions, but I had managed to dissuade him. Anyone who wants to know about a land must also learn to limit themselves to its resources, and a rider must never take more than his animal can easily carry. Besides, we were well supplied with munitions, which were imperative, and the 'nobleman' had a substantial amount of money, which would permit us to cater for our travel needs for many years.

"Now we are alone by the Tigris," he said. "Now dig immediately for fowling-bulls and other artifacts!"

The good man had certainly read a lot and heard about the excavations at Khorsabad, Kufjundshik, Hammum Ali, Nimrud, Keshaf and El Hather and had come to the conclusion that he would enrich the British Museum with one of his own finds and thereby become a famous man.

"At this very moment?" I asked, "That will not work!"

"Why? I have my hoe."

"Oh, you will not achieve much with this mattock. Whoever wishes to dig here first needs to come to an agreement with the government . . . "

"Government? Which?"

"Turkish."

"Pah! Did Niniveh belong to the Turks?"

"Certainly not, since at that time the Turks did not exist. But the ruins now belong to the Turks who own the ground and the earth, although the arm of the Sultan is no longer so mighty here. The Arabian nomads are the real masters, and he who wishes to dig here will first need to establish friendly relations with them, otherwise neither his property nor his life will be safe. That is why I advised you to bring gifts for the chiefs with you."

"The silk robes?"

"Yes; they are most desired and take up little room in transport."

"Well then let us establish friendly relations – but at once and immediately – no?"

I knew that he would remain focused on his excavations and decided not to attempt to deter him from it.

"I am with you. Now the only question remains, which chief to approach first."

"Well – guess!"

"The most powerful tribe is named El Shammar. But they have their pastures far up on the southern slope of the Sindshar Mountains and on the right shore of the Thathar."

"How far are the Sindshar from here?"

"A whole degree of longitude."

"Very far! What other Arabs are here?"

"The Obeïde, Abu-Salman, Abu-Ferhan and others; but one can never determine exactly where one should seek these hordes, as they are always in motion. When their herds have completely grazed one pasture then they take down their tents and move on. At the same time the tribes live in eternal, bloody hostilities with one another; therefore they need to avoid one another and that adds to the uncertainty of their lives."

"Nice life – much adventure – find many ruins – excavate a lot – wonderful – excellent!"

"It would be best if we ride into the desert and ask the first Bedouin we meet where the closest tribe is located."

"Good – well – very nice! Ride now and ask!"

"We can stay here tonight!"

"Stay and not dig? No – doesn't work! Tents down and away!"

I had to abide by his will, and more thought on the matter led me to the conclusion that due to today's conflict it would be better to leave this place. We dismantled the light tents, which were loaded onto the horses of our servants; we then mounted and headed in the direction of the Sabakah Lake.

It was a wonderful ride across a flower-strewn steppe. Every step the horses took stirred up pleasant new aromas. I could not compare even the gentlest and most fertile North American prairie to this place. The direction we had taken proved to be fortuitous, as three riders raced towards us after less than an hour's ride. They made a pretty picture with their flying robes and ostrich feathers. They came towards us amidst a loud war cry.

"They roar. Will they prick?" asked the Englishman.

"No. That is the customary greeting of these people. He who appears timid is not considered a man."

"Will be a man!"

He was true to his word and did not bat an eyelid as one of them aimed the sharp lance tip at his chest and only pulled it away when he suddenly checked his horse just before the tip touched.

"*Salaam aaleïkum*! Where are you bound?" greeted one.

“Of which tribe are you?” I asked.

“Of the tribe of the Haddedihn, which belongs to the great nation of the Shammar.”

“Who is your Sheik?”

“His name is Mohammed Emin.”

“Is he far from here?”

“If you desire to go to him, we will accompany you.”

They turned about and joined us. While we – our servants at the rear – sat in our saddles in a dignified manner, the Arabs raced around us to show off their riding skill. Their prime trick consisted of their ability to reign their horses to a stop from a full run, which could quite easily injure the horse. I believed that I could claim that a Red Indian on a mustang could better their performance. The Englishman liked the exhibition of these people.

“Grand! Hmm, I could not do it – would break my neck!”

“I have seen other horsemen.”

“Ah! Where?”

“On a life and death ride in the American woods, on a frozen river, on a horse that was unshod; or in a rocky canyon, that is something else.”

“Hmm! Will also go to America - ride in the woods – on a frozen river – in a canyon – nice adventure – magnificent! What are they saying?”

“They are greeting us and continue to ask about our destination; they will lead us to their Sheik. His name is Mohammed Emin and he is the chief of the Haddedihn.”

“Brave people?”

“All these people call themselves brave and they are to a point. And it is no wonder. The women have to do everything while the men ride, smoke, rob, fight, gossip and loaf about.”

“Wonderful life – grand – like to be a Sheik – much excavation – find many a fowling-bull to send to London – hmm!”

Moment by moment the steppe became more populated and we became aware that we were approaching the Haddedihn camp. They were, for the most part, still on the move as we reached them. It is not easy to describe an Arabian tribe on the move to new pasture. I had previously crossed the Sahara and part of Arabia and have seen and become acquainted with many western Arabs; here however a different picture unfolded. Just as there exists a difference between the oasis of the Sahara and this land, which in Holy Scripture was called the ‘land of Sinear’ – one can also recognize the difference in the lifestyles of their inhabitants.

Here we rode on an almost endless *merdsh* (field, prairie), which did not bear the slightest resemblance to an *uah* (oasis) of the west. It was more like a gigantic carpet of flowers covering the savanna. Here it appeared that the fearsome *samum* (desert wind) never raged. Here there was no sign of the wandering dunes. Here was no fissured and wretched wadi, and one could believe that here, no *fata morgana* [mirage] possessed the power to fool the tired and lonely wanderer. The wide-open spaces were decorated with fragrant life and the people showed no sign of that 'desert disposition' that no one west of the Nile can escape. There was, over this colorful landscape, no hue that reminded me in the least of the scorched and often bloody gloom and deadly light of the great desert.

We found ourselves now in the midst of a herd of sheep and camels that numbered in the thousands. As far as the eye could see – to the right and the left of us, ahead and behind – surged a sea of grazing and wandering beasts. We saw long ranks of oxen and donkeys that were loaded with black tents, colorful carpets, huge cauldrons and all manner of other things. Old men and women, who were incapable of walking or sitting upright in the saddle without aid, were bound on top of these mountains of utensils. Occasionally one of the animals carried small children, who had been fastened into saddlebags in such a manner that only their heads peeked from the opening. So that the animal remained in balance, young lambs or goats were secured on the other side, these peeped similarly from the tops of the panniers and bleated. Then came girls, clad only in the closely fitting Arabian shirts; mothers with children on their shoulders, lads who drove lambs before them; dromedary drivers who sat atop their beasts leading fine horses by the reigns, and finally numerous riders armed with decorated lances who raced after animals that had decided not to submit to the order of the procession.

The riding camels designated to carry noble women had a strange appearance. I had often seen *jemmels* in the Sahara that carried women in cradle-like baskets; but a contraption such as this one I had never encountered. Two poles, perhaps ten cubits [one cubit = 17 – 22 inches] or more in length, are placed crosswise before and after the hump of the camel and are tied together at the ends with vellum or rope. This rack is decorated with woolen fringes and tassels of all colors and shells and strings of pearls, and extends some nine or more cubits to the right and left of the camel. Likewise decorated is the saddle and the reigns. Between the poles, sitting atop the hump, is a structure, constructed of reeds and covered with fabric, that almost looks like a sentry box and is hung with all sorts of tassel-work. In this *belle-vue* sits the lady. The entire figure reaches an extraordinary height, and if it appeared on the horizon, one might mistake it, due to the swaying motion of the camel, for a giant butterfly or giant dragonfly that beats its wings.

Our appearance caused a sensation in each group that we passed. I was probably less the cause than Sir Lindsay who, like his servants, were recognized at once as European. He would stand out here in his gray-checkered suit, as would an Arab if he appeared in the public places of Munich or Leipzig dressed in his traditional costume. Our guides rode ahead of us until we finally noticed an extraordinarily large tent, before which many spears were driven into the earth. This was the sign that it was the tent of the chief. Everyone was busy erecting tents in a circle around it.

Both Arabs leapt from their horses and entered the tent. A few moments later they re-appeared in the company of a third man. This one had the bearing and countenance of a true patriarch. Abraham must have looked like this when he stepped out of his abode in the Haine Mamre in order to welcome his guests. The snow-white beard hung down to his chest, nevertheless, the old man gave the impression of being a vigorous fellow who was capable of bearing all kinds of burdens. His dark eyes did not examine us in an inviting or friendly manner. He raised his hand to his heart and greeted:

"*Salaama*!"

This is the greeting of an inveterate Moslem in the presence of an infidel, a 'True Believer' would be greeted with *Salaam aaleïkum*.

"*Aaleïkum*!" I answered and leaped from my horse. He looked at me intently because of this word; then he asked; "Are you a Moslem or a *giaur*?"

"Since when does the son of the noble tribe of the Shammar greet his guests with such a question? Does the Koran not say: "Feed the stranger and give him drink; let him rest with you without knowing of his coming or his going!" – May Allah forgive you, that you welcome your guests like a Turkish *khawasse* (policeman)!"

He raised his hand in a warding off gesture.

"The Shammar and the Haddedihn welcome everyone, though not the liar nor the traitor."

His glance designated the Englishman.

"Whom do you mean by these words?" I asked him.

"The men who come out of the western land to agitate the Pasha against the sons of the desert. Why does the queen of the islands (Queen of England) need a consul in Mosul?"

"These three men do not belong to the Consulate. We are tired wanderers and desire nothing more of you than a swallow of water for us and a few dates for our horses!"

"If you do not belong to the Consulate, you shall have what you desire. Enter and be welcome!"

We tied our horses to the spears and went into the tent. There we accepted a drink of camel's milk; the food consisted of thin, hard, half-burned barley cakes – a sign that the Sheik did not consider us his guests. During the short meal his dark eyes gazed coldly at us and he did not utter a word. He must have had sound reason to distrust strangers, and I noticed that he was curious to learn more about us.

Lindsay looked around the tent and asked me: "Evil fellow, no?"

"Seems so." I agreed.

"Looks like he wants to eat us. What did he say?"

"He welcomed us as infidels. We are not his guests yet so we need to be careful."

"Not his guests? But we eat and drink in his tent!"

"He did not give us the bread with his own hand, and salt - not at all. He sees that you are an Englishman and he apparently hates the English."

"But why?"

"Don't know."

"Ask him!"

"Can't, it would be impolite. But I think we will discover why."

We were finished with the little snack, and I arose.

"You have given us food and drink, Mohammed Emin; we thank you and will praise your hospitality everywhere we go. Farewell! Allah bless you and yours!"

He did not expect such a hasty departure.

"Why do you wish to leave already? Stay and rest yourselves!" He bid us.

"We will go, for the sun of your grace does not illuminate us." I said ruefully.

"Your are nevertheless safe here in my tent."

"You mean this? I do not believe in the security of the *beyt* (black tent) of an Arab el Shammar."

His hand reached for his dagger. "You mean to insult me?" He asked coldly.

"No; I only mean to tell you my thoughts. That if the tent of a Shammar does not offer a guest safety, how much less does it offer one who is not a guest!"

"Shall I stab you to death? When did a Shammar ever break the rules of hospitality?" He demanded in outrage.

"It was not only broken against strangers but even against a member of the same tribe."

This, of course, was a terrible accusation I voiced here; but I did not see any reason why I should be polite to a man who treated us like beggars.

"You will not stab me to death, oh Sheik; for firstly I spoke the truth, and secondly my dagger would encounter you sooner than yours would me."

"Prove this so-called truth!" He challenged me.

"I will tell you a story. There was a great and mighty tribe that split again into smaller *ferkah* (sub-tribes). This tribe was ruled by a great and brave chief, in whose heart lived trickery and falsehood. His people were not happy with him and turned away from him one after another. They united with a chief of one of the *ferkah*. The Sheik invited this chief to a meeting. But he did not come. So the Sheik sent his own son, who was courageous, brave and loved the truth, to the chief. The son said to the chief: 'follow me. I swear by Allah that you are safe in the tent of my father. I will offer my life for yours!' – The chief answered: 'I would not go to your father even if he swore a thousand oaths to spare me; you, however, I believe. And in order to show you that I trust you, I will go with you alone.' – They mounted their horses and rode away. When they stepped into the tent of the Sheik, it was filled with warriors. The chief was invited to seat himself next to the Sheik. He was greeted with a meal and the speech of hospitality, but after the meal he was attacked. The Sheik's son attempted to rescue him, but was thwarted. The uncle of the Sheik pulled the chief down and clamped his head between his knees, and so, with the aid of a knife, was the betrayed relieved of his head, just as one might do with a sheep. The son tore his clothes and reproached his father, but had to flee lest he lose his own life. Do you know this story, Sheik Mohammed Emin?"

"I do not know it. Such a story could never happen."

"It did happen and in your own tribe. The victim's name was Nedschris, the son Ferhan, the uncle Hadshar, and the Sheik was the famous Sheik Sofuk of the tribe of the Shammar."

The Sheik became contrite.

"From where do you know these names? You are no Shammar, no Obeïde, no Abu-Salman. You speak the language of the western Arabs, and your weapons are not those of the Arab of El Jesireh (literal 'island' - the country between the Euphrates and the Tigris). From whom have you learned this story?"

"The shame of a tribe becomes just as notorious as the renown of a people. You know that I speak the truth. How can I trust you? You are a Haddedihn; the Haddedihn belong to the Shammar, and you have denied us true hospitality. We will go."

He conveyed his opposition through a movement of his arm.

"You are a hajji and are in the company of *giaur*s!"

"From what do you deduce that I am a hajji?"

"From your *hamail* (a copy of the Koran that is hung in a gold case around the neck. Only a hajji may carry one). You shall be free. But these infidels shall pay the *jisijet* (head tax that the tribes extract from strangers), before they leave."

"They will not pay for they are under my protection."

"They do not need your protection, for they are under the protection of their consul, may Allah ruin him!"

"He is your enemy?"

"He is my enemy. He has persuaded the Governor of Mosul to imprison my son; he has incited the Obeïde, the Abu-Hammed and the Jowari against me, so that they steal from my herds and now intend to unite to destroy me and my entire tribe."

"Then call upon the other tribes of the Shammar to aid you!"

"They cannot come for the governor has gathered an army with which he intends to surround the pastures at the Sindshar and then make war. I am dependent only upon myself. May Allah protect me!"

"Mohammed Emin, I have heard, that the Obeïde, the Abu-Hammed and the Jowari are thieves. I do not love them: I am a friend of the Shammar. The Shammar are the noblest and bravest Arabs I know; I hope that you are victorious over all your enemies!"

I did not intend to form a compliment with these words, rather they voiced my conviction. This must have come through in the tone in which I had spoken, for I saw that my words made a favorable impression.

"You are really a friend of the Shammar?" he asked me.

"Yes, and I lament the discord that has been sown among you, so that your power is almost crushed."

"Crushed? Allah is great, and the Shammar are still brave enough to fight against their adversaries. Who told you of us?"

"I read and heard of you a long time ago; the latest report I received over in *Belad Arab* from the sons of the Ateïbeh."

"What?" he asked in surprise, "you were with the Ateïbeh?"

"Yes."

"They are numerous and powerful, but a curse rests upon them."

"You mean Sheik Malek, he of the outcast?"

He leapt up.

"*Mashallah*, you know Malek, my friend and brother?"

"I know him and his people."

"Where did you meet them?"

"I met them in the vicinity of Jidda and traveled with them across *Belad Arab* to *El Nahman*, in the desert of Maskat."

"You know them all?"

"Every one."

"Even – forgive me, that I speak of a woman, but she is no woman, more a man – even Amsha, the daughter of Malek, you know?"

"I know her. She was the wife of Abu-Seïf but she took her revenge upon him."

"She obtained vengeance?"

"Yes; he is dead. Hajji Halef Omar, my servant, felled him and gained Hanneh, Amsha's daughter, as his wife."

"Your servant? Then you are no ordinary warrior?"

"I am a son of the Uëlad German and travel through these lands in search of adventure."

"Oh, now I see. You do as Harun al Rashid [763?-809 Caliph of Baghdad from 786-809 famed for his participation in the Muslim holy war against the Byzantines and for the splendor of his court.] did; you are a Sheik, an Emir, who seeks out battles and adventures. Your servant killed the powerful 'Father of the Saber', you as his master must be a greater hero than your companion. Where is this brave Hajji Halef Omar now?"

It did not occur to me to speak against his rather favorable opinion of myself. I answered:

"You will perhaps see him soon. He was dispatched by Sheik Malek in order to ask the Shammar whether he and his tribe could live under their protection."

"They will be welcomed by me, very welcome. Tell me, oh Emir, tell me about them!"

He seated himself again. I followed his example and reported to him about my initial meeting with the Ateïbeh, but only as much as I thought necessary. When I was finished, he offered me his hand.

"Forgive me, Emir, I did not know this. You have these Englishmen with you, and they are my enemies. But now you shall be my guests. Permit me to go and order the meal."

Only now that he had given me his hand did I consider myself safe in his camp. I grasped the flask of 'holy' water under my robe and pulled it forth.

"You will order the meal from your *Bent Amm*? (*Bent Amm* means cousin and is the only form by which one can speak to an Arab of his wife)"

"Yes."

"Then greet her from me and bless her with some drops from this flask. It is water from the fountain Zem-Zem. Allah be with her!"

"*Sihdi*, you are a brave hero and a great saint. Come and bless her yourself. The women of the Shammar do not fear exposing their faces before men."

I had of course already heard that the wives and girls of the Shammar where no friends of the veil, and had, during my ride today, met many whose faces were not covered. He arose and beckoned me to follow him. We did not have far to go. Near his tent, stood another. As we entered it, I saw three Arabian and two black girls. The black girls were unquestionably slaves, the others however were certainly his wives. Two of them rubbed barley to flour between two stones, the third, however, directed the work from an elevated position. She was obviously the mistress.

In a corner of the tent, stood several sacks, filled with rice, dates, coffee, barley and beans, over which a precious carpet was spread; this formed the throne of the mistress. She was still young, slim and of a lighter complexion than the other women; her features were regular, her eyes dark and shining. She had colored her lips dark red and her eyebrows black, in such a manner that they met above her nose. Her forehead and cheeks were covered with beauty spots, and on her bare arms and feet, one was able to note dark red tattoos. From each ear a large golden ring hung down to her waist; her nose was also equipped with a very large ring on which sparkled several large gemstones: - this must have been a hindrance to her during a meal. Around her neck hung many thick coils of pearls, pieces of coral, Assyrian cylinders [beads] and colorful stones, and loose silver rings surrounded her ankles, arms and wrists. The other women were somewhat less abundantly decorated.

"*Salaam*!" greeted the Sheik. "I bring to you a hero of the tribe of the Germans, he is a great saint and desires to anoint you with the blessings of Zem-Zem."

Immediately all the women threw themselves to the earth. Even the noblest glided from her throne and knelt down. I let some drops of water run into my hand and then sprinkled it over the group.

"Accept it, you flowers of the desert! May the God of all people keep you lovely and happy, so that your fragrance will quicken the heart of your master!"

When they saw that I had tucked the flask back under my robes they arose and hurried to thank me. This involved the simple clasping of the hands, much like in the west. Then the Sheik commanded:

"Now busy yourselves and prepare a meal that is worthy of this man. I will invite many guests, so that my tent will be full and all will be pleased with the honor they shall receive this day."

We returned to his tent. While I entered, he lingered before it to give his orders to some of the Bedouin.

"Where were you?" asked Sir Lindsay.

"In the tent of the women."

"Ah! Impossible!"

"And yet so!"

"These women permit themselves to be seen?" He asked in astonishment.

"Why not?"

"Hmm! Wonderful! Stay here! Will also see women!"

"That depends on the circumstances. I am considered a holy man, since I have water from the fountain of Zem-Zem, a drop of which according to the belief of these people can perform miracles."

"Ah! Miserable! Don't have Zem-Zem!" He conceded.

"Would not help you either as you do not understand Arabic!"

"Are there ruins here?"

"No. But I believe one would not have to go far to find such."

"Then ask! Find ruins; excavate fowling-bull! Was a horrible meal by the way!"

"It will get better. We will be treated to a true Arabian feast soon!"

"Ah! The Sheik did not appear willing to provide it."

"His opinion of us has changed, I know some friends of his and that has won us his hospitality. But dismiss the servants. The Arabs may be insulted if they are expected to sit in the same room as them."

Chapter 16

Once the Sheik re-appeared it did not take long for the guests to gather. They were so numerous that the tent was truly filled. They seated themselves according to their rank in a circle around the Sheik, the Englishman and myself. Soon the meal was brought in to the tent by the female slaves and served by a number of the Bedouin. First of all a *sufrah* was laid before us. This is a kind of tablecloth made of tanned leather, it is decorated around the edges with colorful braids, fringes and other ornamentation. It also has a number of pockets and can, when it is folded, be used to store food. Next the coffee was brought in. For now, each guest received only a small cupful of this beverage. After this came the bowls of *salatah.* This is a very refreshing course and consists of curdled milk with cucumber slices that are salted and peppered. At the same time a pot was set before the Sheik. It contained fresh water, out of which jutted the necks of three bottles. Two of them, as I soon saw, contained *araki*, and the third was filled with a fragrant fluid, which the Sheik sprinkled upon us after each course.

The next course was an enormous bowl of rendered butter. This is called *samn* here, and the Arabs eat and drink it, preferably as an entree as well as a dessert, and at almost any other time. Small baskets of dates were served next. I recognized the highly valued, compressed *el shelebi,* which is packed much like the fig or the prune back home. They are approximately two inches long and small-seeded. Their aroma and taste are of equal loveliness. Then I saw the rare *adshwa,* which is never, never traded; for the Prophet said of it: 'Who breaks the fast through the daily enjoyment of six or seven *adshwa*, needs fear neither poison nor magic'. Also proffered were the *hilwah* – the sweetest, the *juseirijeh* – the greenest, and *el birni* and *el seihani*. Intended for the less noble of the guests were the tree-dried *balah*, as well as *jebeli* and *hylajeh.* Even the *kelladat el Sham* – 'Syrian necklaces', were offered. These dates are blanched, so that they retain their yellow color, and are then threaded on a string and hung in the sun to dry.

After the dates, a bowl of *kunafah*, noodles sprinkled with sugar, was served. Now the host raised his hands.

"*Bismillah*!" he called and gave therewith the sign to commence the meal.

He reached with his fingers into the pots, dishes and baskets, selected and then placed choice morsels of the food first into my mouth and then into the mouth of the Englishman. I would of course have preferred to use my own fingers but I endured this ritual so as not to unforgivably offend him. Sir Lindsay, upon accepting the first noodle into his mouth, pulled the latter into the well known trapezoid shape and did not shut it until I reminded him:

"Eat, sir, if you do not wish to mortally insult these people!"

He shut his mouth, swallowed the tidbit and then declared indignantly – in English of course:

"Ugh! I do have a knife and fork with me in my cutlery set!"

"Leave it be! We must be guided by the customs of this land."

"Horrible!"

"What does this man say?" asked the Sheik.

"He is entirely charmed by your goodwill."

"Oh, I am charmed with you also!"

With these words the Sheik dipped his hand into the sour milk and thrust a portion, literally, under the Englishman's long nose. So honored, the Englishman snorted a few times to acquire air as well as courage and tried, with the aid of his tongue, to maneuver the gift from the lower half of his face into the opening that should be named the forecourt of the digestive apparatus.

"Terrible!" he lamented at last. "Must I really suffer this?"

"Yes."

"Without defense?"

"Without! But you can revenge yourself." I offered.

"How so?"

"Watch what I do, and then do likewise!"

I reached for the noodles and shoved a portion into the Sheik's mouth. He had not yet swallowed it when David Lindsay took a handful of rendered butter and served him likewise. What I had not expected of the Sheik, since he was a Moslem, was the acceptance of this food without resistance, from an infidel. Certainly he planned to later wash himself and with the aid of a long or short fast to purify himself of this defilement.

While we were both fed in this manner by the Sheik, I lavishly distributed my gifts to those present. They considered this to be preferential treatment by me and voiced their obvious pleasure. Soon nothing was left of the gifts we had brought.

Now the Sheik clapped his hands loudly. A *sinus* was brought before us. This is a very large bowl, some six feet in circumference, engraved with drawings and inscriptions. It was filled with *birgani*, a mixture of rice and mutton that swam in rendered butter. After this came *warah mashi* – a strongly spiced stew of mutton pieces, followed by *kahab* – little roasted pieces of meat on wooden skewers, then *kima* – cooked meat, then preserved pomegranates, apples and quinces and finally *raha* – sugared sweetmeats similar to the type of confectionery we also enjoy as a treat.

Was this the end? Oh no! For as I was thinking that the feast had concluded, the main course was served, consisting of mutton that was roasted on a spit. I could not eat another bite.

"*El Hamd ul illah*!" I therefore exclaimed, stuck my hands into the water pot and dried them on my robe.

This gesture indicated that I would eat no more. Easterners do not share our sense of etiquette regarding the completion of a meal. He who has declared his '*El Hamd*' is excused from further feasting. The Englishman noted this.

"*El Hamdillah*!" he also exclaimed, plunged his hand into the water and - looked at it, somewhat embarrassed.

The Sheik noted this and held his *haïk* out towards Lindsay.

"Tell your friend," the Sheik said to me, "that he may dry his hands on my robes. The Englishmen certainly do not understand much of cleanliness, for they do not wear clothes on which they are able to dry themselves."

I related the Sheik's offer to Lindsay, and he made extensive use of it. Then we tasted the *araki*, and everyone was served coffee and passed a pipe. Only now did the Sheik introduce me to those present:

"You men of the tribe of the Haddedihn el Shammar, this man is a great Emir and hajji from the country of the Uëlad German; his name is ..."

"Hajji Kara Ben Nemsi," I interceded.

"Yes, his name is Emir Hajji Kara Ben Nemsi; he is the greatest warrior of his country and the wisest *taleb* of his people. He carries the waters of Zem-Zem with him and visits all lands seeking adventure. Do you now know who he is? He is a *jihad* (one who goes to fight for his beliefs – a crusader). Let us see if he wishes to march with us against our enemies!"

That placed me into an altogether peculiar and unexpected position. How should I answer? For an answer was awaited of me by all, this was obvious from their expectant gazes. I decided immediately:

"I fight for that which is right and good, against all that is wrong and unjust. My arm belongs to you; but first I must deliver this man, my friend, to where I have promised to lead him."

"Where is that?"

"This I need to explain to you. Several thousand years ago a people who occupied large cities and beautiful palaces lived in this land. The people disappeared, and their cities and palaces lie beneath the earth. He who digs into the depths can learn and see what it was like millennia ago, and this is what my friend wishes to do. He wishes to search in the earth for artifacts and old writings, to fathom their meaning and to read ..."

"And to find gold and take it with him," interrupted the Sheik.

"No," I answered. "He is rich; he has gold and silver, as much as he needs. He only seeks writings and pictures; all else he will leave to the inhabitants of this land."

"And what must you do?"

"I will lead him to such a place, where he can find that which he seeks."

"He does not need you for this, you can therefore march with us into battle. We will show him plenty of such places. The whole country is full of rubble and ruins."

"But who shall speak with him if I am not present? You do not understand his language and he does not know yours."

"Then he should first march into battle with us, after which we will show him many places where he can find writings and pictures."

Lindsay noticed that our discussion was about him.

"What are you saying?" he asked me.

"They ask me what you want in this land," I told him.

"Have you told them, sir?"

"Yes."

"That I wish to excavate fowling-bulls?"

"Yes."

"And?" He asked expectantly.

"They wish me to remain with them and not go with you."

"What else do they wish you to do?"

"To march with them into battle. They consider me to be a great hero."

"Hmm! Where do I find fowling-bulls?"

"They will show you."

"Ah! But I don't understand these people!"

"I have told them this."

"What was the reply?"

"That you should march into battle with us, and then they will show you where to find inscriptions and the like." I explained.

"Well! We go with them!"

"That won't work!" I countered.

"Why not?"

"We put ourselves in jeopardy. Why should the hostilities of these strangers concern us?" I argued.

"They do not. But that is why we may go with whomever we wish," the Englishman parried.

"That is very clever." I conceded.

"Are you afraid, sir?"

"No."

"I thought not! Therefore march! Tell them!"

"You will change your mind."

"Never!" He blustered.

He turned away slightly and that was the unmistakable sign that he had spoken his last word on the matter. I turned to the Sheik:

"I told you before that I fight for all that is right and just. Is your claim right and just?"

"Shall I explain it to you?"

"Yes."

"Have you heard of the tribe of the Jehesh?"

"Yes. It is a disloyal tribe. They have frequently united with the Abu Salman and the Tai-Arabians to rob the neighboring tribes."

"You are correct. They attacked us and stole many herds; but we swiftly followed after them and took back what they stole. Now the Sheik of the Jehesh has accused us before the governor and bribed him. The governor sent a messenger summoning myself and the noblest warriors of my tribe to a conference in Mosul. I had been wounded and could neither ride nor walk. That is why I sent my son to him, accompanied by fifteen warriors. The governor has a treacherous heart and he took them prisoner, he sent them to a place that I have not yet discovered."

"You have asked about them?"

"Yes, but without success, since no member of my tribe dares to venture to Mosul. The tribes of the Shammar were enraged by this betrayal and killed some of the governor's soldiers. Now the governor's troops take up arms against the Shammar and he incites the Obeïde, Abu Hammed and the Jowari against me, although they are not under the control of his highness, they belong under the rule of Baghdad."

"Where do your enemies camp?"

"They mobilize first."

"Do you not plan to unite with the other Shammar tribes?"

"Where shall our herds find pasture then?"

"You are right. You will divide yourselves, entice the governor into the desert and then defeat him?"

"So it is. He cannot harm the Shammar with his army. But it is different with my enemies; they are Arabs, I cannot let them near our pastures."

"How many warriors does your tribe have?"

"Eleven hundred."

"And your opponents?"

"More than three times as many."

"How long will it take to gather your warriors?"

"A day."

"Where do the Obeïde have their camp?"

"At the lower course of the Zab-asfal."

"And the Abu Hammed?"

"In the vicinity of El Fattha, at a point where the Tigris breaks through the Hamrin mountains."

"On which bank?"

"On both."

"And the Jowari?"

"Between the Jebel Kernina and the right bank of the Tigris."

"Have you sent scouts?"

"No."

"You should have done so."

"Impossible! A Shammar would be recognized immediately, and his life would be forfeit if he were discovered. But . . . " He stopped and looked at me intently. Then he continued: "Emir, are you truly the friend of Malek, the Ateïbeh?"

"Yes."

"And also our friend?"

"Yes."

"Come with me; I will show you something!"

He left the tent and I followed him, as did the Englishman and all the Arabs that were present. Next to the large tent a smaller one for our servants had been erected during the meal, and as we passed it I noticed that they too had been served with food and drink. Outside the circle of tents the Sheik's horses were tethered; he led us to the corral. They were excellent animals, but two of them pleased me most of all. One was a young white mare, the most wonderful animal that I had ever seen. Her ears were long, thin and translucent; her nostrils high, flared and deep red inside; her mane and tail were like silk.

"Exquisite!" I cried involuntarily.

"Say: *Mash Allah*!" the Sheik reminded me.

The Arabs are, in relation to an involuntary cry of pleasure, quite superstitious. If someone likes a thing very much, he should say *'Mash Allah'* if he does not wish to offend.

"*Mash Allah*!" I repeated, upon his prompting.

"Do you believe that upon this mare I hunted the wild donkey of the Sindsha until it collapsed from exhaustion?"

"Impossible!"

"I swear by Allah, it is true! These men can attest to it!"

"We attest to it!" called the Arabs in unison.

"I shall only part with this mare at the end of my life," explained the Sheik. "Which other horse do you admire?"

"That stallion. See his bone structure and symmetry, such nobility and rare coloring, a black that passes into blue!"

"That is not all. That stallion has the three highest virtues of a good horse."

"They are?"

"Fleetness of foot, courage and stamina."

"By what signs do you recognize this?"

"The hair swirls on the croup: that is the sign that he is fleet of foot; it swirls from the start of the mane: that shows that he has stamina, and it swirls in the middle of the forehead: that shows that he possesses a fiery and proud courage. He will never leave his rider in the lurch and will carry him through a thousand enemies. Have you ever owned such a horse?"

"Yes."

“Ah! Then you are a very rich man.”

“It did not cost me anything – it was a mustang.”

“What is a mustang?” He asked.

“A wild horse, which one must catch and tame.” I told him.

“Would you buy this black stallion, if I would sell it and you could afford it?” The Sheik asked me

“I would buy it on the spot.”

“You can earn it!” He suggested.

“Ah! Impossible!” I scoffed at this proposal.

“Yes. You may receive it as a gift.” He confirmed.

“Under what condition?”

“When you bring us reliable information as to where the Obeïde, Abu Hammed and Jowari will unite.”

I very nearly cried out with joy. The price was high but the horse was still worth more. I did not take long to reflect.

“When do you demand this information?” I asked.

“As soon as you can obtain it.”

“And when do I receive the horse?”

“When you return.” He said.

“You are right; I cannot demand it beforehand; but then I cannot complete this deed.”

“Why not?”

“Because all will perhaps depend on the horse that I ride, one that I can trust in all respects.”

He stared at the ground. Then with some trepidation, he asked me, “you know that in such a venture the stallion could very easily be lost?”

“I know it; it will all depend on the horseman. But if I had such a horse under me, then no man would catch me or the horse.”

“You ride that well?”

“I do not ride like you; first I would need to accustom a horse of the Shammar to my manner.”

“Then we are superior to you!”

“Superior? Are you a good shot?”

“We shoot the dove from the tent at a gallop.”

“Good. Lend me the stallion and send ten warriors after me. I will not ride further than a thousand lengths of a lance from your camp; permit them to shoot at me as often as they wish. They will neither catch me nor hit me.”

“You jest, Emir!”

“I am serious.”

“And if I take you at your word?”

“Excellent!”

The eyes of the Arabs brightened with pleasure. Certainly each of them was an excellent horseman; they burned with the desire that the Sheik should agree to my offer.

But the Sheik looked at the ground before him, undecided.

"I know what thoughts stir your heart, oh Sheik," I said to him. "Look at me! Does a man separate himself from weapons such as the ones I carry?"

"Never!"

I laid my weapons before him.

"See, I lay them at your feet, as a guarantee, that I did not come here to steal the stallion from you; and if this is not enough, then my word and my friend are also part of the pledge.

He smiled in reassurance.

"Let it be so; ten men you said?" He asked me.

"Yes, or twelve or even fifteen." I agreed.

"All may shoot at you?"

"Yes. If I am shot, no reproach will befall them. Choose your best riders and marksmen!"

"You are daring, Emir!" He allowed.

"That's what you think." I laughed.

"They must only remain behind you?"

"They can ride where they like in their attempt to catch me or to hit me with their bullets." I proclaimed.

"*Allah kerihm*, then you are already a dead man!"

"However, as soon as I halt at this place, the game is at an end!"

"Well, you do not wish it any other way. I will ride my mare so that I miss nothing."

"Permit me to try the stallion first!"

"Do so!"

I mounted and while the Sheik selected the men who would attempt to catch me, I observed that I could wholly depend on the stallion. I leapt from the horse and removed the saddle. The proud horse recognized that something unusual was happening and his eyes glinted, his mane rose and his feet pranced like the feet of a dancer who tries to ascertain if the parquet of the hall is sufficiently polished for a *contre* [contre-dance – folk dance]. I slung a strap around the stallion's neck and then knotted a sling to one side of a tightly bound girdle.

"You removed the saddle?" asked the Sheik. "Why these straps?"

"You will soon see. Have you chosen your warriors?"

"Yes; here are the ten!"

They already sat astride their horses; all the remaining Arabs who were nearby mounted likewise.

"Then we may begin. Do you see that tent, six hundred paces from here?" I indicated.

"We see it." They agreed.

"As soon as I reach it you may fire upon me; and you shall leave no distance between us. Lets go!" I cried.

I leapt onto the stallion – it shot forth like an arrow. The Arabs followed us closely. This was a magnificent animal. I had not yet covered the half the indicated distance before the first pursuer was already fifty paces in our wake.

Now I bent forward and placed my arm into the strap at the neck and my leg into the sling. Just before reaching the designated tent I looked behind me; all ten of my pursuers held their flintlocks at the ready. I now turned the horse at right angles to our path. One of the followers pulled up his horse with the assurance that only an Arab can possess, it stood as still as if it had been cast in bronze. He lifted his flintlock; a shot cracked.

"*Allah Allah, ïa Allah, Wallah, Tallah*!" a cry arose.

They believed that I had been struck, for I was no longer visible. I had thrown myself down along the side of the horse – in the style of the American Indian – and now hung, with the aid of the strap and the sling, on the flank of the horse that faced away from my pursuers. A glance beneath the stallion's neck confirmed that no one was aiming at me. I immediately righted myself on the back of the stallion and guided him to the right, racing onwards.

"*Allah akbar, Mashallah, Allah il Allah*!" The cry went up behind me. The good people were not yet able to explain the matter.

They increased their speed and again raised their flintlocks. I pulled the stallion to the left, threw myself to his side once more and rode at an angle across their flank. They could not shoot if they did not wish to hit the horse. Although this chase looked dangerous, it was, thanks to my outstanding horse, really child's play, but I would not have dared to play this game with the American Indians. We raced a couple of times around the extraordinarily outstretched camp; then I rode, still hanging on the side of the horse, through the group of pursuers and aimed for the spot where the chase had commenced.

When I dismounted, the stallion showed no evidence of sweat nor foamed at the mouth. He truly was priceless. One by one my pursuers arrived. There were in all, five shots fired at me, of course none had hit me. The old Sheik took me by the hand.

"*Hamdulillah*! Allah be praised, that you are not wounded! I had feared for you. There is no horseman like you in the entire tribe of the El Shammar!"

"You err. There are horsemen in your tribe, several in fact, that ride much better than I, much better, but they do not know that a rider may hide behind his horse. If a bullet could not reach me and no man could catch me, then I have this horse to thank. Perhaps you will permit it that we change the game a little?"

"How so?"

"It should be as before, with only one difference – I will take my carbine with me and shoot at the ten men."

"*Allah kerihm*, Allah is gracious; may he prevent such misfortune, for you would shoot all from their horses!"

"Then you no doubt believe that I would not fear the Obeïde, the Abu Hammed or the Jowari, if I had this stallion under me?"

"Emir, I believe it." – He evidently wrestled with a decision, then added:

"You are Hajji Kara Ben Nemsi, the friend of my friend, Malek, and I do trust you. Take the stallion and ride in the morning. If you do not bring me the information, then he remains mine; if you bring sufficient information, he is yours. Then I will also tell you his secret."

Every Arabian horse, if it is above average, has a secret: that being that it has been trained, upon a certain signal, to draw upon its highest degree of speed, and that it will not slacken its pace until it either collapses or is halted by its rider. The horseman does not impart the secret sign to his friend, his father or brother, nor his son or his wife and only makes use of it if he finds himself in the greatest of dangers.

"Only then?" I answered. "Could not a circumstance develop where only the secret could save me and the horse?"

"You are right; but you are not yet the owner of the stallion."

"I will become so!" I said confidently. "And should I not then the secret will be buried within me, so that not a soul should discover it."

"Then come!"

He led me aside and whispered to me:

"If you wish that the stallion should fly like the falcon in the air, then put your hand lightly between his ears and call loudly the word 'Rih'!"

"Rih – that is wind."

"Yes, Rih, that is the name of the horse, for he is even faster than the wind; he is as fast as a storm."

"I thank you, Sheik. I will carry out your mission well, as though I were a son of the Haddedihn or as if I were you, yourself. When shall I ride?"

"Tomorrow, at the break of day, if you like."

"What kind of dates should I take for the stallion?"

"He only eats *balahat*. I need not tell you how cherished horses are to be handled?"

"No."

"Sleep tonight on his body and speak the hundredth *sura* – which is about the dashing horses – into his nostrils, then he will love you and obey you to his last breath. Do you know this *sura*?"

"Yes."

"Speak it!"

He was truly concerned over his horse and I. I obeyed his will:

"In the name of Allah the compassionate! By the dashing horses with noisy snorts, and by them that stamp and spray sparks of fire, and by them that compete with each other to besiege the enemy in the early morning, those that stir up the dust and break through the enemy's ranks, truly man is thankful to his Lord, and he must bear witness to it. Overmuch does he cleave to the love of earthly goods. Does he not know that in those days, when the graves give up their content and are brought to the light, that whatever was hidden in the heart of man will be completely known to the Lord?"

"Yes, you know this *sura*. I have recited it a thousand times to the stallion, in the evenings, do the same and he will know that you have become his master. But now come back to the tent!"

The Englishman had remained a silent spectator; now he stepped up to my side.

"Why did they shoot at you?" he asked.

"I wished to show them something that they did not know."

"Ah, nice, splendid horse!"

"Do you know, sir, to whom it belongs?" I asked, with a glint of humor.

"To the Sheik!" He answered.

"No."

"Whom else?"

"Me." I announced proudly.

"Pah!" He scoffed.

"Truly, to me!"

"Sir, my name is David Lindsay, and I do not permit myself to be fooled; remember that!"

"Good, then I keep all else to myself!"

"What else?"

"That I leave you tomorrow morning?"

"Why?"

"To scout out information regarding the hostility you have heard of. I should seek to discover when the hostile tribes meet; and for that I shall receive, if I am successful, this stallion."

"You lucky beggar! Will ride with you, listen, reconnoiter!"

"That will not work."

"Why not?"

"Your presence would not help, rather it would hinder me. Your clothing ..."

"Pah, would dress like an Arab!"

"Without understanding a word of Arabic!"

"Correct! How long will we stay away?"

"I don't know yet, a few days. I must go far over the little Zab, and that is rather far from here."

"Evil way! Bad Arab people!"

"I will take care."

"Will remain here if you do me a favor."

"Which would be?"

"Don't just scout for the Bedouin."

"For what else?"

"After nice ruins. Must excavate, find fowling-bull, send to museum in London!"

"I will do it, depend on it!" I assured him.

"Well! Done; enter!" He gestured at the tent opening.

We resumed our earlier places in the tent and spent the remainder of the day telling all kinds of stories that the Arabs enjoyed. In the evening, there was song and music, produced by just two instruments: a *rubabah*, a type of sitar with only one string, and a *tabl*, a little drum that made, in relation to the single tone of the *rubabah*, a shocking noise. Then the night prayer was recited and we went to our beds. The Englishman slept in the tent of the Sheik, I however went to the stallion, which lay on the earth, and took my place between his feet. Did I really speak that hundredth *sura* into his nostrils? Of course! I was not prompted by superstition, God forbid! The horse was accustomed to this routine; and by continuing it we quickly established trust between us; by the recital of the words into his nostrils, he learned – how does one say? – the scent of his new master. I lay between his legs, like a child between the legs of a loyal, understanding Newfoundland dog. Just as day was breaking, the Sheik's tent-flap opened and the Englishman stepped out.

"Sleep well, sir?" He asked.

"Yes."

"Not me." He grumbled.

"Why not?" I asked.

"Very lively in that tent."

"The sleepers?"

"No."

"What else?"

"The fleas, lice and gnats!"

The reader who understands English knows what he meant; I had to laugh. [This remark was intended for the reader of the original German text.]

"You will soon become accustomed to such things, Sir Lindsay!"

"Never. Also could not sleep because I was thinking of you." He admitted.

"Why?" I asked.

"Could have rode away without speaking with me first." The Englishman suggested.

"I would have certainly taken my leave of you." I assured him.

"Would perhaps have been too late."

"Why?"

"Have many questions to ask."

"Then ask away!"

I had, during the course of the previous evening, imparted to him all sorts of information; now he pulled forth his notebook.

"Will have myself led to the ruins. Must speak Arabic. Tell me a few things. How do you say friend?"

"*Ashab*."

"Enemy?"

"*Kiman*."

"Must pay. How do you say dollar?"

"*Rijahl fransh*."

"And money bag?"

"*Surrah*."

"Will dig stones. What is stone?"

"*Hadshar* and also *hadshr* or *chadshr*."

In this manner he asked for the translation of some hundred words, all of which he noted down. It became busy in the camp, and I had to go to the Sheik's tent to partake of the *sahur*, the early meal.

At that time much was discussed; I then took my leave, mounted my horse and left this place to which I might never return.

I had decided to firstly search for the southern-most tribe of the Jowari. The best route would be to follow the Thathar river, which almost always flows parallel with the Tigris; unfortunately however, it was very likely that on its shore the herds of the Obeïde were grazing, and therefore I kept further west. I took a route that would permit me to reach the Tigris about a mile north of Tekrit; there I would surely find the sought after tribe.

I had ample provisions; I did not need water for my horse, for the plant growth was moist. I therefore had no other cares besides remaining on the right track and avoiding any encounter with the enemy. Firstly I had a good sense of direction, the sun, and a compass, and secondly I had my telescope, with the help of which I could identify all before I myself was seen.

The day passed without any adventure, and in the evening I camped behind a solitary rock. Before I fell asleep the thought surfaced that it might be advantageous to ride directly to Tekrit because I would be able to learn much of importance without being noticed. It was a very superfluous thought, as I would discover the next morning. I had slept quite soundly and awoke at the warning snort of my horse. As I looked up, I saw five horsemen approaching from the north, heading directly to the place where I was camped. They were so close that they had already seen me. Flight was far from my mind although the stallion would have carried me quickly away. I rose and prepared myself for any eventuality and took the Henry carbine nonchalantly to hand.

They approached at a gallop and halted their horses some paces from me. Since their demeanor did not indicate any animosity, I was unconcerned for the moment.

"*Salaam aaleïkum*!" one of them greeted me.

"*Aaleïkum*!" I answered.

"You slept here during the night?"

"That is so."

"Don't you have a tent under which to rest your head?"

"No. Allah dispenses his gifts diversely. To one he gives a roof of felt and to the other the sky is his cover."

"But you could own a tent; you have a horse that is worth more than a hundred tents."

"It is my only possession."

"Will you sell it?"

"No."

"You must belong to a tribe that has its camp not far from here."

"Why?"

"Your stallion is fresh."

"And yet my tribe lives far, far away, beyond the Holy Cities of the west."

"What is the name of your tribe?"

"Uëlad German."

"Yes, over there in the Moghreb one usually says Uëlad instead of Beni or Abu. Why are you so far from your land?"

"I have seen Mecca and now wish to see Duars and other cities that are in the direction of Persia so that I can tell my people much when I return home."

"Where are you bound now?"

"Always in the direction of the rising sun, where Allah leads me."

"Then you can ride with us."

"What is your destination?"

"North of the cliffs of Kernina, where our herds graze on the bank and on the islands of the Tigris."

Hmm! Might these people be Jowari? They had questioned me: it was therefore not impolite if I also inquired about them.

"To which tribe do these herds belong?"

"To the tribe Abu Mohammed."

"Are there other tribes nearby?"

"Yes. To the south are the Alabeïde, who pay tribute to the Sheik of Kernina, and to the north are the Jowari."

"To whom do they pay tribute?"

"One hears that you come from a distant land. The Jowari do not pay, rather they demand tribute. They are thieves and robbers, from whom our herds are not safe for a moment. Come with us if you wish to fight against them!"

"You war with them?"

"Yes. We have joined with the Alabeïde. If you desire to do great deeds, then you can fulfill them with us. But why do you sleep by the hill of the lion?"

"I do not know this place. I was tired and laid myself to rest."

"*Allah kerihm*, God is gracious; you are a favorite of Allah's, otherwise the 'strangler of herds' would have torn you apart. No Arab would have rested here for an hour, for on this rock the lions rendezvous."

"There are lions along the Tigris?"

"Yes, at the lower part of the river, further upstream you find only the leopard. Do you ride with us?"

"If I will be your guest."

"You are. Take our hand and let us exchange dates!"

We placed the palms of our hands against each other, I then received a date from each of them, which I ate; I handed five of my own dates to them, these were promptly eaten. We then took a southeasterly direction. Some time later we crossed the Thathar, and the flat plain became more and more mountainous.

I became acquainted with my companions and ascertained that they were five honest nomads, in whose hearts no falsehood could be found. They had visited a friendly tribe to celebrate a wedding and now returned home, full of joy over the festivity and banquet that they had attended.

The terrain continued to become more elevated until it suddenly fell away. To the right, the ruins of old Tekrit became visible in the distance, to the left and also in the distance rose Jebel Kernina, and before us stretched the valley of the Tigris. Within a half an hour we had reached the river. It had the width of about an English mile here, and its waters were divided by a large, long island that was covered with greenery and upon which many tents were visible.

"Will you cross over with us? You will be welcomed by our Sheik!"

"How do we get across?"

"You shall see shortly, as we have already been seen. Come further upstream where the *kellek* lands."

A *kellek* is a raft that is usually twice as long as it is wide. It consists of inflated goatskins that are fastened to wooden poles, over which planks are laid and the cargo is carried upon this. The ties are made entirely from willow branches. The raft is steered by two oars that rest in split bamboo that is tied at the top. Such a raft left the island's shore, opposite us. It was so large that it could carry more than six riders and it ferried us safely to the other side.

We were greeted by many children, several dogs and a noble looking old Arab who was the father of one of my companions.

"Permit me to lead you to our Sheik," said the one who had spoken beforehand.

On our way, several men joined us, but they followed at a discreet distance behind us and did not badger me with questions. Their admiring glances were directed at my horse. The way was not far. It terminated in front of a large, spacious looking hut. It was built of willow boughs and covered with bamboo, the interior was dressed with mats. As we entered, a powerfully built, robust-looking man arose from the carpet on which he had been seated. He had been busily sharpening his *sharay* (sharp, Afghani knife) on a stone.

"*Salaam aaleïkum*!" I greeted.

"*Aaleïk*!" he answered and scrutinized me.

"Permit me oh Sheik to bring before you this man," begged one of my companions. "He is a noble warrior, and I dare not offer him my tent."

"Whomever you bring, he is welcome to me." He answered.

The petitioner removed himself, and the Sheik offered me his hand.

"Be seated, oh stranger. You are tired and hungry, you shall rest and eat; but first permit me to examine your horse!"

This was the manner of an Arab: first the horse and then the man. When he returned, it was obvious that one look at my horse had heightened his opinion of me.

"You have a noble animal; *Mash Allah*; may it serve you well! I know this horse."

Ah, that was unexpected and perhaps dangerous! But perhaps not!

"From where do you know it?"

"It is the best horse of the Haddedihn."

"You know the Haddedihn also?"

"I know all tribes. But you, I don't know."

"You know the Sheik of the Haddedihn?" I asked him.

"Mohammed Emin?"

"Yes. I come from him." I told him.

"Where do you travel to?"

"To you."

"He has sent you to me?"

"No, and yet I come as a messenger to you."

"Rest first, before you tell me."

"I am not tired, and what I have to report to you is so important that I desire to tell you immediately." I reasoned.

"Then speak!" He yielded.

"I hear that the Jowari are your enemies."

"They are," he answered darkly.

"They are also mine; and the enemies of the Haddedihn as well."

"I know this."

"Do you also know that the Abu Hammed and Obeïde have united with the Jowari to attack the Haddedihn at their pasture?"

"I know it."

"I hear that you have united with the Alabeïde to punish them?"

"Yes."

"So I come to you to discuss this matter."

"Then I say once again: be welcome to me! You will refresh yourself and not leave us until I have gathered the elders."

In less than an hour, eight men sat around me and tore large pieces of meat off a side of mutton that had been provided. These eight men were the oldest of the Abu Mohammed. I told them openly how I had come to the Haddedihn and how I had become the messenger of the Sheik.

"What proposal do you wish to make to us?" asked the Sheik.

"None. More years have passed over your heads than mine. It is not becoming for the younger to advise the elder."

"You speak the language of the wise. Your head is still young but your wisdom is ancient, otherwise Mohammed Emin would not have chosen you as his envoy. Speak! We will hear and then decide."

"How many warriors does your tribe have?" I asked.

"Nine hundred."

"And the Alabeïde?"

"Eight hundred."

"That makes seventeen hundred. Exactly half as many as the number of the enemy."

"How many warriors do the Haddedihn have?"

"Eleven hundred. Yet often numbers are of lesser importance. Do you perhaps know when the Jowari will unite with the Abu Hammed?"

"On the day after the next *Jaum el Jema* (day of meeting, i.e. Friday)."

"You know this exactly?"

"We have a faithful ally in the camp of the Jowari."

"And where should this union occur?"

"At the ruins of Khan Kernina."

"And then?"

"Then these two tribes will unite with the Obeïde."

"Where?"

"Between the whirlpool of Kelab and the end of the Kanuza mountains."

"When?"

"On the third day after *Jaum el Jema*."

"You are extraordinarily well informed. Where will they go after that?"

"Directly to the grazing grounds of the Haddedihn."

"What will you do?"

"We will attack the tents in which they have left their women and children and take their herds."

"Would this be the wise thing to do?"

"We take back what was stolen from us."

"Entirely correct. The Haddedihn are eleven hundred, the enemy however has three thousand warriors. They would be victorious, they would return as victors and hunt you down, stealing even your present possessions. If I am wrong, say so."

"You are right. We thought that the Haddedihn would receive reinforcements from the other tribes of the Shammar."

"These tribes will be attacked by the Governor of Mosul."

"What do you advise? Wouldn't it be best to destroy the enemies individually?"

"You would defeat one tribe and alert the other two. They must be attacked shortly after their union – that is, at the whirlpool of El Kelab. If you agree, Mohammed Emin will ride on the third day after *Jaum el Jema* with his warriors, descend from the Kanuza mountains and attack the enemies, whilst you will attack from the south so that they will be driven into the whirlpool of Kelab."

This plan was accepted after a much-detailed discussion. A large part of the afternoon had passed and evening approached, so that I was obliged to stay the night. Early the next day I was ferried to the shore and rode back along the way I had come.

Chapter 17

My mission, which had appeared difficult at first, had been successfully completed by such simple means that I was almost too ashamed to tell of it. The stallion should not have been earned in such a cheap manner. But what else could I do? Would it perhaps be better to study the place of the impending battle? This thought did not leave me. I did not cross the Thathar again, instead I rode north on the left shore towards the Kanuza mountains. Only in the middle of the afternoon did it occur to me to question whether the Wadi Jehennem, where I had encountered the horse thieves with the Englishman, was a part of the Kanuza Mountains. I did not know the answer but continued on my way, steering to the right in order to reach the vicinity of the Jebel Hamrin. The sun had nearly sunk to the horizon when I noticed two riders approaching at great speed from the west. When they saw me they stopped briefly and then continued to ride towards me. Should I flee? From these two? No! I halted my horse and awaited them.

Here were two men who were in the prime of their life. They halted before me.

"Who are you?" asked one, casting a lusting gaze at my stallion.

I had never before experienced such a reception from Arabs.

"A stranger," I answered tersely.

"From where do you come?"

"From the west, as you can see."

"Where are you going?"

"Where *kismet* leads me."

"Come with us. You shall be our guest."

"I thank you, I already have a host that provides me with a camp."

"Whom?"

"Allah. Farewell!"

I had been too careless, I had not yet turned to leave when one of them reached for his belt and in the next moment a club flew at my head and I immediately slid from my horse. Whilst my stupor did not last long, the two bandits had time to bind me.

"*Salaam aaleïkum*," one greeted me now. "We were previously impolite and therefore our hospitality was not palatable to you. Who are you?"

Of course I did not answer.

"Who are you?"

I was silent although he punctuated the question with his boot.

"Leave him," said the other. "Allah will perform a miracle and open his mouth. Shall he ride or walk?"

"Walk!"

They loosened the bonds around my legs and tied me to the stirrup of one of their horses. Then they took my stallion by the reigns and we were on our way, abruptly to the east. I was, despite my excellent mount, a prisoner. Man is often a very foolish creature!

The terrain began a gentle elevation once more. We journeyed between mountains and finally I saw the light of many fires in a valley. Night had fully descended in the meantime. We turned into this valley, trekked past several tents and finally stopped in front of one, from which a young man was exiting at that very moment. He saw me and I him – we recognized one another.

"*Allah il Allah*! Who is this prisoner?" he asked.

"We caught him outside on the plain. He is a stranger, he will bring us no *thar* (blood feud). See this animal on which he rode!"

The young man stepped up to the stallion and cried in astonishment:

"*Allah akbar*, that is the stallion of Mohammed Emin, the Haddedihn! Lead this man to my father, the Sheik, so that he can be interrogated. I shall call the others together."

"What do we do with the horse?"

"It remains before the tent of the Sheik."

"And his weapons?"

"They will be brought into the tent."

Half an hour later, I again stood before a gathering of – judges. Here my silence would be of no use, and I therefore decided to speak.

"Do you know me?" asked the oldest of those present.

"No." I replied.

"Do you know where you are?"

"No."

"Do you know this young, brave Arab?" He indicated the young man.

"Yes."

"Where have you seen him?"

"At Jebel Jehennem. He had stolen four of my horses, which I then took back from him."

"Do not lie!"

"Who are you that you speak to me so?"

"I am Zedar Ben Huli, the Sheik of the Abu Hammed."

"Zedar Ben Huli, the Sheik of the horse thieves!"

"Silence! This young warrior is my son."

"You can be proud of him, oh Sheik!" I mocked.

"Silence, I say again, otherwise you will regret it! Who is a horse thief? You! To whom does the horse that you rode belong?"

"To me." I declared proudly.

"Do not lie!" He hissed.

"Zedar Ben Huli, thank Allah that my hands are bound. If it were not so, you would never call me a liar again!"

"Bind him tighter!" he commanded.

"Who will touch me, a hajji, in whose pocket is the water of Zem-Zem!"

"Yes, I see you are a hajji, for you wear the *hamaïl*. But do you truly have the holy waters of Zem-Zem with you?"

"Yes."

"Give some of it to me." He commanded.

"No." I said.

"Why not?"

"I carry the water only for friends."

"Are we your enemies?"

"Yes."

"No. We have not harmed you yet. We only wish to restore the horse that you have stolen to its rightful owner."

"I am the owner."

"You are a hajji and carry the holy water of Zem-Zem, nevertheless you utter lies. I know this stallion well; it belongs to Mohammed Emin, the Sheik of the Haddedihn. How did you come by this horse?"

"It was his gift to me."

"You lie! No Arab gives such a horse away."

"I have told you once that you should thank Allah that I am bound!"

"Why did he give you such a gift?"

"That is a matter between he and I; it does not concern you!"

"You are a very polite hajji! You must have rendered a great service to the Sheik of the Haddedihn to receive such a gift. When did you leave the Haddedihn?"

"Early the day before yesterday."

"Where are the pastures of their herds?"

"I do not know. The herds of the Arabs are sometimes here and sometimes there."

"Could you lead us to them?"

"No."

"Even if we return your weapons and your horse?"

"No."

"Where were you the day before yesterday?"

"Around."

"Well; you will not answer, then you shall see what will happen to you. Away with him!"

I was hustled into a small, low tent and tied up there. To my right and my left, two Bedouin squatted, they later took turns in sleeping. I believed that the decision regarding my fate would be imparted to me this day, but I was to be disappointed; the gathering broke up late, as I heard, without having reached a decision. I fell asleep. A restless dream took hold of me. I did not lie in a tent along the Tigris, instead I was in an oasis of the Sahara. The watch fire flared, *lagmi* was passed from hand to hand and tales passed from mouth to mouth. Suddenly a rumbling thunder was heard; no one who has heard this sound could ever forget it – the thunder was the lion's voice. *Assad-by*, the 'strangler of herds', approached to fetch his evening meal. Again, and closer, the voice sounded . . . I awoke.

Had that been a dream? Next to me lay the two Abu-Hammed Arabs, and I heard one of them praying the holy *fatcha*. The rumbling thunder sounded a third time. It was reality – a lion crept around the camp.

"Do you sleep?" I asked.

"No."

"Do you hear the lion?"

"Yes. It is the third time today that he comes for his meal."

"Kill it!"

"Who shall kill the mighty, awe-inspiring 'Lord of Death'?"

"Cowards! Does he also come into the camp?"

"No. Otherwise the men would not stand freely before their tents to hear his voice."

"Is the Sheik with them?"

"Yes."

"Go to him and tell him that I would kill this lion if I were given my gun."

"You are insane!"

"I am in complete control of my senses. Go!"

"Are you serious?"

"Yes; go already!"

A considerable excitement welled within me; I felt I could have torn apart my bonds. After some minutes the man returned. He untied me.

"Follow me!" he commanded.

Outside stood many men with their weapons at hand, but no one dared to step out of the relative safety of the encampment.

"You wished to speak with me. What do you want?" asked the Sheik.

"Permit me to subdue this lion."

"You cannot kill a lion! Even twenty of us are not enough to hunt him and many would die."

"I will kill him by myself."

"Do you speak the truth?"

"I speak it."

"If you wish to kill him, I have nothing against it. Allah gives life and Allah takes it again; all is written in the book of fate."

"Then give me my gun!"

"Which one?"

"The heavy one, and my knife."

"Bring them both," commanded the Sheik.

The good fellow certainly thought to himself that I was marked for death, and then he would be the indisputable inheritor of my horse. But to me it was a matter of the lion, my freedom and my horse and these three things I could have if I came into possession of my gun.

It was brought to me along with my knife.

"Will you not free my hands, oh Sheik?"

"You will really only shoot the lion?"

"Yes."

"Swear it. You are a hajji; swear it by the holy water of Zem-Zem, which you carry with you."

"I swear it!"

"Loosen his bonds!"

Now I was free. My other weapon was in the tent of the Sheik, and before the tent stood my stallion. I had no more concerns.

It was the hour in which the lion loves to sneak around the herd, the time shortly before dawn. I felt my belt to check if my bullet-pouch was still there, then I walked up to the first tent at the head of the camp. Here I remained standing for a while in order to accustom my eyes to the darkness. In front of me, and to either side, I noticed several camels and many sheep that were huddled together. The dogs, which normally guard the animals by night, had fled and hidden themselves, either behind or in the tents.

I laid myself down on the ground and crawled softly and slowly forwards. I knew that I would smell the lion sooner than see him in this darkness. There . . . it was as if the ground shook beneath me – the thunderous roar sounded from somewhere off to one side and some moments later I heard a dull thump, like two heavy bodies colliding – a strangled screech of distress; the cracking and grinding sound of bone being crushed and ground – and there, at most twenty paces before me glowed two fiery orbs – I knew this shimmering green light. I lifted my gun and despite the darkness, took aim, as accurately as possible, and squeezed the trigger. A grizzly sound shook the air. The flash from my gun had revealed me to the lion, and I had seen it, lying on the back of a camel, mauling the neck with its teeth. Had I struck the beast? A large, dark object flew through the air and landed barely three paces before me. The luminous lights flashed again. Either the leap was badly calculated or the animal was wounded. I quickly knelt, aimed the gun and fired a second and last time, not between the eyes but rather into the middle of one. I then dropped the gun quickly and took hold of my knife – the lion did not come at me; it was mortally wounded by my shot and had been thrown back. Despite this I moved back several paces to reload. All around silence reigned: even from the camp not the slightest sound was heard. Everyone must believe me dead.

As soon as the weakest light of dawn illuminated the body of the lion, I approached it. It was dead and I busied myself with skinning it. I had my reasons not to dally with this task. I had no intention of leaving this trophy behind. The work progressed more by feel than by sight but I finished before the morning light became much brighter.

I took the hide, slung it over my shoulder and walked back to the camp. It was indeed a sub-camp of the predatory Abu Hammed. The men, women and children sat before their tents, full of expectation. When they saw me, a great shouting erupted. Allah was hailed in every possible tone of voice, and a hundred hands stretched out to touch my trophy.

"You have killed it?" called the Sheik. "Really? By yourself?"

"By myself!"

"Then *Shaïtan* assisted you!"

"Does *Shaïtan* assist a hajji?"

"No; but you have magic, an amulet or a talisman, by which you have achieved this?"

"Yes."

"Where is it?"

"Here!" I held the gun under his nose.

"That is not it. You do not wish to tell us. Where does the body of the lion lie?"

"Outside, to the right of the tents. Go and get it!"

Most of those present hurried forth. This was what I desired.

"To whom belongs the skin of the lion?" the Sheik asked with lustful eyes.

"That we will discuss in your tent. Enter!"

They all followed me; there were only ten or twelve men remaining. Upon entry I saw my other weapons at once, they were hung on a peg. With two steps I reached them and pulled them down, throwing my heavy gun over my shoulder and taking the Henry carbine in hand. The lion's hide was, due to its size and weight, a hindrance; but I was going to try and keep it. Shortly, I again stood at the entrance to the tent.

"Zedar Ben Huli, I promised you I would shoot only the lion with this gun ..."

"Yes."

"But whom I shoot with this other weapon I did not say."

"It belongs here. Give it back."

"It belongs in my hand, and there it shall remain."

"He will escape – hold him!"

I raised the Henry carbine to shoot.

"Halt! Anyone who attempts to stop me is a dead man! Zedar Ben Huli, I thank you for the hospitality that I have experienced with you. We will meet again!"

I stepped outside. For a full minute no one dared to follow me. This short period of time was enough for me to mount my horse and to load the hide in front of me. As the tent-flap opened, I already galloped past the camp's last tent.

Behind me and to one side, where the body of the lion still lay, an enraged outcry arose, and I saw that everyone scrambled for their horses and weapons. As soon as I left the camp behind me I slowed my horse to a walk. The stallion shied from the scent of the lion's hide, which he could not bear, and he snorted fearfully. I looked back and saw my pursuers streaming from the camp. I urged my horse to a trot and as the first of the hunters came into range I made ready to spur my horse to a gallop. I decided otherwise though and instead, halted, turned and took aim. My shot cracked and the horse of my pursuer fell dead beneath its rider. It would not harm these horse thieves to learn a lesson. Only now did I urge my horse to speed whilst I reloaded the spent barrel of my gun.

When I turned again, two riders had closed the gap; their flintlocks could not reach me, yet. I again halted, turned, and aimed – two shots cracked and one after the other the two horses fell to the ground. This was too much for the other riders; they reigned in their horses and remained where they were. When I turned once more, after some time, I saw them in the far distance and it appeared as though they only followed my tracks.

For almost two hours I raced directly toward the west in order to lead them astray. I then shifted on to rocky ground where my horse's tracks would not be seen, then turned north and reached the Trigris at the whirlpool of Kelab by midday. The whirlpool was close to the inflow of the Zab-asfal, and just a few minutes ride below the place where the Kanuza Mountains merge with the mountains of Hamrin. This transition occurs by way of a single isolated range, which is separated by deep and narrow valleys. Our enemies would certainly choose the widest valley for their passage and therefore I memorized the terrain and all paths leading to it in the greatest possible detail; I then hurried towards the Thathar, which I reached and crossed in the afternoon. A great desire to see my friends spurred me on; but I had to care for my horse and so I stopped to rest overnight. The following noon I saw the first of the sheep herds of the Haddedihn and I galloped into the camp without heed to the calls that came from all sides. The Sheik determined therefrom that something extraordinary was happening and stepped from his tent as I pulled up in front of it.

"*Hamdulillah*, God be praised that you are with us once more!" he welcomed me. "How did it go?"

"Well," I replied.

"Did you learn anything?" The Sheik asked.

"Everything!"

"Everything? What?" He asked with great anticipation.

"Call the elders together and I will report." I told him.

Only now did he notice the hide that I had thrown down on the far side of my horse.

"*Mashallah*, miracle of God, a lion! How do you come by this pelt?" He inquired with wonder in his voice.

"I peeled it from him."

"Him? The 'Lord' himself?" He said incredulously.

"Yes."

"Then you have spoken with him?"

"For a short time."

"How many hunters were with you?"

"None."

"Allah be with you, that you should not lose your memory!" He scolded.

"I was alone!"

"Where?"

"At the camp of the Abu Hammed."

"They would have killed you!" He exclaimed doubtfully.

"They have not done so, as you see. Even Zedar Ben Huli has left me my life."

"Even him you have seen?"

"Even him. I shot three of his horses."

"Speak!" He commanded.

"Not now, not to you alone, for otherwise I must tell it many times. Call your people and then you shall hear everything in detail!"

The Sheik departed. I was about to step into the tent just then when I saw the Englishman arrive at full gallop.

"Have just heard that you are here, sir," he called from afar. "Have you found it?"

"Yes; the enemies, the battlefield and everything."

"Pah! What of ruins and fowling-bull?"

"That too!"

"Nice, very good! Will dig, find and send to London. But probably fight first?"

"Yes."

"Good, Will fight like Bayard [probably a reference to Seigneur de Bayard - originally Pierre Terrail, 1473-1524: French military hero known for his fearlessness and chivalry]. I found something also."

"What?" I inquired.

"A rarity, writing."

"Where?"

"In a hole, here in this vicinity. A tablet."

"Writing on a tablet?"

"Yes! Cuneiform writing. Can you read this?"

"A little."

"Not I. Want to see!"

"Yes. Where is the stone?"

"In the tent. Get it immediately!" He went in and brought out his precious find.

"Here, look, read!"

The tablet was extremely weathered, yet an inscription, composed of some wedges, could still be distinguished.

"Well?" Sir Lindsay asked, full of curiosity.

"Wait a moment. This is not as easy as you think. I can only find three words that could perhaps be deciphered. They are, if I am not mistaken: *Tetuda Babrut ésis*."

"What does that mean?"

"Stated for the fame of Babylon," I translated.

The good Sir David Lindsay shaped his mouth into a parallelogram that extended to his ears.

"You are reading it right, sir?"

"I think so."

"What do you make of it?"

"Everything and nothing!"

"Hmm! Here is not Babylon!"

"What else should there be?"

"Niniveh!" He suggested.

"It could be Rio de Janeiro as far as I'm concerned! Piece this stuff together yourself; I don't have the time right now." I replied impatiently.

"Isn't this why I brought you along?"

"Very well! Save the tablet until I have time!" I conceded.

"Well! What do you have to do?" He asked, mollified.

"There will be a gathering, where I shall tell of my experiences."

"Will also be there!"

"And I have to eat something beforehand. I am as hungry as a bear."

"Will join you too!"

He entered the tent with me.

"How did you fare with your Arabic?"

"Miserable! Ask for bread – Arab brings boot; demand hat – Arab brings salt; ask for gun – Arab brings turban. Dreadful, terrible! Won't let you go again!"

After the Sheik returned I did not have to wait long for a meal. Whilst I was eating, the guests arrived. The pipes were lit; the coffee did the rounds and then Lindsay pressed:

"Begin, sir! I am curious."

The Arabs had patiently and silently waited until my hunger was satiated; then I began:

"You posed me a very difficult task, but against all expectations I completed it easily. And at the same time I bring you detailed information, beyond what you expected."

"Speak!" said the Sheik.

"Your enemies are already armed. The locations for their unions are determined, and so is the time when this will happen."

"But you could not get this information!"

"Oh yes! The Jowari will unite with the Abu Hammed on the day after the next *Jaum el Jema* at the ruins of Khan Khernina. These two tribes will unite with the Obeïde on the third day after the *Jaum el Jema* between the whirlpool of El Kelab and the foothills of the Kanuza Mountains."

"You know this for certain?" The Sheik asked.

"Yes."

"From whom?"

"From the Sheik of the Abu Mohammed." I told him.

"You have spoken with him?" He asked in surprise.

"I was even in his tent." [See Trans. Notes Ch 17.1]

"The Abu Mohammed do not live in peace with the Jowari nor the Abu Hammed."

"This is what he said. He recognized your stallion and is your friend. He will come to your aid with the tribe of the Alabeïde."

"Are you speaking the truth?"

"I speak it."

Those present leaped to their feet and clasped hands in jubilation. I was almost suffocated. Then I had to relate everything in the utmost detail – which I did. They believed everything, except that I had killed the lion by myself in total darkness – that alone they doubted. The Arab is only accustomed to hunting the lion by day and then only in a large group. I finally laid the hide before them.

"Does this skin have a hole?" I asked.

They examined it very carefully.

"No," came the reply.

"When Arabs kill a lion, the skin has very many holes. I shot twice. See here! The first shot was aimed too high because he was too far away from me and it was too dark for me to aim properly. It grazed the scalp and injured the ear. Here, you can see this. I gave him my second shot when he was two or three steps from me; it penetrated his left eye. You see where the fur is singed?"

"*Allah akbar*, it is true! You let this terrible animal approach so closely that your powder burned its fur. If it had eaten you?"

"Then it would have been written in the book. I have brought the hide with me as a gift to you, oh Sheik. Take it from me and use it as a decoration in your tent!"

"Are you serious?" he asked with delight.

"I am serious."

"I thank you, Emir Hajji Kara Ben Nemsi! I will sleep on this pelt, so I may take into my heart the lion's courage."

"You do not need this skin to fill your breast with the courage that you shall soon need."

"You will fight with us against our enemies?"

"Yes. They are thieves and robbers and have sought my life; I place myself under your command, and my friend here does the same."

"No. You should not obey, but rather command. You shall be the leader of a unit."

"Of that let us speak later; permit me now to take part in your discussion."

"You are right; we need to discuss this as we only have five days remaining."

"Have you not told me that it will take one day for the warriors of the Haddedihn to gather?"

"That is so."

"Then I would, in your place, send a messenger today."

"Why today?"

"Because it is not enough to simply gather the warriors. They must be trained for this battle."

He smiled with pride.

"The sons of the Haddedihn are familiar with battle from childhood. We will overcome our enemies. How many warriors does the tribe of the Abu Muhammed have?"

"Nine hundred."

"And the Alabeïde?"

"Eight hundred."

"Then we number twenty eight hundred men; in addition we have the element of surprise, since the enemy does not expect us; we must win!"

"Or we are vanquished!"

"*Mashallah*, you kill the lion and fear the Arabs?"

"You are mistaken. You are brave and courageous; but courage has twice the value if it is tempered with caution. Do you believe it possible that the Alabeïde and Abu Muhammed might arrive too late?"

"It is possible."

"Then we stand with eleven hundred against three thousand men. The enemy will destroy us first and then our friends. How easily they might discover that we plan to move against them! Then the moment of surprise is gone. And what use is it to you if you fight and only succeed in driving the enemy back? If I were the Sheik of the Haddedihn, I would beat the enemy into such submission that they would not rise again for a very long time and they would pay me a yearly tribute."

"How would you do this?"

"I would not fight like the Arabs, but rather like the Franks."

"How do they fight?"

I now arose in order to speak, a dissertation on European war-craft; I, a layman in the art of war. But I was concerned for this brave tribe of the Haddedihn. I considered it in no way to be a sin if I involved myself in the lives of my fellow men; it was within my power to limit the atrocities that always follow when these half-wild men gain victory. I described firstly their own method of fighting and pointed out the consequences of the same; I then described the dispute at hand. They listened to me attentively, and when I had finished, I noticed the impression my words had made by the long silence that followed. The Sheik was the first to speak:

"Your advice is good and true; it could bring us victory and save many of our lives if we had time to practice it."

"We have time." I assured him.

"Did you not say that it would take many years to ready such an army?"

"That I did say. But we do not want to form an army, we only need to strike the Obeïde and force them into retreat, and to do that we need only two days of preparation. If you send out your messengers today then the warriors will be gathered by tomorrow: I will teach them the unified attack by horse, which will overrun the enemy, and the foot offensive with guns."

I took a camel prod from the wall and sketched on the ground, "Look here! Here flows the Tigris; here is the whirlpool; here are the Hamrin – and here lie the Kanuza Mountains. The enemy meets here. The first two tribes march along the right bank of the river, to their rear our allies quietly approach; the Obeïde cross from the left bank. In order to reach us, they must pass between these mountain ranges; all these paths however lead into the large Deradsh valley, which is called the 'Valley of the Steps' because its steep walls ascend like steps. It has only one entrance and one exit. Here we must wait. We occupy the heights with marksmen, who can attack the enemy without being harmed themselves. We block the exit with barricades, which will also be defended by marksmen, and here in these two adjoining gorges, on either side our horsemen conceal themselves, they attack the moment the enemy is entirely within the valley. At the entrance, the enemy is attacked in the rear by our allies, and should they not appear on time, then the enemy will be driven towards them in flight."

"*Mashallah*, your speech is like the rhetoric of the Prophet, who has conquered the world! I will follow your advice, if the others are in agreement. Whoever is against it, may he speak now!"

No one did; the Sheik continued:

"Then I will send a messenger immediately."

"Be careful, oh Sheik, and let no warrior speak of what this concerns, otherwise it may be that the enemy will receive word of our intent."

He nodded in agreement and removed himself. Sir David Lindsay had listened to this long conference with obvious impatience; now he seized the opportunity to speak:

"Sir, I am also here!"

"I see that!"

"Wanted also to hear!"

"My experiences?"

"Yes!"

"You should have realized that my report would not be in English. But you shall discover the important points."

I imparted to him, in all brevity, my story and the content of the discussion that followed. He was electrified.

"Ah! No wild attack, but rather military body! Evolution! Shock! Tactic! Strategy! Surround the enemy! Barricade! Grand! Lovely! I come too! You general, I adjutant!"

"I would exclude us both from this situation! A general who understands as much about warfare as a hippopotamus understands nets, and an adjutant who cannot speak Arabic! You would be well advised to distance yourself from this matter."

"Why?"

"Because of the Vice Consul in Mosul."

"Ah! Why?"

"It is suspected that he has his hand in this game."

"Should take his hand out! What concern is the Consul to me? Pah!"

The Sheik returned. He had dispatched the messengers and brought back all kinds of new ideas:

"Did the Sheik of the Abu Muhammed say which part of the spoils he expects?"

"No."

"What do the Alabeïde demand?"

"I do not know."

"You should have asked!"

"I did not ask because if I were the Sheik of the Haddedihn I would not be concerned with booty."

"*Mashallah*! What else is there! Who replaces my losses?"

"The vanquished enemy."

"Therefore I must go to his pastures and take his women and children as well as his beasts!"

"That is not necessary. Do you intend to wage war against women? Instead, you do not release the prisoners we will take – if we are lucky – until you receive what you demand. If we gain total victory, then you demand an annual tribute and hold their Sheik or some of his relatives as hostages."

This point was now discussed and the proposal accepted.

"And one last thing," I said then. "We must obtain information regarding the movements of our enemy and his allies. We therefore need to establish a communication link between here and El Deradsh."

"How do we do this?"

"Two warriors, whom you can trust, hide at El Deradsh. They remain concealed and observe everything. Between El Deradsh and here you post other men at regular intervals - four men should suffice; they are careful not to encounter any strangers and they relay to us anything that the first two discover. One carries the message to the other and then returns to his post."

"This plan is good; I will follow it."

"You establish a somewhat longer relay between here and the pastures of the Abu Mohammed. I have already discussed this with their Sheik. He will populate half the line with his men. Do you know the El Farr ruins?"

"Yes."

"His furthest post can be found there."

"How many men will we need?"

"Six will be enough. The Abu Mohammed shall provide the same number. How many warriors do you have here in the camp?"

"Possibly four hundred."

"Could I ask you to gather them. We need to muster them and start the exercises today."

That brought life into the meeting. Inside half an hour the four hundred men were gathered. The Sheik held a long and flowery speech and at the end demanded an oath, by the beard of the Prophet, that no one would discuss the battle preparations with anyone; then he ordered them into rank and file.

We rode down the long row of warriors, each one mounted upon a horse. Each was armed with a knife, saber and the long, feathered spear, which, with better training, could be a terrible weapon. Many also carried the deadly *nibat* (club) or the short throwing spear. Their firearms left much to be desired. Some also carried old leather shields as well as quivers, bows and arrows. Others possessed flintlocks that were more dangerous to the user than to the enemy and the rest had percussion guns with overly long barrels.

The latter I asked to step forward, the others I dismissed, telling them to return early the next morning. Those who remained I asked to dismount and tested their shooting skills. All in all I was satisfied with them. There were two hundred men. I formed them into two companies and began my instruction, which was brief. The men were to march and run in tempo and learn how to perform a rapid-fire maneuver. They were to attack on horseback and goad the enemy, without making a serious stand; everything now depended on training the remaining troops to carry out an attack on foot without the loss of restraint.

The next morning I began with the foot soldiers. For them it was important to execute a united attack with the lance after they had discharged their firearms. I have to say that these men caught on quickly and had great enthusiasm.

Towards evening, we heard that the connection with the Abu Mohammed had been established, and at the same time received word that their Sheik had already heard of my adventure with the Abu Hammed. We sent back a reply and from that moment on the traffic between the posts was continuous.

It was nearly dark when I mounted my black stallion once again to take a brisk ride into the savanna. I had not gone far when I spied two horsemen. One was of average build, the other however was very small of stature and appeared to be immersed in a lively conversation with his companion as he moved his arms and legs about as though he were trying to swat mosquitoes.

I spontaneously thought of my little Halef.

I galloped towards the riders and halted my horse before them.

"*Mashallah*, *Sihdi*! Is it truly you?" Came the astonished greeting.

It really was the little Hajji Halef Omar!

"It is. I recognized you from afar." I replied.

He leaped from his horse and grasped my robe in order to kiss it with joy.

"*Hamdulillah* – God be praised that I see you again, *Sihdi*! I have longed for you like the day does for the sun."

"How is the worthy Sheik Malek?"

"He is well."

"And Amsha?"

"Just as well."

"Hanneh, your beloved?"

"Oh, *Sihdi*, she is like one of the *houri's* of paradise." He crowed.

"And the others?"

"They asked me to send their greetings, if I found you."

"Where are they?"

"They remain on the slopes of the Shammar Mountains and have sent me ahead to the Sheik of the Shammar to plead acceptance into his tribe."

"From which Sheik?"

"That does not matter, the first one I encounter."

"I have already arranged this for you. Over there is the camp of the Haddedihn."

"They are Shammar. What is the name of their Sheik?"

"Mohammed Emin."

"Will he accept us? Do you know him?"

"I know him and I have already spoken to him about you. See this stallion! How do you like it?"

"Master, I have already been admiring it; he certainly is a descendant of the mare of Koheli."

"He belongs to me; he was a gift from the Sheik. Now you can see that he is my friend!"

"May Allah give him a long life for this! Will he also accept us?"

"You shall be welcomed by him. Come, follow me."

We started to move.

"*Sihdi*," Halef said, "the ways of Allah are without understanding. I thought that I would have to search a long time before I would get word of you and now you are the first person that I meet. How did you come to the Haddedihn?"

I told him briefly of the necessary details and then continued: "Do you know what position I hold with him?"

"Well?" He prompted.

"General." I answered casually.

"General?" He repeated.

"Yes."

"Does he have troops?" Halef asked.

"No. But he does have a war." I explained wryly.

"Against whom?"

"Against the Obeïde, the Abu Hammed and the Jowari."

"Those are the thieves that live by the Zab and the Tigris, I have heard much about them that was not good."

"They take up arms against him. They plan to mount a surprise attack, but we know of this and now I am the Sheik's general, instructing his warriors."

"Yes, *Sihdi*, I know that you understand and can do everything, and it is truly good fortune that you are no longer a *giaur*!".

"No?"

"No. You have converted to the True Belief."

"Who told you this?"

"You were in Mecca and carry the holy waters of Zem-Zem with you; consequently you have become a good Moslem. Have I not always said that I would convert you, whether you were willing or not?"

We reached the camp and dismounted before the tent of the Sheik. When we entered, the council was with him.

"*Salaam aaleïkum*!" Halef greeted.

His companion did the same. I undertook their introduction.

"Permit me, oh Sheik to bring before you these two men who desire to speak with you. This is Nasar Ibn Mothalleh, and this is Hajji Halef Omar Ben

Hajji Abul Abbas Ibn Hajji Dawud al Gossarah, whom I have already spoken of to you."

"Of him?" He asked with interest.

"Yes. I have not used his full name but only Hajji Halef Omar." I explained.

"Your servant and companion?"

"Yes."

"The one who vanquished Abu-Seïf, the 'Father of the Saber'?"

"Yes. He belongs to the tribe of the Ateïbeh, whose Sheik is your friend Malek."

"Be welcome to me, you men of the Ateïbeh! Be welcome to me, Hajji Halef Omar! Your body is small but your courage is great and your bravery is awe-inspiring. May all men be like you! Do you bring a message from my friend Malek?"

"I do. He greets you and asks if you will receive him and his people into the tribe of the Haddedihn." Halef replied respectfully.

"I know of his fate, but he shall be welcome to me. Where is he located now?"

"On the slopes of the Shammar Mountains, one and a half days ride from here. I hear that you need warriors?"

"It is so. Animosity has grown between us and those that live around us."

"I will bring you sixty brave men."

"Sixty? My friend Hajji Kara Ben Nemsi said that you were fewer!"

"We have united with the rest of the tribe of Al Hariel during our journey."

"What weapons do you have?"

"Saber, dagger, knife and many good guns. Several even have pistols. How well I handle weapons can be attested to by my *Sihdi*."

"I already know of this. But this man is no *Sihdi*, rather an Emir; remember that!"

"I know it, Lord; but he permits me to call him *Sihdi*. Should one of us go and fetch Sheik Malek and his people immediately, since you need warriors?"

"Your are tired."

"We are not tired. I will ride back immediately."

His companion broke in to his speech:

"You have found your *Sihdi* and must remain here, I will return."

"First take food and drink," said the Sheik.

"Lord, I have a water skin and also dates on my horse."

The Sheik turned to him: "But your horse will be tired. Take one of mine, they have had several days rest and will carry you quickly to Malek, whom you shall greet from me!"

This was accepted and a few minutes later Nasar was on his way back to the mountains of Shammar.

"Emir," the Sheik said to me, "do you know what my warriors say of you?"

"Well?"

"That they love you."

"I thank you!"

"And that they will gain victory if you are with them."

"I am satisfied with them now. Tomorrow we will perform a maneuver."

"How? What?"

"Today I have eight hundred people. Early tomorrow morning the rest will arrive. These will be trained quickly and then we will undertake a mock battle, similar to the one we will have with the three tribes. Half of the men will represent the Haddedihn and the rest will represent the enemy. The old ruins, over there, will be the Hamrin and Kanuza Mountains. I will show your warriors how they should fight with the real enemy."

This announcement doubled the present enthusiasm and when the word was spread outside the tent a great jubilation arose that suffused the entire camp, which, due to the many arrivals today, had increased in number considerably.

What I had forecast had happened.

The following noon, we were completely assembled. I had appointed officers and corporals who immediately instructed each newcomer, after I had determined their place. In the late afternoon the maneuver commenced and turned out to everyone's liking. The foot soldiers shot very precisely, and the shock action of the mounted troops was carried out with elegant certainty. During the maneuver, the last member of our communication chain rode up.

"What news do you bring?" asked the Sheik, whose countenance shone with contentment.

"Lord, yesterday the Jowari united with the Abu Hammed."

"When?"

"Towards evening."

"And our allies, the Abu Mohammed?"

"They are already following the enemy."

"Have they sent scouts ahead so that they are not discovered, as I have advised?" I asked.

"Yes."

The messenger was still with us when another rode up. He was a link in the chain to the valley of Deradsh.

"I bring an important message, Emir." He addressed me directly.

"Which is?" I asked.

"The Obeïde have sent men across the Zab to scout out the area."

"How many men were there?"

"Eight."

"How far did they go?"

"Through to the El Deradsh."

"Did they see our men?"

"No, for they concealed themselves. Then the men of the Obeïde camped in the valley and spoke much." He explained.

"Ah! It should have been possible to eavesdrop on them!" I suggested.

"It was possible, and Ibn Nazar did so." He confirmed.

Ibn Nazar was one of the two men who were guarding the valley of Deradsh.

"What did he hear? If it is important he shall receive a reward." The Sheik said.

"They said that tomorrow, precisely at noon, the Obeïde will cross over to meet with the Abu Hammed and the Jowari, who will be waiting for them. They will advance toward El Deradsh and camp there during the night – they believe they will not be seen there. The next morning they intend to attack us."

"Did these eight men ride away again?"

"Only six of them. Two remained behind to guard the valley."

"Ride back, and tell Ibn Nazar and his companion that I will ride to meet them today. One shall stay and watch the two scouts, the other should ride and meet me at the last post to show me the way when I arrive." I directed him.

The messenger rode off. The first messenger still waited for an answer.

"You heard what was reported?" I asked him.

"Yes, Emir."

"Then carry this request to Sheik Abu Mohammed - I ask that he keep hard behind the enemy without being seen. Once the enemy has entered the Valley of Deradsh, he should attack their rear immediately and prevent them from fleeing. All valleys between El Hamrin and El Kanuza are to be occupied. The rest will be our concern."

The messenger raced away. We terminated our exercises to let our people rest.

"You intend to ride to Deradsh?" asked the Sheik on our return journey.

"Yes." I replied.

"Why?"

"To take the two spies prisoner."

"Can this not be done by someone else?"

"No. This matter is of such great importance that I must do it myself. If these two are not captured and held quietly, our careful plan will be completely ruined."

"Take some men with you." He suggested.

"That is not necessary. I and the two guards at the post will be enough."

"*Sihdi*, I go with you!" said Halef who had not parted from my side.

I knew that he would insist on this and therefore nodded in agreement.

"I don't know if your horse can stand a swift ride. I have to be there and back in one night."

"I will give him one of my horses," said the Sheik.

An hour later we were on our way: I on the stallion and Halef on a golden brown horse, which made him very proud. We covered the distance to the last post in a very short time. Ibn Nazar awaited us.

"You have eavesdropped on these men?" I asked him.

"Yes, Lord."

"You shall receive an additional gift from the spoils. Where is your companion?"

"Close by the two spies!"

"Lead us!"

We rode on. The night was not completely dark and we soon saw the heights, behind which spread the El Deradsh. Ibn Nazar led us to one side. We had to climb through a tangle of rocks and soon arrived at the entrance to a dark hollow.

"Here are our horses, Lord."

We dismounted and led our horses into the recess. They were so safe here that they needed no guard. Then we marched along the ridge until the valley opened below us.

"Be careful, Lord, that no stone falls into the valley, as it could betray us!"

We climbed carefully: I behind our guide and Halef behind me – always in the footsteps of the one ahead. Finally we reached the valley floor. A shape approached us and whispered; "Nazar?"

"It is I. Where are they?"

"Still there."

I stepped up to them and asked; "Where?"

"Do you see the corner of the rock there to the right?"

"Yes."

"They are behind it."

"And their horses?"

"They have tied them up further ahead."

"Stay here and come when I call you," I instructed the two guards and then said "Come, Halef!"

I lay down on the earth and crawled forward. Halef followed me. We reached the edge of the rock undetected. I smelled tobacco and heard two voices speaking softly. When I had crawled right up to the corner, I could understand the words:

"Two against six!"

"Yes. One looked black and gray, was long and thin like a lance and wore a gray gun-barrel on his head."

"*Shaïtan*!"

"No, but rather an evil spirit, a *jinn*."

"But the other was the devil?"

"Like a man, but terrible! His mouth smoked, and his eyes spat flames. He just raised his hand, and all six horses collapsed dead, but with the other four horses, these two devils – may Allah damn them – escaped through the air."

"In full daylight?"

"In full daylight."

"Terrible! Allah preserve us from the 'thrice-stoned devil'! And then he came into the camp of the Abu Hammed?"

"He did not come, but rather he was brought."

"How?"

"They thought him a man and his horse was the famous stallion of Sheik Mohammed Emin el Haddedihn. They wanted that horse and so took him prisoner. When they brought him into the camp he was recognized by the son of the Sheik."

"They should have given him his freedom."

"They still believed that he was a man."

"Did they bind him?"

"Yes. But then a lion came into the camp, and the stranger said he would kill it by himself if he were given his gun. It was given to him and he walked into the night. After some time, lightning fell from the sky and two shots cracked. Some minutes later he returned. He had the hide of the lion wrapped around him, climbed on his horse and rode away through the air."

"Did no one try to hold him?"

"Yes, but the men grasped thin air. And when they rode after him, three bullets fell from the sky and three of the best horses were killed."

"How do you know this?"

"The messenger told us, the one that Zedar Ben Huli sent to our Sheik. Do you believe he was *Shaïtan*?"

"He was."

"What would you do if he appeared before you?"

"I would shoot him and pray the holy *fatcha*."

I stepped around the corner and stood before them.

"Then pray it!" I commanded.

"*Allah kerihm*!" Cried one.

"*Allah il Allah, Mohammed rasuhl Allah*!" Wailed the other.

These two exclamations were all they could manage.

"I am he of whom you spoke. You call me *Shaïtan*; woe to you if you move a muscle to defend yourselves! Halef, take their weapons!"

They quietly let this happen; I believed I could hear their teeth chattering.

"Bind their hands with their belts!" I instructed my companion.

Halef soon finished with this, and I could be certain that the knots would not slip.

"Now answer my questions if your life is dear to you! To which tribe do you belong?" I demanded.

"We are Obeïde." Came the reply.

"Your tribe crosses the Tigris tomorrow?" I asked.

"Yes."

"How many warriors do you have?"

"Twelve hundred."

"What arms do they have?"

"Arrows and guns with fuses."

"Do you have other guns or perhaps pistols?"

"Not many."

"How do you intend to cross – with boats?" I suggested.

"On floats; we have no boats." One of the captives corrected.

"How many warriors do the Abu Hammed have?"

"As many as ourselves."

"How are they armed?"

"They have more arrows than guns."

"And how many men do the Jowari bring?"

"A thousand."

"Do they have arrows or guns?" I asked.

"They have both."

"Do only your warriors cross, or will you also bring your herds to this place?"

"Only the warriors come."

"Why do you wish to attack the Haddedihn?" I inquired.

"The Governor of Mosul has commanded it." Was the explanation.

"He cannot command this; you belong under the jurisdiction of the Governor of Baghdad. Where are your horses?"

"There," one of the men replied, indicating with a toss of his head.

"You are my prisoners. I will shoot you down if you make any attempt to escape. Nazar, come!" I called to the two guards who were still waiting out of sight.

"Bind both men firmly onto their horses!" I instructed them when they appeared.

The Obeïde gave themselves over to their fate and were mounted on their horses without incident; they were then secured to them in a manner that made flight impossible.

Chapter 18

Hereupon I gave the command:

"Fetch our horses and bring them to the entrance of the valley. Ibn Nazar, you remain here in El Deradsh; your companion shall help Halef in transporting the prisoners to the camp."

The two Haddedihn went off to lead the horses down the slope of the valley. We then mounted and returned to camp whilst Ibn Nazar remained at his post.

"I will ride ahead; follow me as quickly as possible." I instructed Halef.

Having said this, I spurred my horse onward. I did so for two reasons: firstly, my presence was required in the camp and secondly, I now had the opportunity to confirm the secret command and determine the top speed of my stallion. He flew across the plain easily, like a bird; the swift pace appeared to be a delight to him, he whinnied happily a few times. Suddenly I placed my hand between his ears ...

"Rih!" I urged him with this command.

At this word he laid back his ears; he seemed to become longer and thinner; appeared to dart between the particles of air. The swiftness of his gallop before could not have been equaled by another worthy horse, but this – this was like comparing still air to a raging gale, like comparing the waddle of a duck to the flight of a swallow. The speed of a locomotive or even a racing camel would not have been able to match the swiftness of this horse and yet the ride was smooth and even. The words of Mohammed Emin were truly no exaggeration when he said to me:

"This horse will carry you through a thousand horsemen," and I felt extremely proud to be the owner of this excellent runner. [See Trans. Notes Ch 18.1]

But it was necessary to cease this extraordinary expenditure of energy; I allowed the stallion to lessen his pace and placed my hand lovingly against his neck. The clever animal whinnied with joy at this demonstration of my appreciation and carried his head proudly upon his neck.

When I reached the camp, I had used just a quarter of the time that it took to reach Wadi Deradsh. Near the tent in which the Sheik lived, a lot of dark unrecognizable shapes were mounted on horses and camels, and inside the tent a pleasant surprise awaited me: - Malek stood before the Sheik, who was about to speak the words of greeting.

"*Salaam*!" the Sheik of the Ateïbeh welcomed me with outstretched hands. "My eyes are happy to see you, and my ear is charmed to hear your footsteps!"

"Allah bless your arrival, friend of my soul! He has performed a miracle in bringing you to us this day." I replied.

"Of what miracle does your tongue speak?" He asked.

"We could not possibly have expected you today. It is three days' ride from here to Jebel Shammar and back!"

"You speak the truth. But your messenger did not need to ride to the mountains of Shammar. After he and Halef left us, I discovered from a lost shepherd that the warriors of the Haddedihn grazed their herds here. Their Sheik, the famous and courageous Mohammed Emin, is my friend; Hajji Halef could have encountered only he and no other, and so we held counsel and decided not to wait for their return but rather to anticipate his message."

"Your decision was wise, for without it we would not have been able to welcome you today."

"We met the messenger halfway along our trek and my heart was happy when I learned that I would find you, oh Hajji Kara Ben Nemsi, with the warriors of the Haddedihn. Allah loves you and I; he leads our feet on paths that cross once again. But tell me, where is Hajji Halef Omar, the son of my respect and my favor?"

"He is on his way here. I rode ahead and left him to bring in two prisoners, you will see him in a short while."

"You were successful?" Mohammed Emin asked me.

"Yes. The spies are in our hands; they cannot harm us."

"I hear," said Malek, "that animosity exists between the Haddedihn and the thieves of the Tigris?"

"You have heard correctly. Tomorrow, when the sun has reached its highest point, our guns will thunder and our sabers will flash."

"You will attack them?"

"They intend to attack us, but we will welcome them."

"May the men of the Ateïbeh lend you their sabers?"

"I know that your saber is like '*Dsu al Fekar'*, ('The Flashing '- Mohammed's sword, which still exists today), which no one can resist. You are most welcome, and all that follow you. How many men are with you?"

"More than fifty."

"Are they tired?"

"Is an Arab ever tired when he hears the clash of weapons and the roar of battle? Give us fresh horses, and we will follow you wherever you may lead!"

"I know you. Your bullets always hit their mark and the tips of your lances never miss their target. You and your men will defend the barricade that will block the exit from the battlefield."

During this exchange, Sheik Malek's people had dismounted; I heard that they had been served a meal and Sheik Mohammed Emin's tent had also been richly provisioned with food. We had not yet finished the evening meal when little Halef entered and reported the arrival of the prisoners. These were led before the Sheik. He looked upon them with contempt and asked:

"You are of the tribe of the Obeïde?"

"We are, oh Sheik."

"The Obeïde are cowards. They are afraid to engage the brave warriors of the Haddedihn alone, and that is why they joined the jackals of the Abu Hammed and the Jowari. They think their combined superiority will crush us; but we shall vanquish and annihilate them. Do you know what the duty of a brave warrior is if he desires to battle an enemy?"

They looked at the ground and did not answer.

"A brave Ben Arab does not approach like a treacherous murderer; he sends a messenger in order to announce the battle so that the competition should be fairer. Have your leaders done this?"

"We do not know, oh Sheik!"

"You do not know? May Allah shorten your tongues! Your mouth drips with lies and falsehoods! You do not know and yet your orders were to guard the Deradsh valley so that I would not receive news of your intentions! I will deal with you and your kind, as you deserve. Call Abu Mansur, the owner of the knife!" The Sheik commanded.

One of those present departed and soon returned with another man who carried a box.

"Bind them so that they cannot move and take off their *marameh* (cloth that is worn on the head instead of a turban)!"

This was done and the Sheik turned to the new arrival:

"What is the honor of a man and a warrior, oh Abu Mansur?"

"The hair that adorns his face."

"What is due to a man who is fearful like a woman, and speaks lies like the daughter of a woman?"

"He shall be dealt with like a woman and like the daughter of a woman."

"These two men have beards but they are women. Make certain, Abu Mansur, that they are recognized as women!"

"Shall I take their beards, oh Sheik?"

"I command it!"

"Allah bless you, you bravest and wisest among the children of the Haddedihn! You are benevolent and gentle to your tribe and just to the enemies of your tribe. I will obey your command," the knife-bearer acknowledged.

He opened his box, which contained a variety of instruments, and took from it a *shambijeh* (a crooked dagger), the bare blade twinkled in the light of the fire. He was the barber of the tribe.

"Why do you not use the beard knife?" asked the Sheik.

"Should I take the beards of these cowards with it and then touch the scalp and the *shushah* (the tuft of hair on the top of the head) of a brave Haddedihn, oh Sheik?"

"You are right; do what you have chosen to do!"

The bound Obeïde fought with all their strength against the impending act, which is considered to be a great disgrace; their struggle did not help them. They were held down and Abu Mansur's dagger was so sharp that the beard hairs were removed as though cut by a razor.

"Now take them outside," commanded the Sheik. "They are women and shall be guarded by women. Give them bread, dates and water, but if they try to escape give them the bullet!"

The cutting of the beard was not only a punishment; it was also an effective means of deterring any escape attempt by the prisoners. They would not wish to be seen by any member of their tribe. The Sheik now rose and drew his knife. I saw by his ceremonial posture that something unusual was about to happen and that perhaps he was about to begin a speech.

"*Allah il Allah*," he began; "there is no God except Allah. All that lives, He has created, and we are His children. Why should they that love each other, hate each other, and why should they, who belong together, part? There are many twigs in the forest that bend with the same wind and on the plain are many blades of grass and many flowers. They are the same to each other, they know each other and do not part. Are we not like them? Sheik Malek, you are a great warrior and I say unto you: '*Nanu malihin* – we have eaten salt with one another'. Hajji Emir Kara Ben Nemsi, you too are a great warrior and have I not said to you: '*Nanu malihin*'. You share my tent; you are my friends and my companions; you would die for me, and I would die for you. Do I speak the truth? Do I speak justly?"

We confirmed this with earnest, solemn nods.

"But salt dissolves and passes away," he continued. "Salt is a symbol of friendship; when it has dissolved and passed from the body, so too is friendship at an end and must be renewed. Is that good, is that sufficient? No, I say! Brave men do not bind friendship through salt. There is a substance that never passes from the body. Do you know of what I speak, Sheik Malek?"

"I know."

"Would you speak of it."

"Blood."

"You have spoken truly. Blood remains until death, and friendship that is bound by blood only ends when one dies. Sheik Malek, give me your arm!"

Malek knew as well as I what this involved. He bared his forearm and extended it towards Mohammed Emin who pierced the skin lightly with the tip of his knife and let a few drops of blood flow into a small wooden goblet filled with water. Mohammed Emin then motioned to me.

"Emir Hajji Kara Ben Nemsi, will you be my friend and the friend of this man who calls himself Sheik Malek el Ateïbeh?"

"I will." I confirmed.

"Then your friends and enemies are our friends and enemies, and our friends and enemies are your friends and enemies?"

"They are." I agreed.

"Then give me your arm!"

I did so and a small cut in the skin produced a few drops of blood that fell into the goblet. He did the same to his arm and swirled the goblet to mix the blood and the water.

"Now comes the toast of friendship – there are three parts; welcome it with your thoughts upon the Almighty, Who knows our minds. We have six feet, six arms, six eyes, six ears and six lips, yet they are one foot, one arm, one eye, one ear and one lip. We have three hearts and three heads and yet they are one heart and one head. Where the one is, there the others are and what one does, the others do as his companions would do it. Praised be God, who has given us this day!"

He passed the goblet to me.

"Hajji Emir Kara Ben Nemsi, your people live the farthest from here; drink your portion first and then pass the goblet to our friend."

I spoke briefly and took a swallow; Malek followed me, and Mohammed Emin drank the remainder. Then he embraced and kissed us and said to each of us:

"Now you are my *rafik* (friend, blood-brother – such a one is worth more than all *ashab* – companions), and I am your *rafik*; our friendship is eternal, even if Allah parts our ways!"

The news of this bond spread quickly through the whole camp and anyone who believed themselves to have the least or slightest privilege came to the tent to bestow their best wishes upon us. This took considerable time, so it was quite late before the three of us sat alone.

It was necessary to give Sheik Malek a description of the terrain, where we presumed the battle would take place, and he had to be made privy to our defense plans. He approved completely and finally asked:

"Could the enemies not flee to the north?"

"They could breach between the river and Jebel Kanuza, which runs beside the Wadi Jehennem, but we will also block this way. Sheik Mohammed, have you arranged for tools to be available so we can erect a barricade?"

"It has been done."

"Have you selected the women who will accompany us in order to tend to the wounded?"

"They are ready."

"Then let us choose horses for our companion and his men. We must go shortly for the day will soon be upon us."

Half an hour later, the Haddedihn were on their way, they were no disorderly rabble, as is often the case with Arab forces, but instead they presented a solid body formed by parallel rows of mounted men. Everyone knew his place.

In front of us rode the warriors; behind us, under the leadership of a fairly robust old man and mounted on camels, came the women who were to form the medical corps. Lastly came those who would man the communication line between us and the pastures of the Haddedihn and those who would act as guards for our prisoners.

When the sun's sphere rose above the horizon, everyone dismounted and threw themselves to the ground for morning prayer. It was a stirring sight to see these hundreds of men prostrate themselves in the dust before their God, who might call upon them to join him in eternity this day.

From the messengers we received word that nothing of note had happened thus far. We therefore reached the great expanse of Jebel Deradsh without incident. Beyond lay a valley that spanned, from west to east, the distance of almost one hour's ride. Those who were designated as marksmen dismounted; their horses were secured to stakes on the plain in an orderly manner; if retreat should become necessary no confusion would result. Not far from where the horses were tethered the camels were relieved of their loads and the tents that were to serve as a makeshift hospital were erected. Plenty of water was available in skin pouches but bandages were in short supply; a situation which caused me some concern.

The communication line that kept us in touch with the Abu-Mohammed Arabs had moved with us so that we could maintain contact. There were almost hourly reports via this relay and the last message informed us that the enemy had not yet become aware of our progress.

Sir Lindsay had barely spoken since last night. There had been little time for me to dedicate to him. Now he stopped at my side.

"Where do we battle, sir? Here?" He asked.

"No, in the valley beyond."

"Remain with you?"

"As you wish."

"Where will you be? Infantry, cavalry, intelligence, pontoons?"

"With the cavalry, but we perform as dragoons because we will shoot as well as use our blades if it is necessary."

"Stay with you." He concluded.

"Then wait here. My troop shall remain here until I fetch them."

"Not go into the valley?"

"No, we will move upstream of this river to prevent the enemy from escaping to the north."

"How many men?"

"A hundred."

"Well! Very good, outstanding!"

I had chosen this post for a reason. Although I was a friend and companion of the Haddedihn, it was not in my nature to kill people who had done me no personal harm, even in open battle. The quarrel that was about to be settled here between these Arabs did not concern me personally and since it was not expected that the enemy would turn to the north, I had requested that I be attached to the section that was to block their retreat in that direction. I would have much preferred to remain at the field hospital; but this was an impossibility.

The Sheik now led his cavalry into the valley, and I joined them. They were divided into two groups and dispatched to the secondary valleys to the right and the left. The infantry followed. One third ascended the heights to the right, another third, the heights to the left, they hid themselves behind the numerous rocks in order to harass the enemy from above. The remainder, which mostly consisted of Sheik Malek and his men, stayed at the entrance in order to man the barricade and engage the enemy from behind this fortification. I then returned and joined my troop of a hundred men and rode away.

Our route was direct until we found a valley pass that permitted us to cross the Jebel. After an hour's ride, we saw the river before us. Further to the right - that is, to the south - there was a location where the mountain touched the river twice and formed a semicircular enclosure. Escape from here would be difficult if one was unlucky enough to be caught in it. I posted my men at this point because here we could detain a force ten times our number with minimal effort on our part.

After I had designated lookouts we dismounted and made ourselves comfortable, Master Lindsay asked me: "Familiar with this place, sir?"

"No," I answered.

"Know perhaps if there are ruins around here?"

"I don't know."

"Ask someone!"

I did so and translated the answer for him: "Further upstream."

"What name?"

"Muk hol Kal or Kalah Shergatha."

"Fowling-bulls there?" he asked in anticipation.

"Hmm! That remains to be seen."

"How much time before the battle?"

"Until noon, maybe even later. Perhaps there won't be a battle for us at all."

" In the meantime will have a look."

"At what?"

"Kalah Shergatha. Dig up fowling-bulls; send to London museum; become famous; what!"

"That will be impossible."

"Why?"

"Because you would have to ride some fifteen English miles to get there."

"Ah! Hmm! Miserable! Will remain here!" He conceded.

He lay down behind a euphorbia bush, but I decided to make a reconnaissance of the area and so I gave the necessary instructions to my men and rode south along the river. My black stallion was, like all Shammar horses, an excellent climber; I could risk climbing the Jebel with him, and so when the terrain became suitable I rode to the summit to gain an overview of the landscape. At the crest I studied the easterly horizon through my telescope. I saw that on the other side of the river there was much activity. On the southern, that is to say, the left bank of the Zab the plain swarmed with horses and men, almost as far as Tell Hamlia. Below the *chelab* (rapids) were several large piles of goatskins, from which rafts were apparently to be fashioned for use by the Obeïde in their crossing. I could not see the shore on this side of the Tigris because of the peak, beyond which lay the Deradsh Valley. Since I still had time, I decided to climb that summit also.

I had a strenuous ride along the crest of the mountain range and it was more than one hour before I reached the highest point. My horse was as fresh as if it had just risen from sleep; I tethered him and scaled up a rock wall. Below me was the Wadi Deradsh. In the distance I saw the completed barricade, behind which rested the defenders; on either side were the hidden marksmen, and below, directly opposite from me, the cavalry sat in their ambush.

I pointed my telescope to the south.

In that direction there squatted tent upon tent, but I noted that these were in the process of being decamped. There lay the Abu Hammed and the Jowari. Possibly the hordes of the Sardanapal, Kyaxares and Alyattes had once camped there also. There, the warriors of the Nabopolassar had knelt when, on the fifth day of May in the fifth year of their ruler, a lunar eclipse was followed by a total solar eclipse, which made the battle of Halys so terrible. There they had probably watered their horses at the Tigris when Nebuchadnezzar moved upon Egypt to dethrone king Hophra, and that these were probably the same waters across which the death songs of the Nerikolassar and the Nabonnad echoed from the mountains of Kara Zshook, Zibar and Sar Hasana.

I saw that the goatskins had been inflated and tied together; I saw the horsemen lead their animals by hand and move towards the rafts; I saw the rafts leave the far shore and land on this side of the river. I expected to hear the cries of greeting from their allies, who leapt onto their horses in order to execute a brilliant *phantasia* (mock battle).

It was desirable to us that they exert their horses so before battle, for when it counted they would be tired.

I must have sat like this for an hour. The Obeïde had all crossed now and I saw that they began to move north. I climbed down from the cliff, mounted my horse and set off on my return trek. The time for decision was upon us.

It took almost an hour to reach a location from which it was possible to descend. I was about to do so when I noticed something flashing on the northern horizon. It was as if the sun were being reflected off glass. We were only expecting the enemy from the south, yet I took my telescope and searched the place where I had noticed the flash of light. Finally – finally I found it. Close to the river I noted some dark figures, which were moving downstream. They had to be riders, and the light of the sun had reflected off of one of their persons

Were they enemies? They were as far north of our hiding place as I was to the south of it. There was no time for contemplation, I had to reach our post before they did.

I spurred my black stallion on and he swiftly descended, as soon as he felt the valley floor beneath his hooves he flew along like a bird. I was certain that I would reach my destination in time.

When I arrived, I called my troop together and told them what I had observed. We moved the horses out of the curved, enclosure. Then one half of the Haddedihn troop hid behind the southern spur while the other half concealed themselves behind the euphorbia and rubber plants in order to cut off any escape of those approaching.

We did not have to wait long before we heard the sound of hooves. Master Lindsay was beside me, listening whilst holding his gun at the ready.

"How many?" He asked.

"I could not count them precisely."

"Approximately?"

"Twenty."

"Pah! Why all the fuss?"

He stood up and sat himself on a rock. His servants followed immediately.

The unidentified group came around the bend led by a tall, powerful looking Arab who was wearing chain mail under his *aba*. This is what I had seen flashing in the sun. He presented a regal figure. Here was a man who had surely never before feared anything, had never before been caught off guard; even now, suddenly confronted with the peculiar figure of the Englishman, he did not bat an eye but simply let his hand drift slowly to his curved saber. He rode forward a few paces and waited until the rest of his troop was at his side; he then beckoned to one of his men. This man was very tall and thin and sat on his horse as though he had never before touched a saddle. I saw at once that he was of Greek heritage. In response to the hand motion the Greek asked the Englishman in Arabic:

"Who are you?"

Master Lindsay raised himself, lifted his hat and performed a half bow but spoke not a word.

The question was repeated in Turkish.

"I'm *Inglis*." Came the reply.

"Ah, then I greet you, noble sir!" was the response in English. "It is an extraordinary surprise to encounter a son of Albion here in this wilderness. May I ask your name?"

"David Lindsay."

"These are your servants?"

"Yes!"

"But what are you doing here?"

"Nothing."

"You must have a purpose, a goal?"

"Yes!"

"And that purpose is?"

"To dig."

"To dig what?"

"Fowling-bulls."

"Ah!" smiled the man thoughtfully. "For this one needs supplies, time, people and permission. How did you get here?"

"By steamer."

"Where is it?"

"Returned to Baghdad."

"Then you disembarked here with your two servants?"

"Yes!"

"Hmm, strange! And where do you go next?"

"Wherever fowling-bulls are. Who is master here?" Lindsay asked, whilst pointing to the Arab wearing the chain mail. The Greek translated this exchange and then answered:

"This famous man is Eslah el Mahem, Sheik of the Obeïde-Arabs, who have their pastures over there." He indicated with outstretched arm.

I was astonished by this answer. This meant the Sheik had not been with his tribe during their maneuvers.

"Who are you?" asked the Englishman further.

"I am one of the English interpreters of the Vice-Consul of Mosul."

"Ah! Where are you going?"

"On an expedition against the Haddedihn Arabs."

"Expedition? Attack? War? Battle? Why?"

"The Haddedihn are an obstinate tribe that must be given a piece of one's mind! They protected several Jesidi when the Governor of Mosul attacked these 'Devil Worshippers'. But how is it that ..."

He stopped in mid-sentence, for one of our horses, which were concealed behind the spur, whinnied and the others followed his example. At once the Sheik grasped his reigns to ride forward and determine the cause. I now arose from my hiding place.

"Permit me to introduce myself to you also!"

The Sheik halted in surprise.

"Who are you?" asked the interpreter. "Also an Englishman? But you dress like an Arab!"

"I am a German and belong to this gentleman's expedition. We wish to excavate 'fowling-bulls' here and study the customs of this country at the same time."

"Who is this?" the Sheik asked the Greek.

"A *Nemsi*." The interpreter replied.

"Are the *Nemsi* 'True Believers'?" asked the Sheik.

"They are Christians."

"Nazarah? But this man is a hajji. Was he in Mecca?"

"I was in Mecca," I answered.

"You speak our language?"

"I speak it." I confirmed.

"You belong with this *Inglis*?"

"Yes."

"How long have you been in this area?"

"Several days already." I told him.

His eyebrows crept together. "Do you know the Haddedihn?"

"I know them."

"How did you learn of them?"

"I am the *rafik* of their Sheik." I said.

"Then your life is forfeit!" the Sheik declared.

"Why?"

"I will take you prisoner, you and these other three." He explained.

"When?" I challenged.

"Immediately."

"You are strong, but Zedar Ben Huli, the Sheik of the Abu Hammed, was also strong!"

"What do you know of him?" He demanded.

"He took me prisoner and held me not."

"*Mashallah*! Are you the man that killed the lion?" He asked in wonder.

"I am he."

"Then you are mine. You will not escape me."

"Or you are mine and will not escape me. Look around you!"

He did so but saw no one.

"Rise you men!" I called loudly.

At once all the Haddedihn rose and aimed their weapons at the Sheik and his people.

"Ah, you are clever like *Abul Hosseïn* (the fox) and have slain the lion, but you will not capture me!"

He tore the curved saber from his belt and urged his horse towards me as he prepared for the lethal blow. It was not difficult to deal with this. I shot his horse, which tumbled to the ground, and then quickly seized him. Now a terrible struggle began, which proved to me that he was indeed an uncommonly strong man; I had to wrest off his turban in order to deliver a blow to his temple, which ensured my victory over him.

During this short contest a battle raged around me, but what was happening could not be called a true battle. I had commanded the Haddedihn to shoot only at the horses; as a result the first volley, which was fired as the Sheik attacked me, killed or maimed all of the horses of the Obeïde. The warriors lay where they had been thrown and from all sides the long, decorated spears of the Haddedihn, who were five times superior in number, were pointed at them. Even the river offered no opportunity for escape as our bullets would have reached any swimmer. When the confusion caused by the first volley was over, they stood around helplessly. I had thrust the Sheik into the hands of Lindsay's servants and was now able to fulfill my desire to end this fracas without bloodshed.

"Don't make any show of resistance, you warriors of the Obeïde; you are our prisoners. You are twenty men; we number over a hundred horsemen, and your Sheik is in my hands!"

"Shoot him down!" The Sheik ordered his men.

"If one of you raises his weapon against me, these two men will kill your Sheik!" I answered.

"Shoot him down, the *dib* (wolf), the *ibn avah* (jackal), the *erneb* (rabbit)!" he screamed in spite of my threat.

"Don't even think about it, otherwise you will all be dead!"

"My brothers will avenge me!" the Sheik shouted.

"Your brothers? The Obeïde? Perhaps even the Abu Hammed and the Jowari!" he looked at me in surprise.

"What do you know of them?" he blurted.

"That they are at this moment prisoners of the Haddedihn, just as you and your men are mine."

"You lie! You are an animal that can harm no one. My warriors will capture you with all the sons and daughters of the Haddedihn and lead you into captivity!"

"May Allah watch over your head and rescue your senses! Would we wait for you here if we did not know what your intentions towards Sheik Mohammed were?"

"How do you know that I was at the grave of the Hajji Ali?"

Deciding to sound things out, I answered:

"You were at the grave of Hajji Ali to gain good fortune for your venture; but the grave is on the left shore of the Tigris and you traveled on this shore to spy out Wadi Murr, where the other tribes of the Shammar are located."

It was obvious that I had guessed correctly. Despite this he broke into derisive laughter and answered:

"Your intellect is rotten and sluggish, like the mud that lies in the river. Release us and no ill shall befall you!"

Now it was my turn to laugh.

"What will befall us if I do not do this?"

"My men will search for me and find me. Then you are finished!"

"Your eyes are blind and your ears are deaf. You have neither heard nor seen what happened before your men came across the river."

"What happened?" he asked in contemptuous tone.

"They were expected, just like yourself."

"Where?"

"In the Wadi Deradsh."

He was obviously alarmed now; and so I added:

"You see that your plan is betrayed. You know that I was with the Abu Hammed. Before that I was with the Abu Mohammed. They and the Alabeïde, whom you have robbed so often, have united with the Haddedihn to trap you in Wadi Deradsh. Listen!"

Just then a dull clamor was heard.

"Do you hear the shots? They are already trapped in the valley and will be annihilated if they don't surrender."

"*Allah il Allah*!" he cried. "Is this true?"

"It is true."

"Then kill me!"

"You are a coward!"

"Is it cowardly if I demand my own death?"

"Yes. Are you the Sheik of the Obeïde, the father of your tribe? It is your duty to stand by them in their time of need; but you wish to leave them!"

"Are you insane? How can I stand by them if I am a prisoner!"

"With your counsel. The Haddedihn are not monsters that lust after blood; they want to repel your attack and then make peace. During that discussion the Sheik of the Obeïde should not be absent."

"Again I ask, do you speak the truth?"

"I speak it."

"Swear it."

"The word of a man is his oath . . . stop, knave!" This last call was aimed at the Greek. He had up to that point stood quietly by, now he suddenly leapt upon one of my men, who had strayed too close to listen, thrust him aside and took flight. Shots cracked behind him, but in the confusion no one was aiming properly; he therefore succeeded in reaching the spur and disappearing behind the same.

“Shoot anyone that moves!” With these words I hurried after the fugitive. When I reached the spur the Greek was already a hundred paces from it.

“Stop!” I called after him.

He looked around quickly but raced on. I was sorry that I was forced to shoot at him; but I intended only to wound him if it was possible. I aimed carefully and fired. It was as though an invisible hand had spun him about on his own axis, then he fell to the ground.

“Bring him!” I commanded.

At this order several of the Haddedihn ran to him and carried him back. The bullet had penetrated his thigh.

“You see, Eslah el Mahem that we are serious? Order your people to surrender!”

“And if I will not give the order?”

“Then we must force them and their blood will flow, a situation that we wish to avoid.”

“Will you later vouch that I only surrendered because you outnumbered us five to one and because you had already captured my tribe in Wadi Deradsh?”

“I will attest to it!”

“Surrender your weapons!” he growled through gritted teeth. “But may Allah cast you into the deepest Jehenna if you lie to me!” He said.

The Obeïde were disarmed.

“Sir!” called Lindsay as this task was being carried out.

“What?” I asked as I turned around.

He held fast onto the arm of the wounded Greek and reported: “Eats paper, the nasty fellow!”

I stepped over to them. The Greek had another shred of paper balled in his hand.

“Give it here!” I demanded.

“Never!” Came the defiant response.

“Pah!”

A bit of pressure on his hand – he screamed in pain and opened his fingers. The paper was part of an envelope and only bore one word - ‘Baghdad’. The man had either devoured the other part of the envelope and the actual letter or had them still in his mouth.

“Spit out what you have in your mouth!”

A disdainful smile was his answer and at once he raised his head to ease the act of swallowing. I grabbed his throat immediately. With the persuasion of my not-so-gentle grip he opened his mouth out of fear of choking. I effectively brought the clump of paper to light. The shreds of paper contained only a few lines of code and it would have been impossible to arrange the pieces in their original order.

Chapter 19

I grabbed the Greek, looked hard into his eyes and asked him; "Who composed this letter?"

"I do not know." He said.

"From whom did you get it?"

"I do not know." He replied obstinately.

"Liar, do you wish to remain here and die miserably?"

He looked at me with terrified eyes.

"If you do not answer, your wound will not be dressed and I will leave you here for the vultures and jackals!"

"I must remain silent." He whimpered.

"Then be silent forever!"

I stood up. That did the trick.

"Ask, *effendi*!" He yielded.

"From whom did you get this letter?"

"From the English vice-consul in Mosul."

"To whom was it directed?"

"To the Consul in Baghdad."

"Do you know of the content?"

"No."

"Don't lie!"

"I swear that I did not get to read a single character!"

"But you suspect what it contained?"

"Yes." He agreed reluctantly.

"Then speak!"

"Politics!"

"Naturally!"

"I may not speak further."

"Have you sworn an oath?"

"Yes."

"Hmm! You are a Greek?"

"Yes."

"From where?"

"From Lemnos."

"I thought so! The true Turk is an honest, unsophisticated fellow, and if he has become otherwise then you bear that blame, you, who call yourselves Christians, are worse than the worst heathen. In Turkey, wherever a swindle or villainous act is performed, there a Greek has his dirty hand in the game. You will break your oath this day either by force or by bribe, you spy! How did you manage to become a dragoon in Mosul? . . . Silence! I have my suspicions, for I know how you achieve all you become! You may remain true to your oath, for I know of the politics of which you speak. Why do you stir up hatred amongst the tribes? Why do you incite, sometimes the Turk and sometimes the Persian, against each other? And all this is done by Christians! Others, who truly follow the teachings of the 'Savior of the World' bring words of love and mercy into this land, you sow weeds amongst the wheat so that it suffocates, but your crop bears fruit a thousand-fold. Flee to your Pope; may he ask forgiveness on your behalf!" [I looked at him in disgust for a moment.]

"You have also served the Russians?" I added.

"Yes, Lord."

"Where?"

"In Stambul."

"Well then! I see that you are at least still capable of confessing the truth, therefore I will not deliver you up to the vengeance of the Haddedihn."

"Do not do it, *effendi*! My soul will bless you for it!"

"Keep your blessing! What is your name?"

"Alexander Kolettis."

"You have a famous name, but you have nothing in common with your namesake . . . Bill!" I beckoned Lindsay's servant.

"Sir?" he inquired.

"Can you bind a wound?"

"That sir, no, but plug a hole, that I can do well."

"Plug it for him!"

The Englishman tended to the Greek. Who knows whether I would have acted differently if I had known at that time under what circumstances I would encounter this person again. I turned to the bound Sheik:

"Eslah el Mahem, you are a brave man, and it is a sorry sight to see a courageous warrior restrained. Will you promise me that you will remain always at my side and make no attempt at escape?"

"Why?"

"Then I can have your bonds removed."

"I vow it!"

"By the beard of the Prophet?"

"By the beard of the Prophet and my own as well!"

"Obtain the pledge from your men also!"

"Swear to me that you will not try to escape from this man!" he commanded.

"We swear it!" sounded the response.

"Then you shall not be bound." I promised them.

At the same time I loosened the Sheik's bonds.

"*Sihdi*, you are said to be a noble warrior," he said. "You have permitted that only our animals be killed and have spared us. Allah bless you, although my horse was more dear to me than my brother!"

I looked upon his noble features and read therein; this man was incapable of betrayal, faithlessness or infamy.

"You have permitted yourself to be maneuvered into this battle against members of your own people by foreign tongues; be stronger next time! Do you wish to have your saber, your dagger and your gun returned to you?"

"You would not do this, *effendi*!" He answered with astonishment.

"I shall do it. A Sheik should be the noblest of his tribe; I do not desire to treat you like a Huteijeh or like a Chelawijeh (despised tribes, that are classed amongst the rabble, somewhat like the *pariahs* in India). You shall stand before Mohammed Emin, the Sheik of the Haddedihn, as a free man with weapons in your hands."

I gave him his saber and other weapons. He sprang up and stared at me.

"What is your name, *Sihdi*?"

"The Haddedihn call me Emir Kara Ben Nemsi."

"Where do the herds of your tribe graze?"

"In the distant west. I am a Frank."

"A Frank?"

"Yes, a Christian."

"You belong to the Nazarah? But you wear a white turban and also the *hamaïl,* around your neck!"

"I am a Christian and yet a hajji, for I was in Mecca."

"So you are a Christian, Emir! Today I learn that the Nazarah are not dogs, but rather nobler and wiser than the Moslems. Believe me when I say that in returning my weapons to me, you have more easily defeated me than you would have with the weapons that you carry and with which you could have killed me. Show me your dagger!"

I did so; he tested the blade and then said: "This steel I could snap with my hand, compare it to my *shambijeh*!"

He removed this weapon from its sheath. It was a masterpiece, double edged, slightly curved and wonderfully damascened; written in Arabic on both sides, was the motto: 'Only upon victory return to the sheath'. Certainly it was created by those ancient and celebrated metalworkers in Damascus, who are now vanished and to whom no one today can compare.

"Do you like it?" asked the Sheik.

"It is worth at least fifty sheep!"

"Say a hundred or a hundred and fifty, for ten of my forefathers have owned it, and it has never been broken. It is yours; give me yours in exchange!"

I could not reject this offer if I did not wish to insult the Sheik. I therefore handed him my dagger.

"I thank you, Hajji Eslah el Mahem; I will carry this blade in memory of you and in honor of your fathers!"

"It will never fail you as long as you hold it firmly in your hand!"

I heard the clatter of horses' hooves and shortly a rider came around the spur that bordered the southern edge of our hiding place. It was none other than my little Halef.

"*Sihdi*, you should come!" he called when he saw me.

"What is the situation, Hajji Halef Omar?"

"We won!" he exalted.

"Was it difficult?"

"It went very smoothly. They are all captured!"

"All?"

"With their Sheiks! *Hamdullillah*! Only Eslah el Mahem, the Sheik of the Obeïde, is missing."

I turned to Eslah el Mahem:

"You see that I spoke the truth?" then I asked Halef: "Did the Abu Mohammed arrive in time?"

"They arrived directly after the Jowari and sealed off the wadi so that none of the enemy were able to escape. Who are these men?" Halef asked turning to the Sheik and his troops.

"This is Sheik Eslah el Mahem, of whom you spoke."

"Your prisoners?" He inquired with delight.

"They will come with me."

"*Wallah, billah, tillah*! Permit me to return at once to bring this news to Mohammed Emin and Sheik Malek!" He raced off at once.

Sheik Eslah mounted one of our horses and the Greek was assisted onto another, the rest of the captives had to walk. In this manner our procession commenced. If there was as little blood spilt in Wadi Deradsh as here, then we could be pleased.

The pass I have already mentioned led us to the other side of the mountains; once on the plain we headed south. We had not yet reached the wadi when I spied four horsemen riding towards us. I hastened towards them; it was Malek, Mohammed Emin and the Sheiks of the Abu Mohammed and the Alabeïde-Arabs.

"You have captured him?" Mohammed Emin shouted to me.

"Eslahel Mahem? Yes," I confirmed.

"Allah be thanked! For only he was missing. How many men did this battle cost you?"

"None."

"How many were wounded?"

"None of our men. One amongst the enemy received a bullet wound."

"Then Allah was merciful to us. We only suffered two dead and eleven wounded."

"And the enemy?"

"For them it was worse. They were bottled up so tightly that they could not move. Our marksmen hit their targets accurately and yet could not be hit themselves; and our horsemen held together, just as you taught them. They rode down the enemy when they burst from the gorges."

"Where are the vanquished now?"

"Contained in the wadi. They were forced to deliver all their weapons, and none can escape, for we have the valley secured. Ha! Now I see Eslah el Mahem! But what is this, he carries his weapons?"

"Yes. He assured me he would not try to escape. You know, of course, that the brave should be honored?"

"He tried to destroy us!"

"He will be punished for that." I agreed.

"You have left him his weapons and so it shall be. Come!" He urged.

We hastened to the battlefield, and the others followed us as quickly as possible. It was bustling at the field hospital and before it a number of armed Haddedihn formed a circle, within which the vanquished and bound Sheiks sat. I waited until Eslah arrived and asked him quietly: "Do you wish to remain with me?"

His answer was as I expected: "They are my allies; I belong with them."

He stepped into the circle and sat down next to them. No words were spoken, but one could see that the other two were startled by his presence. Perhaps they had placed their desperate hopes in him.

"Lead your prisoners into the wadi!" said Malek.

I followed him. When I entered the valley, an extraordinarily striking view opened before me. A breach had been made in the barricade to ease the traffic and on both sides of the valley guards had been posted; the entire valley floor swarmed with captured men and horses and at the rear our allies, who had found an unoccupied area in the wadi, camped. Between them several Haddedihn were busy gathering the horses of their foes in order to lead them out onto the plain where the weapons of the vanquished already lay in a large pile.

"Have you ever seen anything like this?" Malek asked me.

"Something even greater."

"I have not."

"Are the wounded well cared for?" I asked.

"They have been bandaged as you have instructed." He assured me.

"And what will happen now?"

"We will celebrate our victory today and perform a great *phantasia*, as has never been seen here before."

"No, we should not do this."

"Why not?"

"Do we wish to embitter the enemy with this festival?" I asked him.

"Have they asked us if we would have been embittered by their attack?" He responded with a question of his own.

"Do we have time for such a festival?" I countered.

"What would prevent us?"

"Work. Both friend and enemy must be fed."

"We will order this to be done."

"How long do you intend to guard the prisoners?"

"Until they may leave."

"And when should this happen?"

"As soon as possible; we do not have enough provisions for this multitude of friends and foe."

"Do you see now that I am right? A feast should be held, but only when we have the time for it. First of all it is essential that the Sheiks meet, in order to discuss those things that need resolving, and then we must enact these decisions with all haste. Tell the Sheiks that six thousand men cannot remain in close proximity for long!"

He departed and Lindsay stepped up to me.

"Lovely victory! No?" He asked.

"Great!" I agreed.

"How did I do, sir?"

"Outstanding!"

"Nice! Hmm! Many people here." He suggested.

"Obviously."

"Wonder if there are some amongst them who know where ruins are?"

"Possibly; one would have to ask."

"Ask at once sir!"

"Yes, as soon as possible."

"Now, immediately!" He urged.

"Forgive me, sir, I do not have the time right now. My presence is required in council, which is about to commence."

"Nice! Hmm! But afterwards ask! What?" he cajoled.

"Certainly!"

I left him where he stood and walked over to the tents.

There I found ample work because many of the wounded required adjustments to their dressings. When I had provided this I stepped into the tent in which the Sheiks were holding their discussion.

It was quite a lively affair. They could not agree in principle and I believed that my presence was welcome to them.

"You will give us advice, Hajji Emir Kara Ben Nemsi," said Malek "You have been in all lands on this earth and know what is right and advantageous."

"Ask, I will answer!"

"To whom do the weapons of the vanquished belong?" He questioned.

"To the victor."

"And to whom, the horses?"

"To the victor."

"And the clothes?"

"The thief takes them but the 'True Believer' leaves them."

"And to whom belongs their riches, and their jewelry?"

"The 'True Believer' only takes their weapons and their horses."

"To whom belong their herds?"

"If they possess nothing other than their herds then the herds belong to them but they should compensate the victor from their herds for the cost of the war and pay a yearly tribute."

"You speak like a friend of our enemies. We have conquered them and now their lives and all they posses belong to us." He asserted.

"I speak as their friend as well as your friend. You say that their lives belong to you?"

"It is so."

"Do you wish to take those lives?"

"No. We are not executioners, nor murderers."

"And yet you desire to take their herds? Can they live without their herds?"

"No."

"If you take their herds you take their lives. Yes, you even steal from yourselves in such a case!"

"How so?"

"You demand that they pay you a tribute from now on?"

"Yes."

"From what? Can a Beni-Arab pay tribute if he has no herds?" I reasoned.

"Your mouth utters wisdom and reason." He concluded.

"Listen further! If you take everything from them, their clothes, their precious objects, their herds, then you force them to steal and to rob so that they will not starve. And from whom will they steal? First from their neighbors, that is you. What is better, to have friends as neighbors or thieves?"

"The first." The Sheik conceded.

"Then make them your friends, do not make thieves of them! Take from the vanquished only that with which he can do harm. If you take their weapons and their horses then you receive ten thousand various weapons and three thousand horses. Is that too little?"

"It is much, if one considers it."

"They then have neither enough weapons nor horses with which to wage another war. You will rule over them, and they will have to ask for your protection, to be safeguarded against their enemies; then they will also have to help you fight against your enemies. I have spoken!" I concluded my advice.

"Yet more shall you speak! How much does one take from their herds today?"

"Enough to cover the losses that this attack has cost you."

"And how much tribute do we demand from them?"

"One demands only so much, so that they will always retain just enough to live without need. A clever Sheik would see that they never again become sufficiently powerful to seek vengeance."

"That leaves the blood feud. We have killed several of their warriors."

"And they have killed several of yours. Before the prisoners are released, the *chamseh* and *aaman* (relatives) should convene and determine the blood price. You have to pay more than they and can do so immediately because of the spoils you have gained."

"Will they bring the war restitution to us?"

"No. You will have to seize it. The prisoners must remain here until you have secured it. And in order to ensure that the tribute is paid, you must keep some distinguished members of their tribes as hostages. If they fail to pay the tribute then the hostages' lives will be in jeopardy."

"We would kill them. Answer us this final question."

"What is it?"

"How do we divide the restitution and the tribute among us? That is most difficult to determine."

"That is actually very easy to determine if you are friends. The restitution you retrieve yourselves, while you are still together here and then you can divide it according to the head count."

"So shall it be done!"

"You are three tribes, and they are three tribes; even the number of the members of the tribes are almost equal. Why should one of your tribes not receive a yearly tribute from one of their tribes? You are friends and companions. Do you want to squabble and divide over the tail of a sheep or the horns of a steer?"

"You are quite right. But who should retrieve the restitution from their tribal pastures?"

"As many men as are required should participate, of these two-thirds should be your men and one-third the men of their tribes."

"That is good. And what do you desire to receive from this restitution?"

"Nothing. I will move on and have no need for herds, I have weapons and a horse."

"And the three men who are with you?"

"They will also take nothing; they have all that they need."

"Then you must take what we present to you in gratitude. Your head is not as old as ours, yet you have taught our warriors how to gain victory over a great enemy without great losses."

"If you wish to thank me, then care for your wounded foes, who lie in your tents, and see if you can find archeological ruins where one might excavate sculptures and stones with strange writings on them. My companion desires to see such things. Now you have heard what I have to say. Allah enlighten your wisdom, so that I may soon discover what you have decided!"

"You shall stay and participate in the discussion!"

"I cannot say anything other than that which I have already said. You will decide justly."

I went outside and hurried to arrange for water and dates to be given to the captured Sheiks. I met up with Halef who accompanied me to Wadi Deradsh, I wished to examine this valley more closely. The captured Abu Hammed recognized me. Some of them arose respectfully when I passed them, whilst others bowed their heads together and whispered amongst themselves. At the rear of the valley I was welcomed with joy by the Abu Muhammed. They were quite thrilled to have overcome this powerful foe so easily. I went from group to group, and so it was that several hours had passed before I returned to the tents.

During my absence the messengers that had been sent to the tribal pastures had arranged for the breaking of the camp and its relocation closer to Wadi Deradsh. The entire plain already swarmed with their herds and now there was mutton enough for a feast, which was expected in every tent tonight. Mohammed Emin had sought me out.

"Your word is as good as your deeds," he said. "We have abided by it. The Obeïde will pay tribute to the Haddedihn, the Abu Hammed will pay tribute to the Abu Mohammed and the Jowari will pay tribute to the Alabeïde."

"How much restitution does each tribe pay?"

He named the figures: which were significant, but not excessive; this made me especially happy since I was able to console myself with the fact that my words here had not been entirely without influence, averting the otherwise terrible practices which usually prevailed. There was no talk of slavery.

"May I ask a favor of you?" asked the Sheik.

"I will do it gladly, if I can. Ask it!"

"We are going to fetch a portion of the herds from each of the vanquished; to do this the men we send require wise and brave leaders. Sheik Malek and I must remain here with the prisoners. We therefore need three leaders, one for the company of Obeïde, one for the company of Abu Hammed and one for the company of Jowari. The Sheiks of the Abu Mohammed and the Alabeïde are ready to leave; we are missing the third leader. Will you do it?"

"I will."

"To which tribe do you wish to go?"

"To which tribes do the others go?"

"They wish to give you first choice."

"Then I go to the Abu Hammed because I was with them once before. When shall we leave?"

"Tomorrow. How many men do you wish to take with you?"

"Forty men of the Abu Hammed and sixty of your Haddedihn. And I will also take Halef Omar."

"Then choose your men. Will the Abu Hammed need to be armed?"

"No, that would be a grave mistake. Have you already come to an agreement with the defeated Sheiks?"

"No. That will happen later today at the time of the last prayer."

"Keep the respected warriors here and send only ordinary men with us; they will be sufficient to drive the herds."

I went to choose the men that were to come with me and ran into Lindsay.

"Have you asked, sir?" he inquired.

"Not yet."

"Why not?"

"It is not necessary, for I have requested that the Sheiks investigate."

"Lovely! Grand! Sheiks know all! Will find ruins!"

"I believe so! Do you want to come on an interesting ride?"

"Where to?"

"Just south of El Fattha, where the Tigris flows through the Hamrin Mountains."

"What is there?"

"We go to retrieve restitution, which consists of a herd of animals."

"From whom?"

"From the tribe Abu Hammed, they who stole our horses some time ago."

"Precious, sir! I am with you! How many men do we take?" He asked gleefully.

"A hundred." I told him.

"Good! Grand! Imposing troop. Ruins there?"

"Several grave mounds, but on the left bank."

"Not cross?"

"No."

"Pity! Great pity! Could excavate! Find fowling-bulls!"

"We will find something extraordinary nonetheless."

"What?"

"Something delicious that we have done without for a long time – namely, truffles."

"Truffles? Oh! Ah!"

He opened his mouth wide enough to devour an entire truffle pâté in one bite.

"They grow in abundance in that area, and I have learned that a substantial trade in them exists in Baghdad, Basra, Kirkuk and Sulimaniah. They are even traded as far east as Kermanshah."

"Go with you, sir, go with you! Truffles! Hmm! Magnificent!"

With these words he departed to tell his servants of the good news; and I went to choose my men.

It was evening before the three captive Sheiks accepted that they had no other choice than to agree to the demands made upon them. Then the festivities began, for which many a fat sheep had to give up its life. Amidst the jubilation I lay among fragrant blossoms, surrounded by the sound of a thousand voices, yet I was alone with my thoughts. Many centuries ago the Doryphoren had flung their feared javelins here. Here too, perhaps, had stood the tents of the Holofernes, fashioned from gold and crimson and decorated with emeralds and jewels. And over there on the rushing waters of the river had sat the anchored vessels, of which Herodotus wrote:

> *"The boats are of a circular form and are fashioned from skins. They are built by Armenians in the upper reaches of Assyria. The ribs are made out of willow twigs and branches and are covered on the outside with skins. They are round, like a shield, and there is no difference between the front and the rear. The floor of this craft is covered with reeds or straw by the sailors, and many goods, especially palm wine, in as great a quantity as possible are placed thereon, and thus they float downstream. These boats have two oars and at each is one man. The one pulls on his oar while the other pushes. These craft vary in size; some are so large that they can carry cargo up to five thousand talents; the small ones have a donkey aboard; the large ones, many. As soon as the sailors reach Babylon, they sell their wares and then offer the ribs and the reeds of the boat for sale. They load the skins upon their donkeys and return to Armenia, where they build new boats."*

In spite of the centuries that have passed, these craft remain the same; but the people that have lived here are gone. How will things be when as much time has passed again? . . .

The next morning we commenced our journey; I, Halef and one of the Abu Hammed as our guide rode ahead, the others followed behind. Last came Sir David Lindsay. We rode through the Kanuza and Hamrin Mountains and soon saw the small, artificial hillock of Tell Hamlia on the left bank. On the right bank was Kalaat al Jebber, 'the Castle of the Tyrants'; these ruins consist of a few decayed, cylindrical towers that were connected at one time by ramparts. Soon we reached Tell Dahab, a little hill that lies on the left bank of the river; we halted for a noon meal near Brey el Bad, where the rock-face was rather steep.

Towards evening we arrived at El Fattha, where the river had created a channel, as wide as fifty cubits, through the Hamrin Mountains, and when we had passed these narrows, we erected our camp for the night. The Abu Hammed were unarmed, but I still divided the Haddedihn into two halves, who then took turns on watch so that none of the prisoners would escape. If just one succeeded, he would warn his tribe of our arrival and the best animals would then be spirited away or hidden.

At daybreak we were again on our way. The river was wide and had many islands. The terrain of the left bank consisted of many low hills, but on the right, an open plain lay before us, and here beside the river the Abu Hammed were supposed to have their camp.

"Do you have many pastures or just the one?" I asked our guide.

"Only one," He replied.

I read in his face that he had spoken a lie.

"You lie!" I challenged him.

"I do not lie, Emir!"

"Well then. I will make an effort to believe you; but if I discover that you lie to me I will send a bullet through your skull!"

"You would not do this, Emir!"

"I will do it!" I assured him.

"You will not do it, for I tell you that we have perhaps two pastures."

"Perhaps?" I urged him.

"Or for certain; certainly two," he decided.

"Or three!" I suggested.

"Only two!" He assured me.

"Good. But if I find three, then you are done for!"

"Forgive me, Emir! They could have found another pasture in the meantime. Then there would be three."

"Three then?"

"Yes."

"But no more?"

"Three!"

"Ah! Perhaps there are four?" I ventured.

"You will desire ten yet!" He cried in exasperation.

"You are Abu Hammed and will not gladly surrender that which you have amassed through robbery. I will not press you further."

"We have four, Emir," he said anxiously.

"Good. Now be quite, I will see for myself!"

I had, meanwhile, scanned the horizon with my telescope and spotted something moving in the distance. I called the Haddedihn leader who had command of our men to me. He was a brave and decisive warrior, in whom I had complete trust.

"We have forty Abu Hammed with us. Do you believe that thirty of your men can watch over them?"

"With ten, Emir. They have no weapons!"

"I will ride ahead with Hajji Halef Omar to scout around. If I have not returned by the time the sun is just above that bush," I indicated an area of scrub, "then send thirty Haddedihn after me!"

I called the Englishman, and he approached with both his servants.

I said to him: "I have a very important task for you."

"Indeed!"

"I will ride ahead to see how far these pastures of the Abu Hammed stretch. If I am not back in two hours then thirty of our men will come after me."

"I also?"

"No. You remain here with the troop to watch over the prisoners. If anyone makes a move to flee, shoot him down."

"Yes! If one escapes, shoot him and any other that tries to escape."

"Good, but no more!"

"No. But sir, if you talk with the Abu Hammed then ask them!"

"About what?"

"Ruins and fowling-bulls."

"Very well, let's go, Halef!"

We galloped across the plain towards the spot where I had previously sighted the figures. It was a grazing herd of sheep, watched over by an old man.

"*Salaam aaleïkum*!" I greeted him.

"*Aaleïkum*!" he answered, with a deep bow.

"Is there peace in your meadow?"

"There is peace here, oh Lord. Do you also bring peace?"

"I bring it. Do you belong to the tribe of the Abu Hammed?"

"You are correct."

"Where is your camp?"

"There, beyond the curve of the river," he gestured.

"Have you many pastures?"

"Why do you ask, oh Lord?"

"Because I bring a message to all of your tribe."

"From whom?"

"From Zedar Ben Huli, your Sheik."

"*Hamdulillah*! You must bring a happy message," he cried joyfully.

"I bring it. Therefore tell me how many pastures you have."

"Six. Three here at the river and three on the islands within the river."

"Do all the islands here belong to you?"

"Every one."

"Are they all occupied?"

"All but one."

There was something in the tone of his answer and something in the face of this old man that caught my attention, but I did not let him see this and asked: "Where is this one?"

"Directly opposite from us is the first island and the one I refer to is the fourth, oh Lord."

I silently decided to scrutinize the latter, out loud I asked; "Why is it not inhabited?"

"It is difficult to reach, as the river is dangerous."

Hmm! Then it would be ideal for the safe-keeping of prisoners, I thought, and continued my inquiry: "How many men are in your camp?"

"Are you truly a messenger from our Sheik, oh Lord?"

His suspicion naturally increased my own.

"I am. I have spoken with him and the Sheiks of the Obeïde and the Jowari."

"What message do you bring?"

"The message of peace."

"Why did he not send a man of his tribe?"

"The men of the Abu Hammed are directly behind me."

I did not wish to press him further and therefore rode on, but I chose to ride next to the river in order to count the islands. As we passed the third, the river took a turn and before us were the tents of the camp. The entire plain was filled with camels, cattle, goats and sheep. Of horses I saw very few. Likewise I saw few men, and the few who were present were old and frail and therefore presented no danger.

We rode down the avenue of tents.

Before one of the tents, a young girl caressed one of three tethered horses. As she saw me, she screamed, leaped upon the horse and raced away. Should I pursue this fugitive?

I did not do so; it would have been of little use, for all those that had been in the camp now encircled me: the ancient, the sick, women and girls. One old man placed his hand on the neck of my horse and asked:

"Who are you, Lord?"

"I am a messenger, sent by Zedar Ben Huli."

"The Sheik! With what message has he sent you?"

"That I will tell you when you are all gathered. How many warriors were left behind?"

"Fifteen young men. Ajehma will have ridden to fetch them."

"Then permit me to dismount. But you" – and I turned to Halef – "ride on at once for the Jowari must receive the same message."

Halef turned his horse and raced away.

"Can your companion not remain here in order to rest himself and take food?" asked the old man.

"He is neither tired nor hungry, and our orders may not be delayed. Where are your young warriors?"

"Near the island."

Ah, again this 'island'!

"What are they doing there?"

"They ..." he paused and then continued - "They graze the herd."

"Is this island far from here?"

"No. See, they come already!"

Certainly a troop of armed men raced towards us from the river. They were the youngest of the tribe, almost boys; they and the old ones had been left behind. They had no guns, just lances and clubs. The first and also the most comely of them lifted his club and whilst his horse galloped on, he hurled it towards me, and shouted:

"Dog, you dare to come among us?"

Luckily I had hold of my gun and with its butt I was able to parry the club; but the spears of all the youths were directed at me. I did not worry overmuch about that, rather I gave my sable stallion a prompt and brought it hard up against my attacker. He alone, amongst all of them, may have reached his twentieth year.

"Lad, you dare to attack a guest of your tribe?"

With these words I hauled him towards me and sat him in front of my saddle. He hung from my hand with slack limbs, much like a marionette; fear had entered into him.

"Now stab if you wish to kill someone!" I challenged the rest.

They took care not to, as the boy was my shield; but the brave lads were not entirely undetermined. Some of them dismounted and tried to approach me from the side or from behind, as the others kept me occupied in front. Should I wound them? It would have been a great pity to do so. I coaxed my horse hard up against a tent to protect my back and asked:

"What have I done to you, that you try to kill me?"

"We know you," answered one. "You shall not escape us again, 'man with the lion's hide'!"

"You speak very boldly, 'lad with the lamb's skin'!"

An old woman raised her hands and howled, "Is it him? Oh, do nothing to him, for he is terrible!"

"We will kill him!" answered the little band.

"He will tear you apart and then ride away through the air!"

"I will not ride away, I intend to remain here," I answered, and hurled my prisoner into the midst of my attackers. I slid from my horse and entered the tent. With a slash of my dagger I enlarged the opening so that I could bring my horse inside as well, I did not wish to leave him in harm's way. Here I was relatively safe from the stings of these wasps.

"We have him! *Hamdulillah*, we have him!" they rejoiced outside.

"Surround the tent, don't let him out!" shouted another voice.

"Shoot him dead through the tent walls!" called another.

"No, we catch him alive. He has the stallion with him; we must not injure that; the Sheik wishes to own it!"

I could appreciate that no one dared to come inside after me; I sat myself down comfortably and helped myself to the cold meat that sat on a platter nearby. Besides, this involuntary self-imprisonment was not to last for long. Halef had exerted his mount and soon the ground shook with the clatter of thirty sets of horses' hooves.

"*Allah kerihm* – God is merciful!" I heard someone cry. "It is the enemy!"

I stepped out of the tent. Of the entire population of the camp not a one was visible. Everyone had crawled into their tents.

"*Sihdi*!" Halef called in a loud voice.

"Here, Hajji Halef Omar!"

"Have they harmed you?"

"No. Occupy the camp so that no one escapes! Whoever attempts to flee will be shot!"

I spoke these words loud enough so that all could hear them. I intended only to intimidate them. I sent Halef from tent to tent to gather the old people. The fifteen youths I did not need. It took a long time before they were all assembled for they had hidden themselves and came forward shaking and timid. When they sat in fearful expectation around me, I began:

"You have seen the tattoos of my people?"

"Yes, Lord," they chorused.

"Then you recognize their tribe?"

"Yes. They are Haddedihn, Lord."

"Where are your warriors?"

"You already know this, Lord."

"Yes, I know it, and I tell you that they are all prisoners of the Haddedihn, and not a one escaped."

"*Allah kerihm*!"

"Yes, Allah may be merciful to you!"

"He lies!" one of them, whose courage had not been dulled with age, whispered.

I turned to him: "You say that I lie? Your hair is gray, and your back is bent with the weight of your years; that is why I will forgive you your words. Why do you believe that I have lied to you?"

"How can the Haddedihn take three entire tribes prisoner?"

"You would believe it if I told you that they were not alone. They united with the Abu Mohammed and the Alabeïde. The Haddedihn knew everything. When your warriors took me prisoner, I was coming from the Abu Mohammed, where I had been to discuss this war with them. In the Wadi Deradsh we met your warriors and none escaped. Hear what orders I give!"

I stepped to the entrance of the tent in which we were assembled and beckoned to Halef.

"Ride and fetch the captured Abu Hammed!"

They really were frightened now.

"Is it possible, Lord?" One of the elders asked fearfully.

"I speak the truth. All the warriors of your tribe are in our hands. Either you pay the ransom which is demanded for their lives, or they will be killed."

"Even Sheik Zedar Ben Huli?"

"Even he."

"Then you should have spoken to him of the ransom!"

"I have done so."

"What did he say?"

"He will pay it and he has sent forty of your people with me to secure it."

"Allah protect us! How large is the ransom?"

"You shall learn of it. How many heads are in your herds?"

"We do not know!" they answered evasively.

"You lie! Everyone knows the count of the animals that belong to the tribe. How many horses do you have?"

"Twenty, except those that were taken to battle."

"These are lost to you. How many camels?"

"Three hundred."

"Cattle?"

"Twelve hundred."

"Donkeys and mules?"

"Perhaps thirty."

"Sheep?"

"Nine thousand."

"Your tribe is not rich. The ransom shall amount to ten horses, a hundred camels, three hundred heads of cattle, ten donkeys and mules and two thousand head of sheep."

Now the old men raised a terrible wailing. I of course felt sorry for them but I could not help them, and when the figures were compared to what they might have lost under different circumstances, I felt a certain comfort in my heart.

Chapter 20

To put an end to the wailing, I said in a harsh tone:

"Quiet! Sheik Zedar Ben Huli has approved this."

"We cannot give this much!" Someone complained.

"You can! What one has stolen, one can easily return!"

"We have not stolen anything. Why do you believe us to be *haremi*? (robbers – this word is incidentally a label of honor among the Bedouin)"

"Be quiet! Was I not attacked by you?"

"It was only in jest, Lord!"

"Then you play dangerous games. How many pastures do you have here?"

"Six."

"Even on the islands?"

"Yes."

"Even on the island that your young men were near before?" I prodded.

"No," was the response.

"I was told that the herds graze there! Your mouth is full of lies! Who is on that island?"

They looked at each other with embarrassment before the speaker answered: "There are men there."

"What men?" I demanded.

"Strangers."

"From where do they come?"

"We do not know."

"Who does know it?"

"Only the Sheik."

"Who has brought these men here?"

"Our warriors."

"Your warriors? And only the Sheik knows where they came from? I see that I must demand three thousand sheep from you – instead of two thousand! Or would you rather talk?"

"Lord, we may not!"

"Why not?"

"The Sheik would punish us. Be merciful to us!"

"Your are right; I wish to spare you this embarrassment."

A sound came from between the tents: the prisoners had arrived with their guard. At their approach, a great cry of despair arose from all the tents, yet no one allowed themselves to be seen. I stood up.

"Now you see that I spoke the truth. Forty of your warriors are here to fetch the ransom. Go now into all the tents and gather the inhabitants of the camp and bring them here; nothing will happen to them, but I must speak to all of them."

It took some effort to gather the multitude of women, children and the aged. When they had assembled I stepped up to the prisoners:

"See here now, you fathers, you mothers, you sisters and children! Your warriors are under my control and I will lead them away as prisoners if you do not obey the command that I give you now. You have six pastures that are all close by. I will divide you into six groups, each will be guarded by a number of my warriors, each group will go to one of the pastures to gather the animals and to drive them here. In one hour all the herds must be assembled here!"

As I spoke it, so it was done. The Abu Hammed divided themselves into groups under the command of the Haddedihn, and I kept only twelve men with me, one of them was Halef.

"I will now go, Halef."

"To where, *Sihdi*?"

"To the island. You will look after things here and later direct the selection of the animals. Make sure that it is not only the best animals that are taken from these poor people. The selection should be just."

"They have not earned it, *Sihdi*!"

"But I want it done this way. You understand, Halef?" I cautioned him.

At this point Master Lindsay came up to me.

"Have you asked, sir?" he inquired.

"Not yet."

"Do not forget, sir!"

"No. I need to entrust you with another task."

"Well! What?"

"See to it that none of the women escape."

Yes!"

"If one of them so much as tries to flee, then ..."

"Shoot her down!" he finished my sentence.

"Oh no, my Lord!" I exclaimed in horror.

"What then?"

"Then let her go!"

"Well, sir!" he huffed.

These were the only two words he was able to bring forth, but his mouth remained open. I was, by the way, quite certain that just one look at Sir David Lindsay would discourage the women from all intention of flight. In his gray-checkered suit he must have appeared as a monster in their eyes.

I took two men with me and walked to the river. The fourth island stood before me. It was long and narrow and overgrown with thick reeds that were taller than a man. I could not see any sign of life, but the island held a secret that I was determined to discover. The reason why I did not take any Abu Hammed along was to avoid any repercussions for them later.

"Search for a raft!" I commanded the two men.

"Where do you wish to go?"

"To that island."

"Emir, that is impossible!"

"Why?"

"Do you see the strong current on both sides? It would destroy any raft that ventured out into it."

The man was right, nevertheless I was convinced that some form of transport existed between the riverbank and the island, and when I studied the island more closely I noticed that the reeds had been flattened at the upstream end.

"Look there! Don't you see that people have been there?"

"It appears so, Emir."

"Then a vessel must also exist."

"It would be shattered; that is certain!"

"Seek the vessel out!"

They searched up and down the bank, to the left and the right, to no avail. I then searched myself for a long time – nothing. Finally, I caught sight of it . . . not a raft or a boat, but a device whose function became immediately clear to me. Close to the edge of the riverbank, across from the upstream end of the island, a sturdy rope of palm fiber was fastened to the trunk of a tree. One end was tied around the tree; the rope itself, however, was coiled in the thick scrub nearby. As I retrieved it, a deflated goatskin emerged, fastened to the other end, and across the skin a wooden crossbar had been tied, which served as a form of handhold.

"See, here is the raft. This cannot be broken, that is certain. I will swim across while you stand guard here and ensure that I am not disturbed."

"It is very dangerous, Emir!"

"Others have crossed successfully."

I disrobed and inflated the goatskin. The mouth of this was sealed with an attached cord.

"Hold on to the rope and pay it out slowly!"

I took hold of the wooden crossbar and slipped into the water. The current, which was quite strong, gripped me at once; the man holding the rope had to use all his strength to maintain his hold. In order to carry a person to or from the island, the combined efforts of many men would be required. I had to steer for the opposite shore of the island and I landed there without incident, despite being severely buffeted. My first concern was to fasten the rope so that it could not abscond; I then grasped my dagger, which I had brought with me.

A well-trodden path led through the reeds from this position on the island, I followed it and soon came upon a small hut, which was fashioned from bamboo, reeds and rushes. It was a low structure that did not permit a man to stand upright within. Its interior contained nothing but a few articles of clothing. I examined these carefully and discovered that they were the shredded remains of three sets of clothing. There was no sign that the owners of the clothes had been here recently; but the path continued on.

I proceeded along, and after a while I thought I heard a low moaning sound. I hastened forward and reached a place where the reeds had been hacked down. In this cleared area I saw . . . the decapitated heads of three men that had been placed on the ground with their necks intact; at least that is how it appeared to me. The heads were swollen unevenly, the reason for this was not difficult to determine, for as I approached a cloud of mosquitoes and crane-flies rose into the air. The eyes and mouths were closed. Had these decapitated heads been placed here for a reason?

I stooped down and touched one. A faint moan of pain escaped from the lips and the eyes opened and stared at me with a glazed look. In my life I have seldom been truly frightened, but now I was so shocked that I leapt back several paces.

I stepped closer again to examine the situation. In truth, three men had been entombed in the damp, foul ground up to their necks.

"Who are you?" I asked loudly.

All three opened their eyes and stared at me with crazed expressions. One of them opened his lips and croaked slowly:

"Oh Adi! ..."

Adi? Wasn't this the name of the great saint of the Jesidi, the so-called 'Devil Worshippers'?

"Who brought you here?" I inquired further.

Again the mouth opened, but he was no longer capable of uttering a single word. I fought my way through the reeds towards the shore of the island and filled my hands with water. I returned quickly and poured the water into the mouths of the tortured men. They slurped it greedily. I could only bring a little at a time and on the way, much flowed between my fingers, so that I had to return often in order to quench their fearful thirst.

"Is there a hoe here?" I asked.

"Taken ..." one rasped.

I raced to the upstream end of the island. Over on the riverbank my companions still stood watch. I cupped my hands around my mouth, to make myself heard over the sound of the rushing water:

"Fetch a spade, a hoe and the three Englishmen – but quietly!"

They disappeared. I could not call upon Halef because he was needed over in the camp. I waited impatiently . . . finally the Haddedihn returned with the three men I had summoned and an implement similar to a hoe.

"Sir David Lindsay!" I hailed the Englishman.

"Yes!" he answered.

"Come over here quickly! Bill and his companion also! Bring the hoe!"

"My hoe? Found 'fowling-bulls'?" he asked excitedly.

"You will see!" I deferred.

I untied the goatskin float and pushed it into the water.

"Pull it across!" I directed.

A short while later Sir David stepped onto the island.

"Where?" He questioned.

"Wait! First get the others across!"

"Well!"

He beckoned to his men on the other shore to hurry and finally the two strong lads were on the island. Bill had the hoe with him. I secured the goatskin float again.

"Come, sir!"

"Ah! Finally!"

"Sir David Lindsay, will you forgive me?"

"For what?"

"I have found no fowling-bulls."

"None?" – He stood still and opened his mouth wide. "None? Aah!" he lamented.

"But I have discovered something quite shocking! Come!"

I seized the hoe and hurried ahead. With an exclamation of horror the Englishmen stumbled back as we entered the clearing. Now the sight was even more ghastly than before, for the three had their eyes open, and their heads thrashed about weakly, trying to deter the swarms of insects.

"They have been buried!" I said.

"By whom?" The Englishman asked in shock.

"I do not know, but we will find out."

I used the hoe with such haste, and the others desperately scratched and scraped with their bare hands, that within a quarter of an hour we had the three unlucky individuals lying before us. They had been stripped of all their clothes and their hands and feet had been bound with raffia ropes. I knew that the Arabs practiced the custom of burying, up to their necks, people who were suffering from certain serious illnesses, and that this 'packing' was supposed to have certain healing powers; but these men had been bound and were therefore not sick.

We carried them to the shore and splashed them with water. This refreshed their spirits somewhat.

"Who are you?" I asked.

"Baadri!" Came the rasping response.

Baadri? That was the name of a village that was inhabited exclusively by the 'Devil Worshippers'! I had been correct in my original assumption.

"Let's get them across!" I said.

"How?" Asked the Englishman.

"I swim across first to help with the towing and I take their clothing with me. You three then follow me, each assisting one of them."

"Well! Will not be easy." Lindsay said.

"You position him across your arms, in front of you." I demonstrated the position for them.

I rolled the clothing into a makeshift turban and securely placed it upon my head. I then allowed myself to be towed across to the opposite bank. For the two Haddedihn and myself a hard task was about to commence, but for the Englishmen it would be an exceedingly dangerous one. Nevertheless, we succeeded in bringing all six across without incident.

"Get them dressed! Then keep them concealed here. Whilst the other four watch over them, you, Sir David, will quietly bring them food," I directed.

"Well! Ask who buried them." Sir David urged.

"The Sheik of course."

"Beat that fellow to death!" Lindsay said indignantly.

This latest adventure had lasted for over an hour. When we reached the camp, the plain was teeming with thousands of animals. The business of selection was a difficult one, yet little Hajji Halef Omar was up to the task. He had mounted my black stallion, with the intent of being able to move more quickly from place to place, and incidentally, to be admired. The Haddedihn were quite enthusiastic about their work, the captured Abu Hammed however, who were forced to help them, could not keep the silent fury from their countenances. And where the women and the aged sat, hot tears flowed and many a subdued curse escaped from between their lips. I walked up to the group of women. I had noticed one woman who watched my men with quiet satisfaction. Did she hold a grudge in her heart against the Sheik?

"Follow me!" I commanded her.

"Lord, be merciful! I have done nothing!" She wailed.

"Nothing shall happen to you!" I assured her.

I led her into the empty tent that I had previously occupied; there I stood before her and looked hard into her eyes and asked her; "Do you have an enemy within your tribe?"

She looked up in surprise.

"Lord, how do you know this?"

"Be frank! Who is it?"

"You will tell him!"

"No, for he is also my enemy."

"Are you the one who vanquished him?"

"I am he. Do you despise Sheik Zedar Ben Huli?"

Her dark eyes flashed with hatred.

"Yes, Lord, I hate him."

"Why?"

"I hate him because he killed the father of my children."

"Why?"

"My master did not wish to steal," she said.

"And why not?"

"Because the Sheik receives the largest part of the booty," she explained.

"You are poor?" I asked.

"The uncle of my children has taken us into his tent; he too is poor."

"How many animals does he have?"

"A cow and ten sheep; he will lose them this day, for when the Sheik returns, we will be made to bear the entire loss. The Sheik will not suffer, only his tribe will."

"He shall not return if you are honest."

"Lord, do you speak the truth?"

"I speak it. He will remain as a prisoner and the Abu Hammed will be appointed a Sheik who is just and honest. The uncle of your children shall keep what he owns this day."

"Lord, your hand overflows with mercy. What do you wish to know from me?"

"You know of the island over there in the river?"

She paled. "Why do you ask?"

"Because I want to talk to you about it."

"Oh do not do it, Lord, for whoever speaks of the secret will be killed by the Sheik!"

"If you tell me this secret, he will not return."

"Is this really true?"

"Believe me! What purpose does the island serve?"

"It is where the Sheik holds his prisoners."

"Which prisoners?"

"He captures travelers who come over the plains or rest by the water and takes all their possessions. If they do not have any then he kills them, but if they are rich then he holds them and demands a ransom."

"Then he sends them to the island?"

"Yes, in a reed hut. They cannot escape for their hands and feet are bound."

"And when the Sheik receives the ransom?"

"He kills them nonetheless, so that he cannot be betrayed," she replied.

"And if they cannot or will not pay?"

"Then he tortures them."

"What forms of torture does he employ?"

"He has many. Mostly he buries them."

"Who are the tormentors?"

"He and his sons."

The one who captured me was also the Sheik's son; I had seen him among the captives in Wadi Deradsh. I asked therefore:

"How many sons does the Sheik have?"

"Two."

"Is one of them here?"

"The one that tried to kill you when you entered the camp," she confirmed.

"Are there prisoners on the island now?"

"Two or three."

"Where on the island are they?"

"I do not know. Only those men that were present during their capture know."

"How were they caught?"

"They came down the river on a *kellek* (raft) and laid to for the night on the banks not far from here. There they were ambushed."

"How much time has passed since their capture?"

She thought about this for a moment and then answered; "almost twenty days."

"How did the Sheik treat them?"

"I do not know."

"Have you many *tachterwahns* (baskets used for the convenience of women when riding camels)?"

"We have several."

I pulled some coins from my turban. They came from the stash that I had found in the saddlebags of Abu-Seïf. His lovely camel had unfortunately died in Baghdad; but the money had remained with me to this day.

"I thank you! Here take these!" I said, holding out the coins.

"Oh Lord, your grace is greater than ..."

"Don't thank me," I interrupted her. "Is the uncle of your children a prisoner here?"

"Yes."

"He will be freed. Go to the little man that rides the black stallion and tell him from me that he should return your animals to you. The Sheik shall not return."

"Oh Lord ...!"

"It is all right. Go, but tell no one of that which we have spoken!"

She left, and I followed her out of the tent. The selection of the animals was almost complete. I searched for Halef. He rode towards me when I beckoned to him.

"Who gave you permission to ride my black stallion, Hajji Halef Omar?"

"I wished to get him used to my legs, *Sihdi*!"

"He will not fear them overmuch. Listen Halef, a woman will come and ask for a cow and ten sheep. Give them to her."

"I obey, *effendi*."

"Listen further! Take three *tachterwahns* from the camp and saddle three camels with them."

"Who will use them, *Sihdi*?"

"Look to the river. Do you see the scrub and the tree to the right?"

"I see both."

"There lie three ailing men who are to be placed within the baskets. Go into the tent of the Sheik; it is yours with all that it contains. Take from it blankets and place them into the baskets so that the invalids may lie on them in comfort. But no one should discover now, or later, who the camels bear!"

"You know, *Sihdi*, that I will do everything that you demand; but I cannot do all this on my own."

"The three Englishmen are there and also two of the Haddedihn. They will help you. Now give me back my stallion; I will take over the supervision."

After an hour we were finished. While all those present had been focused on the herd, Halef had managed to move the ailing men on board the camels unseen. The entire, extensive caravan of animals stood ready for departure.

I now sought out the young person who had welcomed me with his lance [actually, a club] earlier today. I found him standing amidst his comrades and rode up to him. Lindsay and his servants stood nearby.

"Sir David Lindsay, do you or one of your servants have something akin to a cord with you?"

"Would think there are many cords around here."

He stepped over to a group of horses that were tethered to a number of tent poles, those that had been left to the tribe. With a few slashes he obtained a length of rope with which he returned.

"Do you see that brown fellow over there, Sir David?" I indicated the lad with a furtive glance.

"See him, sir."

"I entrust him to you. He was one who guarded the three unlucky men and therefore he should come with us. Bind his hands behind his back and then fasten him to your saddle or your stirrups; he should learn to walk a little."

"Yes, sir! Very nice!"

"He should receive neither food nor water until we reach Wadi Deradsh."

"Deserves it!"

"You watch over him. If he escapes then our union is dissolved and you may seek fowling-bulls by yourself!" I cautioned him.

"Will hold onto him. Bury him at night!" Lindsay suggested.

"Then lets go!" I said.

The Englishman stepped up to the youth and placed his hand on the lad's shoulder.

"I have the honor, my Lord! Come with us, you rogue!"

He held him firmly, and both his servants bound the lad's hands expertly. The youth was quite astonished at first, then he turned to me and said, "What is this, Emir?"

"You shall come with us."

"I am no prisoner, I remain here!" He said indignantly.

An old woman pushed herself forward.

"*Allah kerihm*, Emir! What do you want with my son?"

"He will accompany us." I explained.

"He? The star of my old age, the glory of his companions, the pride of our tribe? What has he done that you bind him like a murderer in wait for the revenge of blood?"

"Quickly, sir! Tie him to the horse and go!" I urged Sir David.

I immediately gave the sign for departure and rode off. At first I had compassion for this tribe and the harsh punishment they were to receive, but now every face sickened me and when we had outdistanced the cries of despair, it seemed to me that we had escaped from a den of thieves.

Halef had placed himself at the head of the caravan with the three camels. I rode to his side.

"Are they comfortable?" I asked him, indicating the three invalids.

"As though they rested on the divan of the Padishah, *Sihdi*."

"Have they eaten?"

"No, but they did drink milk."

"All the better. Can they speak?"

"They have only spoken single words, but in a language that I could not understand, *effendi*."

"It could be Kurdish." I suggested.

"Kurdish?" Halef repeated.

"Yes. I believe them to be 'Devil Worshippers'."

"'Devil Worshippers'? *Allah il Allah*! Lord, preserve us from the 'thrice-stoned devil'! How can one pray to *Shaïtan*, *Sihdi*!"

"They do not pray to him, although they are named thus. They are brave, diligent, and honest people, part Christian and part Moslem."

"That is why they have a language that no Moslem can understand. Can you speak it?"

"No."

He drew back in disbelief.

"No? *Sihdi*, that can't be true, you know everything!" Halef declared in disbelief.

"I do not understand this language, I tell you."

"Not at all?"

"Hmm! I know a language that is related to theirs; perhaps I can find some words with which I can make myself understood by them."

"You see, I am right, *Sihdi*!"

"Only God knows all; the knowledge of man is but a patchwork. Do I know how satisfied Hanneh, the light of your eyes, is with her Halef!"

"Satisfied, *Sihdi*? With her Allah comes first, then Mohammed, then the devil, whom you have given to her on the chain, and then immediately after comes Hajji Halef Omar Ben Hajji Abul Abbas Ibn Hajji Dawud al Gossarah."

"So, you come after the devil!"

"Not after 'the *Shaïtan*', but rather after your gift, *Sihdi*!"

"Then be grateful and obey her!"

After this admonition I left the little man alone.

Understandably, the return trip took longer than the journey there due to the slowness of the herd that we now had with us. By sunset we had reached a location that was below Jebbar and was, due to the carpet of flowers and luxurious green grass, very well suited for our camp. The main task was now to watch over the herd as well as the Abu Hammed; I gave the necessary orders. Later that evening I had already wrapped myself in my blanket ready for sleep when Sir David Lindsay came to me.

"Shocking! Terrible, sir!" He exclaimed.

"What?" I asked.

"Humph! Inconceivable!"

"What then? Did your prisoner escape?"

"Him? No! Securely bound!"

"Well then, what is so shocking and inconceivable?"

"Forgot essential matter!"

"Well? Speak!" I prompted him.

"Truffles!" He exclaimed.

I had to laugh aloud.

"Oh, that is of course terrible, sir, especially since I saw sacks full of them in the camp of the Abu Hammed."

"Where will we get truffles from now?"

"We will have truffles tomorrow, depend on it!"

"Excellent! Good night, sir!" He said, satisfied.

I fell asleep without having spoken to the three ailing men. Early the next morning I visited them. The baskets had been placed in such a fashion, that the three could see each other. Their appearance had improved and they were able to speak without difficulty.

As I soon discovered, all three spoke very good Arabic, although in their stupor they had uttered words only in their mother tongue. When I approached, one of them got up and looked at me inquiringly.

"You are he!" he exclaimed before I could greet him. "You are he! I recognize you!"

"Who am I, my friend?"

"You are the one that appeared to me when death extended its hand towards my heart. Oh, Emir Kara Ben Nemsi, I thank you!"

"How do you know my name?"

"We know it, for the good Hajji Halef Omar has told us much about you since we woke."

I turned to Halef and chided: "Chatterbox!"

"*Sihdi*, may I not speak of you?" the little one said defensively.

"Yes, but without bragging. – Are you strong enough to speak?" I said turning back to the frail men.

"Yes, Emir."

"Then permit me to ask you who you are."

"I am called Pali, this is Selek, and this is Melaf." He indicated his companions in turn.

"Where is your homeland?"

"Our homeland is called Baadri, north of Mosul."

"How did you get into the situation in which I found you?"

"Our Sheik sent us to Baghdad to deliver a gift to the Governor and to deliver a letter to him."

"To Baghdad? Are you not subjects of Mosul?"

"Emir, the Governor of Mosul is an evil man who severely oppresses us; the Governor of Baghdad enjoys the confidence of the Sultan; we hoped he would present our case."

"How did you travel? From Mosul down river?"

"No. We went to the Ghazir river, constructed a raft for ourselves, rode upon this down the Ghazir until it joined the Zab and from there into the Tigris. We beached on the shore and were attacked by the Sheik of the Abu Hammed while we slept."

"He robbed you?"

"He took the gifts and the letter and all that we carried with us. Then he tried to force us to write letters to our families and ask for ransoms."

"You did not do this?"

"No, for we are poor and cannot pay a ransom."

"What of your Sheik?"

"To him too we were to write, but we declined to do this also. He would have paid but we knew that it was pointless, for we would have been killed anyway."

"You were quite right. They would have taken your lives even if the ransom had been paid."

"We were tortured. We were whipped, were hung from our bound hands and feet and finally buried in the earth."

"And through all this you were bound?"

"Yes."

"You know that your tormentor is our prisoner?"

"Hajji Halef Omar has told us this."

"The Sheik shall be punished for this!"

"Emir, do not punish him!"

"What?" I asked in surprise.

"You are a Moslem, but we have a different religion. We have been given our life again and we wish to forgive him."

They really were 'Devil Worshippers'!

"You err," I said; "I am no Moslem, but a Christian."

"A Christian! But you wear the clothes of a Moslem and even the symbol of a hajji!"

"Can a Christian not also be a hajji?"

"No, for no Christian may enter Mecca."

"I was there nevertheless. Ask this man for he was also there."

"Yes," concurred Halef, "Hajji Emir Kara Ben Nemsi was in Mecca."

"What kind of Christian are you, Emir? A Chaldean?"

"No. I am a Frank." I told him.

"Do you know of the virgin who bore God?"

"Yes."

"Do you know Esau (Jesus), the Son of the Father?"

"Yes." I replied again.

"Do you know the holy angels who stand by the throne of God?"

"Yes."

"Do you know of the holy baptism?"

"Yes."

"Do you also believe, that Esau is the Son of God and that he will come again?"

"I believe it."

"Oh, Emir, your belief is good; your belief is true; we are pleased that we have met you! Show us therefore, your love, and forgive the Sheik of the Abu Hammed his transgression against us!"

"We shall see! Do you know where we travel to?"

"We know it. We go to Wadi Deradsh."

"You will be welcome by the Sheik of the Haddedihn."

After this short discussion our march continued. In Kalaat ul Jebbar I discovered a quantity of truffles, which made the Englishman extremely happy. He collected a supply and promised to invite me to a meal of truffle pâté, which he was going to prepare with his own hands.

When noon had passed, we navigated between the mountains of Kanuza and Hamrin and headed directly towards Wadi Deradsh. I had purposely not permitted the announcement of our arrival in order to surprise the good Sheik Mohammed Emin; but the lookouts of the Abu Mohammed had spied us and had given the signal for a celebration that echoed through the entire valley. Mohammed Emin and Malek rode towards us immediately to welcome us. My herd was the first to arrive.

There is no other way to reach the pastures of the Haddedihn, except through the wadi. Here all the prisoners of war were located, and one can imagine the stares the Abu Hammed bestowed upon us, when they were forced to endure the recognition of their animals during our passing. Finally we were again on the plain and I dismounted from my horse.

"Who is in the *tachterwahns*?" asked Mohammed Emin.

"Three men, whom Sheik Zedar intended to torture to death. I will yet tell you of them. Where are the captured Sheiks?"

"Over there, in the tent. Here they come now."

They had just exited the tent. The eyes of the Sheik of the Abu Hammed flashed maliciously when he recognized the herd, and he stepped towards me.

"Have you taken more than you should?"

"You mean animals?"

"Yes."

"I have brought the number that was ordered."

"I will count them!"

"Do so," I answered coldly. "Nevertheless, I return with more than I should have."

"What?"

"Do you wish to see?"

"I must see!"

"Then call that one to you." I indicated his eldest son, who had appeared at the tent's entrance. The Sheik beckoned him.

"All of you, come with me!" I said.

Mohammed Emin, Malek and the three captive Sheiks followed me to where the three camels, with the *tachterwahns,* had settled. Halef had just let the Jesidi dismount.

"You know these men?" I asked Zedar Ben Huli.

He stepped back in alarm; as did his son.

"The Jesidi!" he cried.

"Yes, the Jesidi, whom you tried to slowly murder, as you have murdered many others, you monster!"

His eyes flashed at me like the eyes of a panther.

"What did he do?" asked Eslah el Mahem, the Sheik of the Obeïde.

"Let it be told! You will be astonished by the kind of man who is your ally."

I described the circumstances in which I had found the three men. When I had finished, all took several steps away from Zedar Ben Huli. As a result, the view of the valley entrance became clear and at that moment three riders could be seen there: Lindsay with his two servants. He was late. Next to his horse he dragged along the youngest son of the Sheik.

The Sheik saw his son and turned to me:

"*Allah akbar*! What is this! My second son a prisoner?"

"As you see!"

"What has he done?"

"He assisted you in your abominable deeds. Both your sons shall stand guard over your head while the rest of you is buried in the earth for two days; then you shall be free again – a punishment that is too slight for you and your sons. Go and untie your youngest son!"

The criminal rushed to the horse of the Englishman and grasped for the rope. Sir David had just dismounted and slapped the hand of the Sheik away and shouted:

"Be gone! This fellow is mine!"

The Sheik tore the gigantic pistol from the Englishman's belt, aimed it and fired. Sir David had turned around with lightning speed, nevertheless the bullet struck him in the arm; in the next moment a second shot cracked. Bill, the Irishman, had raised his gun to defend his master and his bullet penetrated the Sheik's skull. Both of the Sheik's sons leaped upon Bill, but they had been expected and were overpowered.

I turned away, shuddering. This was God's court! The punishment that I had intended for the scoundrel would have been too insignificant. Now my promise to the woman was also fulfilled: the Sheik would not be returning to the camp.

A while passed before all was quiet again. Then Halef voiced the question:

"*Sihdi*, where shall I put these three men?"

"Sheik Mohammed Emin should determine this." Was my answer.

The Sheik walked up to the three.

"*Marhaba* – you shall be welcome to me! Remain with me, Mohammed Emin, until you have recovered from your suffering!"

Selek looked up quickly.

"Mohammed Emin?" he asked.

"So am I called."

"You are no Shammar, but rather a Haddedihn?"

"The Haddedihn belong to the Shammar."

"Oh, Lord, then I have a message for you!"

"Speak it!"

"In Baadri, before we began our journey, I went to a stream to fetch water. Beside the same camped a troop of Arnauts (members of the irregular troops of the Pasha), who guarded a young man. He asked me to give him a drink and as I did so he whispered to me: 'Go to the Shammar, to Mohammed Emin, and tell him that I am being moved to Amadijah. The others have been executed.' It is this that I am to tell you."

The Sheik staggered back.

"*Amad el Ghandur*, my son!" he cried. "It was him, it was him! What did he look like?"

"As tall and as wide as you, and his black beard hung down to his chest."

"It is him! *Hamdulillah*! Finally, finally I have a sign from him! Be happy, you men, be happy with me, for today shall be a feast for all, may they be friend or foe! When was it that you spoke with him?"

"Six weeks have since passed, Lord!"

"I thank you! Six weeks, a long time! But he shall not languish any longer; I will rescue him, even if I have to conquer and destroy all Amadijah! Hajji Emir Kara Ben Nemsi, will you ride with me, or will you abandon me in this campaign?"

"I will ride with you!"

"Allah bless you! - Come, let us speak the news to all men of the Haddedihn!"

He hurried towards the wadi, and Halef came to my side with a question:

"*Sihdi*, is it true, that you go with him?"

"I go with him." I confirmed.

"*Sihdi*, may I come with you?"

"Halef, think of your wife!"

"Hanneh is in good care, but you, master, need a faithful servant! May I accompany you?"

"Very well, I will take you along; but first ask Sheik Mohammed Emin and Sheik Malek if it is permitted ...?

Will the Sheiks give Halef permission?
Will he accompany Kara Ben Nemsi to Amadijah?
What new adventures await along the way?

To find out, read the second part of this continuing Travel Narrative.

Oriental Odyssey II
In the Shadow of the Padishah
"The Devil Worshippers"

Authors Notes

Since Karl May was not very explicit as to exactly when these adventures took place, we will have to know something of the Turkish Empire's history to even guess at the probable historical period.

We know that the Turkish or Ottoman Empire was a dominant power in the Middle East from the 16th to the 19th century, but like all empires seem to do, it crumbled at the edges before its final demise. The rot began to manifest itself in 1820 when Greece rebelled and battled for its independence, which it gained in 1827. A year later, Moldavia, Wallachia and Serbia followed suit. France occupied Algiers in 1829 and then the Turkish Empire was severely weakened after the Russo–Turkish war of 1877 to 1878.

By 1881, France had gained control of Tunis and the British occupied Egypt in 1882. Further conflicts with Greece in 1897 continued to weaken the Empire. In 1908 Bulgaria claimed autonomy and in 1911 Italy occupied Tripoli. Then the Balkan war in 1912 to 1913 reduced the Empire's territory. And by the end of the First World War, the Turkish Empire had lost Arabia, Palestine, Syria, Lebanon and a significant part of its European territories, becoming what we now know as the modern state of Turkey.

With this knowledge, we can conclude that these narratives must pertain to a period after Algiers and before Tunis came under French control. Also we know, from the references to the Russian conflict, that these tales must be set in a period after 1878 and certainly before the British occupy Egypt. And because we also know that Tunis was still, although not ridgidly under Turkish influence, we can surmise that it must have been before 1881. Therefore we can speculate that this novel is set between 1878 and 1881.

Thus the Sultan, or the Padishah referred to in this novel must be Abdul Hameed II, also referred to as "the Damned" who reigned over the empire from 1876 to 1909.

Sultan Abdul Hameed II assumed the leadership of the Turkish Empire and the Khilafaship on the 31st of August 1876 when he was 34 years old. The Turkish people pledged allegiance and loyalty to him. Although Abdul Hameed realised, as he explaines in his diary, that the constant change in leadership after the assasination of his uncle, was indicitive of some kind of conspiracy against the Islamic state.

Into these turmultious times, Karl May set his epic tale of an Oriental Odyssey, a tale of adventure that embodies the struggle of the people with the regime that rules over them.

Translation Notes

The greatest possible care has been taken to render the original German text into a coherent English format. But some passages and concepts just do not lend themselves to fair English translation.

Wherever such passages occur, they have been translated practically verbatim, then changes in the sentence structure were made so that what emerged might be considered intelligible English. The sentence was then further polished and a note was added to explain the foreign concept to the reader.

We (the translator and editor) both feel that in doing this we present a comprehensible (and hopefully enjoyable) English text that retains not only the spirit of Karl May's work but also his unique style.

Below are the concepts that could not be translated without making additions to the original text, as well as other references that elaborate on a concept that is only briefly touched upon within the narrative.

TOPIC	**NOTES**
The Orient	This term was used to indicate the lands where the sun rises (as seen from a European point of view). It is sometimes used to indicate the entire Moslem world from Morocco in the west to Indonesia in the East. More specifically it would refer to the Balkans, Asia Minor, eastern North Africa and the Levant, (constituting Lebanon and Syria, also Greece, Turkey, Israel, and Egypt by today's geopolitical borders).
Ch 1. 1	**Chott** Also Shott. The depression surrounding a salt marsh or lake, especially in North Africa.
Ch 1. 2	**"Because you too have a *tesbih*– rosary."** We feel that this is a reference to the belief, still commonly espoused, that it is easier to convert someone who already has an established faith than it is to convert an atheist.
Ch 4. 1	**Sunnites and Shiites** As you may have discovered, Hajji Halef Omar is a Sunnite Muslim. Sunnites, those Muslims constituting the vast majority in the world Islamic community. The doctrines of the Sunnites were formed toward the end of the 9th century, and their theology was

TOPIC **NOTES**

developed during the 10th century. Both developments occurred, in large measure, as reactions to early schismatic movements, such as the Kharijites, Mutazilites, and Shiites.

Various nuances of interpretation and different schools have developed within Sunnite theology, the Sunnite tendency having been to accommodate minor differences of opinion and to affirm the consensus of the community in doctrinal matters. Four schools of law also developed in the Sunnite tradition: the *Shafi'i*, the *Hanafi*, the *Maliki*, and the *Hanbali*. Shiites are the only surviving major sectarian movement in Islam. The Shiites emerged out of a dispute over the succession to Muhammad.

After the assassination of the fourth caliph, Ali, in 661, the Shiites claimed that Ali was the rightful successor to Muhammad and that the previous caliphs had been usurpers. They maintained that only the imams (the descendants of Ali and his wife, Fatima, Muhammad's daughter) were entitled to rule the Muslim community. This doctrine was rejected by the majority of the Muslim community, who came to be known as Sunnites. The last *imam* disappeared in 880, and Shiites to this day await his return, when they believe that justice will be established on earth. Shiite religious leaders exercise immense influence. They are more likely to take an innovative approach to religious issues and defy political authority more than Sunnites. Shiites adopted an esoteric interpretation of the Koran, believing that beneath the explicit and literal meaning of the Koran are other levels, which are known only to the *imam*, who can reveal them to chosen followers.

Ch. 4. 2 **Bastinado**

A beating with a stick or club, especially on the soles of the feet.

Ch 4. 3 **The term 'Slipper'**

unter dem Pantoffel stehend. – To stand under the slipper (literally) corresponds to being 'henpecked' – i.e. A henpecked husband. It should also be noted that the term *Pantoffelheld.* - Literally 'Slipper Hero' is used to describe someone who is 'under the thumb', at the mercy of, in the power of, in the hands of, at the feet of, etc.

The original German text stated;

Da wollte sich mir die Überzeugung aufdrängen, daß der

TOPIC **NOTES**

Pantoffel im Oriente dieselbe zauberische Kraft besitzt, wie im Abendlande. Der Wekil sah seine Autorität bedroht und machte einen Versuch, sie wieder herzustellen:

The conclusion was forced upon me, that the slipper in the Orient had the same magical quality that it had in the West. The *Wekil* saw his authority threatened and attempted to reclaim it:

Of course, 'magical quality' (zauberische Kraft) is a tongue-in-cheek expression.

O Du beglückende Pantoffelherrschaft, Dein Zepter ist ganz dasselbe im Norden wie im Süden, im Osten wie im Westen!

Oh the delightful reign of the slipper, its scepter is identical in the north as in the south, in the east as in the west!

As for *' beglückende Pantoffelherrschaft'* – i.e. 'delightful reign of the slipper' is likewise a tongue-in-cheek expression. Obviously Karl May thought the entire situation quite amusing.

Ch. 6. 1 **"A Saxon! One could burst with happiness! And you have become a Turk?"**

Because of the dialect and phrase used the above is only an approximation for: "Een Sachse! Da sollte man doch gleich vor Freede 'n Ofen einreißen! Und Sie sind man wohl een Türke jeworden?"

After additional research, it was discovered that the act of demolishing an 'Ofen' [oven, stove] was an arduous task, due to the immense hardness of the long fired clay, that was once assigned to prisoners as a punishment. The sentiment of the statement is therefore relaying that one is so happy that once could perform this difficult task with ease.

Ch 8. 1 **Jehovah Sabaoth**

Sabaoth – (In Hebrew, plural form of "host" or "army"). The word is used almost exclusively in conjunction with the Divine name as a title of majesty: "the Lord of Hosts", or "the Lord God of Hosts". According to some scholars the "hosts" represent, at least primitively, the armies of Israel over whom Jehovah exercised a protecting influence. Others opine that the word refers to the hosts of heaven, the angels, and by metaphor to the stars and entire universe (cf. Genesis 2:1).

TOPIC	NOTES
Ch 8. 2	**"Because here lives *Melek el newth*, the Angel of Death. He who enters the water here will either drown or receive the seed of death. Each drop of this water is one tear from the hundreds of thousands of souls that perished because they tried to slay *Sidna Musa* - Moses and his followers. Every boat and every ship hurries past here without stopping; for Allah, who is called *Jehuwa* by the Hebrews, has cursed this place."** It should be noted that whilst this may have been common belief at the time Karl May wrote the original text, it is now believed that the crossing took place further north, in what is known as the 'Sea of Reeds'. These swampy marshes are located to the north of Suez.
Ch 8. 3	**Maria Theresa Taler** Silver coin first struck in 1780 and minted until the 20th Century, all coins, however bear the date 1780 – distributed throughout the Levant, Middle East and north and east Africa – particularly Ethiopia. Maria Theresa, Empress of Austria-Hungary and Bohemia from 1740-1780. Coin diameter 41mm, weight 28.07 grams, .8333 fine silver.
Ch 11. 1	**'Bear-killer'** Refers to one of Kara Ben Nemsi's weapons, a large, heavy, double barreled gun given to him by U.S. gunsmith, named simply Mr. Henry. (See the notes on the Enigma of the Henry Carbine).
Ch 11. 2	**Selan-Dib** Also referred to in this text as **Sinhala Dvipa** Referes to the island of Ceylon, now known as Sri Lanka. According to tradition, Vijaya, a Hindu prince from northern India, conquered the island in 504 BC, naming it Sinhala
Ch 11. 3	**The month of Pilgrimage** Dhu al-Hijjah 12th lunar month of Muslim calendar 8th – 13th days of this month covers the arrival of the hajji in Mecca.
Ch 11. 4	**Celebes** Also known as Sulawesi, island of eastern Indonesia, situated east of Borneo and west of the Moluccas. Celebes consists mainly of four peninsulas separated by deep gulfs. The island has a number of active and latent volcanoes. The Portuguese first sighted the island in

TOPIC	NOTES
	1512, but from about 1607 the Dutch gradually obtained supremacy. In 1946 Celebes was included in the autonomous state of East Indonesia, now the Republic of Indonesia.
Ch 12. 1	**"Watch out! As soon as you touch the saddle the hedjihn will rise, first with the forelegs, so that you will be thrown backwards. Then it will raise its hindquarters and you will be thrown forwards. You will have to counter these movements with your body."** It is possible that Karl May never saw a real camel rise and may be excused for this mistake – just ask yourself how a cow rises and see if you get it right without ever having witnessed it. Actually, a camel rises from a prone position to the knees first, then the hindquarters and lastly the forelegs. Really there are three 'jolts' that have to be endured. Therefore, the first 'jolt' will throw you backwards – because the camel's body moves forwards. The second 'jolt' would throw you forwards – because the camel rises at the rear; and the final 'jolt' would throw you backwards again – because the camel rises from its foreiegs, which are still in the kneeling position. But even then, these 'jolts' are not as severe as they are described in this passage.
Ch 13. 1	**Altan or Altar?** The text we used for the basis of our translation used the word 'Altan' – meaning balcony; this did not make sense in the context of the sentence. The word could have been mistyped and should perhaps have ended with an 'r' instead of an 'n'. The intended word could have been 'Altar' – meaning alter. The latter fits the described circumstances much better and was thus used in the translated text.
Ch 15. 1	**Girl-Robber** Karl May originally wrote this word in English. Therefore there is no translation. The associated travel narrative where this adventure is told is entitled "*Am Stillen Ozean*" – "On the Pacific Ocean"
Ch 17. 1	**"I was even in his tent."** This was referred to previously as a hut, not a tent.
Ch 18. 1	**"This horse will carry you through a thousand horsemen"**

TOPIC **NOTES**

Actually Mohammed Emin said: *"... Er läßt seinen Reiter nie im Stich und trägt ihn durch tausend Feinde. Hast Du einmal ein solches Pferd besessen?"* - "... It never leaves its horseman in a lurch and carries him through a thousand enemies. Have you ever owned such a horse?"

NOTE:

"Dieses Pferd wird Dich durch tausend Reiter hindurchtragen, und ich fühle mich unendlich stolz, der Besitzer dieses ausgezeichneten Renners zu sein." - "This horse will carry you through a thousand horsemen, and I felt extremely proud to be the owner of this excellent runner."

The additional words attributed to Mohammed Emin could be a type setting error in the document we are working from. Probably the dialog is a paraphrase of what Mohammed Emin said and the pride, in this case, belongs to Kara Ben Nemsi – rather than Mohammed Emin. We believe that this is correct and have changed the text accordingly for the sake of readability.

The Enigma of the Henry Carbine.

The famous superior weapon that is used with devastating effect by the hero of these Travel Narratives was initially mentioned in the first book of the Winnetou Series. Here Karl May described the manner in which he (alias Charlie a.k.a. Kara Ben Nemsi) obtained both the Henry Carbine and the heavy double-barreled "Bear-killer" gun from a gunsmith named simply Mr. Henry.

At no time in the original text did Karl May elaborate on Mr. Henry's full name. Any assumption that is was D. Tyler Henry, the inventor of the Henry Lever Action Rifle, the patent of which was later bought by the Winchester Rifle Company is quite erroneous.

In the Winnetou text Karl May wrote the following about Mr. Henry:

Er schien mit dem Gewehrlaufe fertig zu sein und nahm aus einem Kasten ein polygones Eisenstück, dessen Ecken er abzufeilen begann. Ich sah, daß jede Fläche desselben ein Loch hatte.

He appeared to be finished with the rifle barrel and now took a many-sided piece of iron from a box, the edges of which he started to file down. I saw that every flat side of it had a hole.

The description of this iron piece that would become part of the mechanism of the Henry Carbine is indeed curious - we do not know at this time how many sides this iron piece had, yet we are told that each flat side had a hole.

Karl May wrote further:

Er guckte eine längere Zeit in alle die Löcher hinein, drehte das Eisen nach verschiedenen Richtungen, hielt es einige Male an das hintere Ende des Laufes, den er vorhin fortgelegt hatte ...

He looked for some time into each of the holes and turned the iron piece in different directions placing it occasionally at the rear of the barrel he had previously laid down ...

Mr. Henry then said;

Es wird ein Stutzen, ein Repetierstutzen mit fünfundzwanzig Schüssen.

It will become a carbine, a repeater-carbine with twenty five shots.

When Charlie the hero of the story questions this capacity and the quite embarrassing size of a twenty-five shot magazine, Mr. Henry responds;

Nur eine Kammer; ist ganz handlich und geniert gar nicht. Dieses Eisen ist die Kammer

Just one magazine; its quite enough and its not at all embarrassing. This piece of iron is the magazine.

We can therefore be quite certain from the above writing that this iron piece Mr. Henry was working with will eventually become a kind of magazine that will hold twenty-five shots. We do not know it's size, or how the rounds will be stored in it. As Mr. Henry continues his explanation, the matter becomes even more perplexing;

Dieses Eisen wird eine Kugel, welche sich exzentrisch bewegt; fünfundzwanzig Löcher darin enthalten ebensoviele Patronen. Bei jedem Schusse rückt die Kugel weiter, die nächste Patrone an den Lauf.

This iron piece will become a sphere that moves eccentrically; the twenty-five holes in it contain just as many bullets. After every shot the sphere moves on, the next bullet aligns with the barrel.

From the brief description given it is quite difficult to visualize the working mechanism, it is left to the reader to imagine how it might work. Certainly this weapon is not 'The Henry Rifle', for in that rifle the rounds are stored serially in a tube magazine that is positioned below the barrel, the loading of the bullet from that magazine is achieved by a manual movement of a lever.

When Mr. Henry agreed with Charlie on the issue of what such a twenty-five shot repeater-carbine could do and promises that he would only fashion a few of these weapons by special request, the extreme rarity of this mystic weapon is assured.

The same mystique surrounds the heavy double-barreled Bear-killer gun. We initially know that it is quite heavy, but we do not know what kind of gun it is. Only much later do we discover that it had two barrels. We still do not know the caliber, weight and size of either weapon.

Karl May's skill as a story teller is such that despite the lack of description of these two weapons, which play such an important part throughout all of the stories, the reader is not distracted from the tale. In fact, one can imagine handling these guns without a second thought about their construction or function.

ABOUT THE AUTHOR

Michael M. Michalak was born in Germany in 1953 and became interested in the works of Karl May after receiving the first Winnetou book from his father. Ever since then he has been a Karl May fan. Since English translations of the Karl May books are few and usually abridged, Mr. Michalak undertook to translate the entire Orient saga of Karl May's works. The translation started in January 1999 and the initial book took one year to complete. During the following year, an extensive editing effort was undertaken to polish the translated work and ready it for publishing.

This first book of the Oriental Odyssey series covers the first part of "In the Shadow of the Padishah", subtitled "Through the Desert". It is the first and only unabridged translation of a Karl May work by a modern author.

Mr. Michalak emigrated to Australia with his parents in 1965 and now resides in the United States of America.